MW00913143

RUN IN THE FAM'LY

THE UNIVERSITY OF TENNESSEE PRESS / KNOXVILLE

RUN
IN THE FAM'LY

A NOVEL

To The Giessings,
dear family friends.
Peace,

[signature]

JOHN J. MCLAUGHLIN

17 Oct 2007
McLean, VA

| TENNESSEE | PETER TAYLOR |
| BOOK AWARD | PRIZE FOR THE NOVEL |

Co-sponsored by the Knoxville Writers' Guild and the University of Tennessee Press, the Peter Taylor Prize for the Novel is named for one of the South's most celebrated writers—the author of acclaimed short stories, plays, and the novels *A Summons to Memphis* and *In the Tennessee Country*. The prize is designed to bring to light works of high literary quality, thereby honoring Peter Taylor's own practice of assisting other writers who care about the craft of fine fiction.

An excerpt of this novel first appeared, in slightly different form, in *Hunger Mountain: The Vermont College Journal of Arts & Letters*.

Library of Congress Cataloging-in-Publication Data

McLaughlin, John J., 1971–
Run in the family : a novel / John J. McLaughlin. —1st ed.
      p. cm.
"The Peter Taylor Prize for the Novel"—T.p. verso.
ISBN-13: 978-1-57233-595-0 (acid-free paper)
ISBN-10: 1-57233-595-5 (acid-free paper)
  1. African American men—Fiction.
  2. Oakland (Calif.)—Fiction.
  3. Fathers and sons—Fiction.
  4. Criminal behavior—Fiction.
  I. Title.

PS3613.C5756R86 2007
813'.6—dc22   2007017904

Mom and Dad—fierce, abiding love
Tim, Maureen, Brian, and Anne—faithful joy and mercy
Kathy, Annika, and JJ—our journey together

Well, then, says I, what's the use you learning to do right, when it's troublesome to do right and ain't no trouble to do wrong, and the wages is just the same?
—**MARK TWAIN,** *Adventures of Huckleberry Finn*

To yoke me as his yokefellow, our crimes our common cause. You're your father's son. I know the voice.
—**JAMES JOYCE,** *Ulysses*

He did not want his father's kiss—not any more, he who had received so many blows.
—**JAMES BALDWIN,** *Go Tell It on the Mountain*

The stone that the builders rejected has become the cornerstone . . .
—**PSALM 118:22, MATTHEW 21:42**

CONTENTS

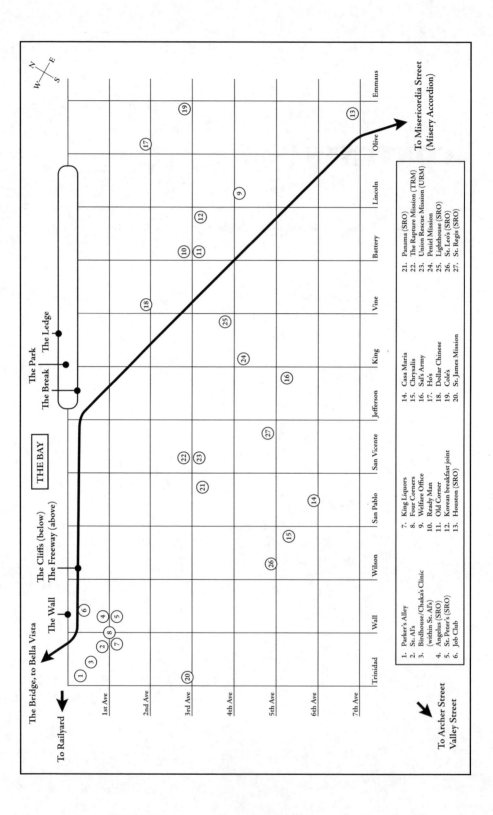

PROLOGUE
VOICE IN THE FLATLANDS

Nobody knows where he comes from. Not for sure anyhow, not to stake his life on. I ain't no different. I've got stories, just like everybody else, things I remember, fix-up right nice for the telling, and mix-in there with things I heard from other folk, who heard it from other folk and on down the line. That's how I know who I am. Who my people are, how I got here. Or that's how I tell it, anyhow. Don't know for sure, but what else I got? If a man wants to believe something, time comes around when he's got to have a little faith.

But I've got other stories too, the kind you can't pretty-up except by killing them dead and starting all over again. I've tried but it don't work. I try forgetting but I've got dreams I just can't shake. I slip away, leave all that shit behind like sticking trash under the seat on the bus, but sooner or later it comes back around. I'm just walking along on a street like this and quick as that I hear that engine gun and those brakes shout and that door slide open, quick as that a bag is flying and I can smell it even before it hits me in the chest, and there's a voice from inside saying *this is yours boy don't you try leaving it behind.*

The dreams about the man hanging in the maple started back in Chicago, in Granddad Lenny's house he passed on to Daddy—back before the time I want to forget, before we made the move to California. Daddy moved us all out here, me and Paula and Cheryl and Momma, because he said the cold was killing us, but he never asked me. I could have stayed there my whole life. I had the dreams there, but they weren't never so bad as when we got to that house on Valley Street. Nothing was. My whole life got turned upside-down once we got to the Flatlands—and even before.

Two nights from California, I was riding back in the hole, under that tarp in the bed of Daddy's truck. It was back twelve years ago, when I wasn't but eleven, but I've got it in me fresh as today. Just like the fight at the window, just like the game with Keisha and Lydell, like getting put out of Momma's house and then George's hall, like all that shit I wish I could forget. It's all here, in my dreams and walking around with me like my shadow right out on the street, and sometimes I don't know if I'm just remembering or living it all over again.

I can still feel that cold metal under me, those ridges running right down my back biting through that sorry-ass rug Daddy put down. I can still hear that tarp whip-slapping and those plywood walls creaking, smell Paula next to me and my sneakers too. I can still feel the hum of the wheels coming up through the floor, the road moving under us smooth enough to sleep if it wasn't for Daddy hitting those bad spots and the whole truck jolt-jangling like a motherfucker and keeping me awake.

Paula always tells it straight, if you give her a chance, sometimes even if you don't. She's fourteen now, one up on Cheryl and three on me, but it ain't years that does it, because Momma's got plenty of those. Ain't about being tall neither, because she ain't never gonna reach Momma and I'm catching her fast, but can't nobody stand up to Daddy like she can. That's why she's back here now, in the hole with me, under this tarp and inside all these boxes, taking the bumps and fighting me for the blanket. She got here for being tough. I got here because of my face.

That's what she says, but I don't need her to figure that one out. I ain't been riding in the front like she has, ain't heard everything she's telling me now, but I heard it with my own ears before we even left, when Daddy made me haul the plywood out to the truck and hold it steady while he nailed it into the sidewall all the way around. *This gonna be your hole*, he told me. That hammer was booming between the words. *Ain't sharing my seat . . . no pussy-faced pretty boy . . . time you showed me something . . . started to be a man.*

I'm showing him now. Been riding like this all the way from Chicago, freezing my ass off because there's only room for three in the seat and Daddy is driving and Momma and the girls are girls. Been showing him since a couple months back now, when I started getting my height, losing that kid fat and putting some muscle on. But not like he's got, not that barrel chest and cement-block shoulders. I'm getting what Momma gave me, turning out long and lean, and that's why Daddy's been saying I'm changing on him, looking like Momma's son. That's why he's been saying he's gonna have to do something so I don't turn out all wrong.

He's been saying it up in the front seat too, since the first night, and Paula and Cheryl have been bringing it back to me when they take turns here in the hole. Cheryl never gives me as much as Paula, because she just wants us all to get along, and she sure never gives it back where it came from. But Paula does. Daddy always says he can't believe a girl who's his spitting image could have been born talking back like her. I can't neither. She's dark like him—no cream in her coffee like us other three, Momma says—got those big shoulders, got that big butt, but biggest thing on her is her mouth. She'll fight anybody on anything, but I ain't never seen her put up no fight for me—and damn-sure not nothing that would put her here in the hole. I almost can't believe it when she tells me. When Daddy started in on me she told him what kind of man was he anyhow didn't have no job and lost his own home, and he stopped this truck quick as that. I thought all these boxes were coming down on Cheryl and me, but Daddy's ropes held good. It was Paula's night to sit up front in the seat with that heat blowing on her, but just like that she lost it, and it don't seem to bother her a bit.

"Least I can lie down flat now," she says. "Don't got to be falling asleep sitting up."

"Girl, you crazy," I say. "You ain't slept a minute back here this whole trip and I ain't neither. Now you got two nights of this coming."

"Don't matter none to me," she says, pulling the blanket to her, trying to steal my share. With that butt of hers, she could steal it all and still freeze her ass. "I'll sleep in the motel."

I pull back, but I don't get it all, at least not as much as I do with Cheryl. It's better sleeping next to Cheryl in the motel too—she doesn't kick like she's trying to hit a field goal from fifty like Paula does. She's sweeter all around—got cream *and* sugar in her coffee. Got Momma's skinny bones just like I do, and the lightest face in the family. She's taller than Paula now and catching Momma quick, but you'd never know it when she's asleep—the girl don't take up no room at all. Soon as we pull in and Daddy says let's get it set up, I'm staking my claim and Cheryl's too. Gonna grab that cardboard and that extra tarp, run and pick out the spot and set my piece just the way I want it. When Daddy walks over he'll have the two umbrellas, the baseball bat, and that piece of tubing, he'll knock them into the ground and we'll get the tarp over and the cardboard under and that motel will be open for business.

We sleep days because Daddy says driving at night is easier on the engine. He slept in there with us till yesterday—all I know is I woke up and the sun was still shining but he wasn't snoring no more, he had his boots on and was crawling out. He went back to the truck and Momma told him stay there, and Paula says she ain't cooking with no more beans while we're on the road. At least in the motel all that farting stayed under his blanket some, but in the truck it sank good into the seats, and riding with the windows down didn't hardly help at all.

"But they fighting about more than just them beans," Paula says. "Ain't you heard it?"

"I ain't heard nothing," I say, lying like a motherfucker. I want to know what she knows.

"Well then you deaf *and* dumb, boy," she says. "They talking plenty about you. That's why we're *making* this move. It ain't just because he lost that job like he's been telling you."

She pulls on the blanket again, and this time I let it go, let it slide off my legs and over to her side till it's hardly on me at all. Whatever keeps her talking—it ain't too cold for me yet. I move over, lean in smelling-close, just how girls like it when they're telling you a secret. Paula and Cheryl and Momma have been washing their face in those bathrooms when we fill up with gas, but ain't none of us even been near a shower since we started out. Don't bother me none, because Momma makes me shower too much anyway when we're at home, but the girls have been crying about it the whole trip—and now I know why. Paula better tell this story right quick. She says my sneakers are bad, but her funk could stop a train in its tracks. Gonna kill me before the cold for damn-sure.

"Sometimes he's drinking," she says. "I know you got to know about that."

"He ain't no drunk," I say.

"Just listen, Jake," she says. "I ain't saying he's doing that all the time. He don't even need it to act crazy. Look at how he lost that job—he wasn't drinking then, and he about broke that man's jaw."

"He *did* break it. But so what? He was supposed to give Daddy the raise-up and he didn't. Daddy was just showing him you can't fuck with a man's family."

Paula shifts her shoulders and hips, gets in a little tighter. "That what you believe? Ain't you heard him saying he don't want to look at your face no more?"

"Yeah I heard him," I say. "I'm sitting back here, ain't I? Now what you got to tell?"

She shifts again, like she's trying to get those ridges to lie right on her back. The truck rattles, and the blanket drops off my shoulder. She puts it back on me. When she does, I can feel her arm shaking.

"You scared?" I say.

"I just know something," she says, looking straight up at that tarp still whip-slapping steady as can be. We hit another hole, and I feel the boxes by my arm move in. "The other night he was in the kitchen. Told her he was gonna break her jaw, said he wasn't gonna hit easy like he did on that man."

"Naw, girl. Daddy ain't gonna hit no woman."

"He raised his hand, Jake. He would have done it if I wasn't there. Cheryl saw it too."

"You lying, girl," I say. "Both you all are. What's it got to do with me anyhow? You said you had something worth telling."

"I do," she says. She puts that cold-shaking hand on my arm. "It's just—I don't know, I can't tell it straight. It's just there's some things I can't tell you. Only Momma can. Or Daddy."

"Why?"

"I don't know, I don't know. But something's gonna break loose—I can feel it." She pulls in even closer, but I can't see her eyes to know if she's lying. "Only been one other time he raised his hand to her."

I push her, shove her back good in the shoulder, and pull hard on that blanket. "Must have been some long time ago then, girl. About a hundred years back. That ain't *my* Daddy."

She shakes her head at me. "You don't know what you saying, Jake."

Quick as that there's a *boom* and the truck drops and it's like we're riding over rocks. The tire's blown. We're shaking—everything's shaking like a motherfucker—tarp slapping, metal crying, Paula shouting and grabbing me biting those nails into my shoulder right down to the bone, those boxes rumbling too and Daddy's ropes holding tight but they can't work no miracle and one falls, two now, right down on my leg and maybe Paula's too.

The truck stops, the front door creaks open and slams. Steps come quick on the road, clips click down the side to the back, and that tarp is up just like that. When it peels back that sky is big as the world and blacker than old Auntie Thelma sitting in the dark, even with all them stars. But Daddy's eyes shoot me right quick, smoke-gray and burning. He grabs my shirt.

"Get up, boy. Get the light, get the jack."

"Hold on, Daddy. Them boxes fell on my leg."

He shakes me. "Don't give me none of that pussy shit! Move your ass now!"

I pull my foot out from under the box and stand up. It's burning a little, but it's all right. The flashlight was here right beside me but it must have taken off when the tire blew. I turn around to the front, where Daddy packed the toolbox, right behind the boxes at me and Paula's heads. I tell her to get up and give me a hand getting the ropes off.

Momma's door opens, and the cab light comes on. Cheryl climbs up here into the hole to help us with the ropes, and Momma goes and stands in front of that shining headlight.

"What you hit?" she says to Daddy.

"Didn't hit shit," he says. "Motherfucker just blew." He slam-bangs that metal side wall. "Jake! Where that light at?"

The knot in my hands is cold like it's frozen-through, and I can't budge it. "I can't find it. Rolled off someplace."

"*This* is the light you oughta been after, Curtis," Momma says. I look at her but she ain't looking back—she's got her finger pointing at that broken headlight, that place where Daddy hit the tree a few weeks back, gave the hood a slumped shoulder like an old man. Her eyes are dead on Daddy. "Didn't I tell you to fix it?"

"Shut up, woman! All you know is talking. You can't drive nohow—can't even ride a bus across town without fucking it up. So where you gonna go without me?"

"You had it coming!" Paula says. She pulls hard on that rope—I can't tell if she's getting it loose or what.

Daddy looks up. Quick as that he slap-grabs the plywood wall, pulls himself up on the roof, jumps down here in the hole. The truck shakes. He grabs my shirt again. "I *told* you, boy—get the light, get the jack. Now watch how a man does it."

Soon as he gets his hands on that rope I hear Momma come running. "Don't you touch my children, Curtis! *None* of them!"

Paula's hand goes up, and the light from the cab catches it. Got a fist set to come down on Daddy, but Cheryl moves quick, wraps her arm over Paula's and pulls her back into the boxes. "Don't be mad at her, Daddy."

He looks at them and laughs. "What you stopping her for?" He gets that first knot loose and whips the rope down to the floor. "Go on and hit me if you want, girl. See what good it does you."

Daddy pulls a box out from where he just loosed the ropes. He looks at the girls and throws his chin out toward Momma. "Now get on down there."

"You all stupid or something?" I say, stepping up next to Daddy. "We got men's work to do."

"Ha! So what *you* gonna be doing?" Paula says.

Daddy puts a hand on my shoulder, holds it there, squeezes me good. Feels good and warm like drinking down some of Momma's soup. I look at my sisters and I know I've got something they don't, I know I'm Daddy's only son.

"Gonna be getting this truck back on the road, that's what," he says. I turn to him, look up at them smoke-gray eyes and those wide shoulders and that Cubs hat and those stars all behind, and I know he's right.

"I'll get the tire off," I say. "Don't need no light."

"That's a good boy," Daddy says, then he luck-smacks me on the ass, just like he always did when we were shooting from downtown at that hoop on the maple and I hit two in a row going for three. "Hurry up now. And get your sisters on down there with you."

I pull the girls up onto the roof, and we all slide down to the hood and hop off. Momma stands with her arms crossed right by that broken headlight on Daddy's side. Daddy's got Granddad Lenny's toolbox out from behind those boxes and waiting to drop it on down.

"You ready, Jake?" he says, leaning over that plywood wall, holding the box by the handle. I stretch my hands up, but even with all my growing I'm still too short. "Give with it, bring it to you," he says. "Soft hands, just like catching that football."

But it ain't like that at all. Big and cold and heavy as a motherfucker, and those corners bite my hands, and those clips rattle-clack good and loud when I pull it into my chest and it about knocks me over. I shuffle back, but I keep my feet and squeeze that box hard as I can. I look at Daddy. He's all shadows, but I can hear him laugh.

"That's it, boy. You getting stronger. Now move—you know what to do."

I get down on the ground in front of the tire, unlock the box clips, lift the tool tray out and take the jack out of the bottom. I know what to do, but I ain't never done it myself, and sure not in the dark like this. I've ridden all around with Daddy in this truck, and we've hit some flats before—even one time going down to Mississippi—and he's shown me how to change it quicker than the engine can get cool, but that was just with me helping the job, not running it.

The tire looks like it got its guts shot out—broke-open across the treads and sliced down the side like a big onion got burnt blacker than coal. The wheel must have cut right through it after it blew and Daddy pulled us over. It's smoking, still hissing, and I know if I touch those steel cables I'll burn myself something good. I set the jack under the axle and start cranking it up till it gets a good hold. I get it lifting a little, but not much—can't even get that tire off the ground. I go at it till my arm's shaking, but I can't crank it but a couple inches more. The truck rocks when I let go, and I roll out of there quick as I can before it all falls on me. But it holds, just keeps rocking with Daddy up in that bed moving all around loosing ropes lifting boxes talking to himself steady loud fast like he don't even know I'm here.

"I can't get it," I say. "When you getting outta there?"

"What you talking about, boy?" He throws a box down on the bed, and the truck rocks bigger than before, and I think that jack's gonna come shooting right out and then I'll have a whupping coming for sure. "I'm getting the spare out. Use this and crank it like I done showed you."

The tire iron catches the cab light when it's in his hand, but it blacks-out quick again soon as he throws it, and I can hear it flying feel it coming like I was pulling it in on a line and the girls are shouting look out now and I make to run but it catches me, right square in the shoulder, clang-bangs loud when we both hit the street.

"What you trying to do to him?" Momma moves quick. She kicks the tire iron away, kneels down and puts her hands soft on my face and tells me I'm gonna be all right, didn't nothing touch my head. Paula and Cheryl come around behind me. Momma stands me up, brushes my shirt off, and hugs me close, and even with my shoulder hurting it feels good. She shoots a finger at Daddy. "Don't you start your shit again! We going to California now—you said so yourself. You told me that Chicago story was dead and gone, so don't you go bringing it out here. Leave it behind."

"You don't know what I said, Janice," Daddy says. "He's *my* boy. Don't you tell me how to be his Daddy."

He throws the spare out at us, underhand like shooting the ball granny-style, but it still falls quick, hits hard flat on the street right where we're standing. Momma goes one way, the girls go two others, but I stay right where I am, let it land right up against my leg.

Daddy jumps down off the roof, picks up that iron and holds it right up in front of my eyes. "Show me something better than what you got in that face, Jake," he says. He takes my arm, puts my hand on the iron and squeezes his down over it. "Show me you're a man."

Those eyes burn, hot as a couple of matches in my face, and that smoke gets thick and black as that sky behind him. I put my other hand on that iron and pull it away, spin around and get it in the jack. It cranks easy now, and I can feel my hands getting hot, my arms too, but it's all right because the truck is lifting up quick.

Cheryl tells me to watch myself, then Momma's in there with her and even Paula too, but Daddy shuts them up, tells them ain't nothing gonna hurt me now without his say-so and ain't nobody running the family but him. But I don't even look back, just keep on cranking till it's up and set and then I swing that iron around and fit it on the lug nuts and start getting them loose. Top one first, then down to the right, then up to the left and back over again, making that star, getting each one of them a little bit at a time so they all come off easy and smooth. I hear Daddy *that's it boy, that's it,* but I don't even have to look to see him because that face is right in the wheel, those eyes are watching me work. I'm hitting a rhythm, getting hot all over now, till I get to that last one—the motherfucker won't move. I skip it and hit all the others again and come back around to it, push it till I can feel my shoulder about to burn through my shirt, but it won't give me a damn thing. I feel those eyes but I skip it again, hit all the others one more time then pick them off with my fingers and put them in my pocket. They're hot enough to burn through too but it's all right.

"What you doing, boy?"

"You told me put them in your pocket so they don't get lost on you," I say. "Especially at night."

"What's that one still doing on there?"

"It don't move."

"Bullshit. Kick it."

I put the iron back on it, stand up, and pound my foot down on that T-bar, but it pops right off, jumps off the wheel and heads at Momma like it got shot out of a sling, hits her smack across the leg.

Daddy goes upside my head from behind, knocks me into the truck. "What you doing to my woman, boy?" He steps in, gets smelling-close, grabs me by the collar. "Cheryl, go on and bring me that iron."

"She ain't bringing you shit," Paula says.

Daddy lets me go and turns quick. Momma picks the iron up and rubs her leg. "It ain't nothing, Curtis. Quit your damn show and get that tire changed so we can get where we going."

Daddy looks at Momma, points at Paula. "You teach her to talk like that?" He looks over at Cheryl. "And she teach you to stand there when I tell you to do something? Get me that iron. *Now,* girl."

Cheryl looks at Momma, looks at me, then back at Daddy. "But, Daddy, you got to promise—"

"Let him come get it himself," Momma says, holding it out. "If he's a big man like he's talking about, he can walk over here a few steps."

"I'm sorry, Momma," I say. "I didn't mean—"

He turns on me again. "You *sorry?*"

I step back, come up against the wall of the truck, cold just like that floor. "I just kicked it like you said. I didn't think it was going nowhere."

"Naw, boy, naw," Daddy says, shaking his head, stepping with me. "You don't even know what you sorry about. After all this time."

"Leave my son alone!" Momma moves in close now, pointing that iron. "This ain't about him."

"You ain't hurt, are you, Momma?" I say. "I didn't mean it to hit you."

Daddy leans in, gets smelling-close, eye to eye. He talks soft, so only I can hear him. "Shut up, boy. I'm talking to you now. You don't know what you sorry about, do you? I'll tell you right now—you weak. I saw it in your face the second you was born, and I see it right now." He brings his hand up, two fingers out straight and flat like a knife, and he drags it soft across my cheek, barely touching but it's hot as a motherfucker anyhow. "You got a pussy face, Jake, even worse than your Momma. I should have put my brand on you long time ago, made you ugly like me. Like a man."

"I told you don't touch him, unless you want me taking *your* nuts off."

Momma holds the iron up, and Daddy must feel it coming because he turns quick as a cat and smacks it out of her hand, knocks it straight down, and then he's moving, he's running, Momma is too and we all are, going down on the street to grab it. He's down first, right with Momma, but I'm on his back, and Paula and Cheryl jump in too, we're all reaching down trying to grab it but Daddy's too strong, he pulls it up, rips it right out of Momma's hands and then he picks her up, pushes me off the girls off and quick as that Momma's back hits *whap* against the truck door but the glass holds her.

"So now you want them, huh woman? Well go on and take them if you can! I'm gonna whup you like I should have done before!"

He steps in and the iron flashes up, catches the light from the cab and goes black again hanging over his head, over Momma's, hanging hard and heavy and gonna leave his mark for sure. I still ain't a man but I can hold a hammer good, and my sisters ain't moving an inch so I snatch it up out of the toolbox right here on the ground and run, run at that light that iron that man don't even look like my Daddy no more but I know he is, run and swing because it's coming right up out of my bones and can't do nothing else, but he feels me coming he turns quick and that free hand grabs the hammer and he swings me like I was on the end of a string crashing rolling right into my sisters. That iron goes up again and we're all yelling, goes up and gonna come down now and break it all open, and don't know where it comes from but I just say it *mercy Daddy have mercy,* and it flashes down quick and hard that side mirror shatters and Momma screams the girls scream but it's nothing but glass, and Daddy turns and throws the iron against the truck clangs on that sidewall like a motherfucker bounces out in the street slips into the dark, and the sound hangs don't know how long all around us till it dies.

* * *

Next day we didn't stop when morning hit, not to sleep anyhow. Daddy pulled into the stations every now and again to put air in the spare and gas in the tank. The tire needed it every damn time too—had a leak worse than the window in my room in our Chicago house. Daddy said he had to keep checking it, so he drove slow, kept the window down and looked over his shoulder every now and again because that mirror was gone. He said we were across the state line, so why set up the motel and wait till night to get where we're going—a man oughta see his new land in the light of day.

I hadn't never seen nothing like it. Brown brown brown, all the time and every which way, rolling up and laying flat and going wider than I could see without spinning my head around, rocks and grass and trees and sand and all kinds of colors up close but just brown from way back. All this wide open space, but the mountains held it all in like it was their stadium. All them ridges and curves made them look like old God was flexing his biceps, and they were damn-sure taller than all Chicago's downtown towers stacked up together. And soon as I got to thinking there couldn't be nothing taller than that, I saw more mountains behind those.

I sat up front, just me and Daddy and some boxes in between. Momma said she wasn't having no more of it, made me make the hole in the back big enough for her and the girls and stack some boxes between Daddy and me. I can still see his hat, his hands on the wheel, the back of his head when he checks the tire. And I can hear him too—but he don't say a thing, not to me. Just some coughing now and again and that aw shit when the spare needs air.

When we pull into the station, Daddy stays with the truck, Momma smokes her cigarette out by the street, and me and the girls hit the john. Cheryl gets there first because I let her, and I tell Paula to get in front of me so I don't have to hear none of her crying about put the seat down this time around.

"You learning something now," she says.

"Yeah you learning too, girl. I told you he ain't gonna hit no woman."

She shakes her head. "You a damn fool like I ain't never seen."

"You got some other story, go on and tell it," I say. "What about that other time he raised his hand to her? What happened then?"

The door opens, Cheryl comes out. Paula shakes her head again and goes in. "There wasn't no other time."

The door shuts, locks quick. I look over at Momma by the street, standing tall and skinny, that one arm crossed and the other sitting straight up on it holding her cigarette between her fingers. She tilts her head back and blows smoke up into the air, into that sky sitting over those mountains, and it climbs into that blue blue blue but when it gets there it's gone.

Back on the road, Daddy tries talking, says we won't have no snow out this way, no cold neither. I don't say nothing back, and just like that it's quiet again, just his coughing and the engine humming and the air slipping in my side because the window won't close right. But the sun's coming on strong now, so it feels good. I lean my head against it and close my eyes. I can still see all that brown and those mountains all around, but soon enough it's getting dark, going black, and I don't know if I'm dreaming or what but I see Daddy throw Momma against the glass and that iron's in the air. He holds it there high and cold-cocked back and just like that it freezes—it all freezes, no running no shouting no nothing. That iron hangs there big and dark like a limb on a tree, and I know I've seen something like that before.

* * *

When we get there, we find a house on Valley Street. It's small but it holds us. Daddy and Momma get one room, me and the girls get the other. After a couple weeks, Paula says she ain't playing this no more, she ain't letting no boy see nothing he ain't got a right to, so we put a sheet up across the middle. Cheryl gets some tacks and walks back and forth between me and Paula up on our chairs.

"I don't know what we doing this for," I say, pushing those tacks into the ceiling. "You all ain't got nothing a boy wants to see nohow."

Paula don't even look. "Ha! Yeah we gonna see who's getting a date first around here."

Cheryl hands me up some more tacks. "You better watch it, Jake. Don't expect no help with the girls, talking to us like that."

I step down and move my chair to the middle, toward Paula, gonna try to finish my half before she does hers. "I don't need no help from you all. Gonna have me three girlfriends before the month's out."

Paula laughs, takes some more tacks from Cheryl. "We gonna see about that. Don't think you getting no help from Daddy neither."

"That ain't all he ain't getting," Cheryl says. She goes to the door and closes it, and now she talks low. "Momma says if Daddy don't get some work soon we ain't gonna make the rent."

"What you mean?" I say.

"I mean we ain't got no *money*, Jake," Cheryl says. She looks at Paula. "Am I lying?" Paula shakes her head. "What you think Momma's been fixing that beet stew all month for?"

"So she can make Daddy shit blood," Paula says.

We all laugh, and Cheryl covers her mouth. Daddy's been crying about them beets every time he comes out of the bathroom, saying they're tearing up his insides something awful, but Momma keeps telling him they just get into some folk worse than others, they make it look like blood but really it ain't nothing, it ain't nothing at all. Must be I'm one of them folks too, because it don't hurt coming out but it sure looks like it should have when I flush it down. I didn't even waste my time asking the girls if it happened to them too—I ain't met a girl yet gonna tell you what her shit looks like.

"'Cause she can throw any old thing in there and they'll just cover it up," Cheryl says. "And pretty soon we ain't gonna have nothing to throw in—ain't even gonna have them beets."

"He'll get some money!" I say. "He told me he's getting him a real man's job."

"Yeah? When that gonna be?" Paula says.

"He got to get to know some folk, and that takes a while 'cause we ain't got no people out here."

She shakes her head again. "That what he telling you? Well we ain't got no *nothing*. Why don't you ask him why we moved out here anyway."

Cheryl shushes her. "Don't say that!"

"Don't say what?" Paula jumps down off the chair and throws the door back open, bangs it against the wall. She points out into the hall. "It's only Momma out there, and she knows it better than anybody."

"Now you gonna tell me, ain't you?" I say, jumping down too, moving toward Paula, toward that door. Cheryl grabs my arm but I knock her off. "Gonna tell me about that other time."

"What the hell's going on here?" Momma comes in like she was shot out of a gun. She spins Paula to her, pushes her head back and squeezes her cheeks together in her hand. "You fixing to ruin this house?"

Cheryl's hands shoot straight out. "Don't! We'll take it down, Momma! We'll take it down!"

I stop dead where I am, almost don't know what I'm saying when it comes out. "Where's my daddy? What he do?"

"What?" Momma looks at me like she don't know me, then she looks at Paula and jerks that hand away like those cheeks were a couple of hot stove rings. "Leave it up," she says. She steps back quick, crosses her arms tight like she just went cold, and just like that she's gone, down the hall. "You all shouldn't be living together anyhow."

The front door slams, and then it's quiet. Nobody moves, nobody says nothing. I look at the sheet, still hanging low in the middle.

We all stand there a minute, then Cheryl moves over to Paula, puts her arm around her. "You all right, girl?"

Paula rubs her mouth. "Yeah I'm all right." She steps up on her chair and holds her hand out. Cheryl bends over and picks some tacks up off the floor. Paula puts them in and just like that they're done, it's done, that sheet is up and they're walking out with those chairs, quiet as can be. Cheryl doesn't look back, but Paula does.

"Now you got your answer, Jake," she says. "You done seen and heard all you need, so don't ask nobody no more."

Soon as the girls leave I duck behind the sheet and hit the bed—don't change out of my clothes, don't cut off the light, I just turn my face to the wall and pull the blanket up over my head. That night I'm by myself on my side of the room, and the dream comes around but it don't go far—I ain't even out of the basement to see the maple yet, ain't even seen if the man with no face is hanging this time—when something slams inside the house and I'm up. Must be late now, because the light's out and the girls are in their bed, but I get my sneakers on and I'm around that sheet and out the door, right out into the hall at the top of the stairs. The light's on in the kitchen, and I look in and see Momma sitting at the table, smoking, blowing it up into the light where it all disappears. "What you want?" she says.

"Nothing," Daddy says from behind me, slamming the door and coming up that little set of stairs into the hall, moving right by me and into his room. I didn't see him till he said it and maybe he didn't see me neither. I hear him in the room, opening things, closing them, moving them around, looking for something. Quick as that he's back out, coming back toward me, that big tall shadow moving fast.

"Go back to bed, Jake," Momma says. "There ain't nothing to see now."

I move out of his way, step into the kitchen, but his hand sets down on my shoulder, squeezes it, good and hard like that night with the tire. He spins me, turns me to the stairs, and my feet are moving before he even says it. "Let's go, boy."

I hear Momma's chair push back. "Don't you get him caught up in this, Curtis!"

"Ain't nothing gonna hurt him," he says, and pulls the door shut behind us.

Outside it's cold, it's dark, the streetlights are buzzing. The truck is right out front, still running. Daddy says get in, and we're gone.

We turn through some streets, and soon enough I don't know which way we came from. "Where we going?"

"Gonna show you something, boy." Daddy looks at me, and the streetlight catches him quick and then fades away. Just then a train whistle blows—loud and hard like a smack upside the head—and I jump. I've been hearing them at night, just like I did in Chicago, but never close like this to get right inside me.

Daddy laughs. "Why you shaking? You cold?"

"Naw," I say, and look back at the street again. Can't see no train, just buildings all around, a bus passing us going the other way, somebody getting across the street up ahead and slipping away into the dark.

"Here, now go on and take this," he says, sliding one arm out of his jacket and then the other. "Don't you know better than going out of the house with nothing but a shirt?"

I put it on, zip it up halfway, push the sleeves up so my hands pop out. It's big, but not like when I was little—used to be I could fit two of me in here, but now I bet if I stood up it wouldn't even hang past my ass. I zip it up all the way now and grab it at my chest, pull it tight down on my shoulders. It's got that Daddy smell—no smoke like Momma, none of that sugar-fruit perfume like the girls. Just a cold deep down in it, and sweat down even deeper, the way you smell coming home from a long walk in the snow.

We turn again, and just like that it all opens up. Still plenty of streetlights, but the buildings clear out, and now I see where that train was crying from. It's the railyard. Daddy pulls up to the fence, shines the headlight out over all those sets of tracks. A whistle goes again and then it's right here—those bells start in and that metal starts clacking and those cars go rolling by right through the light. It's long, like most every train I saw in Chicago, and after a minute I look back over at Daddy. His hands are on the wheel, arms locked straight. His chin dips down into his chest the way it always does when he's giving you that look through his eyebrows, but he's looking out into the yard. I can't see his eyes and can't see nothing out there but that train, but I know it's got to be something.

"Why don't you work in this yard, like you used to back home?" I say.

He shakes his head short and quick. "Naw, boy, ain't no life in it no more. Work like that ain't what it used to be. Whole industry done gone to shit. They just use a man up and throw him away."

"I could help you. You wouldn't get so tired."

Daddy laughs, looks at me. "You just a young man yet, got to be in school. What your momma gonna say if she finds out you cutting to come down here?"

"She already wants to whup me." I look back at the train, still rolling, still clacking and crying. "You do too. That's what Paula says you all fighting about—see who's gonna get at me first."

"You believe that, boy?" I feel his hand on my shoulder, that same squeeze, but I shake him off. I feel it back on again and I turn on him, get my fists up and I'm ready to go now, make him fight me like a man, but then I see it. He's holding it out, and my fists fall open. It's that scarf, the one he always wore when the cold rolled in back home, the one our Mississippi people put Granddad Lenny on the train with when he was going north, way back then before Daddy was even born. I didn't even see him wearing it till now.

"Go on and put it on you now," he says. He puts the truck in reverse, turns us around, and we're moving again. "You look like you still cold."

Even in the dark I can see it. Even if the streetlights weren't flashing in I could just close my eyes and see it with my fingers, maybe even without them, see that deep dark blue and all the other colors sewn into it. I put it around my neck, wrap it loose, slide my fingers down that row of leaves sewn in all the way around the edges and feel it against my cheek. I hold the ends in my hands and I see that tree and that pond and I know that fish is around someplace. Strangest scarf I've ever seen, but you can't find another one like it. That's because it's made from a story.

Daddy told it to me first time he let me wear it, and it's still with me. Wasn't always torn like it is now. When Auntie Thelma made it, she knit it all one piece, one big loop, without a seam. Wasn't till later it got torn, Daddy doesn't know how. Everything she sewed in—the yellow hickory and the white egrets at the pond and the fish with no face and those leaves going yellow red rust black and back green again all around—that's all from some dream she and her own granny had. Daddy said sometimes there ain't no explaining dreams, and I know he's right. What I know for sure is how it got here and where it came from. What I know is Granddad Lenny and Granny Jo-Jo were coming north to start out on their own, she had Daddy in her belly and he had the scarf around his neck to keep him warm and remind him where he came from, who his people were. He wore it till he died—when Daddy was my age now—and then it was Daddy's. Lenny had said it was always meant for him, once he got to be a man.

It's got the Daddy smell like the jacket, but it's different too. The snow's down in there, the sweat too, but there's something else. Could be because those women made it without a seam, could be because Lenny wore it, but I think it's the blood. And not just from when Daddy broke the boss-man's jaw and came home with that cut over his eye. First time he showed it to me I could smell it strong as it is now, and something in me knew it had been down in there long before then.

"Why you kill that man, Daddy?"

He looks at me, and the streetlight flashes in and disappears. "What you talking about?"

"That boss-man," I say. "You broke that jaw of his and near about killed him."

"Yeah but I didn't. He had it coming but I let him off easy." He makes a turn and the railyard is gone now, just those buildings again. "Look boy, that's all done and gone now, you hear? That's what I'm telling you. What you think I'm showing you this for?"

"I ain't seeing nothing at all," I say. I turn and look out my window, put my face on the cold glass and hear the wind slipping through. We pass an alley, and I see two men standing on top of a dumpster, reaching down in and throwing stuff out on the street.

"Look Jake," he says, and I do. It ain't all the time he calls me by my name. Both his hands are on the wheel again, arms locked straight. His voice is soft now, so it must be something. "You know you a handsome boy now, don't you? Ain't your momma told you that? Don't pay no nevermind to none of that junk I was talking before—you gonna be a man's man, I know it. You come from good people."

"Why don't we go back to where they at then, Daddy? What we doing out here where we ain't got nobody?"

"We're here now, boy, ain't no going back," he says. "We ain't doing nothing more than what your granddaddy did. You think he had people in Chicago when he got there? Didn't have no-damn-body. Everybody *followed* him. Sometimes a man's got to make his own way." He puts his thumb in his chest, looks at me quick. "That's what I'm doing. That's what I *have* to do. But don't you worry, boy, I'll take care of you. We gonna make it work out." He sets his hand back on the wheel and points out into the street. "Now let me show you something."

We make another turn and then he cuts the lights and pulls over to the curb where the street ends. Don't know what we're gonna see like this—the only light working is back the other end of the street and don't hardly reach down here. He tells me to get out and keep quiet. I can hear the water someplace close, like it's smacking up against a wall, and up above me there's some kind of bridge, real tall with big old concrete legs holding it up, going off into the dark either way I look. A car horn shouts out up there, then a zoom-clack running one end to the other and then it's gone.

I pick up a rock and throw it up in the belly part of the bridge, just to see what it sounds like smacking in there, but it just knocks some pigeons loose. One heads down the way the car went, one flies straight up over top, another one comes down at me like he's gonna get me back but Daddy raises his hand and just like that he's gone.

"Your momma wants to be living on that side." Daddy steps around the truck, comes up next to me in front of the broken headlight. His eyes catch the light from down the street, but quick as that he turns and points up at the bridge, out the same way that car ran off. I look harder now, and way out in that dark I think I see some lights but I can't know for sure. "She says folks got nice things on that side. Got nice jobs and they all buying nice things."

"That where we going?" I say. "I thought we don't got no money."

"Who said that?" He grabs my arm, bends down and gets in smelling-close. Those eyes are dark shining hot now. "I'm taking care of this family, boy. What you need that you don't got?" He stands up, pulls me, and we're walking now, into the street and under the bridge. "You want to see folk that ain't got no money? Look around you, boy—look all up this street. Come morning time you gonna see men standing on every corner under here, damn-near the length of this bridge till it gets to uptown. What they doing? They waiting for work, waiting for somebody to drive along here and give them a job for a day. You go up a few blocks from here, you got the same thing. Men signing in at a labor hall so somebody can put them to work and throw them away when they done." He stops. He shakes his head and spits on one of these bridge legs. "Your momma's trying to tell me I oughta get me some work like that. You think that's any way for a man to live, Jake?"

I look up the street and all around me. Ain't nobody around but us, but I can picture them all just like he said, folks out on the street like I saw in Chicago, walking standing sitting with a big old bag shaking a cup and taking whatever comes around just to make it through. But I thought it was different in California, I thought everybody made it good out here.

"Why them folks like that?" I say, looking at Daddy. "Why they out here?"

"'Cause they ain't got nobody!" He slaps the bridge leg, turns square on me and puts his finger in my face. "*Nobody!* Ain't nothing worse than that. They all done lost their families and ain't got nothing now. I'll tell you something, boy— that ain't gonna be me. I'm keeping this family together, and we staying right here. Your momma wants to live across that bridge, she gonna be living there by herself. She ain't breaking up this family no more."

"What you talking about—we always been together!" My hands are shaking, and I grab the ends of the scarf and pull down hard as I can, and my throat gets tight but I can't stop the shaking. Behind me there's wings flapping, louder closer *thwap thwap thwap*—I duck and feel that pigeon whip by. It lands just down the way, starts looking for something on the ground.

Daddy grabs my hands. "Hey boy, it's all right." He pulls my fingers back slow, gets the scarf loose. "Hey now, you gonna hurt yourself like that. It's all right." He unwraps the scarf off my neck, shakes it out, and hangs it loose back on me, flat down on his jacket. He puts his hand on my throat, strokes his fingers on it a couple times and it's nice and cool, feels all right.

He takes his hand away. I put mine right where it was and look up at him—no jacket no scarf, just a black shirt and pants and those eyes going up the street and down now, hiding out in the shadows when he turns his head, coming back smoke-gray and hot when he leans in smelling-close.

"I'm gonna show you now, Jake," he says. "You still a boy but there's some things you got to know."

His hand comes around from behind his back, and when I see that gun nose pointing at me I'm ready to run, but he grabs me. "It's all right," he says. "I ain't gonna hurt you. Ain't never gonna hurt you."

He tells me he ain't even got his finger on the trigger. I breathe in big, take a good look. It's small, fits right in his hand, and the color is just the same as his eyes.

"You know how to use it, Daddy?"

"I'm gonna tell you this now, so you can't say I never did," he says. "But don't go telling nobody about it neither. This is just for you and me." He snaps that gun up in his hand, slides his finger down the nose, spin-flips it and holds it with the handle facing out to me.

"You my boy, Jake," he says. "You my only son. A man's got to protect what he loves, and if you love something enough you'll kill to keep it, or die trying. When you get to be a man yourself you'll know what I'm telling you is true."

"But what about Momma?" I say. "You said she was gonna break—"

"Naw, boy. This ain't about her no more." He puts his hand on the scarf, right down on my shoulder, and when he squeezes I know I ain't running nowhere no more. "All you got to know is I'm doing what I got to do. Back before you was born, somebody tried to break this family up but I protected you. I saved us all."

"So you *can* use it then," I say. "You killed a man."

"I did what I had to do," Daddy says. "That's all you need to know."

He steps back, spin-flips that gun again, and points the nose straight up. He cocks his arm at his side, runs two fingers down the barrel like he's giving it a shine. "You want to see if I can use it? Let me show you what kind of shot your daddy is."

He steps out and points it down the street, at that pigeon still walking around in the dark.

"What you doing, Daddy? It ain't nothing but a bird."

"Don't you worry, boy. It ain't nothing at all."

He clicks the hammer back, locks his arm straight out and then it's a crack-flash *boom*—white light, something old burning, and that shot sound bouncing all around like thunder.

But those wings keep flapping. That pigeon does a couple circles up high and lands again a little farther down the way.

Daddy puts his arm up again. "Stupid motherfucker," he says. "Don't know what he's got coming."

I put my hand out. "Let me do it."

Daddy puts the gun down, clicks off the hammer. "You think you can shoot this?"

"Give it to me."

He tells me to come here, and I do. He puts it in my hand, stands behind me and reaches his arms around like he always did, teaching me to shoot on the hoop he nailed to the maple out behind our Chicago house. But I push those arms away. Don't need that no more. I hear him laughing behind me saying you can't even see that thing now it's too dark too far away but when I pull that hammer back he just fades out, I don't hear nothing but that metal whispering singing soft like Momma used to put me to sleep way back then but I'm wide awake tonight. I hold it out straight, look down the nose out into the dark and can't see nothing at all can't hear no wings flapping but I just wait, I breathe in big let it out slow and then I see him, and the longer I look the bigger he gets, the longer I look the more I see that heart right through the skin and hear it beating creeping right up the barrel *boom boom boom* feel it making me sweat under this scarf and right down to my hand. I see it, gonna hit it dead-on, but I can't. I wait for him to flap his wings out again because one of them can grow back and he's nothing but a bird. I wait and wait and then he does and I tear it right off.

"You missed him," Daddy says.

I run into the dark, right to where he's laying. He's crying worse than a cat fell out of a tree, and flapping that other wing like a motherfucker. He gets up in the air a foot, comes right at me and his blood sprays me good, but quick as that he's down again.

Daddy comes up behind me. "You hit him! That's a good boy. Go on and finish it now."

I turn around and look up at him. "I can't, Daddy."

He quick-grabs the gun from me. "He's mine then."

"Daddy have some mercy on him!" I say. "He's nothing but a bird."

"I *am* having mercy, boy. I ain't gonna let him live with that pain."

He pushes me away, takes a step back, and shoots. I want to close my eyes, but that bird's blood is on me now. The shot misses and the bird flaps harder, gets up in the air a second then drops again, but Daddy steps in close now and this one goes right to the heart.

* * *

Way back then, I didn't know where Daddy took me that night, but I do now. Same place I am today. Right here in Oakland, the Flatlands, wrong side of the water, wrong end of the bridge. It's all different for me now—I'm a working man, I found me a girl, and I've got a son of my own—but some shit ain't changed at all. Prez Reagan is gone, Read My Lips Georgie too, but folks say Slick Billy ain't gonna be no different. He ain't been in but a few months now, but I still ain't seen nothing trickle down my way but some pigeon shit and a whole lot of rain. Folks say Georgie never finished the job with old Saddam Insane, and Billy knows us folks on the county can read his lips but we don't pay his bills, so it ain't gonna be long before that GR gets cut till you can't cut it no more.

When we drove back that night, Daddy pointed at that labor hall, and I saw those green doors, same ones I started walking through a couple years ago. It's just like he said, they just use a brother up and throw him out, but it's work, and that's something. I've got me a moving job now and it's pretty steady, but there's days my back just wishes I was sitting in that hall doing nothing but drinking coffee and shooting the shit.

He dropped me home on Valley Street that night, took back the jacket and scarf, and left me standing there at the door. Didn't say where he was going, didn't tell me when he got back the next night neither. I asked Momma and the girls, but they wouldn't give me nothing.

But it didn't take long. The courts on Archer Street had lots of stories. I heard about Daddy pulling boosts, with Dereck and all alone, and I knew that's where the rent was coming from. Now and again I threw in a story of my own, but I never told nobody about that pigeon, not even Lydell. I knew I could shoot a gun better than any of those brothers, even if Daddy couldn't do it to save his life, but nobody would have believed me if they asked me how I learned.

Lots of stories, but there was one I never heard, not at the courts, not from the girls, and sure not out of Momma. I never heard, but I never asked neither, because he told me don't go talking about that night. I figured if I kept that promise, that missing story would just come right on home to me on its own. But all that waiting never did me no good. He never told me no secrets. Never told me who it was tried to break up the family, never told me who he killed because he loved me so much.

But I know better now. Nobody ever broke up the family better than he did. He's doing time for it now, upstate in Folsom, and even with these seven years gone by he'd still probably say he did it all just to keep us together, still probably say it was me that put him there.

He can cry all he wants, long as I don't have to hear it. And long as he ain't around, nobody's gonna know I'm his son. I'm taller than him now and I'm skinny like Momma. I ain't got his face, and I sure ain't never ending up in no prison. This voice is the only thing he ever gave me I've still got left. I can't shake it, can't run from it or lie it away—not even Momma could tell us apart if she wasn't looking.

But she ain't here. Nobody is that knows nothing. Long as Daddy ain't around, I can spin out any story I want—ain't nobody gonna know where *I* come from.

PART I

CHAPTER 1
PLAYIN'

Clouds rolling in, the kind that make an old man's bones ache, all dark and full-up with rain. Breeze blows cold coming down the street, whips right on past us under the freeway and straight to the water. Cold like you wouldn't think it could be now that it's spring going on summer, the kind that gets down inside you if you ain't doing nothing but standing still.

We turn right out of Parker's Alley and head up the street, toward First. Noel shakes her head at me and switches William to her other arm. "He don't know this child from nothing," she says. "First it's one thing, then it's something else he told us the time before there wasn't no way it coulda been. And every time he's got something new we gotta pay for."

I look at her, walking tall beside me, fixing her hand under William again to get a better hold. She's my girl, and we ain't married yet but William's our little boy, just hit a year old couple months ago. She's pretty like you write a song about—cream coffee skin and not too thin, and a smile I could feel before she even flashed it, first time I met her, down at the labor hall. But all this with William is starting to show on her now. She don't look like she used to, she told me again this morning, and she keeps saying there ain't no sense in fixing-up with make-up if you've got to slap on so much you come out looking set to trick. Most times I tell her she's lying, she looks fine as she ever did, but when I let it slide today she put a smack on my ass before I even knew I forgot.

I put my hands in my jacket pockets and cross them over my belly. The zipper broke about a year back when Mr. Jerry was good and torn-up and tried to take this jacket right off me. We're coming out of the Birdhouse now, the St. Al's clinic, and like most times we're walking this walk I don't have much to say. I heard the doc just like Noel did, and even if it wasn't old Doc Charlie who else we gonna believe? That nurse Chaka was standing right there too, didn't say nothing different, and everybody knows she's seen it all. And I've been up nights just like Noel has, listening to my little man coughing like ain't no kid this young ought to be, that sound hitting me like somebody banging on our door and I'm locked-down on our bed can't get up to stop them. Might as well kick me right in the balls for how I'm feeling after a night like that, carrying that sound with me, like glass breaking, most everywhere I go.

"*God bless you, Jesus help you,*" Noel says, sticking her lips out and talking low and white like the doc. "Well Jesus better come and help *his* ass when I tie that white coat around his ankles and leave him hanging up there with them pigeons."

I tell her to give William to me, and just like that he starts in on his crying, but maybe I can get a laugh out of Noel and he'll catch on too. The Cliffs are behind us, back down the street, and I spin around and head toward them. It's the same bridge on the same street Daddy showed me all those years back, but now I know what us Flatlands folks call it. The pigeons and crows been jammed up in this overpass long as anybody can remember, long before me and Daddy scared some off with that gun. Gone and made their own project up in there, don't need no light or heat or nothing, and folks say soon as the government finds out they're gonna get the pigeons to build the next SROs and save them taxpayers some *serious* money. Folks say you can count on them birds dropping every time a foreign car passes over, and come rush hour you'd think it was damn-near snowing right here in California. They say back in the day when there was a couple of banks and dressing-up restaurants down here, Old Willie White Shoes used to take a brush to the walk every morning. He was the one gave it the name, said it reminded him of that place he went in England where the birds shit so much they turned a whole hill white. Don't know who believes that, because they say Old Willie never got farther than his TV could take him, but it stuck. When those places moved across the water Old Willie went with them, and these days you can't find a city crew to clean this walk at all. This stretch along Wall right down from the alley is the worst of it, but you can't get anywhere downtown in the Flatlands without crossing through the Cliffs, what with the freeway cutting right through and those exits shooting off. You're gonna get hit sometime, don't matter what you do.

I hug William to my chest and pull my jacket over him, and I tell Noel let's go dodge them bombs, see who can hold out longest. I start running before she can even say a thing, get right down under there where I can hear the cars zoom-clacking and the birds caw-cooing and I shout up to them to bring it on.

"Get in here, baby!" I say, but Noel just walks slow. "Let's see what you got. Come on now—can't beat me if you don't play!"

I juke and jive, shuffle and swing, spin around smooth enough to dance between the rain if I needed to—but I hope I lose quick. William is still crying and Noel's still got her mind on what the doc said by the look of her, but if I can just get a bird to drop one down, hit me right on the nose, maybe that will get a laugh out of her, maybe then I can tell her it's gonna be all right, and pass William back to her while she's still laughing and calling me a fool. Maybe then I could quick-slip away and go take care of business, wouldn't have to hear no more about nothing until I got home.

But looks like all the Mercedes stayed home today, don't like going out in the rain, not even on the Friday before Memorial Day. I look up, but nothing's coming down.

Noel takes him right from me, puts him to her shoulder. He gives a scream like he's been saving it up all day. She looks at me with those big eyes open wide, like she's about to let them flow. Her hand comes up quick right at my collar, yanks me to her, up against the bridge leg. She pulls me like I'm some kind of doll, and if she weren't holding the boy I'd slap her one good. She puts her back against the bridge leg and brings me in close. Without even looking she brings her shirt halfway up and slides William to her breast, and his crying stops right quick.

"Just tell me he's talking crazy, Jake," she says. She bites down on her lip and looks up, shooting her eyes up into that space out from under the Cliffs, looking at those clouds moving fast. "Some other doc would have told us different."

"It ain't nothing. This boy's gonna be fine." I reach over and put my finger real soft on his cheek. "He's a good old boy, just can't shake this nasty cold he's got." I smile big, lying like a motherfucker, and do another little swing and juke, looking for something to break in her eyes.

She screws her face up sour and shakes her head. "Don't gimme that. This boy turned *blue*, Jake—blue as that water! You weren't there but I was!"

I turn my hands up. "Is that what this is gonna be? I wasn't there? Well what you think I'm out here doing when I ain't there?"

"You been hearing him nights just as good as me. And I know you ain't stupid."

"Yeah but he coughed it up, didn't he? He can do it again. And that doc even said himself it's hard to say for sure."

"He's *got* it, Jake. He's got that asthma, or he's getting it soon." She turns her head back down the street toward the alley. "That guy is just afraid to say it," she says, pointing with her chin. "But I ain't."

I look down the street too, just let my eyes walk on down the walk, through the Cliffs along the water, down the same way I shot that pigeon all those years back, past the corner of Wall all the way down to King, where the freeway turns off and starts cutting through the downtown nobody wants to see with the window down and the door unlocked. Every now and again the wind slaps the water up against the wall, makes it hang in the air like a bird just gliding, then drops it smack down on the street. I see some dude down there in an army camo jacket—like he's trying to disappear or something right here in the city—walking along with a pole in his hand. His hair is going gray sticking out from under that cap, but the brother's sure got a rhythm going. Little old-time swing like Daddy used to have when we first left Chicago, and even almost like Laurence, but the dude's too short. He swings that pole back till the tip near touches the street, brings it up and across him and taps the wall, and it's like he's pushing a button because the water comes right over. The old guy slides up flat against the wall, lets the water drop on the street, starts that swing, and does it again. I can't make out his face from this far, but sure looks like he's laughing under that cap.

"So what's it gonna be, Jake?" Noel says, shaking me. "You listening to me? What you gonna do—what *we* gonna do?"

It's getting late now, I can feel it. Time got away from us waiting down in the alley, like it always does. I look over her shoulder, across the street at the Angelus, just let my eyes climb up one window at a time till it disappears behind the freeway. Plenty of nights I stayed up in there listening to them cars roll by, and even when they got quiet there was always somebody knocking, somebody trying the handle down the hall and *shit brother where you been* and it was party time with the girls and the dope and there ain't no sleeping while that's going down. Downtown in the Flatlands, there's an SRO on every block, and the door's always open. That's why me and Noel are sticking together the way we are. Let that doc come out here and find one building ain't got roaches top to bottom. Every-damn-body around here has some kind of cough—who's he joking?—and if he could hear Mr. Jerry he'd about fall outta his chair.

Just as I'm looking over at it some brother comes tripping out the front and across the street, and it's been a while. That dude in the black jacket I used to know from up at the labor hall. He spits on the sidewalk, runs his hand across his nose, bends halfway over and shakes his head like he's trying to get water out of his ear, does it both sides. It's that old routine, hasn't changed at all, and when I start laughing Noel looks over too. He stands up straight and does that dance he said he learned running track—back when he could *fly*, brother—two steps up two back, two up two back, arms pumping like a motherfucker. The whole time his head is rising, just going up up back back like he's in that zone, gonna break that tape, and when he does that chest goes out and the fists are up and he's bouncing around like Ali. Then he claps his hands together, rubs them real fast, licks a finger and puts it up. He closes his eyes and starts turning a slow circle. That finger comes down, and points right at us, and quick as that he's coming.

Noel puts her shirt down and hugs William into her chest, but I know this dude's seen something. He puts a foot up on the curb, bends over slow till his elbow sits on his knee and his chin sits up on his hand. That long finger comes rolling out and his eyes follow it up her body till he's about looking through his eyebrows to look her in the face. "You that la-dy," he says, pointing, with that voice of his, all low and scratchy out of the back of his throat like he lost it way back when and ain't never figured out how to get it back. "You that *girl*."

His eyes move over to me and he smiles. He stands up straight and claps those hands, snaps into that dance, two steps up the curb and two down, two up two down, but it's only a couple seconds before he's worn out. "You all done got *busy!*" he says, pointing at William. "Been a while now I been hearing stories, and now look at my luck, heh heh."

He moves his hand toward her, and when Noel jumps back he just laughs. I put my hand on his shoulder, strong enough so he knows it's time to go. "Ain't you got someone expecting you down there?" I say, pointing to the alley.

"Aw brother," he says. "Ain't we worked together? Well ain't we at least *tried* to work together? 'Cause you know, if it weren't for Blue, I'd have been out on them jobs with you every day! Damn, how long it been since I seen you? Ain't *nobody* up at the hall seen you around lately."

"Quit talking your shit," I say. "Get on outta here."

"I'll be looking for you now," he says. "Now that you got some stories to tell."

He's flying now, must have got himself a good spook for lunch. He turns back to Noel, but I put both hands on his shoulders and pull him back. Noel quick-steps around the bridge leg and out of sight.

"Aw brother, sweet little cake like that you can't eat it *all* yourself," he says.

"She's too much for you, old man," I say, walking him back across the street. "Besides, I ain't seen you down here in a few months now. She needs a man can stick around."

He lifts his arms up, smacks my hands off. "Stick around? Boy, you think I'm crazy? I got to get me in some *treatment* every three-four months or so. Do like them preachers say and get clean, get up outta this mess." He looks across the street at the Angelus. "Then you come back around town shined-up and squeaky-clean and all the girls are so glad to see you they ready to *give* it away. And shit, not even no preacher man gonna turn down a bite of *them* apples. Ain't nothing sweeter than getting dirty once you done got clean."

He walks on, but only gets a couple steps before I see that grin again. "She too much for me, huh? Think I'd die coming? That's the best way to go. You ever get ready to put her out, you just let me know."

I wave him on and watch him walk down the block toward the alley. I head up to the corner where Noel is waiting. The dude in the black jacket starts singing, loud enough so it bounces around under the Cliffs. "My dick is hard, and my balls are smokin'. I need a shot of pussy, and I ain't jokin'! Don't you go thinking I'm old now!"

Noel looks across the street, shifts William on her hip. "You gonna make it?" she says.

"I'll make it," I say.

I reach over and kiss them both. Noel just gives me her cheek like usual, holding still a second from that little rocking she does to help William fall asleep. I take my jacket off and hang it on her shoulders. They cross the street, and Noel sits down on the bench to wait for the bus.

When you're in the game, there's times you gotta run. I quick-step across the street and head up the block past the Angelus. Got to see my caseworker, if she's even there at all, get in there and keep it going another little while till we get through.

* * *

Everybody's got a game just like they've got a cough once you get down here, don't matter where you come from. Noel picked it up quick herself, and soon enough she knew good as I did that it ain't so easy putting it down. Hardest game to shake is the one folks play right here under the Cliffs—the Four Corners. That's why me and Noel keep playin' our own. All that time I was staying in the Angelus I'd see folks playin' the Corners, running up and down back and forth across them streets so much you'd think why didn't they just take old Willie's brush out there and do a little work while they're at it? Folks who've been around a lot longer than me say if Prez Reagan had ever took a look down here he would have named them streets himself, called them Trickle-Down Lane and Tax-Free Ave—just check out all the *business* going down, a man gets Empowered like a motherfucker in that Zone. But not even old Ronnie would have tried to steal the name of Parker's Alley. That's Doc Charlie's, and it ain't for the taking, even if he's gone now, even if nobody ever saw him blowing a horn, even if most everybody who went in his Birdhouse still came out singin' the blues. Doc Charlie was a good man, and that St. Al's clinic is *still* the only place they'll take those coupons or take you in for nothing at all—but they can't heal you like that Jesus on the wall. Closest thing you've got to a miracle in Parker's Alley is the Job Club, the needle exchange across Wall, behind the Angelus. You give them some junked ones, they come back clean. You get yourself some of them, or a pipe, and you're ready to go to work, jack, start playin' the Four Corners. First you get a room up in the Angelus, cheapest SRO in town and enough rock going in and out to build a quarry. You get your check to start out the month and see how long it lasts—a day, half a week, maybe a full one but sure as hell not two. When it's smoked you roll on over to the St. Al's, the place you go when they won't take you in noplace else. It's big, got three floors and plenty of mats, and they'll even take you when you're still spooked as long as you don't got no works or liquor in your pocket. They're good people, even clean up your vomit with you, but you break one of them Commandments you'll be out quick—and folk do all the time. Ain't nothing that makes you want to pick a fight or a pocket like getting the shakes. When they put you out of there, or if you just can't get a space—some days, by the time they let in all the grandpas and vets in chairs and ladies screaming at somebody who ain't even there, there's hardly room for anybody else—you roll on down to the Cliffs, third corner, bottom of the barrel. You find yourself a cardboard condo or whatever bags and blankets are in the dumpsters, stake out the driest place you see even though those birds got some smart bombs better than Stormin' Norman's army had when Read My Lips Georgie couldn't finish off Saddam Insane, and listen to all that zoom-clacking and coo-cawing and brother gimme a dollar and how about a drink until you're ready to Surrender like the first Step says, till it's *good God almighty never again*, till you climb up Wall, cross First and knock on the St. Peter and see how long you can stay clean till you're ready to get dirty again. Ain't easy playin' that, even harder breaking out, putting that game down. Maybe that's why that dude jumped a couple years back, the one folks say tried flying over to the St. Peter on Thanksgiving night and ended up all over First, thanking God he had enough junk in him not to feel it too much.

But Noel ain't like that, and I ain't neither. We're just trying to find a way to bring this boy up, any way we can piece it together—the county, the stamps, my job, and two caseworkers in different parts of the Flatlands who don't know we're together. We're playin', just like anybody else—but this game we've got is all our own.

Still some long blocks to the county office. I'm hoping to catch a short line in there, but I still have to hustle if I'm gonna beat these clouds. I'm off today, Friday, ain't working again till Sunday when we head out to the desert—and it sure better be warmer than this or I'm coming right back. The wind picks up again, colder now, but those clouds aren't taking the ride. Just hang up there, blueblack and heavy, like an old man sitting steady with something he's been waiting to tell you all day.

I stay on First, a block up from the water, and at the corner of King I see him again. Walking along, swinging that fishing pole nice and easy, tapping the wall and sliding up against it when the water smacks down. Now *that's* playin'. I don't know the brother but just watching him walk I know him good enough, I know there was probably a time at the hall he cracked me up with something good, got going with a story that had everybody hanging on and falling over out on the corner, not even thinking about how we couldn't get any work. Not everybody sees it like I do—especially folks like George, folks who look down here and don't even want to see it. Playin' ain't just working, it's getting by. Sure plenty of folks are gonna try to work something like me and Noel, cheat 'em 'cause they cheating you, but there are times you're out on that corner all day and ain't no kind of work coming your way, and if you can't play it and get a laugh you'd better just get on outta town. If you can't go back to your cardboard condo under the Cliffs at the end of the day and see ain't a pigeon missed it and figure hey at least I'm keeping that street under there clean, maybe I can charge the city for that—if you can't do that, before too long you'll be walking around dead. Playin' is getting by when there *ain't* no getting by. It's saying maybe I ain't got shit in my pockets but at least I'm a man.

Crossing King I see him come up on the Break, and slip right on through the wall. A while back, maybe ten years ago or whenever Prez Reagan was in his first go-round, a storm knocked the water through the wall right here, washed the whole park out below. Never got fixed-up after that, folks say, because that was when some money started packing up outta here and crossing the bridge, some real money, and pretty soon those nice folks from Bella Vista didn't want to come down here and hear all them ships and trains and breathe in that air that ain't nice folks' air no more. After that they said the park was shut down, but they know who's down there and how they're getting in. The old man slips through, but I can't follow him now.

I quick-step and get a little rhythm going, try to walk myself warm. The blocks are just about empty this afternoon, nothing but folks checking the curbs for butts with a drag left in them or stopping in front of a hotel and looking up to the top. The traffic is light like always, until I come up on the other overpass, a couple blocks from Battery.

Underneath I hear them passing over, heading out for the weekend, zoom-zoom-zooming so quick I can't make out one from another. Walking slow now, stopping, standing in the middle of all those bridge legs, looking down the block, the sound gets bigger till I can't hear it no more. Nobody down there by the Ready Man that I can see from here, nobody out there crowing on the old corner across from the hall. Nobody leaning up against those green doors, ducking out from the wind, probably nobody behind them neither. I put my hand on a bridge leg, same one I ducked behind couple years ago, my breath all gone and my hand busted open and George back behind those doors cleaning his own blood up off the floor. Just standing still, looking down the block, that cold runs right up my arm and makes my shoulder ache, right in that old spot, and I get moving again because I don't have no time to be an old man yet.

The office is a couple blocks up—you follow the freeway up the little rise to Fourth, turn off and walk till you just about lose the sound of those cars. I hustle in the door, and inside it's a whole different noise. Kids crying and mommas shushing them, phones ringing and nobody answering them, folks sitting and waiting and waiting.

In here, it's all about the waiting. I put my name down to see my caseworker, and sit in one of the chairs. Five rows of them on each side, those blue plastic seats stuck on a piece of metal and all welded to another piece running across the floor. No matter what you do—sit down, lean back, get up again—everybody in your row feels it. The seats aren't even half-full, but it looks like most of the caseworkers are out today. I take one on the end of the only empty row and keep a look out for the fat folks. One time a dude in here sent our whole row flying, sat down right quick in the first seat by the door and popped us outta those chairs like a jack-in-the-box. Plenty of folks fall asleep in here, but you won't catch me doing that no more. Besides, the waiting always gives me a little time to see over across the glass, see if I can get a quick look and figure how the story needs to go that day.

Could be like pissing into the wind, the way Rhonda is coming out. I see her head first, hair pulled back like always and those braids swinging with all the colored beads, pushing some dude in a wheelchair, coming fast. Past the glass and right up to where the chairs start, and her eyes go tight when she shoves him away and says, "Get out!"

The dude rolls right up next to me and wheels around, turns right on a dime looking back at her. He's got a vet's cap pulled low, dark green with yellow letters, and a flag pinned on the brim. "Damn, girl," he says, and right off I know he's from someplace else, not Mississippi like Auntie Thelma and her "damn chiiiild" with that "i" about as long as the river it comes from, but somewhere back South. He pats his legs twice, and I see they don't go past his knee, either one of them. "What's it to *you* now, huh? Maybe if you *gave* it to me I'd *grow* me some."

Rhonda just flips her hand in the air. Her pants swish high, and she disappears. The dude looks at me and turns his hand over, empty side up. "Shit, now a *white* girl gonna *give* me that ten dollars." He leans over and touches my arm, smiles big. "Down there at Payless this morning, that pretty little thing just didn't know *what* to say when I told her let me try on some wing-tips. Them blue eyes just about fell out of her head. I could hear that manager laughing his ass off when she went to ask him about it." He reaches for the pack on the back of his chair and pulls them out. That leather shines like new metal, smells good enough to make me hungry. "That girl was just about crying, she leaned over close enough to kiss me and said she hoped they fit me good," he says. He shakes his head, pulls his hands down inside his jacket sleeves and holds up his arms. "Shit, next week I'm gonna tell her some gook found me over here after all this time and cut my hands off, so can I get me some gloves?"

He whirls around again and rolls himself to the door, and when I open it for him I hear Rhonda call out for next in line. The lady in front of me gets up, holds her baby to her chest and stretches the free arm to the two kids, gives them a finger each, the pointer and the pinky. Maybe there's some candy waiting for them back there, because they hush up quick. The lady is older, thirty or somewhere up there, and she's dressed nice, now that I get a look at her. Navy jacket, slacks to match, nice red blouse setting them off. Brown leather shoes that would sure clock across the floor if there weren't this carpet over it. She's tall and she walks steady with her arm stretched behind her, and the kids have to run to keep up. I watch them all till they disappear behind that cubicle wall.

I look down at my boots, the ones I got at Sal's Army back before I met Noel and before I even started working out of the labor hall. They ain't talking yet, but might not be too long—that sole on the right one looks itching to come loose. They're all right for now, this moving job with Bills ain't hard on them like construction or some other work I've done, but one of these days I oughta do like Noel says and get me a new pair, something that could take the work and maybe even be good to step out in, with a good shine and some pants just long enough to show off the laces. I settle back in the chair, put my hands in my jeans pockets, and try thinking about how she's doing at that other office. Doesn't make any sense, but going to two offices was the only sense we could make of this mess, so I used my old Angelus room number on my application and Noel put down our apartment on hers, that basement hole I've had a couple years now and the roaches have had since as long as they've wanted. Keeping separate is the only way to stay together. Noel just keeps telling them she don't know who the daddy is and don't want him around if she did, and she gets her check, some stamps, and some coupons. I watch my ass, make sure ain't nobody even *in* here same time as me who's ever seen me with Noel—and that ain't easy—and the county throws me that General Grief every month, enough to get some diapers and milk, because that boy can't do on just one a day. The moving job with All Things gives me five and a quarter, a buck up from minimum, but I ain't worked ninety days yet and won't see no kind of raise till Bills gets the OK from corporate. Up until William was born, the apartment manager gave me that basement room for next to nothing, all I had to do was keep the halls clean and sweep the walk out front. But he's gone, and now the rent takes my whole moving check at once. Just sitting here thinking, I know we're gonna be a little short this month because of that paint I bought for our place. Ever since that time we walked around town when I was first getting to know her, and she saw that man selling flowers, I've known there's something about yellow for Noel. Her eyes went big and her lips kissed the air, so I got her those flowers, right on the spot—don't know what kind, just they were yellow. I still don't know from flowers, but there's times I'll see some and if I've got a couple dollars on me and the man has some yellows, I'll take them. So that day I went looking for the paint, it was easy—except I got blue for the bathroom so I could at least have some part of the place looked like a man's. But it's still sitting there, all those gallons and rollers and brushes, and our walls are still dirty green and cracked like motherfuckers. With no real windows down there we need something to give the place a little light. I've been wanting to surprise her, have her come back to it one day, our place all bright and all those cracks sealed up, but how am I gonna do that when she's home most all day? How am I gonna open them cans and get it done before she smells it, before she starts going off saying what you doing buying that when this child ain't got milk?

"Robertson! You coming or what?"

I look up and see Rhonda standing there with the clipboard, scratching the pen back and forth across the page. She hangs it up and walks back, and her legs make that high swishing, that black nylon sweatsuit she wears now and again. The tall lady turns her shoulder to squeeze past her, and the kids follow behind, still running to keep up.

It's tighter back here than the last time I was in. Folks moved all the cubicles around, all these stand-up walls that reach to your shoulder, and you'd have to have some NFL moves to get through here fast. Rhonda is already behind her desk, looking down at her fingers all out in front of her. My file is there, still closed, and she folds her hands on top of it. "You need something today, Mr. Robertson?"

I take the letter out of my pocket, the one I picked up in the box I still keep at the Angelus. "Says here you need to talk to me."

"Sit down." She opens the file. "Yes, that was sent out—"

"Twenty-fifth of April," I say.

"Twenty-*fourth*," she says, her finger on the page, looking up at me now. "I *know* when I sent it out. Any reason you waited a whole month to read it?"

"Yeah well if you'd put it in with the check I would have got it next day," I say. "You *know* the postmen get them *brown* letters there on time."

She doesn't laugh, just shakes her head. "It doesn't work that way. Anyway, it's the *what* we're talking about right now, Jake, not the *when*."

"Rhonda?"

A girl comes up to the opening between the dividers. She's one of the case-workers too, but she sure looks like a baby. She's got blond hair, thin and shiny, smooth pale skin. She looks at me, starts to say she's sorry for breaking up this fine chat I'm having with my good friend Rhonda—good ole soul sister, looking-out-for-me Rhonda—but she stops, and I know she knows something.

She looks at Rhonda, and I can make out the edge of that big smile. "Um, he called."

Rhonda's eyebrows go up. "When?"

"*That's* what I was gonna tell you," I say. "I been trying to get in here but I'm busy as a motherfucker out there."

Rhonda snaps the file shut and hands it over the desk. "You want to take it yourself, Jake? Save me the trouble of tossing it out."

I look over at the girl, who ain't smiling no more, then lean back and look up at the ceiling till she pulls it away.

Rhonda breathes out loud and slow through her mouth, dialing the phone. She looks up at me, puts that little radio on my side of the desk, and turns up the volume. She checks her watch and spins around in her chair, facing the back wall now. "Hey baby," I hear her say.

Nothing but some ads playing on her radio. I pull the antenna out all the way, move the dial around, but nothing. Rhonda looks back over her shoulder, waves her hand at me to stop, but she's too busy talking. No music I can find, just this jingle and that one about something you gotta have—but it's nothing you can kick back to, relax and find a groove, nothing that can get your mind off where you're at.

I run into one about some kind of car when Rhonda hangs up. She checks her watch again. "All right, let's do this quickly," she says. She picks the file up off the desk. "Tell me why I should keep this case open."

"Wait hold on," I say, putting my elbows on the desk and snapping the letter open. "Says here we're gonna *discuss*, not close."

"Well, where have you been all this time?" she says. "How long am I supposed to wait for you to show up?"

"Lady, I just *got* this thing," I say. "And I just got done telling you I'm out there working like a—"

"Rhonda?" The girl pops her head in again. "Um, sorry," she says, looking at me, her eyes going all the way down to my boots. She smiles quick like she don't mean it and looks back at Rhonda. "Um, did you talk to him?"

Rhonda laughs. "Yeah, I'm gonna go pick him up at his office in a minute. You know what he tells me now? He's thinking of *selling* that car." She leans forward, shakes her head. " I don't know about that brother anymore. First I thought he had these nice eyes and he tells me he's got color contacts. Now all this about his car—" She waves her hand in front of her.

"Can you, um—" The girl puts her hand to her head, thumb up at her ear and pinky at her mouth.

She steps out, and Rhonda picks up the phone. The radio is still going, still spinning those ads. She puts her purse up on the desk. "So Jake," she says, looking at her fingers again, straight down in front of her face. "Tell me what it is you're out there doing."

"I told you I'm working," I say, then stop myself, almost getting stupid. "You know—looking for a job is a job and all that," I say, tapping the side of my head. "I ain't one of them dummies falling asleep reading the classifieds."

She puts her hand up and leans into the phone. "Oh," she says, looking down at her desk. Her head starts nodding. "I see."

I could walk out right now and it might all be the same, for all I know. She's fixing to leave, get her nails done and pick up her man, and she could throw my shit right in that can without anybody ever seeing. And who am I? Who's gonna believe me any way I tell it? Doesn't matter if I 'fess up about the job and she cuts me fifty cents to the dollar and I slide off GR in two months, doesn't matter if I tell her I'm just some joker getting the work search form signed for my two-twelve and the stamps. Doesn't matter, but I need to try some kind of riff.

"Look," I say. "If there was jobs out there I'd have me one by now. I'm trying to play by the—"

"Let me see your arms!" she says, slamming the phone down, smacking her fist on the desk. "Let me see what kind of work you're doing!"

I jump back in the chair. "Now where you going?"

"Let's see them!"

"Look, lady, the closest I ever been to some tracks was a railyard," I say, folding my arms across my chest. "Let's get to talking about my case now."

She stands up, puts both hands on the desk, and leans across. Her eyes look straight at me, straight through me, small and dark. Her face goes flat, like that lady with the kids, just all flat and you don't even know her from nobody else at all.

"You done been caught, *booooy*," she says, talking low, stretching her mouth out crazy on that last word, trying to sound like the dude in the wheelchair if she could. "Down in the alley with the users and losers."

Doesn't make no sense, won't matter now, but I try to get up in those eyes, see if I can wet them down somehow.

"You got a kid too, don't you?" I say. She straightens back up. I lean into the desk, putting my arms up on it. "You know what it's like. You think I'm gonna be getting spooked in that alley when I got me a little boy now?" I push my sleeves up and slap them muscles hard. "Go ahead *look* at these arms then, if you want to see what kind of man I am."

She purses her lips and breathes loud out her nose. She checks her watch. "All right, Jake, all right." She picks up the file. "Come back in next week, and I'll see if there's some way we can keep this open. Maybe get you into some treatment, switch you over to SSI."

I jump up. "What kind of shit is that? I don't need no crackhead check!" Rhonda shakes her head, turns around and opens the cabinet. I jump up on the desk, slide quick on my knees to the edge, take the file right out of her hand.

"Jake Robertson is a working man," I say. "He got him a son named William and don't matter how many jobs he got, we need this here money." I grab a pen up off the desk. "Now write that! Write it!"

Rhonda steps back, catches her leg on that file cabinet door and falls back on her ass, smacks up against that green cubicle wall. A picture frame comes down quick, falls glass side down on her hand.

I stand up on the desk and rare back with that file, set to throw it down on her. She puts her hand up, with the blood coming, and I let it drop. I look around, at the green walls and the desks and all the folks looking up at me, look out to the waiting room too, and in that glass in-between I can see myself. Just me in this old shirt that looks like something Daddy would wear. I kick that wall down, right at him, but when it hits the glass it's like throwing a rock into still water, and he's gone and I'm gone too.

I jump down. Rhonda yells, other folk yell, but I'm too quick. I take the file, I take her purse, and I'm out past those blue chairs, into the street and gone.

* * *

I dump the purse in the first block, grab the bills and turn the corner. Nothing but make-up and some credit cards anyway, and who needs that down here?

Running with the bills in my hand, running into the dark, turning corners now, and now, and now again like I'm following I don't know what, getting tired but keeping on till it just comes up out of me, hot rushing bitter nasty, full-up thick and I can't breathe till it's out. I stand up straight but it comes again, and again, and my legs get like mashed potatoes. I catch myself on some wall and ease on down till I'm sitting looking at that vomit. Can't remember what I ate today, but it's sure enough all there. I pull the bills open—nothing but three Georges, sweating as bad as me now, and what can I get with that? Loaf of bread, pint of milk, and a ride on the bus if the driver lets me come up short.

I ball them back up and throw them into my mess, try to kick them away but my boot just splashes it around. The bills come apart from each other, slow and easy, and I think if I could see old G.W.'s face on them he'd be laughing like a motherfucker. Three bucks. Sure it was easy, sure I was worked-up, but what kind of fool steals three damn dollars? What kind of fool passes on a chance to keep his check going—even if he does have to go playin' about being a crackhead—just so he can say that ain't me? What kind of sorry ass fool wants to go telling the truth—because that's what I would have done if she'd let me, if she hadn't gotten me worked-up, would have spilled it all about William and Noel and her check and my job—when he knows you can't work and keep a check, can't keep a family without work, can't keep it all unless you're playin', when he knows all he's doing is saying *this is who I am*, but ain't nobody listening?

There's a bird crying, one of those gulls maybe, and looking around I know I'm near the Break, on the wall. I look up the block and see the freeway, the lights on the cars zooming away going white to red, and the streetlights down here brighter now, even with the fog rolling in. The wind picks up and I think I smell something burning on the other side of the wall, some kind of fish maybe. There's times down in the park after dark when somebody's got a piece of meat and they make a little fire and cook it up, even if it's gonna draw a crowd. Folks figure even if they have to share, at least they'll get something. Maybe that old man in the army jacket caught something. I pick up the dollars, shake them off, and stand up. Might as well try to use them, because that bitch sure won't want them back now.

The wall is tall, and thick too. Not like you'd think it would be to keep this park out of sight and hold all that water back, but it still takes you a couple steps to get through the Break. When I come up on it, get set to go down, my shadow comes up on the wall and I turn quick to see who's there. But it's nothing, just me, just some light that got behind me from someplace I didn't see.

The Break is thin but it's enough. I go sideways, and right when I do, right when I get my hands on that cold dark wet falling apart inside of the wall with the rebar rusted-out, the wind comes through, up from the water, bringing that fish. Dude must have caught something good. It's dark, and Noel might have a plate ready for me at home already—and if William is good and quiet it could be something to really sit down to—but after that vomit I don't want to wait that long. When a man is hungry, sometimes there's nothing else.

I jump down on the grass and send water flying, and have to kick my boots up out of the mud. The gulls scatter, a whole mess of them at the edge of the grass, where it drops off into the water. I look around, but no fire, just some streetlight caught in the puddles in the grass. And the smell is gone too, like it wasn't even here at all.

Nobody around, not that old man, not nobody that I can see, but I walk over to the edge to get a look. There's another wall that drops down below the grass, and when the tide is low folks can stand on a ledge down there. Used to be a time when the ducks would come right up to you, but these days some folks just like to sit and wash off where nobody can see them except those big ships coming in. Maybe the old man saw me coming, maybe he could see I was fixing to get me some of what he had.

I walk slow and quiet as I can, squish-stepping through the grass, around the puddles and the junk. It's everywhere, bottles and wrappers, vials and a baby doll, a book puffed-out and a sneaker talking like the worst of them, and anything else folks or the water used up and didn't want after all.

Near the drop-off I get on my knees, wash the bills in a puddle, and lean full-out over the edge to see if the old man will take something for that fish. A gull takes off, screaming like I scared it from out of a dream, from down below. Now I know.

"Jerry! What you doing down there, man?"

The dude I saw before is long gone, but now I've found old Jerry, found him trying to get lost again. Can't even tell if he's still alive. He's on his back next to the ledge, one arm in the water and one over his eyes, and his skin's so white it shines.

Real quick there's glass breaking from I don't know where and some water washes up over Jerry, and steps land hard and fast behind me. I turn around and the fist gets me right in the jaw.

I fall back and smack my head on the edge. And just like that this dude is on me, black hood and clothes but eyes shining like a train cutting through fog. I hit him in the chest but it's like a wall, and before I can get in another one that pipe is up and coming down. I duck my head to the side but it catches me on the shoulder, right on the bone, right on the spot. Burns like a motherfucker but I push through, turn over and kick up where Daddy taught me to and follow with a straight fist to his head. The dude is strong but he's still a man, and he falls over with his hands over his balls. I jump up and go to his head, right left right till he spins away and I don't want to chase him. He's big but he slips quick through the Break, and he's gone.

The ground is cold, and sitting down, lying down, the water gets through, through my hands and legs and cools my shoulder, runs all the way to my head. I'm drifting—cooler, colder. Red leaves are falling, the maple is bone-clean. Colder, colder, blueblack dark, down in our basement, that house in Chicago, walking over that cold floor in bare feet up to Granddad Lenny's workbench, and all the tools fall off the wall, fall into the shadows on the floor full of nails, old and rusted as a dead man, and I can't walk, that door bangs open and I stop dead, the light bright from all the snow, and out there the tree is bare as the black body lying at the root, out there someone's moaning like a bird lost its wing and I know he's still got some life left.

Jerry's cough snaps me out of it. Like a gun going off, so big you can't figure how a guy this old and thin could have it in him.

I push myself up and my shoulder burns again but I'll live. I let myself down onto the ledge and kneel next to Jerry. He's on his side now, holding the cap out over the water. I sit him up and the puke comes right out, but it's clear and not even stinking, like the man didn't have nothing bad in him—or he'd already been busy getting it outta him all night. By the smell of him I know it's been one of those nights that turns into three or four for the old man. Sixty-five looking like eighty-five, can't be carrying even two pounds for every year, and Jerry still drinks with the best of them—if you believe his stories.

The cough comes again, two three shots, and my face gets wet with the spit. I tap his face, making his head bob, till his eyes come open. Good and red where they ought to be white, but makes that gray in the middle look clear and shiny like a couple of polished silver bullets.

"Jerry?" I say, not even sure he sees me. "Yo Mr. Jerry man you gotta go to the *hospital* if you want to find a new liver. Can't come looking for that down in the park."

He's a good man, a nice man, and I know he'd laugh if he was in his right mind. His eyes go halfway shut again and he looks over at his green cap on the ground. Lifts it up, shows me the empty inside, but then his chin hits his chest and it falls back down.

"Come on now, Jerry," I say, tapping his face again. "There you go with that hat again. Now I know what you *really* out here doing. But you ain't no young buck no more. You can't go chasing skirt like the kind's gonna leave you flat on your ass by the water no more."

His eyes pop open, shining like the light of day, and he spits in my face.

But it's nothing I ain't seen before. I pick him up, lift him over the ledge onto the grass, climb up myself, and hitch him over my shoulder. My boots sink deep into the grass, and the rain starts down as we head toward the Break.

I put Jerry up on his feet. "Gotta slide through this little stretch yourself," I say. It's good and dark now, and through the Break I can't see nobody around, just some shadows standing still out on the street. He looks past me, out at the water, then takes his hat off. He puts his hand inside it, dark green now soaked-through, grabs quick around like maybe some little fish got stuck in there. But it's nothing. I take his hand out nice and slow, start to turn his shoulders so he can slide through. He moves against me. "Might be down there tonight," he says. That gray hair he says used to be blond back in the day is standing up like he stuck his finger in a socket. "Just another hour, it might come up." I give him a steady-soft push and hold him tight behind in case he trips. "No it won't," I say. "It ain't there tonight. Whatever it is, it ain't there."

Through the wall, back out on the street, I'm standing in the rain with this old man who couldn't tell you his ass from his jawbone right now, couldn't walk a block if you spotted him a mile. The shadows hold still and heavy, and some even disappear into the dark, into this rain falling harder the longer I stand here. I look around, but the block is empty as a church on a Monday—not even God's gonna hang around on a street like this, night like tonight.

I put my hand on Jerry's back, try to ease him down off the curb, but he ain't having it. "I can't," he says, grabbing my arm. He turns to me. The rain is dripping steady off his nose. "I can't see a goddamn thing out here."

For a skinny old man he's still got a grip like a motherfucker, but setting my hand over his he finally lets go. Can't weigh much more than a sack of cement, but when I pick him up I wish I had Bird or one of the boys from the moving crew to help me. I heft him up, feel it in that old spot where the dude hit me just now. The wind picks up, and I think I see some red leaves shoot down the curb, but I don't trust my eyes much further than I can spit when it's pouring down like this.

Don't even know what I'm looking to find, just carrying this old fool to some-place dry if I can. And it ain't the first time neither. Back when I first moved into that basement hole, I used to see Mr. Jerry coming and going with that green cap pulled low, hear that cough from inside the Otis or behind his door. But I never got his eyes till that time I was mopping the fourth floor. I heard the Otis door open, the gate squeak pulling back, heard somebody say *shit* from inside there. Soon as I saw Jerry step outta there I knew he'd break his neck on that wet floor, so I went running.

Didn't think about falling myself. Just lucky I didn't take him with me when I went slide-slipping past the Otis into the stairwell, and lucky I caught the railing at the top. That old man just shook his head, gave me those gray eyes, and asked me was I gonna go slower walking him down to his room. He didn't let me inside, but just opening the door I could see there wasn't noplace to sit down anyhow. Dude had an honest-to-God junkyard in there—so much shit I couldn't even make out one thing from another, except for a pile of bags, and when he closed the door on me right quick I just stood there listening to him walk slow through the junk until I heard another door shut inside. I didn't see him again for near a couple more months, when I found him with the bags and started putting it all together. I was on my way to the Ready Man to pick up some work, and there he was under the freeway on San Vicente. The building super had cut me out of my work, hired some corporate outfit to do it Mexican-style, fast and furious and cheap, and I was taking whatever else came my way. It was a warm summer morning, and I knew there'd be plenty of good work going out, but I saw him lying there—how was I gonna walk on by? There he was, old Mr. Jerry, lying dead drunk under the Cliffs, hugging a couple of full-up black plastic bags. I couldn't have woken him up with a winning Lotto ticket, so I just got down and put him on my shoulder, got him on the bus, took the Otis up to his floor and found his keys in his jacket pocket. Couldn't find the bed at first but I got him lying belly-down so he wouldn't choke himself, and I left some food outside his door. Coming back the next day the food was right there where I left it, so I picked Jerry's lock. Don't remember how long it took me to find a spoon and that hot plate under all that mess, but once I got a little soup in him, Jerry started spinning out some stories. And man, he had some to tell. You'd never know it looking at him, especially the way I found him under the freeway, but the old man used to run with all the big cats back in his day—King and the Kennedys and all them folks you hear about heating things up. He showed me his picture with Martin, a book by somebody named Day, and a letter the Prez wrote him—even let me run my finger over the back to see the man used a real pen signing it. He met his woman Helen down in San Diego, and it was her that got him out of that Navy bullshit and moved them back South so they could be right down in it. She passed not too long after those government motherfuckers killed all the good fighters, Jerry always told me, but they had already come back here to California, and he wasn't leaving again just to run. Somebody took her from him, she just disappeared one day and never came back—so who can blame an old man for getting drunk now and again? Who can blame him for going out trying to find a piece of those good old days, filling up his room with all kinds of shit, looking for some clue, even if he rides out that drunk for three-four days and needs somebody like me, some stranger, to come pick him up and put a little soup in him? Who can blame him if his life done floated away and he wants to spend what he's got left swimming out after it?

I've come up on old Mr. Jerry plenty of places—early morning on the steps of St. Al's, late nights against the lot fence next to our building, and any old time under some freeway bridge. But I never found him down in this park, never about to fall in the water like tonight. There's been times he looked wet, his jacket soaked tight to him and his hair a mess like birds took up in it, but I always figured it was from the rain or some booze that missed his mouth. But maybe this ain't nothing new, maybe the old man really is fishing for something he can't find out on the streets. Maybe that's part of the story he don't want to tell.

The rain don't have pity for no man tonight, so when I see it, just sitting there in the alley soon as we cross back over King, it's like a lady walking in late and all in white on Easter Sunday just so she can turn all the fellas' heads. Lord have mercy, I say to myself, ain't she *fine*.

She's a white Benz, from way back when they still had the sharp lines, and just looking at her I know she ain't had a man taking care of her who knows about cars. I walk quick as I can without shaking Jerry too much, because maybe he's still holding something that could end up all over me. I set him down nice and easy, just like loading a sofa out of a truck, lean him up against the front door and hold him steady with one arm. The back door window is busted-out. I open it right up and get Jerry inside.

Now I wish I had my jacket back. I lay Jerry down across the seat, put his head down away from where the rain comes in, but it won't stay out without no window. I jump in the front to see what's there. Maybe a map or some plastic bags, something to cover that space.

I look around on the dash, in the glove box, the ashtray, on the floor, but nothing. I even feel around the clutch and pedals and up behind the wheel, but just loose wires there like a fistful of baby snakes.

I look back at Jerry, mouth wide open but his eyes still dead shut. He's got a little wheeze going now, like William sounds when it's coming on. Even in here, that cold is gonna get inside him good and deep, and a man his age can't take that.

I look at the wheel again. I put both hands on it, turn it back and forth, run my finger over that silver star right in the middle. I get down on the floor, put my hands up in the wires, feeling for the right ones. It's been a long time since Lydell taught me, since I was running with the boys on Archer Street, since those days in his Olds. Been a long time since I saw Daddy up in Folsom or even heard any stories about him down here in the Flatlands. Been a long time since I thought I'd be thinking like this, but running the wires through my fingers I know it's just too easy.

And it's a fine car too, pretty as I'm ever gonna get my hands on, even if Jerry wasn't back there needing to get home.

I close my eyes and find them. It's my lucky night 'cause they're already cut and ready to go, and it only takes a few tries to turn the engine over. Somebody must have dumped this thing here not too long ago, the way me and Lydell used to when the boost went bad.

Don't have to worry about that tonight, as long as this rain keeps up. No police I know is gonna be down here looking for trouble, and even if he is, he ain't gonna do nothing that means he has to get up out of his car.

Jerry coughs loud right as I'm gunning the engine to get it warm, keeps it up till we're out of the alley and into the street. The wind and rain come through good and cold, and I just hope I ain't making it worse for the old man. But there's no sense pulling over now.

And this girl don't run so bad once you give her a chance. A little slow out of the blocks, a little loose around the corners, but this ain't like some Lazarus I used to pick up on the freeways outside the city, ain't some car somebody left for dead. This baby is hot, I know it—no matter how cold the wind blows in here. And I sure could make her a whole lot hotter. Clean her out, patch up the seats, spit-shine the chrome and give her some fresh paint—nothing a man like me couldn't do with a stack of bills and some hard work. Spice this thing up, treat her right, she'd be a *fine* ride. Ain't she a *Benz* after all? Better than Daddy ever had, better than me and Lydell ever boosted, and sure good enough for Noel and my boy.

But it's been a long time. I work through the gears, take the corners nice and easy, watch the streetlights float on by, and I know it's been a *damn* long time. Those freeway lights were all yellow on the windshield riding nights in Lydell's Olds, and I could never see the stars from in there. That window in our house had Daddy's shadow in it damn heavy even after he went back up to Folsom that last time, even after we got it replaced. Lydell always told me I was the best one he ever taught—I even put Daddy to shame—but that was way back then, when I was still in the house and didn't know nothing. This is easy right here tonight, but I'm a man now, got Noel and my own boy to take care of. And she told me herself she didn't want to hang around no stupid nigger playin' with her like some schoolgirl. If she knew all the stories I've been keeping from her, she'd leave me drop-dead quick. Shit, seeing me in this car she might do it anyhow.

But if it's easy like this, even after all this time, maybe it ain't so stupid. That GR check is gone as a motherfucker—I know that. How am I gonna get us outta that basement on six an hour? How am I supposed to bring my boy up right like his momma wants, and how am I supposed to get her all the nice things a lady ought to have, when we're fighting the roaches for what we got in the fridge? How am I gonna sleep tonight if I leave this car down here in the Flatlands for somebody else, when I ain't slept good in a year because my boy can't breathe?

Jerry starts up hacking again, and I'm sure glad we're getting close. Next thing you know, I'll come home with whatever he's got.

Soon enough I come up on the Misery Accordion, and pull into the drive next to our building. I cut the engine and the headlights, but the rain pops hard and steady on the top, and the front stoop bulb lights up the water washing down the windshield. When I turn around to look at Jerry, the window over his head is almost bright as day—damn-near scares me.

I heft him up on my good shoulder again but feel a shot go through my other one. Don't know what I'm gonna do if it don't heal up for that big job this weekend, because you can't fake having two good shoulders with some rich lady's armoire looking at you. I feel it in my shoulder, in my legs walking up those steps to the front door, in my hand going cold digging in my pants for the key. I work the key in the lock, back and forth. The door, the handle, the lock—they're all gone cold, and when it finally gives I think maybe those red leaves will whip up right there inside in the dark and I'll put Jerry down and he'll be that man under the tree, his body gone all to ash frozen and swollen up, and that bloody white shirt and the scarf around his neck.

But it's nothing. Just the hall inside. The Otis on one side and the stairs on the other, catching the light from the stoop bulb. I shut the door behind me, pull open the Otis and step in. I close the gate, and just as we start up, I hear Noel calling me.

I try to stand Jerry up, but he ain't having it. I carry him out, take him to the end of the hall, hold him up against the wall with one hand and pick his lock with the other. Inside it's all upside-down inside-out like usual. Cutting on the light would only make it harder to find the bed. I carry him in, kick stuff out of the way, feel around with my foot till I hit the mattress, and clear it off—papers and bottles and shoelaces and toilet handles and every other thing you can't even think of. I know tomorrow he'll be yelling at me, saying he had it all in order. He's a smart dude, but he's a class-A junkman, if you ask me, and if he were *really* smart he'd get on one of the city trucks and get *paid* to pick up all this shit.

I turn him belly-side down, step out through the junk, and pull the door shut. Down the other end of the hall I hear the Otis in motion. I know who it is.

The gate rattle-slides, and Noel steps out. She holds the door open, waiting. Even from down here I can see she's got William in her arms asleep, and that little line between her eyebrows is good and sharp.

My boots squeak like a couple of frogs, and I'm still dripping rain. "Hey baby," I say, getting close.

"You better hey baby your way into this elevator right now," she says. "Where you find that old fool this time?"

"Hey now, talk soft," I say, talking soft now myself. "You gonna wake my little man."

Noel kicks my leg, hard right on the bone. "*I'm* the one put him to sleep," she says. "You ain't got nothing to say about it." She steps inside, does a little scoop with her head. "Let's go, Jake."

"Now wait a minute—"

"I ain't waiting no minute," she says. She reaches out and slams the gate. It cracks like a whip, and through the holes I see William jump. Quick as that he's crying, and Noel puts him up to her shoulder. "I already been waiting long enough."

"Noel!" I put my hand through, and that burning runs quick right down to my fingers. "I'm coming," I say. I open the gate, step in, put a finger up. "But you've got to give me one minute. Just one minute."

We're quiet riding down, but William ain't. At the bottom Noel lifts up her shirt and puts him to her breast. I open the gate again, and she looks at me. "All right," she says. "Your minute's about up."

I open the front door. The rain is softer now but it's still coming down. Noel stops in the doorway. I step out to the stairs, and I can feel myself smiling. The Benz is right there where I left her.

"Look what I got," I say.

William coughs, twice and three times, turns his head and sends the milk spitting into the rain. Noel puts her shirt down, grabs him to her, and walks back inside.

* * *

That night a new dream comes around. The old one hasn't snuck in when I'm sleeping in I don't know how long, just little pieces of it pop up in the day here and there, now and again, and I guess I can thank God or somebody for that.

It's not like the other one. I can see everybody's face. I know who they are. Down at the park, George and Laurence, Lydell and Daddy, all got me backed up to the edge, and I can hear the water smacking up against it, feel it cold on my legs spraying me working its way through my jeans. I'm holding William, and Noel is holding on to me. They're coming, walking tall, slowing down getting close. They spread apart, like a net catching air before it hits water and goes looking for fish. Noel squeezes in tight. Slow, all of them, till George makes a move at me. But quick as he does Daddy's on him, one-two-three head gut head, and George is down with his face in the grass. I hold my ground when Laurence comes next and Lydell too. Daddy moves like a young man again, lowers his shoulder and drives through Laurence, throws him off like a sack of potatoes. In a couple steps he's got Lydell, grabs that shirt collar from behind so hard Lydell's neck splits it like a knife.

Daddy spins him around, goes to his gut, and Lydell's ribs crack like sticks in a fire. When he rips the shirt all the way off him I figure it's that old dream slipping into this one, but he just tosses it in the water and leaves Lydell on the ground. Daddy steps at me, and Noel tries to take William, but I won't let her. *Give it up, boy,* Daddy says. *It's just you and me now, and I'm your Daddy.* Noel keeps grabbing at William, and I want to give him over but my arms done gone stiff, no blood in them at all. Noel keeps grabbing, shaking me, and Daddy steps up puts his hand on my head and smiles. *You're my boy, ain't you,* he says, and Noel's screaming even louder now when Daddy's hand presses and I fall back into the water. The blood runs to my arms and I hold up my little boy, runs fast and hot, hot as that sand all around me where the water's supposed to be, the sand splash-whirling up everywhere till I can't see, I'm sinking in it, filling my eyes nose mouth sinking, splashing, holding William up, trying to hold him up out of it just as long as I can.

* * *

Before it's even light, I'm up. William slept better than most times last night, and the Sandman still owes me about three months' pay, but I couldn't get another wink now if I tried. Going to the labor hall today, the Ready Man, see if I can make peace with George and get a day's work. Folks say he remembers the Alcatrazzed dudes even better than those keys around his neck, but I've got to try something. Payday ain't coming for another ten days, and with my pay it ain't much of a day anyhow. With no more county Grief coming in, won't be too long before we're out on the street, if something doesn't change.

But first I've got to take care of the Benz. When Noel sees me putting my pants on she smiles just as little as she can, and turns over. That soft pretty smile like she always had those first days we started hanging together, just having fun. Her face smooth as can be, no worries making wrinkles in it like trucks grooving-out the freeway. These days, just about anytime I see that smile it's for William, so catching it now makes me think maybe she's dreaming eyes open, or maybe she don't even see me at all.

Jerry's door is unlocked, just the way I left it. Don't have to worry about it—anybody trying to break into this room last night would have broke their neck before they took three steps. I push the door open slow and quiet till it creaks, put my head in and see if the old man is still breathing. The streetlight comes through the windows, and I see Jerry looking right back at me. And it ain't with no pretty smile like Noel had. "Get the fuck outta here, you son of a bitch," he says, and he reaches down to the floor. I slip back and pull the door shut right as he throws something smack-bang into it.

Just like usual. The old bastard paints me the motherfucker first, saying why don't I just let him be. But I wait through it, and then I get some of that good food his daughter leaves, and even if there's none of that there's always Jerry's stories.

I take the stairs back down, get a little blood moving. Got to take care of business quick and get to the hall—always plenty of work on a Saturday, but the best jobs go first. I roll my shoulder to get it loose, but it's still hurting. On the first floor I put both hands on the stair railing and try a couple push-ups, but it's no good, the pain is like a hot knife. When I'm on the job I'll just have to fake it best I can—couldn't do no real work today if I wanted to.

The Benz is still outside, but I've got to get it gone. I jump down the stoop steps and open the driver's door. The wind must have whipped in that rain because my ass gets wet right through my jockey shorts just sitting down. Damn shame for a car like this, all this nice red interior soaked through and splitting like an old man's shirt that can't hold his gut no more.

I feel up under the wheel again and try the wires. Feel dry in my fingers, but maybe they're just playin' me—or the battery only had enough juice in it to get me back home. Just that clicking sound from the starter to the battery, can't even get the engine to think about turning over. Like it was snapping its fingers just as cool as can be listening to some blues, snapping singing saying you can try that shit all you want boy, this motherfucker ain't goin' nowhere.

I hop back up the stoop and run down into the basement, pop open the janitor's closet. The shadows jump every which way around the floor, and I know it's the roaches thinking I'm come to kill them. I push the paint cans to the wall, reach behind the brooms and buckets, and pull out the box with all my old stuff. Plenty in here that could come in handy if the Benz had a working battery. If she were a Honda, all I'd need is this big flat-head, just like Lydell taught me. I pick through it but there's nothing, nothing that can get that car moving right-quick now like I need it. If the sun comes up and that car is still outside this building, you never know who could come looking for it.

Dark inside our room. I cut the light on, hop over to Noel's side of the bed and give her a shake.

"Get up, baby," I say, squeezing her shoulder. "You got to give me a little push."

She turns on her back, puts her hand over her face, then opens her fingers slow and gives me one eye. "I'll push you real good," she says. "What time is it? I thought you went to work."

"Just get up for one minute," I say. I step over to that corner where we hang our clothes, take down her jacket and a pair of pants, look for her shoes on the floor, and bring it all back over to the bed. "Just put this on. Ain't time to talk about it."

She pulls her hand away, and that line between her eyebrows is good and sharp. "There ain't, is that right?" she says. "Well, *I* got all day. Looks like you do too, ain't going to work or nothing." She sits up and pulls the sheets tight up to her chin. "Had all night, come to think of it, but you were out doing your thing—"

"Get *up!*" I throw the clothes down on the bed. William cries from his crib. "I'm trying to help us out here, goddammit. Get up!"

"Well you sure helping *him* out plenty," Noel says. She pushes her sheet off, and puts her arms out toward the crib. "Give him to me, Jake."

"Just leave him be! You want to keep that car, don't you? Ain't that what you want?"

"You talking crazy now, nigger. Give me that baby."

I kick her jacket over against the crib. "Get him yourself," I say, and walk out. She gets up, and at the door I look back. Just in that second I take it all in, those cement walls I haven't painted, the sink with the water running dirty, the cold coming in from this empty space at the bottom of the stairs, slipping in under our door and walking all around the room with nowhere to go, trying to find its way out again but that little window is shut-down solid so we stay good and invisible down here, and who'd want to look in anyway?

"I found us a ticket *out* of this motherfucker," I say, pointing up the stairs. "You don't want it, then *fuck* it, *keep* living down in this hole. And tell everybody *I'm* the one put you down here. Tell them it was Jake Robertson did it."

I run up the stairs. Outside the streetlights are still buzzing, but I know just looking at that sky the sun is coming.

I try the wires again just in case she was fooling before, but nothing. I take the brake off, jump quick out of the seat, and get to the front grill. I bend down, get set, put a man's push into it and roll the Benz out of the alley. My shoulder starts burning good enough to set her on fire, but I keep going.

Got one shot at it. The Misery Accordion is about the only street in the Flatlands with any kind of rise to it, and we're at the top of it here. From 23rd to 26th it's nice and easy down the hill, no other streets cutting across, all the way down till you hit MacArthur, the junkie park. Not much, ain't no hill like over in Bella Vista, but it's enough to put her in second and pop her. If she don't want to turn over by the time we hit that park, I'll just leave her there and pretend I never saw her at all.

I keep pushing, move her out into the street, toward the curb on the other side where those crackheads set up a tent every now and again.

"What the hell you doing?" Noel says from the stoop. The door slams behind her.

"Get on down here, you gonna find out," I say, and keep pushing.

The Benz is out to the middle of the street when Noel comes up next to me. She's holding William. "You going somewhere?"

"Yeah," I say, still moving. "Yeah, I'm fixing to take this down to my caseworker, see if she'll put me back on that GR if I give it to her." Getting close to the curb now. "Now jump in there and turn that wheel for me."

"What you talking about? You lose the check, Jake?"

"Cut me off like a small fish on a good day, didn't even let me keep the worm," I say. Then I stand up—it's there. "You want to turn that wheel or what?"

"Cut you off?" Noel says. "She find out about the job?"

"Shit, I *told* her about that." I get down good and low. "But then when I pushed her over and scooped her purse she got real nasty." I give the Benz everything I've got, to get those back wheels up on the curb.

Noel screams, and William jumps right in. She quick-steps over to the driver door. "You *hit* that lady, Jake? You *stole* from her? Look up at me!"

I do. "Get in the car, Noel," I say. "It's real simple—you don't need but one hand to turn that wheel. I'm gonna do all the rest."

She hugs William tight to her. "I ain't driving nothing till you start talking."

I push the Benz one more time, all my shoulder can take, and jump up and go for the door. "Go on back inside then," I say, and slide behind the wheel.

The car rolls right off that curb, right past Noel and William, quicker than I thought it could. The wheel don't come around so good neither, even if I had two good shoulders. It rolls right back to the stoop, quicker than I can turn it, and just like that the front end catches the stoop railing, and I hear the headlight crack.

Noel is at the window, and William is screaming like I don't know what. "Get outta there! You all right?"

I open the door and push right past her. I slide across the hood to the front end and see the glass on the step, just like the thing poked the girl's eye out and left it all in pieces. I get down again to push. I look up at Noel. "You got one more chance," I say. "Just get in there. Set him down on the seat and we'll talk it all out soon as we get this girl running."

"Who the hell you talking to?" she says, turning William away and looking over her shoulder. "We ain't getting in no car like this."

I stand up. "Why the hell not?" I smack my hand down on the hood. "This is what you want, ain't it?" Then I point back at the building. "Or is *that?*"

Noel takes a step back, then another. She follows my finger to the building, to our room down there, then her eyes come back to mine. She shakes her head. "I don't know who you are no more," she says.

"Aw, cut the bullshit, Noel," I say. "I'm doing this for *you!* For *him!*"

She shakes her head at me again, keeps stepping back.

The stoop door comes open like a gun going off, and that cough sounds out like another one, two three times till I look up and see Jerry coming down the steps at me. "Put something into it!" he says, climbing in the Benz and getting behind the wheel. He puts both hands on it, and even through the glass I can see his knuckles going hot red and white. "Are you a man, or what? *Push* this son of a bitch!"

Maybe somewhere out on those streets Jerry found a good shoulder somebody couldn't use no more, maybe he's got it up there in that room of his with everything else. Because that's what I'm sure gonna need—and a brand-new one would do even better. Feels like somebody driving a four-inch nail right into that collarbone when I push again, but I push through and through, step and step and get the Benz moving back across the street, and step and step and see Jerry cranking that wheel his hands whirling, and when she comes up against the curb I run around front and get in the other side. Noel yells something but I can't catch it because Jerry coughs when I slip down on the floor and grab for the wires. We start to roll forward, and I hear Jerry cranking and those tires biting the pavement turning rolling slow. I try the wires but it's just that clicking sound. Jerry yells and tells me to hold off till we get some speed and I yell back to just quit coughing and turn this motherfucker straight. I hold the wires and wait, watch his foot slam the clutch down and smell those pants and shoes he's been sleeping and pissing in all these days in the rain. We're moving now, the old man's got us going. I hold the wires and wait. Jerry throws it into second, hitches up straight in that seat and slaps his hand on the dash. He laughs and lets out a big *whooo-eee* like he's some kind of cowboy. I look up at him, and he's smiling, and behind that green cap the streetlights go by buzzing yellow and I see the top of the building where the crackheads make their caves and that one with the orange tarp hanging off the top balcony saying rooms for rent, building for sale, and I know we're getting close so I try the wires again but nothing and now it's just lights moving faster and I ask Jerry how far we got but he just says get it done, and the lights are all gone and the park's coming up and Jerry says now or never and she catches, she roars like a tiger, we pull the corner and we're running.

We're running. I turn around to see if I can see Noel up the street, but the rain is running thick down the back window like little rivers come spring. She's too far gone anyway, and I know she knows I'll be back soon enough.

The Benz sounds good as gold, and I start thinking about how I could spice her up, put a little money into her and have myself a sweet ride. Wouldn't take long to do it either—could look up some of the old boys from Archer Street and find me some good parts real cheap.

But that's thinking crazy. Right now I just need to find someplace to keep her on ice a few days till I get my shit together. I tell Jerry to pull her over, I'll drop him back off at the building.

"No sir, sonny-boy," he says. He throws her into fourth and we fly through a yellow-gone-red across Chavez, heading back toward the freeway. "You've got some listening to do."

Here we go. Old man Jerry gonna try to pull the Daddy shit on me. "Look Jerry, I know it's early, and I know how much you like sleeping—even if you had to be in your bed instead of under some bridge. But can't I get a thanks or nothing?"

"It's not about that, not about that at all," he says. He looks over at me, and his eyes are big and gray and white-hot, like clouds with the sun fighting hard behind them. "Don't you know what day it is, Jake?"

All kinds of shit I could tell him now. Yeah this is the day I got my GR cut off, got me three dollars and a chance at six months in the county bullpen, got me an old car that maybe don't run and a chance at losing my place if I don't lose my girl and my little boy first. Good God Praise Jesus, *this* is the day the *Lord* done made, let us get up and *shout*, motherfucker! But I hold off, let him talk. This is how his stories begin.

There was the story about King when that day came up, about how Jerry and his old lady weren't but two hundred miles from Memphis whey they heard, and they drove ninety the whole way to get there but getting close they slowed down, didn't want to believe it was true—because they knew their marriage was gonna come apart too, just like everything else. There was the story he told me on Vet's Day about being down in San Diego squaring off with some old Navy boys he used to be an officer to, getting in each others' faces till somebody just snapped and Jerry ended up with the butt end of a rifle across his jaw. Broke it, but he laughed when he told me it didn't shut him up. Sometimes it's no kind of special day at all, except to him, now and again when he picks up some piece of junk on that floor and tells me where he found it all those years back. The man's got a mind for days, that's all I know. And that's how the stories come.

"I bet you think I'm some kind of crazy son of a bitch hanging out in that park," Jerry says. "But you don't know what it's all about yet."

"Hey old man, I've known you're crazy since I first saw you," I say. The sky is getting lighter, and I see the freeway up ahead. "I just don't think you oughta go *swimming* down there."

Jerry hits a hard left, and I smack against the door, feeling that nail in my shoulder again. He throws it back up through the gears, and we whip right under the freeway, through the lights, straight at that park wall. I grab Jerry's shoulder. "You gonna get us killed!"

He shakes it. He hits the brakes, downshifts and grinds it like a motherfucker, and then takes it nice and easy, just like that, right up to the wall, banging through those potholes in the old entrance, nice and slow right up to the water and that ledge where I found him. He cuts the engine and looks at me. "I'm not getting anybody killed anymore."

He gets out of the car and starts walking down to the ledge. I tell him to get his ass back here because I ain't saving him no more, but he just shakes me off. "Come look at this," he says. "I think you're ready for it now."

Walking to him, all I can hear is the water hitting against the wall. Jerry sits himself right down on that ledge, getting his ass good and wet all over again, letting his feet hang over those steps that disappear into the water. When the waves hit, the water just about covers him, and he just lets it, closes his eyes under that green cap when it comes, and the drops run down his face. I stand next to him and watch the waves come in, smacking harder, and I feel the water sneaking down in my boots and pressing my jeans cold against my knees. Clouds rolling out, fat cool white and way high, passing right over, and the sky is big and getting lighter blue blue blue in those spaces in between.

Jerry hits me on the leg. "You looking for something?"

"Naw," I say, and I look down at him looking up at me. That wet face he ain't shaved since who knows when, that stinking-ass liquor still strong. "But if you don't start getting to what you want to tell me I'm gonna let you find the bus this time around."

"No you won't," he says. "You're not going anywhere."

I laugh. "Is that right?"

He grabs my arm, pulls me down smelling-close. "That's *right*," he says. "You *are* looking for something, Jake. And it's right here."

The story comes. The sun is coming, I'm cold, I'm wet, that car is sitting there telling the world to lock-up my sorry ass, but it comes, so I set tight. I listen. I let old Jeremiah, old Mr. Jerry, crazy class-A junkman tell me some story he might just be making up as he goes, just riffing it like a motherfucker, just walking along talking and picking up whatever's lying around like he does on these streets, some story he might have told a thousand times but it always comes out new, some story might not even be true, but it takes you somewhere. He takes me all around and back, San Diego and meeting Helen and that little sister she helped out when his buddy threw the beer can at her, quitting the Navy and getting hitched and following the *movement* even past Memphis, all that story I've heard before. But right here this morning he picks up something new, he leans in and gives me those eyes, gray-white sun behind the clouds, he jumps down on the bottom step and cups two hands of water and lets it fall back down, cups them up again and says *Look, look can't you see it, Jake.* He holds it up in front of my face, just clear water and his old cracked hands showing through. Holds it up and says *This, this is what I've got after all these years.* He found her out, some other dude, a brother, a Panther, some man came and rocked her world with how he was gonna change it. *I've come looking but it's this.* And she bought it all, left the ring right there next to the sink, right on the towel still wet, and Jerry was all alone. *This.* But he held it, held it because he couldn't believe. Held it till he *did* believe, and even longer, when the Panther got shot and she came back, found the house empty because Jerry had already holed-up in that room and started collecting. *This.* She asked around, found him in the middle of all his junk, chased him begging him right down to this ledge.

"Right here, Jake," he says. He leans in closer, smelling-close, his breath going right up my nose. "Right here is where I pushed her off, and I threw the ring in too, right at her head."

Then he pushes back, puts his hand over his face, and breathes in sharp through his nose. "As soon as I did it, I knew I'd fucked up. I wanted to get her out, Jake. But the cold got in too deep."

A wave hits, spray falls down over us, but we don't move. Jerry keeps squeezing his face with his hand, and the other one is crossed over and tucked under his arm. Another wave hits, and another. The old man stays still. I feel something warm, real soft and quiet on my back. I turn around and the sun is just breaking free, climbing over top of those buildings on the other side of the freeway. I look over at the Benz. Smoke is coming steady from under the hood, turning the windshield white.

Jerry grabs my shoulder from behind, the hurting one. "Help me out here, Jake."

"Don't *touch* me there, crazy motherfucker," I say, shaking him off.

"Listen," he says. "You've got to find something."

"No, you listen here," I say. "I been looking after you better than my own kid. What the hell you want from me? Dive in there and fish out that ring? Find your old lady? Go around picking up shit for you so you can keep feeling sorry for yourself?"

He waves a finger in front of his face. "It's not about that anymore, Jake," he says. "Not about me." He points. "I can see it in you."

I look up at the sky, bluer all the time. "Lord have mercy."

"Don't try to run from it," he says, and puts that finger right in my chest. "It's right here, and it will find you."

"Long as it ain't with the police, I'll be all right," I say. I stand up. My shadow goes right over him, but he keeps his finger pointed back at me. I shake my head and walk to the Benz. "Now I've gotta get to work, old man."

"Leave it," Jerry says. "It will be there. There's other ways to get where you're going."

I get inside and try the wires, but the Benz just coughs like she was kin to Jerry. I slam the door and point back at him. "Look what you got me into, you old bastard, bringing you down here. I *need* this thing."

Jerry laughs. Laughs till he's hacking, till he spits something in the water, and even then he's smiling. "Goes back way beyond that, sonny boy. You got in this long before you ever met me. Leave it down here now and get going."

"So where am I going?" I say. "Back to that hole we're living in? Back to that five and a quarter job I got?"

"Get out of town," Jerry says. A wave comes smacking up. "Don't you have any dreams, Jake? Get following them."

"Who the hell are you now, my high school guidance counselor? Gonna tell me to get on the GI Bill too?" I slam down on the hood again, and she coughs up more smoke. "Well let me give *you* some motherfucking advice. You see that little boy you walked past this morning? He's got himself a cough damn-near bad as yours, you crazy coot. So why don't you go on and do *me* a favor and go looking for something. Go find me some way I'm gonna make me some motherfucking *money* and I'll get *all* us losers outta this sorry place. How about *that?*"

Jerry turns back around, looks out at the water. "Just leave it. Leave it and get going."

Just my feet. That's all I've got now. I walk up through the grass, through the Break in the wall, through the streets, leave Jerry behind.

Under the freeway, I throw a rock and scatter a whole mess of pigeons. They all go the same way—down the street, back up Third toward the labor hall. Where it all went down with George.

But it's too far away still. Can't do a thing unless I walk there, and if I don't do it fast, all those jobs will be long gone real soon. Fact is, as warm as the sun's getting now, I could have already missed my chance.

Maybe I should just get home, get some rest before the big moving job tomorrow. When I get there I bet I'll hear the Misery Accordion, coming around to cheer me up. That damn ice cream truck comes around any hour day or night, playing that Entertainer song all out of tune. Our street sign says *Misericordia*, something in Spanish, but with that truck coming through so much with that sorry-ass music, Noel and me couldn't hold back, had to play it somehow. Can't even get no decent blues music on our street.

But if it's there, maybe I could boost it. Wouldn't that be something—driving that baby out on the freeway to go get it stripped, playing the Entertainer the whole way. Even if I couldn't get nothing much for it, might be worth it just to rip that song box out and smash it myself. Or just to see if I could boost it at all.

But that's crazy, that's thinking worse than Jerry—I couldn't get enough money out of that thing to fill up the Benz with gas. I just need to get home and tell Noel I dumped the Benz in the water, because that ain't me, I don't run no nigger games like that no more. I just need to get up smelling-close and let her see it's her man standing in front of her, even if I've got us in some hard times. Need to get talking about her and me and our little boy, and how we're gonna get playin' something serious right quick. Just about us—don't want to get into it with her or nobody else about Jerry or nothing he said. Don't even want to think on it myself.

But first I need to give it a shot at the hall. Ain't nobody thinking about no dreams around there.

CHAPTER 2
THE OLD CORNER

Running, hustle-stepping, moving—got to get there. Trying to beat the clock but need to keep my breath too, because nothing gets you the shit jobs at the hall like looking like you'll take them. I *will* take one, that's for sure, but the more money I make today, the better. You don't get the good jobs unless you look like a man—hungry, not desperate. But the only way I'm making a dime is if I turn George around, and I ain't doing that unless I'm breathing easy and thinking straight—not like the last time.

Slipping under the freeway, coming up on Third and Battery, I spot a man I ain't seen since I last saw George. Laurence, on his old corner. Or right across from it, now that I think on it, on the crowing side of the street. It don't take going to night school to pick him out before you can see those big hands or that salt in his hair, or before you hear that laugh coming from way down in his belly. Just one look at how he moves, and you'll know. From a couple blocks away, you'd think he was dragging a limp leg and spreading seed in a field, the way he bends to the side and lets that left arm sway back and forth when he struts. I even heard some fella a while back say the man looked like he must have done a little time on a chain gang. But nobody paid much mind to that, since everybody around the hall knows Laurence can't let nobody tell him what to do for too long, no matter what he's got to do to get out of it.

He's out now. Last time I was down here, a couple months before William came, everyone said he was across state when I asked for him. Told me he'd been two-stepping with AA, finally busted loose and got locked-down after he broke the no-contact with his old lady down in Fresno. Was supposed to do eighteen months in Folsom but I don't doubt he got a bus ticket back here in about half that time, knowing how good he is at playin' Mr. Getting Myself Right. I should have seen some of that when I first met him, and damn-sure should have seen it the day I ran into him at St. Al's then ended up flooring George up here at the hall, swinging at that Mexican punk Gustavo. Should have picked him out for what he was then.

It's easier to see now. Getting closer, I hear him going on some story, cracking everybody up. There's five fellas standing in front of him, two or three smoking but none of them crowing that I can see—don't wave down none of them vans going by. I don't know any of them, but I figure either they ain't hungry or they already got tickets inside.

When I get to the curb catty-corner to the hall and across from Laurence, I see him bend down a little, reach in front of him with one hand and pull it back like he's opening a door. Then he freezes, leaves his hand hanging there while he turns his head around. All the fellas break up at that, and one dude even slaps another one on the back. I cross over, to Laurence's curb, because he's gonna see me anyway.

His head's still turned, showing me the back, but I can hear him now. "You looking for something too, motherfucker?" he says. You'd think the fellas weren't hardly laughing before, the way this one gets them.

"It was *just* like that," one of them says, a short brother with a blue Dodgers cap. "I about thought that old man was gonna drop over, the way he looked at—"

"Hey man," another brother says, and slaps the Dodgers dude on the chest. "Whose story we listening to?"

Just then I step up on the curb, and you'd think Laurence could feel it, as quick as he turns around.

For a second I hardly know him. His beard is shaved close, and there's a scar on his cheek still looks fresh, creeping up out of the whiskers and under his glasses. Somebody got him good—you don't get that running into no door. But then he smiles, and all the old lines in his forehead and around his eyes come back, deeper now than I remember. And I can smell him, without even getting smelling-close. It ain't fresh—probably from last night—but it's strong. "Jake," he says, and puts out his hand. "Goddamn."

When we shake, I know right off Laurence ain't been out long. The iron's still there, enough to break your hand, but the skin's softer, almost like a kid's. There's always plenty of weights to throw around in the pen, but you can't get sandpaper hands like Laurence used to have unless you're putting in some real work on an eight-to-five. That last day I saw him, Laurence could have lit a match in his palm. But now, when I let go, my hand almost slides out, like I never had a good grip at all.

Nobody's laughing no more. Laurence turns back around to the fellas standing looking at him, and he puts his hand on my shoulder. "All you all know who this is, don't you now?"

I try to step off the curb again and get on my way, but Laurence makes his hand tighter. I ain't looking for no new friends when there's work going out.

"Good seeing you again, old man. But you know I need to go sign in before it gets too late."

Laurence breaks up, and the other fellas do the same. Now I'm the joker. "Gonna sign in?" he says, pointing over at the hall. "Over there? You got a key?"

"Could be," I say. "If George can open up to a little mercy."

"Mercy, my ass," Laurence says, laughing again. "You better know some Houdini shit if you think you getting out of that mess, Jake. Ain't no razzamatazz getting *you* outta Alcatraz."

He takes a beat-up pack of cigarettes out of his shirt pocket, something you'd find in the trash if you looked hard enough. The plastic crackles when he takes one out and throws the pack in the street. It lands right on one of those fading lane lines. I look at Laurence, and he's looking back. "Might be something in there if you want it," he says.

Walking across, it looks to me the paint's fading everywhere, as far down Third as I can see, and Battery too. Driving this road you've got to have some kind of sense of how to stay straight yourself, with nothing here to tell you. I step over Laurence's pack. I could stand a smoke right now to cool my nerves, but I never pick anything up off the ground like that, don't matter how bad off I am.

It's funny how when you come back someplace you can almost see it like it's your first time around. Especially if it's been a long while, or something big happened since the last time. I remember feeling like that when I brought Noel back from the hospital with William. All of a sudden our place looked too small, and after a few minutes I started getting a headache from all that racket on the street that most times I'd just let slide. I thought maybe I'd opened the wrong door. I step over the glass on the walk now and come up on those old double green doors and take the handle, just like I did lots of mornings before. But pulling them open I wonder if it's still the Ready Man. Hardly a man in here, and the ones that are I don't know at all. The place is all mopped up like it's the end of the day already, those old metal chairs are all against the walls, and I smell some kind of spray a lady would put in her bathroom instead of all the good-morning sweat and that motor-oil coffee they always had going in here. Blue's desk is in the usual spot, stopping me right when I step in, but he ain't at it. Just two men working behind the glass in the back, where they take the calls from folks looking for somebody like me do to a job for a day. They've both got a phone to their head, yapping away. I start back there to see if I can catch some of what they got going this morning.

One of the dudes looks up. It's hard to tell, with the light coming off the glass like it does, but I don't think I know him. Tall Chinese guy, solid top to bottom, with a mustache thick enough to make up for that hair he's losing in front. I don't remember anybody but white dudes working behind the glass, except for George. He comes outside right quick, and his shoes are loud on the floor. "Help you with something, buddy?"

"Could be," I say. "Let George know Jake Robertson wants to talk with him."

He gives me a quick look up and down, pulls a face like he's smelling something, and folds his arms over his chest. "What's it about?"

"Look, this ain't no family visit," I say. "What you think a man comes in here for?"

The guy shakes his head. "So is that the word outside now, with all those losers holding the sidewalk in place? Just come in here asking for George and you get put to work?"

I'm about to tell him he don't need to get uppity just because his shoes shine nice, sitting on the other side of the window all day. But I hear the door open in back, and sure enough it's George, still wearing his tie and tucking his shirt in tight and hanging those keys around his neck. Just looking at him you'd think the brother got lost from somewhere up in those hills across the bridge. But when he gets to talking you find out pretty quick he's wise to most all the ways fellas down here keep getting up and messing up. At least that's how George said it that first time I sat down with him, the day I had to wait all day for nothing because he wanted to test me. There was a time when I could joke with him, but the way he walks over now, pulling his tie knot tight, I know it ain't the right way to go.

I put out my hand. "Long time, George, long time."

"Who's he?" George says, looking at the Chinese dude.

The dude laughs and looks at me. "That's what I thought."

"George," I say, working quick now, "it ain't been the same not seeing you. How's that boy of yours doing—he still playing ball at State?"

George pulls those bitty glasses out of his pocket and goes to look at his watch, but he stops first and picks at something on his cuff, something I can't even see, then flicks it away. When I was coming here before, I wouldn't have known he had cuffs at all—his shirt was always rolled-up over those old carpenter's arms thick as pipes. He looks at me over his glasses. "It's getting on now," he says, pointing at his watch. "And you've got the wrong man, young brother."

"This ain't right," I say, shaking my head. "You can't go acting like you don't know me no more."

George shrugs and puts his hands up, all full of nothing. "Well, what do you want me to say?"

Somebody opens the door in back now, an old white guy with gray slicked-back hair. The phones ring like a cage full of birds in the morning. "Call for you in your office, boss."

George turns around, and something in me knows that's all I'm gonna get from him. He goes half-running, his shoes shuffle-shushing over the floor.

The Chinese dude points at the green doors. "You know the way, don't you?"

I look at him. He ain't kidding. And George is already behind that door. "Sure I do," I say.

It's a walk I've done before—leaving the hall with no ticket, nothing to show for coming down here. Sometimes in the winter I wouldn't even go up to the window, because I'd hear there wasn't nothing going out as soon as I got to those green doors. But even those times there'd be folks in here who I could rap with some, bum a smoke off, or get a cup of coffee for at the Korean breakfast place across the street. Today I'm just on my own.

When I push the doors open and look over to the corner, I see Laurence looking back. Got his hands in his pockets, one foot on the curb and one in the street. All those fellas are still there—nobody gone to get a bus, nobody waving down any of the cars. Nobody's doing nothing they weren't doing before. Except Laurence—he looks like he's making his way somewhere, maybe over here.

I step back in and shut the doors. I walk right up to the window again and knock on it. The Chinese dude looks up from the ticket he's writing, turns around quick and says something that gets a laugh from the old guy before he opens the little slide-door at the bottom so I can hear him. "Hey stranger," he says, looking back at the ticket. "Long time no see. What do you need?"

"How about that ticket right there?" I say. "That would do me for today."

"Got your paperwork?" he says, still writing away. "Résumé, references, stuff like that?"

I lean down and look through the hole. "Hey man, I'm Jake Robertson," I say. "You don't see me standing right here? You want something on me, go check my file, 'cause I don't know about any of that shit right now. I just know about working."

He gives me his eyes, takes a big breath. He puts the cap on his pen, folds his hands, and sits his chin on top of them. "I did check your file," he says. "Who are you kidding, buddy?" he says. "I know who you are. You got nothing for us, and we got nothing for you." He holds up the ticket. "You see this?" He puts it up against the glass. "See it? This is what work is."

He puts a book over the slide-door hole, and goes back to writing.

That's what work is, all right, just like the man says. Here I am in this empty room, in between what's behind the window and what's outside those green doors, with no work. Here I am on a Saturday morning, trying to get something together, trying to get a little extra just to get enough, and I can't reach through that glass and grab it.

I turn around, look over at the green doors, and go sit in one of those chairs on the wall. You can't get around the waiting, don't matter where you go. There's been days when I've sat in a chair like this—they've got them all over downtown—hoping my name would come up for some food, a mat in the missions, or a ticket when I'm here at the hall. And there's been times when I've walked out with nothing, times I know they've got it right there on the other side. I look down at the floor and can see something looking back—it's still the same old floor, but I guess this little shine goes with the smell today. Just sitting here a couple minutes, it finally comes to me, the last time I smelled something like this coming off a floor.

There's nothing like a prison when it comes to waiting, don't matter if you're wearing the blues or not. Last time I saw Daddy was up in Folsom, maybe six or seven years ago, when I was seventeen. He'd been in a year already, and Momma got us together for his fortieth, made us wear Sunday clothes, and put us on the bus. It was the first time, and the last time too. There was something wrong in there that day, the air-conditioner was broken maybe, wasn't no wind moving through at all. They'd just been cleaning the floors when it went out, so that smell was still hanging strong. I didn't even want to breathe in. When I finally got my turn to sit down with him and we picked up those phones across the glass, I asked him if he could smell it too, and he said yeah, let's keep it short. He looked harder to me, bigger in his shoulders and chest from all the iron he'd been putting up—made me wonder if I still could have thrown him up against the window like I did that night. But there was something in his eyes too, like I couldn't really see them straight, and I didn't know if it was just the light coming off the glass. We didn't say much—I told him how the A's were doing, but he said he got all the news he needed on the inside. We never said a thing about what happened, how he got in that place, behind that glass. When it was time, I didn't know how to say goodbye, so I just put my hand up on the glass. But Daddy just looked me right in the eyes and said what's that about boy. He set that phone down, stood up, and buzzed for the guard to take him back. On that bus ride home I spun it around in my head, played it up back and side-to-side, but by the time we got back to Valley Street I wasn't even sure if I'd seen him at all.

Laurence had that same something in his eyes when I saw him just now. Like he's keeping something behind them. I still don't know what Daddy was thinking, because when we all left that day nobody said nothing about nothing, except Momma, who just went on about ain't this a fine way to pass a birthday. Don't know for sure, but I bet if I saw him today he'd still say it was all my fault, still say what kind of boy turns his own Daddy in, still want to reach right through the glass and pull me in with him. Don't know what Laurence is thinking neither, but I still ain't going back out there to pick that shit up out of the street.

I get up and quick-step it to the door George went behind. It's locked, but I can see him at his desk back there. He's up quick, coming at the door fast as a train jumped its tracks.

"Look, George," I say. "I don't even need a ticket today. Let me just sit down with you a minute."

"Sit down?" He pushes me full-on in the chest, steps in smelling-close and gets that rich man aftershave up my nose. "You think you're my prodigal son or something? You want me to have you over for supper now?"

"So a man can't even get a chance in here no more, is that it?" I say. "You don't have mercy on nobody."

"*Mercy?* You want *mercy* now, Robertson?" he says, taking those glasses off and bringing his voice down. I stand up straighter, finally hearing my name. George sees it. He puts those keys up under my chin. "That's right," he says, "I know who you are. Think I'm going to forget that? Think I just let all that go?"

"Oh I see it now." I feel that cold brass on my skin, pressing in, biting. "Can't nothing change with you, I guess, except maybe the way you dress."

George is quiet a second. He sucks on his teeth, then he takes a quick sharp sniff, and his whole face goes tight. "Nothing changes with me?" He drops the keys back on his chest and shoots a finger in my face. "Look who's standing here in the Ready Man again. Look who still can't get himself up on his feet without somebody being his daddy. *Aw come on please George, just gimme a job—*"

"You don't know a goddamn thing anymore," I say, smacking his hand. "I *got* me a motherfucking job. But now I got a kid and he got—"

He laughs and crosses his arms. "Must be some good job, for you to be down at my place again." He cocks his chin up, puts his finger back in my chest. The door opens behind him and Blue and the Chinese dude come out, shoes clacking. "Listen here, Jake. We've got work for folks who are trying to better themselves, going someplace. I saw something in you, but what did you show me? You went and played the nigger fool, that's what you did. Now you come in here and want to talk about having mercy because you can't take care of your family." He leans in smelling-close again. "And what do you have for me? You think you're special because you're strong? Every day I've got fifty men who can lift a box just as good as you." He taps the side of his head. "It's like I told you before, Jake, if you want to get ahead you've got to work smarter, not harder." He points over to the green doors. "Now get out of my hall."

Just like that he turns away and those dudes are on me, lifting me dragging me, opening the doors and pushing me out. They pull them whap-bang shut again, and I can hear the laughing all the way from the corner.

But not from Laurence. He's not there, he's not looking at me. He's standing by himself now, up against the wall of that Korean breakfast joint, right across the street. He's watching the cars head up Third to the freeway. I wait for one to pass and then I cross over.

He's still looking down the street when I step up on the curb, but he takes another pack of cigarettes out of his pocket and puts it in front of me. "I told you he still knows who you are," he says, turning his head at me over his shoulder. His glasses catch the light and then let it go. "But he don't know what all I know."

The pack is new but I push it away. "Buy me a cup of coffee," I say.

We get a table at the window. Could have any one we want—this place ain't doing no business today. Laurence tells me they just don't make their eggs like they used to. But he orders them anyway. "Sure better than the ones upstate," he says, laughing. "Your old man used to say it was like eating the scraps off re-tread tires somebody painted up yellow."

I put my cup down. That's Daddy right there—*Gimme the re-treads, Janice, and make 'em hot.* Just about every Sunday morning, and Momma would always toss a shell his way or pour on the Tabasco to get back at him. I sit up straight, look at Laurence, but he's busy stirring sugar into his coffee.

"Used to get everybody with that one," he says, "even the guards. But it didn't do nothing to get him any different food. Not like the way he said little Jake could sweet-talk his momma into giving him what he wanted."

Laurence looks up, calm as can be, waiting. He tilts his head and his glasses catch the light again. I push my cup to the edge of the table while he takes a sip. "I'm listening," I say.

When Laurence tells a story, his hands get to work. Showing you who folks are, how they move and talk. After a while you start to think it wouldn't be the same story without them, like he wouldn't get the words out if he couldn't let them dance around in front of him. I see Daddy, with his smoke-gray eyes, blue Cubs hat, and that scarf. With his big shoulders and that wrinkle that goes straight down his forehead when he gets worked-up, with his mouth running when he gets to drinking.

"They stuck us in the same class together," Laurence says, locking his fingers together like a web. "Anger management. All the DV dudes had to do it."

Laurence had to go to AA too, but that didn't stop him from making pruno and sharing it around. First time he gave some to Daddy, they got drunk right quick.

"He was asking me what Oakland was like now, 'cause he hadn't seen it in a few years," Laurence says. "I started into all that about how many more Mexicans there were now, maybe because I had so many of them in my pod. Saying how those folks are eating the jobs faster than you can say three dollars an hour, and before you know it brothers won't find no work at all unless they take something for less than the Mexican will." Then he points at my hand. "And then I told him I knew this young brother," he says. "It just came to me then, because I was thinking about how maybe the only place to still get something going is at a day-labor hall, but that kind of work ain't moving you up nobody's ladder. And when something goes wrong there, it's bad news." Laurence puts his cup down and smiles to himself. "Don't know why, but I threw your name in there somewhere, laughing about that counting to a hundred bullshit. Said one time I was down there, this brother Robertson just reached back and popped one of them Ponchos—or tried to anyway, got himself in a heap of trouble when he took out the boss man instead."

Daddy sat up at that, the way I did hearing about the eggs.

"That's how he knew," Laurence says. "Maybe it was only because he was all loosed up with that pruno, but when he heard that, everything started coming."

I put my hand up, because I know where it's all going, and I've been there before. I don't need to get back there again, thinking about our house on Valley Street, nights when I'd be sleeping like a rock until the truck pulled in and it would start. In the kitchen, a chair pulled out from the table, some glass clinking, then Momma's slippers going down the hallway. Some talking, some shushing, then the chair again. Talking getting louder until it's not talking no matter what Momma says the next day, something breaking on the floor, always something breaking, and my sisters creaking our door open and sliding out. The cold floor when I run out after them, when I'm eleven twelve fourteen, when I'm sixteen, that light shining bright in the hall because everyone's already in the sitting room shushing and shouting. The sound of Daddy's hand hitting her shoulder instead of her face because he can't aim when he can't hardly see straight, and when I'm sixteen, that thud when she goes down, and that night, when I'm sixteen, when I'm thinking maybe he ain't so bad he won't do it again, we just talked the other day and he said he was proud I was starting to be a man, his only son and Momma's too even if she always had a word about how I fucked up. But he does it and I grab the collar on that shirt all full of sweat and it's easy, like pulling a fish out of water, and he don't say a thing but I couldn't hear him if he did because I just want him out, and he goes up against that big glass window and it cracks until it almost breaks.

"Save the scrapbook stories for the jokers on the corner," I say, putting a dollar down and getting up from the table.

The door opens once I'm on the sidewalk, but I don't look back. "You know what he told me?" Laurence says. "*The boy's still got it.*"

There's a fireplug near the curb, and I stop and put my foot up on it. My feet are starting to ache from doing nothing all morning. That's the way it always is with these boots—they start feeling like handcuffs for my feet if I can't get some work going, if I can't move around and break a little sweat into them. I loosen the laces, let some air in, move my toes around. I look at Laurence, start walking back to him.

"Maybe he does," I say.

* * *

It's a cool morning, like it almost always is in the summer, and some clouds roll in while we're walking. The sun breaks through at first, and I can follow my shadow on the sidewalk, but soon enough the clouds get heavy and it just disappears.

Going around the block, getting more of the story, it's almost like looking at a Polaroid, when somebody shoots it and you watch it all come together out of the dark. But this one ain't focused right, can't make up its mind how to come out. Daddy's been upstate seven years this time, I know that, but you can't keep up with somebody you ain't hardly been to see or heard nothing about in all that time. Sure I've thought about him since then, but not much, and when I do, I start to ask myself if I really remembered what his face looked like, if his voice really sounded like mine, or if I was just making it up because I didn't want to think I could forget. Now that Laurence is catching me up on those years, I see there's some things I wouldn't have even thought to make up.

Laurence wasn't around to see it, but Daddy told him there was a time he was meeting pretty regular with a chaplain, a big fella everybody called Danny Mac. Started when he got put in solitary for fighting, kept up for three years. Danny Mac got Daddy started working in the library too, till he fell and broke his wrist trying to stack some books up high. The warden said it was his own fault, and when they didn't let him work again, he figured it wasn't no use talking with Mac no more, since all the big guy could tell him was to be patient with the folks who was doing him wrong. Laurence had come in by then, and Daddy started hanging with him instead, a brother who was still deep down in it, who really knew where he was at.

"It was like we was both young men again," Laurence says. He stops and lights a cigarette and looks around breathing it out. "He told me he started getting something back, something Danny Mac was trying to wash away. I could see it too—that fire."

I don't say nothing, just watch Laurence take another drag.

"And that's what he was telling me," Laurence says, looking right at me now. That scar is good and red, from his nose to his cheek, and not even those big glasses or that skin near dark as Daddy's can cover it up. "Can't nobody say you ain't his son, 'cause you got it too. Nobody, not even your Momma."

I feel a little breeze come through. "That so?" I say. "What's some old man who ain't seen me in all that time gonna know about it?"

Laurence cocks his head. "He ain't seen you yet?"

The breeze picks up, sends a flap through my shirt and moves a loose wrapper between me and Laurence, down the sidewalk. Just looking at him, the way he's leaning forward, the way the wrinkles come up in his forehead, I know where he's going, but I try playin' him anyway. "How's he gonna see me from behind all those walls up there?"

Laurence smiles, the way he does when he's telling me something he thinks I should have known. That scar stands up and shines. "Shit, Jake," he says. "He's out."

And been out. Near three months now. Laurence figured I knew, maybe heard something about him. The day Daddy got released, Laurence says, he told him he was going to take some time to get around the state, look for something he needed to find.

"I figured he meant you," Laurence says.

"Naw," I say, and start walking again. I catch up to the wrapper and kick it in the street. "He's just talking about getting work or something. He don't want to see me."

"That's what you don't know," Laurence says, keeping up with me. "Or it's one thing you don't know. Curtis is coming, and he'll be telling you the rest himself."

"He ain't gonna find me," I say. "Besides, I got nothing to say to him."

"Don't you want to tell him about your little chat with George?"

I spin around and head the other way—ain't gonna hear no more about that hall. But Laurence stops me right quick, grabs my shoulder, and turns me back to him.

"He give you that shit about you ain't no prodigal son? Gave it to me too—been giving it to every man he's putting out these days. Looks like old George done got himself some religion, huh Jake?"

"What you want from me, motherfucker?" I say, smacking his hand off. "Quit talking your shit and leave me alone."

"Leave you alone?" Laurence says. "As I recall, you came up to *me*. Fact is, Jake, I think *you* the one wants something here. But I don't think you want to be alone. You walk away now, you *will* be—good and alone. And that's your problem. But you stick around, maybe we can work together."

I cock my head, point to his scar. "So how did George give you that?"

He laughs. "You're too smart, Jake," he says. "I can't lie to you, I know that, so I won't even try. George told me he had a deal I couldn't refuse, but I did."

Nobody knows who the rats are. Just George and whoever takes the bait, till he cuts them loose. Any fool who's ever been locked-down knows you can't get no lower than a snitch, and it's the same code out here on the street, but George knows there's always somebody for sale in the Flatlands. And he's screwed enough folks to know somebody's always got a bead on him too. He likes to get the new folks to rat for him, keep you from making any friends, but I never went for it because of what Laurence told me before I walked in those doors that first time. Laurence never did neither—not at first, and not last week, when George threw him the deal. Turns out the old lady at the job Laurence was on called George and damn-near called 911 when she saw Laurence taking those beers out of the fridge.

"George told me he'd give me another chance, since I'd always worked so good for him. Said he had a job needed doing, and if I didn't want to get Alcatrazzed then I was his man. Said all this time's gone by and he still didn't have nothing on you, and he's getting itchy for some payback."

"Bullshit," I say. "I just got in his face right now and he didn't do a thing. If he wanted a piece of me so bad he could have taken it." I laugh. "Or tried to—he couldn't do shit to me without somebody holding me down."

Laurence shakes his head. "Look, Jake, try to understand now. I ain't talking about no street fight. This hall belongs to *George*. You got him in his own *house*, with a full house watching. You don't know how many brothers been coming around since then asking for George just so they can laugh at his ass. He wants you, but he don't want some OK Corral showdown. He wants to do it quiet, cut you someplace you don't even feel till you already done bled half to death. And believe me, he's gonna be there for that other half."

I cock my chin up again. "He can't touch me," I say. "How's he gonna get me?"

"Don't know," Laurence says. "Don't know for sure, because I told him to find another man before he even got telling me the plan." He pulls off his glasses, runs his finger down that scar. "Man near went crazy on me, hit me with those keys— little bit closer, and I'd be trying to find me a glass eyeball. Called up the Panama and had my shit out on the street in no time. But that don't matter, Jake, because I ain't no rat. I told George I know you, I know your daddy too, so throw me some other deal or throw me in the Alcatraz with Jake."

I look closer, and that purple-blue around the red ain't the shape of any set of keys I know about, but quick as that Laurence has the glasses back on and his finger pointing down Third toward the hall.

"He gave me that same line—you ain't no prodigal son. Shit, that's what I oughta be telling *him*. Look down that way, Jake. You see his name on it? Naw— that's *our* hall. *We* the ones doing the work. He ain't doing nothing but selling us. And what's the motherfucker doing with all that money? Is he helping a brother out? Naw—just spending it all on himself. But he don't want us to see them fat pockets, so he went and got himself a house in Bella Vista."

"George went across the bridge?" I say.

"And it's time we did too, Jake," Laurence says. "You and your daddy and me. Time to go get back what's ours."

I step back, put my hand up. "Naw. I'm a family man now. I ain't got time for no games."

Laurence laughs. "I ain't talking about bringing him no fatted calf," he says. "But I sure do aim to eat me one." He steps in smelling-close, and he's strong as before, that cheap wine and that hand on my shoulder again, but even if I tried breaking away now I don't know where I'd go. "Us three gonna have us a feast. Now don't you tell me a family man like yourself don't want to bring some of that home."

I shake my head. "I ain't going in on that. You said yourself he's got rats out on me. He's gonna know we're coming."

"I said he's *trying*. But he ain't got nothing yet. Ain't got nothing on me neither, and I know because I'm *always* checking my back."

Laurence tells me to think on it, page him when I get back from that job in the desert, and if I see Daddy before then tell him to do the same. He puts his beeper number on a piece of paper and puts it in my hand.

I turn around and start heading home, start running, hustle-stepping, moving when I hit the first corner and Laurence is good and gone. The clouds look like they'll hold, but the breeze is blowing strong now so you never know. I ball that paper up and throw it in the street, and I hear it skip-roll along the other way behind me till I can't hear it no more.

* * *

Too early to go home. Or too long since I've been home. Don't know what it is, but I'm just following my feet now, and they're taking me to Valley Street. Ain't but a couple miles or so from the Misery Accordion, and I'd take the bus if I could but walking ain't never hurt me yet. Either way I'll be back in that basement hole by the end of the day.

That Benz could get me there in no time. Could get me anyplace I want—across the bridge, across the state line, anyplace. Plenty of room in there for Noel and William too. I could spread a map across the dash and just tell them pick someplace. Find us someplace ain't got no roaches and sheets you've got to boil every week, someplace a man can work for more than four and a quarter and buy his family some nice things.

But it's gone—ain't no sense thinking on it. Just got to keep walking.

My name's still in the walk out by the street, and the house looks the same as it did when I left, when Momma put me out. The empty drive with the hoop torn out, that peeling paint job and those sagging gutters, that window in front.

I go around the side, around back to the kitchen, to see who's home. Word got to me that Momma left three or four years ago, a year or so after I did, went back to Chicago and took Paula and Cheryl with her. Cheryl sent me some letters, but I never wrote her back, don't even know if she'd still be there now if I did. Somebody else must have moved in here after us, maybe another family like ours, but I hope not.

I press up on the kitchen window to get a good look. Not much light, can't make out much except that there ain't much to make out. The door to the hall inside is open, and I can see into the sitting room where we had the couch and our eating table, but it's just the floor and the walls now, and when I knock it sounds like it goes all around the house and right back to me without having touched nothing at all.

Those houses over in Bella Vista are all full-up with nice things. That's what folks say, that's what I've seen with my own eyes when we've done moving jobs over there. Daddy never went for homes, just the little groceries and corner liquors, and Lydell only taught me about boosting cars, but that don't matter. I'm better than both of them—they both knew it from the start—even if I ain't touched that game since I don't know when. I bet I could clean out a house by myself, wouldn't even need Laurence and Daddy, wouldn't even matter if it belonged to George.

But ain't no sense in that neither, that's thinking crazy too. That shit got them all in jail, gonna do the same to me. I just need to do my work, get my raises while we hold our breath a little while, and we'll make it through.

I go to try the front door, and step on a sign that fell down on its face. It's small, it's black, and the orange letters tell me my old house is for rent. I read the bottom—a number with the name of some joker to call about it, some corporate outfit you see on TV. I fold it up into my pocket, and I walk through the grass until I find a rock. It's solid, good and heavy in my hand. I toss it up in front of me as I'm walking back to the curb, just to see how it flies, and when I'm at the street, when I can see the house looking back at me, I throw it right at the big front window, the same one that held when I put Daddy up against it, but this time I'm stronger, dead-on and through.

CHAPTER 3
EMPTY HOUSE, FULL-UP

The room is cold, the floor is too, when I get out of bed and step over to the fridge. Too dark to see the clock, but I can always feel it in my bones when it's too late to go back to sleep, even if that alarm ain't started shouting yet. Don't have to be over in Bella Vista till eight, but the Sunday buses are always slow getting across the bridge, and I don't want to go back to that dream anyhow.

I open the fridge, and when the light hits the floor I see some roaches hustle under, probably laughing their asses off at my big fool self and leaving me some more shit gonna get in William's lungs, but I ain't going chasing them now. The light inside don't do me much good, just shows me what we ain't got. Nothing in there but some baloney and mustard, a little bread, a little milk.

I put the bread and meat on the table and start making a sandwich. The old dream came around last night, that one I just can't shake, don't matter what kind of hole I'm living in. I was back in Chicago again, in our basement, walking through all Granddad Lenny's tools on the floor, coming out up into the snow and there he was—that man without a face, hanging from the maple, at the end of Daddy's scarf and that bright white shirt all full-up with blood. He hung there coughing, hacking worse than old Jerry, shaking loose those last red leaves. I ran out to him like I always do, but then he was gone, it was all gone, I woke up, and it was William coughing loud and sharp like breaking glass.

This sandwich ain't much, but it's gonna have to do. Noel don't have but a couple more dollars of food stamps to last us till Thursday, when her check comes in. I take some wax paper down off the top of the fridge, cut the sandwich in two, wrap up my half and put Noel's back inside. The bright light in there shows up the bones good on my hand, and when I squeeze it, the muscles and veins stand up too. Holding it, I can feel the blood pumping up my arm all the way to my shoulder. Still sore from down at the park, but it's good enough for now, good enough to get me through this job and into next week.

But what the hell are we gonna do then? Last night me and Noel sat up late talking it all out, trying to figure something. Don't matter how you look at it, we've got to change our game—ain't no way to make it on what we've got coming in, not with everything William needs now. We could save the rent by going to the shelters, but I've been in that rut before, and I know it sucks a man down better than quicksand, even when he's on his own—it's harder pulling out when you're carrying a family. If we go that way and split up—if I get a mat at the St. Al's and Noel takes William to the Casa Maria—we'll keep her check, but we won't see each other except on my days off. If we stay together, check into the Sal's Army family place, we'll lose the check—won't take long for word to get to Noel's case-worker she's got a working man around. But playin' the shelters like that don't make sense beyond a month or two, because even if even if this basement hole ain't nothing but a roach motel, if we leave it somebody's gonna take it right quick, and who knows where we'll find a room after that. Best thing we could come up with is for Noel to take William and hop on over to the Luby, that women's safe house they think no man can find, stay there a month or two playin' them about how I'm beating the black off her and get them to buy the nebulizer and boil those sheets. If she can score all William's asthma toys off them, then I can hold on to this room, sleep better than I would on those St. Al's mats, and go to work in the morning getting closer to my raise.

We said we'd sleep on it. I don't know how Noel slept, but my old dream didn't tell me a damn thing, and I sure didn't wake up with no winning Lotto numbers in my head. Went to bed looking at my hands, got up doing the same thing. All that muscle in there, all the bones and blood—what good does it do me? What's the use being young and strong if I can't put it to no use? I'd give a man my hands if he could give me a way out of this mess—shit, I'd give him all my blood if it could just get my little boy better.

He starts coughing again and Noel wakes up, rolls over and pulls him out of the crib. She sing-shushes him and looks over at me, tells me to give her the milk.

"Ain't much to give," I say. "Why don't you give him yours?"

"Because I'm getting him off it," she says. "It's past time for that, I told you already."

The other sisters have been telling Noel she's crazy a long time now, letting William keep biting her titty when she can get that formula with her stamps. But Noel always does things her own way, and on this one I couldn't blame her, because there ain't nothing like momma's milk and it don't cost a dime. That's why I can't figure why she'd go changing now, with the mess we're in.

"Just give him some," I say. "You're still in my house."

She pulls her ugly face, bunches those lips up tight and presses those eyes thinner than a Chinawoman. "You calling this a house now?"

"We can't do no better right now," I say. "You know it as good as me."

"Is that what you got up to tell me? Is that what it comes down to for you? Keep him in this place so you can keep making the rules?" She shakes her head, turns her back to me. William's little head is sitting on her shoulder, and I get his eyes. "Grow up, Jake. Be a man for your boy."

"By letting him go? Letting him stay in a shelter?"

William's eyes stay with me, and just like that he starts fussing, reaching over Noel's shoulder out at me and pulling a face like he's set to cry again.

"Give him to me," I say, and lift him up out of her arms, put him to my chest and start that little bounce-hop that always gets him quiet—or does most times. He goes with it now, puts his head over my heart, and his fussing knocks off right quick till he's just humming like the way a pigeon sounds cooing through the roof.

Noel gets the milk out and turns on the hot plate, runs some water into a pot and sets it to boil.

"So what we gonna do then, Jake?" she says.

"I don't know," I say. I walk to the door, just three steps, then back again past the bed and the fridge to the bathroom, ain't but five or six more, keep that bounce-hop going and keep my boy quiet. He's breathing smooth now. His eyes are still open, but I know if I stay at it, I'll get him back to sleep.

But just like that he's squirming again, fussing, pushing back off me and kicking his legs. I hold him out from me, and those legs pump like a couple of pistons in a brand-new car. Maybe today's the day.

I set him down, stand him on his feet and let his legs hold him. I tell Noel to back up to the door and put her arms out. We've been waiting a while for him to walk, but he never gets more than a step or two before he falls. But if he's good and hungry like she says he is, he'll get it for sure.

"You'll see," I say when she tells me he ain't ready for this yet. I pat him on his butt and point out at Noel. "Go on now, boy," I say. "You can do it."

Noel looks at me and shakes her head, but then she gets down on her knees and puts that smile on, holds her arms out wide. "Come to Momma."

William gives that little laugh of his and his hands fly up like he's cheering himself on. That gets me and Noel laughing, and he sees it and laughs some more.

"Go on now, boy," I say again. "Walk on over there."

He takes a step, he takes another one, and those hands go up again and that laugh comes when Noel claps, but then he's down, drops straight on his butt, and that laughing stops.

I stand him up again. "Keep at it, boy. You was going good."

"Ain't you got a job to get to?" Noel says. "Can't you see he ain't ready yet?"

"He's ready," I say, looking at him. "Go on now."

He takes a step to Noel, but that's all this time because quick as that he looks back at me and tries to spin around, but he just ends up on the floor. Noel scoops him up and starts walking with her eyes on that pot, but I put my hand out and tell her to give him one more chance.

"Third time's the charm," I say. "Let him try walking toward me this time."

She pulls that ugly face again, gets those eyes so tight I don't know how she can see me at all. "You show up late to that job you gonna lose it. Ain't no time for games."

I put a finger up. "Don't you tell me about my job. It's still early. This here's my boy, and if I want to see him walk before I go to work, that's what I'm gonna do."

"Once more, Jake," she says. "And that's it."

"That's all he needs."

Noel steps back to the door and sets William down. I take the bottle of milk off the hot plate, crouch down, and hold it out.

"Walk to me now," I say.

William's hands shoot out and that laugh comes again and he's off. Stepping to me—one, two. He's smiling big, those legs are holding, I know he's gonna make it. Stepping again—three, four, at the edge of the bed now. Noel claps, and I slap my leg and tell him keep coming. He does—five, six, to the middle of the bed now, halfway to me, better than he's ever done before. He knows it too, those little eyes light up and shine just like those couple teeth in his mouth. I know he's gonna make it, we are too. I can feel him in my arms already, feel his head over my heart again, feel my hands up under his arms when I lift him up toss him up let him fly a second and catch him again, let him fly and hear him laughing clear and free because he made it, he's walking now. I can feel my hands letting him fly when I get back from this job and we'll be a little bit closer, won't be in this hole much longer now, let him fly because I'm his daddy and I'm getting him out starting us fresh pulling us through.

He steps again—seven, and then he tries to run and his head gets ahead of his feet. He falls smack down on his chin, and for just a second he's quiet and I think maybe he'll bounce right up, go back to the door and try again and make it all the way this time. But that scream comes, loud and sharp like glass breaking, and Noel scoops him up and swipes that milk off me before I'm even on my feet.

"Time to get to work," she says. She opens the fridge and pulls out the ice tray, cracks out some cubes for William's chin. I put my boots on, look at my hands when I open the door and pull it shut again, squeeze them to feel the blood pumping through, but I can't feel nothing at all.

* * *

When me and Bird are putting the last boxes into the truck and locking-down the door, I hear the Daniels' kids inside their house, getting one more run-around. An empty house can make a whole lot of noise, and sometimes there ain't nothing kids like better than showing they know how to stir up a racket. I oughta know—William's a champ at that. The boy and the girl are trying out the echo, seeing if maybe they shout loud enough their voices will keep bouncing around till the next family moves in.

We started straight-up at eight this morning, and now that we're done I'm ready to trade-in for a new shoulder, maybe a back and a pair of legs too if they got any. I lie down on the grass right by the fence and look at the clouds. They're big, moving slow and going yellow now. I hear Bird light a match, and I want those kids to shut up so I can have a minute to think. This is just about the only time you can catch Bird being quiet—he says it's against his religion to talk when he's having a cigarette. Nichols, the white guy on the crew, always tells Bird to smoke more.

Just when I start to drift off a little, Bills and Mr. Daniels come down the stairs and walk outside. I don't even need to look to know, because Bills can't get down a flight of stairs without sounding like he's rolling a strike, and Daniels—he told us to call him Morris, but none of us do—promised us all at lunch we'd have some beers in bottles at the end of the day. He's wearing a green polo shirt tucked into some nice pants, and he's carrying a six in each hand. When he walks the bottles make that nice soft clink the way cold beers are supposed to. I'll take one if he gives it to me, but I'd rather get the tip.

Daniels is an Oreo if I ever saw one. Ain't that he's a bad dude, it's just funny watching him, because he thinks he can hide it. When we got here this morning, he was packing bags into his minivan, and it didn't take long to spot. He let us meet the whole family, but he talked for all of them, his woman too. He shook hands with all four of us, just a straight shake with Bills and Nichols first, then he stepped over to me and tried some soul-brother number I couldn't follow. When I took my hand back he laughed and slapped me on the shoulder and said I was too young to know that one, but it must have been something he saw on TV because Bird's about his age, forty or somewhere up there, and he didn't know what the man was doing neither.

I sit up against the fence while I'm waiting for Daniels to give me mine. Over here in Bella Vista, other side of the bridge, things are different—ain't like the Flatlands. This fence is solid, ain't nothing like that Archer Street chain-link with the holes and those soft spots you could lean back into while you were watching the game. It's wood and it's thick, it stands up tall and plants in deep, keeps you out of sight. Everybody around here's got some kind of fence, but if they all had them like the Daniels you wouldn't know there was anybody living in these houses at all. I'm taking it all in while I've got the chance—only way someone like me is getting in here is if I'm cleaning something or stealing it. Lydell brought me out across the bridge when we boosted the car, but that was way back then, and don't matter what kind of plan Laurence has on George, I'm a working man now, and I ain't coming back here unless I've got an honest job to do.

Daniels hands out the beers and passes the opener. He knocks bottles with Bills and slaps him on the back. "These boys worked real well today," he says, taking a sip. "Real, real well. I hope you know we appreciate it."

Bills nods and has himself a sip too. Nichols has been working for him going on eight years now, and he says all that time he ain't never seen the little man meet a beer he didn't like. Never known him to turn down his momma's cooking neither, and it shows. Bills takes off his cap and his glasses, wipes his hand over his face and back through that little bit of hair still hanging on up top before he fits them both back on. "Tell you what," he says. "This here team's the best I've had since I don't know when."

"It's all on account of the new man," Bird says, and looks at me. "Ain't he something else, Nick?"

"Oh yeah, got that right," Nichols says. He pulls his bottle up quick and takes a couple long sips until that little smile of his fades. Bird does this with all the customers, and you'd think Nichols wouldn't think it's so damn funny anymore. But he loves to watch Bird work the tip, especially a tough one like this. We all do, and even if Bills says company policy don't allow it, he never stops him, just as long as Bird don't slow the job down while he's at it. If you take him to the letter, Bird's done it all—fought in Vietnam and been all across Asia and Europe, sold cars with his brother in Atlanta, played clubs in Kansas City, and had fifty-yard-line seats at every Super Bowl in the seventies. He's the kind of man Lydell might have turned out to be if he wasn't locked-down in Texas. I asked him once or twice what's a man of the world doing moving furniture in Oakland and sporting a set of teeth Dracula wouldn't want, but he shook me off and said he got cleaned-out in a nasty divorce, don't you ever go getting caught in no mess like that yourself, brother.

Bird looks up at Daniels, takes his cigarette case out of his shirt pocket. "Want one?" he says. "Rolled them all myself. And I always wash my hands before I do."

He talks too much for me, but Bird tells a good story, and all the time I've been with this outfit I've hardly seen a customer yet he couldn't shoot the shit with. But Daniels wouldn't have nothing to do with him the whole day today. Bird tried, for damn-sure—tried asking him what kind of classes he taught at the college, if he knew much about animals out in the desert, and if him and his wife had ever been over to Paris, when he heard him call her Collette. Daniels just laughed at Bird, slapped him on the back once or twice, until Bird asked about the lady. It was right before lunch, and we were all in the same room, getting set to take the paintings to the truck. Mrs. Daniels had wrapped them up in brown paper and written names in black on the front. Bird said he knew most of them, the lady was definitely into old-time French and African. When Daniels came in to check on us, he told us he sent the family to the movies so he could help us out. We all knew he wasn't no working man, and he wouldn't do much—his arms were buff from that health club but he couldn't hide that gut he got sitting at that college desk. He told us be careful with the paintings, but we had to teach him how to turn corners and take the stairs, and he almost cracked his anyhow when Bird asked did the Mrs. have any roots in Haiti. The dude spun around quick and missed whacking the corner on the door frame by an inch. He looked at Bird and said what we all figured he'd been thinking since the morning—Don't talk to my wife, best if you don't even talk *about* her. He ain't looked at Bird since.

But somehow he took to me, and we rapped a little at lunch. Maybe he wanted to talk to a younger brother, maybe he thought he could do me some good. Whatever it was he got himself on a roll—I got through a whole burger before Daniels even stopped to breathe. Most of what he said was boring so I just kept nodding—getting passed over for some spot at the college and all the friends his wife had made here she'd be leaving. But I woke up when he asked me didn't I wish Bush had beat Slick Billy back in November, because it ain't right for hard-working men like us to be paying so folks on the county can get something for nothing. I told him that shit's fucked up, *brother*. But he didn't get it, just laughed and told me let him know if I needed anything. Bird was standing in the shade over against the truck, close enough to read it all, he told me later. *You tell him about Noel or something? Dude thinks you want to be like him.*

That's why Bird thinks the tip's gonna be good. He knows I need it too, so does Nichols—they both know I've got a kid and All Things don't hardly pay more than that four and a quarter bullshit until you've put in three months, don't pay you more than six until you've given them a year. Bills always says he'd pay more, but it's corporate who decides all that. So they're all working it for me today, gonna let me keep it all instead of splitting it like usual. Anytime we get one it's never big, but it's enough to bring home a bottle of wine—cheapest they got, and I always tell Noel I tried getting her fancy favorite kind but that grocer don't speak no French good as me—and a pack of cookies for William to chew on. Bird says he's keeping track of what all our customers give, just to see what's going down in California, just a little experiment. Says he's gonna write it up someday in one of those papers he's always showing me, little papers from neighborhoods all over the state, even down to LA. He told me he's written stuff before, but he don't want to bring those copies on the job in case they get dirty.

Daniels doesn't look at Bird or the cigarette, just puts his hand up. "No thanks," he says. "It's been a long time since I touched one of those."

Bird stands up and hands one over to Nichols and Bills. I take one too. It ain't much like me to buy my own, but most times I don't turn down a free one. It tastes all right on a break or at the end of the day.

Bird takes a drag and blows it out between his teeth. "Yeah we sure work better now we got Jake," he says. "All it takes is one family man on the crew to get up a little more *motivation*. Rubs off, don't it, Nick?"

Nichols just nods and takes another sip, then he looks over at the house when the kids start making a racket coming down the stairs. They run right through the middle of us and head around back, like maybe they think that big swing set is still back there. That was the first thing we broke down this morning, but at lunchtime I saw Daniels out back just looking down at those places the kids had worn the grass away, just dragging his foot in the dirt and kicking up dust.

"You have kids, Robertson?" he says to me.

"Just one," I say.

He puts the beers down on the grass. "Let me show you something inside," he says, and points a thumb at his house.

I look at Bird and Nichols, but they're both laughing, or trying not to, especially Bird. Whenever his lip is down over his teeth you know he's dying inside. He nods to me and rubs two fingers to his thumb.

Daniels tells the fellas to help themselves to the beers. I follow him inside. His shoes are loud on the floors. It's a nice-looking house from the outside, but when it's cleaned-out like this any fool can see the bones are cheap. Ain't nothing but one of them California middle-class specials—just some tin they throw up quick and call it gold, and when you get down to it all you're paying for is that fence and some neighbors that leave you alone. Beats our hole in the basement, and I'd damn-sure take it if they were giving it away, but when I get us out of the Flatlands I want to be living someplace real.

We go up to a little bedroom in the back, the room with that clown wallpaper. It's nice and warm in here now with the light coming in. The window's open and I can hear the Mrs. playing with the kids out back. Daniels' shoes clock going across the room. He stands by the window and looks outside. "Did you move this room, Robertson?"

I tell him me and Nichols did. I remember I saw the boy's name on all the boxes.

"So what do you know about that scratch on the floor?"

"Where?"

He points. "Right next to where the bed was. Look closely."

I take a couple steps and bend down near the middle of the room, acting like I can't see nothing. Gotta try playin' him now. Daniels bends down with me and points right to it—two big marks maybe a couple-three inches long apiece, one slashing and crossing over the other in the middle, right where the varnish is coming up. I saw it before, but I fucked up, didn't say nothing to Bills right off the bat. Corporate says to check out every room before you start the job, especially a nice place like this, check the walls floor paint glass and rugs, and get down all the marks so there ain't no doubting what's yours and what ain't. I saw it, plain as day on that first sweep through, but those kids were yelling and my head was pounding and by the time I was outside again strapping my belt on, it was out of my head.

Now I'm fucked. I ain't doubting me and Nick made a racket up here moving the kid's bed and all them drawers, but we didn't cut into the floor like this. Bird would back me, Nick probably would too, but I don't know about Bills. I'm still the new man, could be cheaper to cut me loose than get into a fight with Daniels—corporate could come down hard on him when they hear somebody from Bella Vista's got a complaint. Now it's me against Mr. College Professor. All that brother shit before wasn't about nothing but setting the nigger up.

"It ain't nothing," I say, standing up. I move to the door. "You hardly see it."

He stands up quick and grabs my arm. "Hold on, where are you going?"

I smack his arm away. "What you looking at me for, man? Get the fuck off me."

He laughs and lets go, puts both hands up in front of him. "All right, all right. Take it easy now. Just asking you a question."

"I ain't got time for no questions. I got work to do."

"Fine, let me get right to it then. You know how to fix this?"

I give my mustache a quick stroke and point at him. "What I tell you before? I don't know nothing about it. You got a gripe, bring it to Bills."

He pulls a face like he didn't hear me right. "Gripe about what? I'm the one who screwed it up worse than it was. Just look at it."

He gets down and shows me where he took sandpaper to it after he gave KJ a good whupping. He tells me he found his boy's name carved in a tree out back, and next thing he knew he heard some scratching behind this door. Daniels damn-near wore off his arm trying to sand it out before he saw what he was doing.

"My boy is meticulous," he says, laughing again. "He got in there pretty deep. Trying to get back at me, maybe." He stands up again, shakes his head. "You know, it bugs the hell out of me every time I see it. You'd think a bunch of primitives lived here."

"Yeah well you moving now," I say.

"Right, but we still have to sell this place. If we put carpet down in here it won't match the other rooms," he says, turning his hands up. "You see my problem now, Robertson? I thought I'd ask you, because you look like somebody who might know how to take care of that."

I shrug. "Too deep to buff it out. You could take the piece up, but you do that you gotta take them all up if you want it looking nice in the end."

He crosses his arms, nods some, looks down at the floor. "Right, right. That's what I thought."

"You finished now?" I say. "'Cause I'm going."

"Wait, hold on again," he says. "Let me just ask you one more thing. Where are you from?"

I stroke my mustache again. What's this fool need to know? "Got family from Chicago," I say. "But I can't hardly remember that place."

"Really?" he says. "I remember everything about it."

Turns out he's from Gary. In our neighborhood we always thought folks in Indiana were hayseeds, even if they did come from a city. But Daniels don't seem much like that—not with his way of talking and that ugly-ass minivan. I stand a minute, listen to him go on about Chicago, and I can tell he knows something. He says it was always a big thing when his old man would drive the family in for a weekend. They'd go to the same park by the lake, buy hotdogs from the same stand, play touch football till it was dark.

"I don't know why, but I can't get that off my mind lately," he says. "The whole time since we've been packing up I've been thinking about how I used to look at that place. Even though I haven't been back since Dad's funeral."

Wouldn't be so bad listening to the man if I thought the tip was coming, or at least if I could sit down. But I don't see it happening. So I just put it to him. "Hey Morris, what you telling me all this for?"

He pulls that face again. Bird would say I'm playin' like a champ now, calling Daniels by his first name right at the end like we some *soul* brothers now. Daniels turns around, closes the window, and locks it. He walks over to me slowly, hands in his pockets, his shoes clocking on the floor. He shoots his eyes over to the middle of the room. "It's like you just said, Robertson. That mark doesn't come up. My wife and I moved into this place when she was pregnant with our little girl." He looks around at the walls. "This house is all my kids know."

I nod at him. I was down too when Daddy packed us up for California. But that was different—we *had* to, wasn't no work for him in Chicago no more. Mr. College Professor can get any kind of work he wants. "So why you leaving then?"

He shakes his head and breathes out loud. "You mean why am I telling *you*? Is that what you want to know?" He steps around me, through the door, still shaking his head. I hear him go down the stairs, his shoes clocking in the middle of all these empty walls, till he gets to the bottom and calls his wife and kids, tells them to get in the car.

* * *

Next morning we start out early, headed for Bethel, by way of Fresno and Bakersfield, then east again into the desert. It's a little town not too far from that college where Daniels got his new job, I think, somewhere about a hundred miles from Barstow.

We set out from Oakland about four, and we'll be crossing into the valley by the time the sun comes up. Bills and Nichols drive the trailer together, and me and Bird follow behind in the van. It's a dark-blue number All Things bought way back in the eighties, just two seats up front and an empty space in back where Bills took out the benches so he could haul extra stuff. On this job, most everything fit in the trailer—this van ain't even half-full today—so last night we had to stick the phone books behind the loose panel to keep it from rattling. Most times we just shove some boxes up against it and it's all right. And I bought a couple packs of cigarettes so Bird's mouth won't get to feeling too empty neither. It's about eight hours to where we're going, and I figure I ought to try to get back at least a little sleep on the way.

Early mornings Sundays and holidays it's always quiet on the road, even in California. It's Memorial Day tomorrow, and most folks are probably gonna remember they need to catch up on some sleep. I do, too, but won't be today. I get a couple winks while Bird drives the first few hours, and somehow I feel pretty good when I wake up and see the sun between the hills and those long shadows stretching out onto the freeway. Cold, but good. The sun gets powerful real quick out here, but it's bright before it's hot. Bird gives me some coffee from his thermos. No doubting later on today when we're working and my shirt's soaked-through I won't believe I ever touched something this hot, but for right now it's just what I need.

Noel kissed me when I left this morning, told me to come back quick as I can. I couldn't bring her home no tip last night, and the only thing I could tell her today was to stay put till I get back, because we're gonna make it. This sun feels good now, but I don't know if it can make me believe that. And if it's shining now in the Flatlands, how's she gonna see it with that window all shut up?

Looking at the back of that All Things trailer for so long, Bird can't help but want to talk about the job. I take over driving and listen to him. I don't mind, for a little while. When I ask him why he thinks a man like Daniels wants to pull up out of a nice place like they got and settle down where he's gonna sweat to death, Bird asks me back if I remember the fence. I sure do. Daniels told me yesterday he built it himself one summer, but I don't believe it. It's a professional job—those boards were so tight you couldn't fit a dime between them. I can always tell when Bird thinks he knows better, the way he gives a little smile and kind of rolls his eyes back. He says he wouldn't put it past Daniels to have done it, seeing how bad the dude wants to keep everything out. But he knows Daniels don't trust the fence no more—can't I see that for myself?—and now he's taking the family to some old-timey place, someplace where ain't no niggers like us two gonna climb up over. When I say to Bird that it don't sound so bad, getting out of the city, he asks me then how come that dude and his wife couldn't stop telling Bills they've been living by the Bay since before they got married, the kids don't know nothing else, how come they kept walking around like they was checking the house for ghosts.

The farther we go, the hotter it gets, and the more I feel like I'm running on dead time. That's what I call it when my mind's going but my body's not, when I can't sleep but there's nobody to talk to, not much to look at. Bird falls asleep pretty quick after he quits on Daniels, and for the first hour or so I'm glad for it, because I've got the radio and I'm tired of all his yapping. But then all the stations start to fade till there's nothing but country, and listening to Bird would beat the sound of those cowboys crying about old dead Yeller any day. After he falls off, all I've got is the back of that trailer and the wide-open road.

Out here the freeway doesn't turn a whole lot, so I don't have to think too much about the wheel, except to keep it steady when the wind picks up. And it does, too—strong enough to give this van a kick. The mountains run slow on both sides, like some old stone walls, but there's plenty of flatland between them for the wind to get up some speed. Ain't many trees, and all the bushes and rocks lie pretty low to the dirt, so there ain't much to stand in the way. And just brown brown brown, just like twelve years back, sitting in the front of Daddy's truck. I ain't been out in the desert but once since then, ain't hardly left the city at all.

Now I remember why—I don't like it, not a bit. Don't like the heat, don't like how it takes forever to get from one place to another, and can't stand all the places my mind gets running to in between. Running back now to the cab of that truck and all that wide-open space out in front, back to the side of the road and that tire iron clanging on the ground and flashing in the air. Back to Momma laughing reading Daddy's letter from Folsom, saying he was seeing a chaplain now and getting himself together and couldn't we come up for his fortieth, back to that Greyhound hot as a motherfucker on the way back home and that sweat soaking my shirt running down to my hand he left hanging on the glass. Back to that basement hole, looking at those empty shelves in the fridge, holding my arms out to William and watching him fall. And back to that dream again—but that ain't never left me alone.

By noon most of the shadows slip away, but it seems like there's more mountains now, getting darker, sharper, coming closer to the road. Makes me wonder if they're gonna come together someplace up ahead and close me in.

After Bakersfield we turn east, and Bird keeps snoring. But it's all right, because taking in the view out here keeps me awake better than listening to him. We're in the real desert now, and it's sure got plenty for a place so full-up of nothing. The only thing worth looking at on that Greyhound to Folsom was the mountains, but I couldn't see them till we were almost there because of the smog. Somebody on that bus told me about a lake close by, but we never made it there. It was hot as a motherfucker that day, like today, and it would have been nice to cool down after how that visit went. Now the road starts winding, but we hardly see another car pass us, so it don't matter if I slip over the lines now and again while I'm taking everything in. The ground looks drier than a week-old chicken bone, and there's some places where it's cracked just like a big pane of glass that somebody got thrown up against but didn't go through—a thousand pieces and who knows what's holding them together. I don't know how anything gets by out here—those Joshua trees that sure look like palm tree–cactus muts to me, all the little bushes, or the animals. Some signs start to pop up along the side saying you can exit and get a look at a dry lake, and each one's got a different name. But I don't really believe it until the road rises and I get a good look at a big one for myself. It's like the top of a candle you let burn a while—big circle with a raised edge, and the ground inside is sunk down and the same brown as the outside. Guess there used to be *some* water in these parts. Maybe the desert folks want to remember it, put up a marker they way you do when somebody you know passed, so other folks stop a second and don't go walking all over the place you put them in the ground to rest.

Sometimes the road sinks low too, down even with the lakes. About fifty miles outside of Bethel I see a sign saying we're crossing into Gilead County. We pass through some places where a couple rock walls shoot straight up on both sides and the desert disappears. Ain't no balm around here now, not even one of them Joshua trees. The sun's just about straight overhead, so the walls light up gold like some old honey, but I still feel like I'm in a tunnel, the way they squeeze in. I can hear the truck rattling up ahead, the sound bouncing all around. Bird sleeps through it, but I can't get out of there quick enough. And even when we're out of the tunnels, when it all opens back up, the sound's ringing in my ears.

In the afternoon, before we start getting the stuff inside, I do the walk-through real quick on this new place. It's got cheap bones, just like the other house, might even be a prefab they ship in from Mexico these days, and even if it doesn't have that fence like back in Bella Vista, I bet they put down a fortune for it. Can't get something for nothing in California no more, can't hardly get nothing for something. I check all around for scratches this time but there ain't any I can see—but I know it won't take long for the kids to make this house their own.

The work doesn't take long. Tonight we just put the stuff inside, in whatever rooms Bills tells us to, till the family comes tomorrow morning and shows us how they want it all straightened up. Around nine we lock the doors and go for pizza and beers, Bills' treat.

It's good to fill up, eat till I can't get anymore down, because it ain't often these days I get to do that. After we put away two big pies and a couple pitchers, the other fellas start racking up a game of eight ball, but I tell them I've got to see a man about a horse while I can still lift my leg. Somebody's using the john inside, so I go out back and look for a spot. Ain't no trouble finding a place that could use a little water, but once I start walking the air feels good. The music from the joint gets softer, and the light does too, till pretty soon the windows just look like little candles in all this darkness.

Bethel is a nowhere place, if you ask me. Funny name too—I wonder if I'm gonna find some ladder out here, if God's gonna send me an angel to fight with or some dream I've got to follow. If he does, I sure hope it don't go down with me like happened to old Jacob—don't want to go home with no bad hip *and* shoulder. And whatever dream he sends sure better not be worse than the one I've got inside me. Who knows, maybe I'll end up with something good. Maybe God will tell me what he gave me these hands for after all.

The only lights around are the ones I just left behind, and after you get out here where I am now, you can't find nobody to talk with to save your life. When we were finishing up at the house tonight, Bird started off on a riff about some kind of rat they've got out here. I guess just because the sky's all full of stars in the desert don't mean you can't have rats like they do in the city. But this one is different, Bird was saying, because it's just a bitty thing but it's famous because it don't need to piss but once its whole life. When I got up from the table, I told Bird I could use what those little dudes got, but now that I've found a spot and can let myself go, I feel all right. Feels so good, really, that I can't even believe anything, even some rat, can live without doing the same every now and again. Some of them never get a chance to because they die too early. For the ones that do, that piss is so strong it just about burns a hole in the ground. I guess that's what happens when you spend your whole life holding on to something, waiting and waiting and waiting to let it go till it's either gonna burn right through you, or whatever gets in its way.

After I finish my business, I head back to the motel corporate got us, the Peniel. Ain't in the mood for no more pool, no TV neither. I just get right to bed.

I fall off quick, but it don't last long. When I wake up from my dream, it's past two, too late to stay up too early to get up, but I'm wide-awake and gonna be that way awhile. Bird's in his bed and snoring, but my head won't stop. Ain't never left Noel and William alone before. I told her to lay low, and she ain't no fool anyhow, but trouble's got a way of finding you sometimes in the Flatlands. Especially with that Benz sitting out in the street.

I head back outside, shut the light off again for Bird. Maybe walking will get my mind off things, maybe I'll see something out here that will tell me it's all gonna be all right. Either way I'll get some blood moving, get some air, and maybe that will help me get sleepy again.

The moon's out now, but it's just a slice, so I have to walk slow. I can hear that sand crunching under my feet, feel it hard on top and soft when I sink down in. Seeing those dry lakes before makes me think there could be smaller ones just about anywhere. Could be the kind that haven't lost all their water yet, the kind you can't spot in the dark till you're right in them, slipping down into that soft spot in the ground that's been waiting for you, holding on to just a little bit of rain from God knows how long ago just so when the time comes the ground's still got a little something to take you in past your ankle or your knee or even all the way if it's been waiting long enough.

It's good going slow. The moon ain't much but it's enough when I walk like this. Can't see those mountains no more, none of them bushes or cactus neither unless I walk right into them. But this place is alive for sure. Just breathing in I know that—this air cleans me right out. Things are moving out in the dark, running creaking and croaking, and even if they don't come close I can see them.

Walking, just walking. Got all night if I need it, or as long as this moon stays up if the sun don't get here first. Don't know what I'm gonna find, but it sure feels like something got me up out of that bed just now. Something out here waiting, been waiting a good long time.

PART II

CHAPTER 4
AT THE READY MAN

Sand crunches under my feet, whisper-shouts when it's just rolling smooth and fine, but gets talking good and loud in those crusted-up spots with the rocks on top. In the city you wouldn't hear it at all, but out here in the desert at night that sound just fills up the air, fills up your head too. Makes me think of that glass I walked over the first time I went through those green doors on Third and Battery, maybe three years back. I can't think when it was for sure, but I know it had already been a couple years since I'd seen Daddy, a couple since I'd been out on my own too, getting a mat at the St. Al's or whatever mission would take me, renting a room in an SRO when I could pay for it. And I know it's still walking around inside me, still fresh and smelling-close as living it all over again. Plenty of memories are like that, and my dreams are too—won't leave me be, don't matter if I'm under the Cliffs or in that basement hole or out here in the desert. Can't shake them, can't make that past stay past.

Things start early at the Ready Man, that's what everybody knows. You don't get there before six, you'll be on the shit jobs for sure, if there's any work left at all. If not you'll be crowing across the street, waving down those vans and fighting other dudes for the scraps.

I thought I'd be first in line, but when I get to the corner I can see a few brothers standing around, leaning up against the building, smoking or just looking at the ground. The sun ain't up full yet, but I can make out the dude in the black jacket up on his toes, knocking on a window, trying to yell something inside. All the windows are dark, and everything else on this street is rolled-down.

"Hey Blue," he says. "Tell George y'all gotta get me out today. Ask him who he got on that moving job." He comes down on his heels, turns his hat around and pops back up to the window. "Come on," he says, louder, "I know y'all ain't *doing* nothing yet."

The windows light up yellow and everybody shuffles into line, moving back from the double green doors, down the sidewalk toward me. There's maybe fifteen, twenty men here, a few white guys thrown in I didn't see before. Don't know how I missed this one in front of me. Short old dude, got a hunched back, gray hooded sweatshirt and this dirty red and blue knit hat that's pointed on top. Pulled down over his ears, so it's like his ugly brown beard is crawling out from under there.

"Ain't you gonna be hot in that hat, my man?" I tap him on the shoulder.

He turns around, coughing. Dude looks like he got a broken nose for his birthday every year since he was twenty. "Come again?"

"I said that's some kind of hat you got on."

"Tyler's been wearing that since he got his first check from the county," the brother in front of the old guy says, turning around. He's tall—got to be six-three or four, even without those boots. That salt and pepper beard is high on his cheeks, almost up to his glasses. "Goddamn President Johnson himself came out and gave it to him, said, 'Here you go Mr. Maltain, wear this hat around and show all them nice people how we're keeping you warm.'"

"Aw, fuck you, Laurence, it's just in the summertime," the old guy says, frowning, shaking his head. He looks at me. "I mean *California*, kid, and this place has the coldest summers you ever seen. Late fifties, I was a young man like you—"

"No, unh-uh," Laurence says, putting his hands on the old guy's shoulders, turning him back around. "At least let the dude get his coffee before you start up on that again." He looks at me and tilts his head to the side. "We do a yard work job together, maybe two–three months ago?"

"Naw," I say. "I ain't worked outta here before."

Tyler turns around again, wiping his nose. "Just make sure you got yourself a sweater around, son. Sun goes down, wind gets going, fog comes off the Bay . . ." His eyes get real wide and he waves his hands around in front of him, wiggling his fingers, sucking in air through those yellow teeth. "Gets in your *bones*." He puts a finger on my chest.

"Don't touch him," the tall brother says, pulling Tyler's hand back. He gives me a quick wink. "That's his clean shirt. Man's trying to get himself a job today. You remember what that's like, don't you, Tyler? Getting sent out on a job?"

The windows get brighter. The man in the black jacket is right at the door, rubbing his hands together, bouncing around like he might piss his pants. "Blue my man Blue, when y'all gonna open *up* 'cause it's al*ready* quarter to six and you know I got me a family to feed."

Laurence picks his voice up. "Yo man, your old lady still serving you up the pipe before you come down here?"

The other dude looks back and shrugs his shoulders, turns his hands up. "Don't you know it? Goddamn Eve and her apple." He laughs and looks back inside. "All right how's that hand Blue? You gonna hook me up with that job ain't you? Cause you *know* I'm the hardest working man out here . . ."

One of the green doors swings open, and out comes this white kid in jeans and a sweater. Almost as tall as Laurence. He pushes the door against the wall and kicks in a doorstop underneath. His right hand is all wrapped up.

"Call him Blue," Laurence says to me. He looks over his shoulder and takes a couple steps back to catch up with the line moving to the desk. "And tell him this here's your first time signing in." He pushes his glasses up his nose. "See, you got to get yourself an interview with this dude named George, as soon as possible."

I step in, over some broken glass that crunches good and loud, and get a look around while I'm waiting my turn. The kid sits up right inside the doors, at this desk that's about chest-high to everybody. Behind him is a big hall with fold-up chairs on the sides, and in the back I can see a couple of guys in button-ups behind some glass, talking on the phone and writing stuff down.

Looking at him again, Blue ain't no kid—might even be older than me. His hair is wet and combed back, and he's got some crow's-feet around those eyes. He nods at everybody when they come in, doesn't talk unless they talk first. Except for Tyler.

"All right, old-timer, what's the word?" he says.

"The word," Tyler says, picking up a pen, "is work. I'm ready for whatever you got today."

"Yeah? Well, I don't know that there's too much happening," he says, looking down at the desk. But when I step up next to Tyler, I get Blue's eyes. "You got ID?"

Tyler acts like he's got juice with Blue. "I just been talking with this young man," he says. "Fine, upstanding, God-fearing—"

"Look Tyler," Blue says. "You want to get sent out today, you best get back there and start pleading your case. But you want to get your breath in shape first." He reaches down and comes up with a little toothbrush in a plastic wrapper. "Because you know Marcelo can smell that shit halfway across the room."

Tyler snaps up the toothbrush and starts saying something. Blue puts a hand up, doesn't even look at him. "Save it." He breathes deep, looks at me, flicks his eyebrows up. "ID?"

I show him my California and my Social Security. "That tall brother with the glasses told me I gotta talk to some dude George about getting an interview."

"Laurence? He's not running the show down here." He looks at the cards with his wrapped-up hand, then pushes them back across the desk. "Are you still at that address on your ID?"

"I moved."

"Are you at one of the missions? A halfway house?"

"I got my own place."

"Have you ever been to Voc Rehab, ever had to see a psychiatrist?"

"Look at me, man," I say, taking a quick step back. "You see me standing here, don't you? I ain't crippled, right? And I ain't talking no bullshit like that old dude."

He shrugs. "Just stuff I have to ask everyone." He reaches under the desk and comes back with a white piece of paper. "I need you to fill this out."

"I'm just looking to get eight hours today, you know what I'm saying? So how 'bout you tell George there's a man out front needs to see him?"

He laughs. "Right. You go by Jacob?"

"Jake."

He writes on the paper. "Look, couple things you need to know, Jake. First, George doesn't talk to new guys until eight o'clock. Other thing is nobody gets sent out on a job their first day."

"If I can't get sent out today, what am I doing waiting till eight?"

"I'm giving you a chance to get some work here, Jake. You got something better to do today, go do it."

"What am I supposed to do for the next couple hours?"

He picks up the paper and a pen and leans toward me. "First thing is to fill out this application. After that, I don't know—sit in here, go outside and smoke, get some breakfast across the street." He checks over my shoulder. Somebody else comes in the door. "Look, I need to let this next guy sign in. Just make sure you give me that pen back."

Waiting, always goddamn waiting. I sit in a chair, trying to get comfortable, looking over the application. Can't get a damn thing in the Flatlands without filling out some paperwork, even if you're off the county. I look at some the questions: Am I taking drugs? do I have a record? do I have a place to stay? when was the last time I worked? All this shit just to do some day labor. I put it down, look around, think maybe I should just walk on out of here, back over to that office building up on Lincoln and see if my old boss will give me that mopping job back. It was easy, better than some other jobs I've had doing security with no gun or cleaning up in a restaurant. I could do it again, and I'd tell him I wouldn't be late no more, wouldn't talk back or throw nothing when he told me what to do this time. But when I think on it, I know he's probably got twenty guys like me coming in and asking him every week. What makes me better than them? Only reason I got the job last time was because I showed up right after the other brother quit. At least here in this labor hall I can tell a lot of these dudes been playin' a long time, gonna get some cash to run the Four Corners and won't see them around here till it runs out again. At least in here I can maybe show this man George I'm doing something different.

"They got you signing a confession already?"

I look up from the application and see Laurence standing and finally showing some teeth underneath that beard. He sits down next to me and leans forward, elbows on his thighs. "They want to know it all," he says. He shakes his head. "They say they got all these restrictions they gotta keep to, but you know they make you write all that shit down just so you don't forget who you are."

Across the room the dude in the black jacket is slumped down in a chair, legs straight out in front of him. His hands are on his stomach and his head is against the wall, looking up at the lights.

Laurence sees me looking. "That brother over there got put out of here for a couple months 'cause he was drinking on this job they sent him out on. Was raking leaves for this old white lady and she told him he could come inside when he wanted to, take a piss or get some water. Dude ends up coming in after half an hour and gets into her liquor cabinet. Didn't surprise no one at all. Then he comes back here and starts some shit when they told him he was on restriction. That's how Blue got that hand." He sits back and laughs to himself. "And *that* didn't surprise nobody neither. Of course, if that had been George's hand, that dude would have been Alcatrazzed for sure. Wouldn't let his ass come nowhere near this hall again. This place really belongs to brothers like you and me, 'cause *we* the ones doing the work, right? But George thinks it's his, and sometimes I think he'd just about kill a man for telling him different."

"So they sending that dude out on jobs again?" I ask.

"It don't take much for them to send you out, even if you're just coming off restriction," he says. "They told him to go to some meetings, get himself a sponsor, they'd let him sign in again. If they knew what they were talking about, they'd wait till he comes back with one of these." He reaches into his pocket and takes out a silver coin with a little AA on it. "You ask me, a man's got to have at least ninety days before you take him serious again."

I look at the coin in his hand. He turns it around in his fingers, and when it catches some light I can see the places where it's good and worn down. "How come you were on him before about smoking rock?"

"When we were in line?" Laurence says. "I was just talking. But if he *is* still smoking, you got to give the brother credit for making it down here this time of the month." He puts his finger down on my paper. "They ain't gonna pay no attention to nothing you put on this," he says, tapping it now. "Unless you got a felony or something. First Monday of the month, when all the county checks are coming in, and you're trying to get some *work*—damn, they're gonna *kiss* your black ass." Laurence makes his voice higher and starts talking white. "'Young man in a nice shirt? We could put this one in the *brochure*.' You know what I'm saying? All these jokers behind the glass are really trying to do is get some stories for their kids. 'Guess what son—I put this *homeless* man to work today. Isn't that something?' Don't you worry, they'll get you some jobs."

I shrug. "Yeah but Blue over there said I ain't getting no work today."

"Blue just runs that attitude with the new folk so you don't think you can fuck with him. If they've got a job needs doing, they'll put somebody on it, don't matter how long they been around."

Tyler comes out of the bathroom with the toothbrush wagging in his mouth, running somebody's ear down about something.

"Even that old man ends up with a ticket now and then," Laurence says. He checks his watch. "I've got a couple hours before I need to get to this job. Let's go across the street."

Down the block, this Korean woman is lifting up her roll-down. She pulls hard on the chain, hooks it to the side, and slaps the lock back on.

We get a booth. "New owners," Laurence says. "I give them a week or two more before they get a guard out front. That old bastard Tyler followed me in here last week, got himself about three or four refills on his coffee, then starts walking outta here like he don't know nothing about paying. Lady looks at me, and I tell her hey he ain't my date so she walks up behind him real nice with this 'Pay please? pay please?' But you seen Tyler, you know once he's going he's gone, and he walks back across the street like he can't even hear." He pushes his glasses back in place, leans into the window, and squints across the street. "He see us come over here?"

I get coffee and some toast. Laurence gets milk, because he says he stopped drinking coffee. At least he's trying to. He takes a long drink and wipes his mustache. He leans back, says he wants to tell me a story. When he does, his glasses catch some light and for a second I can't see his eyes.

The coffee's too hot to drink just yet, so I listen. Even if I don't know this brother, even if he's trying to hand me down some bullshit wisdom, right now, ain't nothing else to do.

"You see these hands?" he says, holding them out, showing me both sides. I see the scar on his right one, running from his thumb to his wrist. The last three fingers on his left are crooked at the joints, and the nails are all yellow and thick. He spreads his elbows wide on the table, and he looks at his hands, like maybe they're a couple of old pictures and he's got to give himself a second to let the story come back.

"Last fifteen years, these hands ain't seen nothing but a whupping," he says. "I was a young man like you when I got hired as a longshoreman at the docks, just unloading the crates, loading them back up. Straight forty, good pay with the weekends off, all that." He shows me the scar again. "This right here was my own damn fault and the company still took care of it. You know, from the *outside*, somebody could look at me and think everything was cool. Had a good job, the old lady and me were getting along, the kids doing all right. But after a little while I started hanging with the wrong crowd, you know what I'm saying?"

Here we go. I should have seen this coming, should have known by the coin. Another addict who needs to tell somebody the good news. I dump some sugar and three or four creamers in the coffee, and watch it turn almost white.

If Laurence had been in our church when I was growing up, folks would've said he had the gift of bearing witness. If he got up there on Sunday and started telling this story, I bet he would've had those hat-pin ladies pulling out their hankies. When he told about working at the dock, breaking his hands to feed the family, he'd have the whole church shaking their heads and doing that quiet little *umn umn ummmn*. When he told about letting the bottle—the *devil* in that bottle—break him up on the inside, he'd get some amens. And when he got to the part about hitting his wife, hitting his kids, using those broken hands now to break the family apart, Momma'd be right there with the old ladies, and Daddy'd hold her hand on her knee so all us kids could see it.

I don't know what it is that makes me stay here in this booth. I listen to his whole story, let him tell me about how he was cheating on his wife, how she left him and took the kids down to her brother's in Fresno. More than I'd ever tell somebody I just met. But I've met plenty of guys in recovery, and some can tell you more one-day-at-a-time stories than you'd ever want and give you their clean time to the day and rattle off the Twelve Steps just like the Ten Commandments. Laurence is coming up on ten months now. His boss at the docks had eleven years clean, so he knew what was up when Laurence missed three days in a row, and he canned his ass right then. Told him he needed to get into some treatment, take that first step and admit he was out of control. If he could come back with a piece of his one-year cake, he could get his job back. That's what Laurence is working for now, trying to get that year. All this day labor stuff is just to get by, put food in his mouth and send a little something to the kids.

He drinks the milk good and slow. He tells me his old boss saved his life—he was the only one who cared about him enough to tell him he was fucking up. His wife just hit the road, and nobody else in his family talked to him after that, until he got sober. Probably wasn't their fault, because he wouldn't have been listening anyway.

A couple cars start coming down the street, and from our booth Laurence and I can see some dudes walking out those green doors to catch a bus to their job. Laurence leaves a swallow of milk in the glass. When he tells me the rest of his story, about how he thinks it's all gonna end up, he looks out the window, up at the clouds, making circles in the air with the bottom of the glass. Holding it up, swirling that little bit of milk around inside. He'll have his old lady back, his kids too, and he'll put his pension from the dock into their college fund. It's bullshit you can smell from down the block, but something about Laurence makes me listen. Maybe because I want to believe what he's saying, that if a man gets back in touch with his soul, he can pull himself up off drinking or the county or anything. If a man gets tight with God again, he can find all those things that broke off from him and smooth them back into place.

Back across the street, one of the green doors opens and Tyler steps out in the street with his head down. One of the brothers standing against the wall quick-grabs the hood on his sweatshirt and pulls him back to the curb. A car goes by, honking like a motherfucker.

"I ain't paying for nothing of his this time," Laurence says, pointing at me. "You can deal with that lady."

Tyler pushes into the booth, next to Laurence. The Korean woman behind the counter takes some scrambled eggs off the grill and puts them under a lamp next to a tin of bacon and sausage.

"Come on and gimme a plate of eggs," Tyler yells to her.

"She ain't bringing you shit," Laurence says. "You think she don't remember your dopey-looking ass from last week?"

"Easy there, big fella." The old guy takes off his hat and puts it in his lap. His hair is mostly gray with some blond running through it, straight down and thin except where it sticks up on top. He licks his hand and tries to smooth that down, but it won't go nowhere. Then he grabs a napkin from the box and blows his nose in it, a good six or seven shots before he gets it all out. He squeezes it up tight and leaves it on the table. "I'll just tell her to start me a tab."

"Start *you* a tab," Laurence says.

"That's right." The cigarette wags in his mouth again and some ashes fall on the table. Tyler takes out his pack. "Three left. Want one?" He takes the first butt out of his mouth, lights the new one with it, and throws it on the floor. He calls for the eggs again.

The woman doesn't look. "Look, you act nice and maybe she'll give you a cup of water or something," Laurence says.

"No no no, I want some *breakfast*," Tyler says, slapping his hand down. "Today I'm going to work."

"What you talking about?" I say.

"Marcelo gave me a ticket."

Laurence turns. "What ticket? I know you ain't on the moving job with me."

"No, just doing janitorial at the Houston." Tyler smiles, and when he does, his big beat-up nose wrinkles like some old grapes. "Eight hours today, and the manager might need somebody again for tomorrow."

I point at him. "What you know about being a janitor?"

He waves me off. "Hey kid, I can do every job in the book." He looks at Laurence. "Now don't you start with this 'you got lucky' shit again."

"It's just numbers, old man, one-two-three" Laurence says, counting off his fingers. "It's summertime, so they got jobs. It's early in the month, so most folk are out partying. And you ain't had no work in about a month. If one two three adds up, and you don't got a pipe in your mouth when you walk in there, you got yourself a ticket."

"No no no, don't gimme that shit," Tyler says. "It's like the good Lord says, good things come to those who wait."

After a couple minutes of the old guy going on about how he'd been praying for God to help get him some work, Laurence snaps up and squints out the window. He cocks his head so the side of it touches the glass, and he strokes his chin. "Will you look at that."

From that distance, there was no way to know. I couldn't make out much about her, couldn't see the dimple she was hiding in her cheek, couldn't hear that high voice that could be sweet and soft or could make you back right off if she wanted it to. From where I was, it was just her walk, just her chin up in the air and her legs taking her smooth and fast down the walk. She was on the other side of the street, headed toward the group of brothers hanging outside the Ready Man. I turned all the way around, just to keep my eyes on her, just to see those nice-fitting jeans and that jacket that came down just over her hips and bounced soft on her ass when she walked. She wasn't a pro—they're all make-up and smiles when they come around. This sister looked serious as a heart attack. She walked it too. Looking for work down here, lining up for day labor with all these mother-fuckers, she looked damn-near out of her head to me.

This was the first time I saw Noel, and I almost thought when she went through the doors it would be the last. Thought all those dudes inside would eat her up. Don't know what I was thinking when I went across the street, if I was trying to save her or just get me some.

The green doors are open, and all the men on the sidewalk are crowded in behind her. When I get across the street I hear the old man saying something about how he ain't seen a woman down here by herself since last year, and that lady had her ass grabbed so many times she was back the next day with a knife, saying any finger touching her without her say-so was going home with her. Tyler says after that nobody touched her, and she didn't come around again.

She's at the desk with Blue. The brother in the black jacket is standing next to her, leaning in, smiling and trying to catch her eyes. But she acts like he's the invisible man. She holds up a piece of paper for Blue.

"Look at her with that application." Laurence gives me an elbow. "Girl's gonna get your place in line."

Blue unfolds the paper and checks out both sides, then hands it back to her and points toward the back of the hall. She slides past the brother in the black jacket.

I push through the other brothers to the desk. "You sending her back before me?"

Blue looks up and folds his hands in front of him. "Is your application filled out yet?"

"Naw man, that don't mean shit." I look at her, walking to the back. "You better hold up, girl."

"Look buddy, there's plenty of other people we can put to work today. So why don't you stop whining and wait your turn?"

"Yeah, plenty. Like mister eighty-year-old man back there, and this fucking girl—"

Now Blue's eyes get thin. "It's like I said. If you've got something better to do, get out of here. And give me back my pen."

I want to smack that pen upside his head and tell him I don't need it anyway. But I don't. I've seen what happens to folks who put up an attitude with their caseworkers or anybody else that's got juice. You fuck with them, you get fucked back.

She's at the window at the back of the hall, talking to some white guy behind the glass. Her hair is pulled back loose and is just a little darker than her skin. When the door opens, she steps up and says something to the brother holding it.

He's short, ain't too young neither—maybe Daddy's age. Got big shoulders, a nice button-up with a tie, and some keys hanging down from his neck, right over his belly. His beard is shaved tight, but even if it weren't I could see that jaw cut like a rock. He must be George.

She says something to him, and he pulls those little reading glasses off and looks over her shoulder at me. He talks to her and she nods, then he follows her inside and closes the door.

I sit down and get back to that application. I ask Laurence what I should say about my record. Never got caught for taking the car from Bella Vista with Lydell, but I've been in on a couple of petty thefts since then.

"Shit, that ain't even worth remembering." He checks his watch. "Just tell them you're clean. And act like you're Mr. Getting Back on My Feet, you know, like you'd make them proud if they'd just give you a *chance*. George loves that shit."

The old man comes our way, his hat back on, the toothbrush in his mouth now instead of the cigarette. Laurence sees him and slaps me on the shoulder. "I gotta catch my bus. You have fun talking with these folks."

He hustles out, and Tyler yells at him, "You owe me that pack now! When am I gonna see it?" The old man sits down next to me, smelling-close, coughs and spits behind the chair next to him. "He told me a couple weeks ago he'd buy me—"

"Ain't you got a job to go to?" I say.

He squints at the clock. "The Houston's just a ten-minute walk."

I shake my head. "Don't you want to go change your clothes or something?"

He looks at me, feels like a long time. I know the old man ain't got more than what I can see right now. But he doesn't go off and tell me some shit about living in his cardboard condo and ain't taking no charity from nobody because he's got *pride*. He just looks at me.

Tyler starts telling me about the hall like he's going through the family scrapbook. He points to the bathroom, says before they put in the toilets ten years ago there was just this big tub back there and some pipes on the wall that leaked into it, so you'd have to hang it out with all the fellas when you needed to piss, and of course some guys got stuck with names they didn't like. The chairs didn't come until the seventies, and it's been these same metal fold-up ones ever since. Some of them are bent-up from some fights in here, usually when one guy's drunk and starts talking smack about somebody he's got to share his ticket with. And sometimes it's over a lady.

She comes out again with George right behind her—a goddamn escort to the street. Good thing for her, since she took my place in line. They walk straight up through the hall, right through all the brothers up out of their chairs for a better look. George's keys bounce on his belly and jingle-sing. I go over to the green doors, and when she pushes through I catch her peeking at me so quick she probably doesn't think I see.

George follows her outside, and when he comes back in everybody wants to know if he gave her a ticket. "I don't wanna have to go take it from her if you ain't gonna send *me* out," the brother in the black jacket says. George laughs, keeps on walking to the back. "That girl would kick your ass to the curb."

I take my paperwork to the window and slide it under. A Mexican guy a little older than me checks out my application. His hair is short and tight, but he's not wearing a tie. No accent neither. "Did the guy at the front desk give you a time?"

"Said I was first up."

"You? George just met with that young lady there."

"That's what I'm talking about. You all gave her my spot and now you got me behind schedule."

"Behind schedule," he says, nodding slowly. "What kind of schedule are you on?"

I bend down and talk through the slide-door at the bottom of the glass. "The one where your landlord says, 'Pay me now.' The one where your stomach says, 'Feed me now.'"

He just looks at me, holding the application.

I put my finger through. "You go ask Blue if you want—he took my name. Now how about you help me out here and take that back to George, tell him you got a man out here who can show all these dudes what working is all about."

"Get your hand out of my window," he says, and walks to the back.

George meets me at the door, and I go back to his office. I sit in a low chair, looking up at him. There's some files on one side of his desk, papers on the other, straight-stacked and tight as bricks in Bella Vista. He pulls those little glasses out of his shirt pocket, puts them on his nose, and looks over my paperwork.

"Your name is Robertson, huh?" he says. "Where you from?"

"Look," I say. "I ain't living in no mission like these other dudes. I'm clean, and I know how to—"

"No," he says, shaking his head. "I said where you *from*? Where are your *people* from? I used to know some Robertson folk when I was in Chicago."

"Shit, Daddy brought us out here such a long time ago I can't even remember where we came from."

George rolls up his shirtsleeves, puts his elbows on the desk. "That so? What's your daddy's name?"

I look long and slow back over both my shoulders, then cock my chin up at him. "You see anyone else in here asking you for some work? We gonna get talking or what?"

He laughs, leans back in his chair. "We sure will. Lady we just had in here says you're giving her a hard time, Robertson. Says you're calling her bitch this and ho that, trying to scare her off."

"Naw man," I say, and I sit up and grab my own shirt. "Look at me, mister George. I ain't come in here to waste nobody's time." I remember what Laurence told me. "Look, I just got laid off last week. It wasn't nothing to do with me, it was just numbers, you know? I just want you all to give me a little *chance*, you know, get me some work so I keep my ass off the streets."

He looks at me over his glasses. "You know how many brothers come in here and give me that line?"

"Yeah but none of them work like me. You call up my last boss—he'll tell you," I say. George looks at the backside of the paper where I filled in about my other jobs. I'm just hoping Laurence is right, that none of that stuff matters, that George won't make that call. "And how many folks you got coming in here first week of the month?"

He laughs again, pulls those glasses off. "You ever worked day labor before, Robertson?"

"Man, any job you need done, you just give it to me," I say. "Some of the fellas already told me the routine. Send me out this morning if you got something for me to do."

"You don't want to listen to those jokers out there," he says. "Shit, my own staff can't even keep all the steps straight—so how are you going to let some fool in the line tell you what you got to do? You've got to look out for your*self*, Robertson."

George gives me a whole mess of little stuff to remember. Sign in at six. Don't come down here fucked up. Keep that mustache trimmed. Wear working-man's clothes and bring your own bus fare. And don't ever forget, out on a job, the boss is the boss—the hall doesn't want any calls about some worker with attitude. The way he's telling me all this, it's like he's got his own little church in here, and he's passing out the wisdom to the folks coming through the door. But pretty soon, it's more like he's up in the pulpit, bringing the law down on me. I've run into brothers like this before. They start making it, they get a job or something where they're in charge of some people, and they can't stop thinking about how they're supposed to be an example. Especially to their own kind. So when George gets around to his own story, I'd already seen it coming. He tells me how when he was a young man like me he was putting himself through school out in St. Louis, roofing houses part-time. Some guys on that crew were just getting by, drinking their checks, not doing anything for their families, if they had them. Not doing anything to better themselves. For the longest time the boss did those guys wrong, George says, letting them miss days, show up late, do work that had to be done over.

"He should have been kicking their ass," he says, making a fist. "You want to help somebody, you can't treat them like no pussy."

So he tells me he sees something in me. He sees how I brought work clothes in my bag. He sees how I'm here early in the morning, early in the month—just like Laurence said he would.

"So you got a ticket for me now?" I say, thinking I didn't have to push George over at all, he just did it to himself.

But he shakes me off, laughing. "You and that girl Noel must have been talking before you were fighting."

"We weren't *fighting*—"

"No—I know, I know. Ladies coming through here are real sensitive. Every one of them thinks if a man out in that hall's talking to her, he's trying to get her to give him her job or her pants. I was just seeing how you'd stand up to it, Robertson."

"That still don't answer my question."

"Blufort told you, didn't he?" George waves a hand in front of him. "Nobody goes out their first day."

More waiting—now it's through the rest of George's preaching. But at least I got the girl's name out of him. I just keep quiet and keep nodding, like doing the amen bobs when I used to sit next to Momma in church. Preacher would say something that didn't make no sense, but I'd look at Momma, and do what she did. If one of my sisters or I asked her about what the preacher was saying, she'd tell us we had to put our trust in the man.

George slaps a hand down on his desk. "So," he says. "It's real simple, Robertson. You respect me, I respect you. If you're on board with that, come on back tomorrow, I'll see what I can do."

"What about right now?" I say. "I need to make me some money—I'll work hard for you."

"I know you will," he says. "But I want to see you work smart too. *That's* what going to get you someplace. That's what got me here—I know how to read a man. You come back around tomorrow, I'll know you're not just playing."

I do, but the rain comes back quicker, and the only thing George can tell me is be patient. I sit in the chairs, drink some coffee, bullshit with the other fellas in here till I'm the only one left. After a couple hours George tells me the rain washed all the work away today.

I catch the bus back to the Angelus. It's quiet inside, just a few folks sitting here and there and nobody saying nothing, just that engine gunning. I sit in the back, look out the window, and round about Lincoln I see some kid brothers pull up next to us at a light. They've got the windows down, pumping some jams, and the kid in the back looks up at me. He's got that tall fade like Lydell wore that one summer. He throws his chin up, throws a little laugh with it, and I know I couldn't get him to come up and trade places with me on this bus if I paid him. The wind kicks in, smacks the rain hard on the glass, and then they're gone. But I can't help thinking about that night, with Lydell and Aaron over in Bella Vista, back when I was fourteen. Pull the lock, turn the starter, push the gas—in and out, easy as pie.

Up in my room that night, I fill a cup of water at the sink and stand at the window. I see the Cliffs down there, look out across the water to those lights in Bella Vista, watch the cars going each way across that freeway bridge in between. Soon enough the wind kicks in again, whips the rain against the glass and makes it all blurry. I stand back, and with the light on in here, I can see myself in the window if I look at it right. I start thinking of all the shit that had made me want to go straight, start seeing some of it playing in the glass. The nights in the county youth, the party Momma had for me when I finally got my diploma at summer graduation, the time I caught the bus to Folsom and visited Daddy and he left my hand up on the glass. And then I see those little brothers in the car again, and the one with the fade is looking at me stuck on the bus. And then me and Lydell are ripping out in that Nissan and taking the freeway to the chop shop in Hayward, and I'm standing in our kitchen on Valley Street with a pocketful of money, telling Momma I'll give her whatever's left over after I get me some nice sneakers.

I drink down the water, cut off the light, and get in bed, turn away from that window. But even with my eyes closed I can still see it—just like the times in our Chicago house when the ice would hang down off the gutters and I'd look out the window at the maple and think I'd see that man hanging there. I watch it all running out and washing together, till I don't know what's what, if I'm still awake or dreaming.

* * *

Late. I walk fast from the bus to the hall, and when I get there I check the clock. Six-thirty, and most everybody is already signed in. That good rain storm that hit last night kept me sleeping right through my alarm. But it oughta mean there's plenty of work going out today, even for me.

Noel is in the back of the hall. Talking to Marcelo and George through the window, with a group of brothers behind her. Only thing I can see between all those shoulders is a red bandanna and her hair coming out of it on her neck. The dude with the black jacket jumps back quick, and now I can see her better. She's standing straight, and the way she's got that little thing going with her head and shoulders, there's no doubting this girl's got it together. I've seen sisters stand up to a man one-on-one, tell him to go fuck himself when he starts coming on, but never anybody who'd take on a crowd like this with no girlfriends around. Must be six or seven brothers trying to tell her she's so fine all at once. But Noel doesn't run. She keeps looking straight ahead, like all the smack they're talking doesn't mean a damn thing.

Marcelo opens the door. The brother with the black jacket says something that makes all the brothers crack up, and they give her some space and she goes to the back.

"She's going by 'Brass Zelda,'" Laurence says, shaking his head and laughing.

"That her handle?"

"Well it ain't the one *she* picked, but it's good and stuck. You could've been here for it if you made the line-up." He points across the room, to where the brother in the black jacket is standing next to the old man, who's squeezing out his hat again. "See that brother over there with Tyler? The man's got tracks all up his arms like you never seen and he puts down a forty-ounce like soda pop, but he's still the sharpest set of jaws in the hall." Laurence looks back at me. "So I'm standing in line with him a couple minutes before Blue opened up this morning and we see that girl walking up the sidewalk. Dark pants, white sweatshirt, and that cherry bandanna on top—the dude over there, he says it looks like we got a walking sundae this morning. Says he's gonna take a bite out of that ass, have himself some whipped cream. I say Lord help me, to myself you know, because I got my wife and kids I'm trying to get back to, but I got to tell you I was thinking about having me a little snack myself. So she walks up to the back of the line and that brother asks her what's she doing hiding that pretty hair under that bandanna and she says she's going to work. Then I tell her I saw her in here the other day but didn't nobody get her name. She looks right at me and she says 'Zeke.' When he hears that, brother next to me says 'Zeke? What you got inside them pants?' She looks at us like fuck both you all but she don't say nothing but 'Zeke.' So that brother keeps on. Anytime somebody comes around with a handle he don't think is cool, he's right on it, slaps them with a new one. He says we got us a Zelda thinking she's Zeke, like she's got some balls up in them pants somewhere. *Brass balls*, coming down here and talking like she does."

"What she saying Zeke about?" I say.

"Attitude. Like 'You can't touch me, motherfucker.' Shit, I bet her momma told her to say it."

"Ain't no momma gonna send her daughter looking for work down here."

"Naw man, listen. I seen her *hands*. She ain't done no hard work in her life. She's just down here trying to prove something. You go talk to her, you'll see what I'm saying."

I want to tell Laurence he's got her wrong, but the speaker comes on. Just this buzz at first, real loud and crackling. The hall goes quiet and folks look up at the speakers in the ceiling. *Robertson*. Loud, fuzzy, like the guy has the mike inside his mouth. *Jacob Robertson*. I go to the window, and Marcelo waves me to the door.

I see her inside, sitting in the same chair I had sat in a couple days ago. She doesn't turn around, just stays still, one leg crossed over the other, her clean sneaker hanging in the air. I stand next to her, in front of George's desk. Feels like we're gonna have some little apology session, like George is gonna make me say I'm sorry for the shit I said to her if I want a ticket today. But I thought she was taking a job from me. Was I supposed to let that go?

"There's a yard on the north side needs some work," George says, writing out two tickets. I look at mine a minute before I put it in my pocket. See my name, official as can be, right there on the paper. Almost as good as getting paid.

Noel walks out, and I'm right behind her. Right past the brother in the black jacket, past the old man and Laurence and all the looks we get. We walk under the freeway, toward Jefferson to catch the 73 going north. We pass a fat brother trying to get his cardboard condo to stay up. Being under the freeway is no good if it's raining and the wind is blowing, unless you're with a camp of folks and you draw an inside space. Even then the top of your box can still get wet. I heard this one story about some dude who thought he was smart and damn near covered his whole box with some new garbage bags he found. Cut them into strips and laid them tight all over, tucked everything in so wasn't no water going to get in there at all. Trouble was, he liked his beans. Got himself a Mexican plate that night and didn't get out of the box in the morning—motherfucker farted himself to death in there. Driest dead man you ever seen sleeping out in the rain. This brother here would kill for some garbage bags, but right now it's just him and his falling-down box. He's kneeling next to it on the long side, the way it's falling, trying to prop it up with some slats from a mango crate and a piece of cement block. Seems like most of the shit folks throw away or forget about ends up under the freeway. He's got another one of those slats standing up in the middle of the short side, and that's sagging too.

Noel is still in front of me, and she steps it up when we pass this dude. He pushes the sharp end of the slat through the side, but it doesn't hold and the box falls toward him. He looks up at us.

"Sweet *Jesus* I got to get me some *insurance* on this motherfucker! Piece of the rock and all that shit, you hear?" He's on one knee and the bottom of his foot is all white on the heel and under the toes. He's got on a blue shirt with white stripes, a button-up that isn't buttoned-up, and when he turns to us his belly hangs over his dark green pants. "Can you all give me a little something? Help me out?"

"Go try one of the missions," Noel says, walking on.

"Bitch, trying and failing are the same fucking thing. What you know about the missions?"

She doesn't stop, but I do. He looks at me. His skin is about medium but he's got a little pink in his nose and under his eyes. "Hey man, I ain't mean to be talking no shit about your old lady."

"She ain't mine, I'm just walking her to the bus."

"Oh that's good, that's good," he says, nodding real big. "God bless you. Good man." He coughs toward me, four, five times. St. Ides on an empty stomach—I know that breath in a second.

"But the bitch *do* got a fine ass, you hear?" he says. "Don't know if I oughta be smacking that or her mouth." He looks at me, smiling, squinting his eyes. I don't say anything. Then he gets serious again. "Hey man, young brother like you got to have a little something extra on him. Can you help me out?"

He sits there with his shirt open, one hand scratching his chest and the other holding up his condo. His thumb is in the hole where he punched through with the slat, right in the middle of that GE noise in the fancy letters, *We Bring Good Things.* . . . It's real soggy, barely holding together. I know what he wants with my money. Ain't looking for no bacon and eggs change.

"Come on, man, how about just a little dollar or two?"

I reach in my pocket. Noel finally stops and looks back, puts her hands on her hips. I look back at the brother, still holding up his condo. He could go down to one of the missions, get himself a hot plate, maybe even meet some nice folks that might help him get dry if he wants to. I know he could, I've seen a couple other folks get up from where he's at. But there's no use preaching at him, he's a grown man. I think about how much I need for the bus, and I put fifty cents in his hand.

"That all you giving me!" He starts to get up, and the condo falls his way and hits the cement block. He stands it up, and I walk to where Noel is waiting at the end of the block. She looks at me and just shakes her head a little and starts walking again, turning up Jefferson now, before I catch up. The fat brother yells from behind us, and it kind of bounces around under the freeway, but I still hear it straight. "Hey man, God bless you anyway! And tell that bitch to have herself a nice fucking day!"

At the stop, three Mexican ladies stand with us. One of them looks about thirty, and she's nice-looking—nice skin and big eyes and a red shirt that fits real tight. She has a boy next to her, a teenager, could be her kid. All of them have little plastic bags, maybe got some lunch inside. When I used to take this bus, it was early like this, before seven. Lots of Mexicans would hop on downtown and either get a transfer if they were cleaning houses or something in Bella Vista, or ride to the end of the line in the Garment District. I know because one morning I met this lady and she told me all about it. I was just minding my business until she asked me what time it was, said she was running late. Before that I never heard no Mexicans on the bus say something I could understand, just all this Spanish. This lady had one of those plastic bags in her lap so I asked her where she was working. She told me she sewed shirts but she was hoping to find a family to take care of across the bridge.

The bus comes and we get on. Noel doesn't even look at me. I try to think of something to say, just so maybe we can be a little friendly before we get on this job together.

The bus ain't even half-full. Noel sits right in front of the back door, on the aisle, with nobody in the seat by the window. She's sure as hell telling me something. I sit one row behind her, across the aisle from the door, and the pretty lady and her boy sit right behind me. I put my legs up on the empty seat next to me and watch the street go by.

At the last stop in downtown, a brother gets on behind two more Mexican ladies. He's got a shoulder bag and he's wearing a white T-shirt inside-out. The tag sticks out in back, and one of the sleeves is torn. There's a picture with some writing or something on the front but I can't make it out, the way he's wearing it. He puts a couple coins in the box and starts walking back. The bus doesn't move. The driver's a white guy, old enough to have grown kids. He looks at the brother in the big rear-view, says he needs more money. "Let's go, buddy. You're putting me off my schedule."

This driver must be new. I've never seen any of them acting like they're worrying about being on time. And any driver with experience downtown knows what this brother's all about. Walking around this early in the morning with that nappy head and that little bag all zipped up, the brother's damn-near obvious. Any dude like this tries to cut you short on the fare, a driver's got to stand up and take it from him or kick his ass off. No hesitation. You let him slide, or just sit there in your chair and talk to him so everybody starts looking, you're giving him what he wants.

"Who you talking to?"

"The fare's one dollar ten. You put in thirty-five cents."

The brother stops at a seat in front of Noel. "You lying."

"Says it right here on the machine, buddy. You got the fare or what?"

The brother puts his bag down. "I *got* the motherfucking money, junior. Just finding me a seat." He walks slowly to the front, grabbing the top handrails along the way. He pulls some coins out of his pocket and dumps them into the box.

"The machine doesn't accept pennies," the driver says, looking in the rearview again. The brother is at his seat.

"Then you make 'em into nickels yourself, junior. I done gave you the dollarten already."

The driver closes the door, pulls away from the curb and calls the next stop. The dude sits against the window, like I am, and unzips his bag. He starts singing to himself in his scratchy voice. *I'm a player, got two strikes. Get number three, if you likes.* After a minute he looks at Noel behind him.

"That motherfucker talking about he don't take no pennies," he says to Noel. "What he want? Food stamps instead?"

I can't see her face from back here, but I know she's not looking at him.

"Motherfucker's looking to get knocked *out*. And I'm ready to go on ahead and do it."

"Then what you sitting here for?" she says. "Just go on up and talk to the man. That breath you got's liable to kill him."

The brother sits up, pulls his bag into his chest. "I'm gonna wax his ass and then I'll drive this motherfucker my*self*. You watch me now."

"I'm watching."

He looks at the front, then turns back to her. "Say girl, who you talking to like that?"

"You, fool. You said you're ready to kick ass and I'm sitting here waiting to see it. Nothing else on this bus for me to watch."

The driver calls out the next stop, and I see his eyes in the rearview. Nobody pulls the cord.

"Girl, don't you start fucking with me."

He's louder now. He puts the bag down on the seat, someplace I can't see it, and starts to lean over the back.

"Hey man," I say, "the girl's got some problems." She looks at me. "Can't even tell a brother her name. Now how's a sister like that gonna treat a man right?"

He nods and points at me. "Now there's a brother talking some *sense*. 'Bout time somebody heard what I'm saying."

"A girl like her don't understand what a working man goes through, bringing home the money for his family like you and me do."

"Ain't that the truth," he says, and he stands up. "Let me show you something." He puts his bag over his shoulder real slowly and walks to the seat right behind the door, across from the lady and her boy. He sits down and leans into the aisle. He puts his foot next to mine on the empty seat. His shoe is black. A hole in the bottom, and no laces.

"This right here," he says, and he lifts up his pant leg. His skin is real ashy and there's a line from his ankle to his knee. "This right here used to be where I had me a motherfucking bone. Goddamn gook shot the shit out of it." He knocks on his leg. "Flew my ass outta there and gave me a new shin, told me not to walk too close to no big magnets." He laughs and pushes his pant leg down again. "Brothers like me and you done made some *sacrifices*."

His foot is still next to mine. He looks in his bag. I open the window to let some air in. "So where you going to?" I say. Maybe if I keep him talking, he won't go back up front. "What kind of job you got?"

"*Job?*" he says, and laughs. But he's not smiling. "Look at me, boy." He pulls the forty out of his bag and takes a sip. It's about half-empty. "You think I ain't got no self-respect or something?"

The driver calls another stop, but nobody pulls the cord.

"You just like that girl? Think I'm just some chump you can fuck with?" He takes another sip, but we hit a bump so some of it gets on his shirt.

I should just wait him out. If I'm cool and keep nodding like I hear what he's saying, then maybe he'll just talk himself out.

"'Course I *could* be working," the brother says. He's wiping his shirt with one hand and holding the bottle with the other. The beer swishes all around inside. "I got some skills these companies be dying for. But what I gonna wear to the motherfucking interview, now I got this shit all over my shirt?"

The driver makes a turn and calls out a stop, and the Mexican boy behind me pulls the cord. The bell rings and the sign at the front of the bus lights up. Some women up there move into the aisle, waiting to get off.

"Used to have me a job before I went downstate," the brother says. "But I got laid off. Now they hiring Mexicans for three dollars an hour." He looks at the lady and her boy. "Ain't that right?"

The lady says something to the boy in Spanish. The boy nods and they stand up.

The brother's leg is still across the aisle. "Where you going now?"

The boy stands there looking at him. He puts his hand on his mother's shoulder.

"Don't speak no English, right?" the brother says.

"We're getting off here," the boy says.

"Then I'm coming with you. Your momma's a pretty little thing." The brother looks at me. "Reminds me of my old lady, the way she got that look on her face," he says. "Bitch tried to throw my ass out just 'cause I got locked up. I said, '*You the* one I was trying to get the money for, bitch.' Even sold the Purple motherfucking Heart for her sorry ass."

The lady and the boy move out into the aisle. He still has his hand on her shoulder. He makes a little move with his head, looking at the brother's leg. "Please," he says.

Noel turns around in her seat when the brother gets louder. "Oh now he want to be all nice," he says to me.

"Hey man," I say. "They ain't done nothing to you. All they want to do is go to work."

The brother smacks the bottle with his free hand. "That's what I'm *talking* about." He stands up and points at the lady. "Taking my job. Two-fifty an hour and shit."

The bus slows down. The lady says something to the boy again. He pulls a dollar out of his pocket. He reaches around the lady and holds it out to the brother. "Please," he says.

The brother smacks the kid's hand, and the dollar falls. "I ain't asked you for nothing!" he says. "I ain't shaking no cup!" He looks at me. "You hear me ask them for something?"

I can feel Noel looking at me. Wanting to say something about the dude under the freeway and his falling-down condo and his St. Ides breath and the fifty cents I gave him.

The Mexican lady shouts at the brother and points at him. Her boy pulls her away and wraps his arms over her, and they take a little step back. The brother holds the bottle in front of him and sticks a finger back. "You keep screaming that shit I'm gonna break your head."

"What you want to do that for, my man?" I say. "This ain't nothing but a misunderstanding. You go off like you talking about, you gonna get your ass locked up."

The bus moves toward the curb, and Noel steps out into the aisle. Her face is tight and she's looking at the brother like she's got something to tell him. But the brakes squeak real loud and the bus stops short before she gets a word out. The brother loses his feet, she puts her hands out to stop him from falling on her.

He turns around real quick. "What you *touching* me for?" Noel just looks at him. "What you trying to start now, bitch?" he says. The doors open, and some people get out in front. The green light over the back door is lit, the breeze is coming inside, but nobody back here is moving.

"Fuck all you all," the brother says. He's standing right between me and the door now. "You think I'm scared to go downstate again? I don't give a fuck about that shit." He shrugs his shoulders and looks at me. "Hey brother, I told you I got two strikes. Third one's coming. Don't make no difference to me if it's now or later."

"Why don't you just sit down and let us all get to work?" I say.

"Why don't you tell me who I'm gonna take this shit out on," he says, shaking the bottle at me.

The back door closes. The boy yells, "Wait!" The bus starts to move.

"Hold the door!" Noel says. "Somebody trying to get off back here!"

I can see the driver's eyes. The light goes on and the door opens again. "Let's go, I'm on a schedule," he says.

"Who's it gonna be?" the brother says.

I stand up, step in smelling-close. "Right here. Bring that bottle to me. I'm the only one here knows what you talking about."

He stands there in front of that open door, lowers the bottle to his hip. The breeze moves through his shirt. His eyes go thin, digging right into me. "You a crazy stupid motherfucker. Look at you shaking."

He throws the bottle at the window in front of me, and the smash-cracks go every which way, like some spider on a joyride. Like that night on Valley Street with Daddy, before I pushed through.

He turns, and quick as that he's out the door. The lady and her kid wait till he's gone, then they step over the glass and down to the street, holding hands.

I smell the beer on the seat, dripping to the floor. Noel takes my hand. "You all right, Jake? Let's get moving."

I remember how it went when we got outside, got away from that bus and sat at the stop for the next one. I remember she took my hand again, said she'd just about needed a crowbar to pry me off that handrail on the bus, but it was all over now, I could stop shaking. I laughed her off, said I wasn't afraid of nothing—the other dude was the one went running. She laughed back and told me her name, said she wasn't no Zeke to me no more.

We sat together on the next bus and talked. I remember how she started, saying she was only telling me all this because we was gonna be working together now. I said that's fine, that's the way I want it, just partners on the job.

Most of the time she looked at her knees, or out the window, or at the seat in front of us. But every now and again she'd stop and look at me, maybe wait for me to say something back. Her momma was the one got her into this thing at the labor hall, she said. Came up from LA to check on her baby, try to make up and bring her back home. Her daddy was some big dude in construction who spent all his time watching people build his buildings, so he didn't have time to watch her momma get around with some other brothers in the neighborhood. Noel said she wasn't no daddy's girl, but her momma couldn't have no hold on *her* no more if she was gonna treat him like that. Her daddy sent her a letter when she got up here, said he didn't blame her one bit for leaving. Her momma tried to make her come back to LA, told her to get back to where she belonged and find herself a man and a job because there wasn't no way she was gonna make it up here by herself. Noel said when she heard that, everything just clicked. She was at the labor hall the next day, ready to do a man's work.

We pulled a long day. Just about anything that man wanted done, we took care of business. Shoveled the mud out of his driveway, stacked the branches and raked up the leaves, even pulled some weeds out of his garden and planted stuff in the dirt. We worked some good hours in that garden, digging holes and putting in seeds and flowers. Worked up a sweat like a motherfucker—we were dripping so much, almost didn't need the hose.

When we finished up, the old guy thanked us and gave us a good tip. Back downtown, we split that and got a couple of burgers, ate them outside because it was still light out and the breeze cooled us down. We had to walk different ways to our transfers. I was getting the 16, she was catching the 2. She put out her hand and I shook it, and before I turned the corner, I watched her walk to the end of the block. She just glided, and her shirt moved around in the breeze like the sails on those boats in the Bay. I saw her untie her bandanna, and her hair came down on her neck, and she stopped at the corner, waiting for the light to turn. She snapped it out and folded it and wiped it across her neck, behind her ears, all over her face.

CHAPTER 5
ARCHER STREET GAMES

Sunday mornings, before we knew anything for sure, we'd skip church and play basketball. I'd get Noel up early and we'd walk from the Misery Accordion to Archer Street, all the way down to the court where I used to hang with my boys and do some of that shit I wish I didn't remember. Noel told me she didn't feel right missing service—good memories, she always said, the only time her family was always together when she was little. But I told her we didn't have no family no more but each other, and no God we found in some Flatlands church was gonna change that. Couldn't bring back her daddy or mine, couldn't keep her from getting sick in the mornings. Couldn't serve up no miracle just because you wanted Him to.

I ain't no old man, but I'm too old to hang around the court anymore, too old to know what's going down now. But I guess it's the same thing it was when I was fourteen, when we played basketball and the dozens, smoked weed and boosted cars and talked shit about how the police couldn't touch us, didn't matter how many dudes we knew were in lock-down. Probably different sneakers and haircuts today, different music too. But I don't even have to watch them play to know everything else inside that fence is just the same.

That's why we'd come early. For what we had going on, for what we were trying to decide, the court wasn't a good place. But I didn't know where else to go.

The weekend before she started that office job she was so nervous about, we went looking for some clothes. When she took some dresses into the ladies room at Sal's Army, I found a ball down in the basement. It was torn up and lopsided, but it was only a dollar. She told me her daddy had taught her to play, even coached her for a couple years until she had too many little sisters for him to do anything but stay at work all the time. But she didn't think she'd want to play again, even shoot around, because she was trying to put all that away now.

She was better than I thought. She said she was rusty, but I never saw a girl who had a jumper like hers. She put them up with so much arc they almost drew rain on the way down. If she was hitting, the ball came through like a rock, making that chain net ring. When she was off, I'd just back up and watch because the ball could go damn-near anywhere.

If we were just shooting around, it was easy to talk. That's why I wanted to go to the court instead of sitting up in some church and listening to somebody tell me the same old thing I heard before. Me and Noel had to decide what we were going to do, what would be the right thing and could we even afford it. When we'd get to arguing, I'd tell her if she could beat me one-on-one I'd take her side. That's how me and my boys used to settle things on this court. I'd let her get a few easy buckets, then I'd pour it on until it was all over. She never quit—she'd chase down every rebound and hack the shit out of me on D—except for our last game. I remember she was trying to get position, backing into me, trying to work me off-balance so she could hit her little turn-around. Just like that she ran over to the fence and puked. First time she ever got sick out here. She just stood there bent-over saying that's it, she was the winner now and I couldn't have no more say.

Maybe it was something about the court—that's what I thought at first. Thought maybe some of the old ghosts inside those fences had gotten her good and turned her insides upside-down. *Girl,* they'd be saying, *don't you know what Jake done on this court?* I didn't know it could go on this long. Noel didn't either. But one of her girlfriends at the office, the sister, told her some women got it worse than others—some got it almost till the baby came—and it was all just part of being a momma. Told her she probably had a boy in there, because a boy makes a momma sicker than a girl. All those sister's little stories helped Noel get through for a while, better than anything I could say. She didn't believe me when I said I wanted to have it. Hard to blame her. Ever since that little test came up blue, all she could see walking around these Flatlands was sisters everywhere holding babies—waiting at the bus, waiting outside the county office, waiting in the grocery stores trying to buy diapers with food stamps—with no men around. No way she could have known that I'd stick it through, that I'd be by her bed letting her cuss me like a motherfucker when she pushed William out, and that I'd still be around a year later, playin' best I could, just to keep us together.

* * *

That summer after me and Lydell got the car, I was on Archer Street every day. I was fifteen, didn't know any way else to pass the days but hanging on the fences and playing ball.

When school lets out in the Flatlands, nobody goes home. Nobody I know has much they want to run right back to. These days I'm staying out of the house as much as I can too. Daddy's been down in the county pen for a few months now—second time in a year—but Momma hasn't done a whole lot of cleaning up. She left that picture of all five of us hanging on the wall in the front room, and never got around to patching up that hole in the kitchen wall where she threw the pan. The court's the only other place to go. When I'm here, I always get right in the game if I can, keep away from those fences. I ain't telling Lydell that, but I know the fences are where everything gets started. Standing around out there, leaning back into those soft parts that give so much you almost feel like you're floating, ideas just start coming, and nothing ever seems too crazy.

There's two courts in here, but ever since Aaron bent a rim on the far court trying to dunk, nobody runs games over there unless they have to. If they do, it's usually the little brothers or the ones with no game. Halfway through the summer, I got picked to play on the near court. It was my first time running with the big dudes, and my shit was weak. But ever since then my game keeps going up and up. Ain't been talking to Lydell much this summer, since we boosted the car—just playing ball, playing ball.

Two dudes from the varsity are on the near court when I get there, just shooting around. I'm thinking I'll go out for the team come winter. The taller brother with light skin is in my math class, and he's got on that gray practice jersey he wears around the halls sometimes. I go to the other end, lace my sneakers up tight, and start doing my warm-up, taking free throws. Nobody else is around yet.

They start getting serious. The taller brother rebounds for the other one, who takes jumpers from way outside. Boom boom boom from the right corner, nothing but the bottom of that chain net. Then he moves to the top of the key, hits three more. "Train's up and running," he says, and moves over to the left corner. His name's Rasheed, but everybody at school calls him the Conductor during the season. He's a senior, starting point guard for two years running. Folks even said his momma wears one of them train hats to all the games.

He hits his first jumper from that side, misses three in a row after that, all off the back of the rim. Pervis, the tall dude who's rebounding with those long arms, laughs and says something I can't make out. Every time he gets called on in class, the teacher tells him to say it louder. I figure he doesn't speak up because he feels stupid being in there with all us freshman. Plus he hardly ever gets the right answer. One time he asked the teacher why couldn't she hear him, was she was fucking deaf or something, and she didn't have to ask him to say *that* again. Nothing came of it though, because most teachers know how they're supposed to act with the players.

Rasheed misses two more in and out, then puts up an air ball. Pervis catches that and just holds it. He shakes his head and starts laughing. Rasheed bounces in the corner with his hands in front of him. "Gimme that ball."

Just then Lydell pulls up in his black Olds. He's had it a few months now and he's been bringing it here every day. He got it with some miles on it but he keeps it nice, washes it at his folks' house and won't let anybody smoke in it unless they blow out the window. Some dudes say he bought it legit, paid cash with what he had left over from some boosts. Maybe he did. If I'd been hanging on the fences more I'd know the whole story inside-out.

He gets out of the car with Aaron and Jenkins. And Grantwell, that little dude everybody calls G now. He's been trying to grow himself a mustache since I knew him in junior high. And his voice is still cracked—maybe he won't ever sound like a man. Some dude I was playing against this summer told me he heard G went in on a boost with Lydell on the east side.

"Gimme that motherfucking *ball*," Rasheed says from the corner. Pervis is still laughing.

Lydell steps inside the fence. Those red sneakers are flopping like usual, because he only laces up when he picks up a game. He stops and leans right back into one of the soft spots. "Ten dollars says you miss the next one."

"You get that money ready, 'Dell," Rasheed says, "soon as skinny-ass clowning motherfucker over there gives up the ball."

Jenkins and Aaron step inside next. Neither of them ever say much. First time I heard Aaron talk was when he and Lydell told me to go with them to get the car, and I said yes quick as I could because I thought he'd whup my ass if I made him talk any more than he had to. Jenkins is wearing his usual—no shirt and that gold cross around his neck. Aaron's eating something, like always—an apple, I think. Neither of them look over at me.

"Pervis," Jenkins says, leaning back next to Lydell. "What you acting all goofy about?"

Pervis palms the ball and points at Rasheed with it. "Dude's our captain and he can't hit a jumper."

"Who you talking to, boy?" Rasheed says, walking toward him. Pervis is only a sophomore, but he's a starting forward, and he's got some good inches on Rasheed.

Lydell starts laughing. "My ten's still on the table," he says, "when you all decide you're gonna throw down. And it ain't on you, Rasheed."

"Shit. I ain't fighting his sorry ass," Rasheed steps up to Pervis and takes the ball. Pervis lets him. "We gonna play for it. Show this chicken-leg motherfucker what the game's all about."

Rasheed goes to the top of the key. Pervis steps up close, checks the ball, and gets low on defense, with his fingers up and his arms out wide like some bird. Before Rasheed makes a move Pervis slaps him real quick on the leg. "Bring it, little man."

Lydell snaps up off the fence and walks over just inside the line of the court. "We gonna see who the boss is now."

The players go at it. Rasheed starts right, then crosses over quick and gets a step on Pervis to the hole. But those long arms save the big man, and he pins

Rasheed's lay-up to the backboard. Then he gets him on his hip at the free-throw line, leaves him standing with a spin move, and dunks two-handed.

Lydell just shakes his head and flashes a smile, standing there with his arms crossed. "Look at Pervis riding that train to the bank."

Pervis takes the ball because we always play winner's outs on this court. I've seen some dudes get skunked 11–0 before, trying to D-up somebody who's unconscious, never even getting a shot of their own. The way Pervis struts after that dunk, he acts like he's gonna pour in ten more buckets like rocks in the Bay. He dribbles with his left, his weak hand, and tries a crossover. Rasheed slaps the ball away, through Pervis's legs and toward me.

When somebody's on top of their game, when they can't miss—no matter where they put it up from, they're unconscious. I know it when I see it, and Rasheed had it right then. It's almost like being out of your head. Wouldn't make no difference if there were police sirens screaming or a line of sisters on the fence just waiting to give it up—you don't know about nothing but the game. I get like that too, when I'm playing my best. Not really thinking, just moving, following something inside. You don't know you're in that zone until you come out of it, and sometimes you can't remember everything you did.

Rasheed dribbles back down court and starts going after Pervis. He jab-steps like he's going to the hole again, then pulls up and sinks a jumper. Then he hits two, three, four more. When Pervis plays him tighter, Rasheed blows past him and lays it up, slapping the backboard.

Games are always tight when money's on the line. The sweat is pumping good now, dark spots on their shirts and shiny streaks on their faces. Pervis finally gets it together and starts coming back. He stops buying Rasheed's fake and swats the jumper into the corner, then scoops it up before it goes out. When he makes up his mind to take it inside, ain't much anybody around here can do about it. Even when Rasheed starts hacking at the ball and putting his shoulder in the big man's back to keep him out of the lane, Pervis still works in far enough to get the easy bank shots. At 10–9, Pervis pulls up from outside and hits the front of the rim. Rasheed forgets to box him out, and Pervis goes right around, snatches that ball out of the air and jams it through the hole, just like that. He hangs on the rim so Rasheed can get a good look, and when he comes down, the basket shakes in place.

Lydell walks over with his hand out, and little G follows him. Rasheed doesn't look, just picks up the ball. "You a lucky motherfucker, Pervis. We gonna play two out of three."

Pervis lifts up the bottom of his shirt and wipes his face. "Naw, I'm going home to eat."

"Yeah you better eat, boy. Else next time you stand up against that fence you gonna slide right through one of them holes."

"After that I'm calling up Dominique to bring me some dessert."

"You outta your head." Rasheed gets louder. "She don't even know who you are." Maybe they've been talking about her. Lots of brothers are. She's a sophomore, a fine little thing always wearing shorts that let her legs go way up.

"That's why she's always looking at me from her locker, right?" Pervis points to G. "Dude over there done seen it plenty of times."

Little G just nods his head. Lydell laughs. He don't hardly go to class twice a week and even he knows about her. "Looks like the Conductor having some trouble keeping his caboose on track."

"You ain't going nowhere," Rasheed says to Pervis. "We gonna play again."

"You sure?" Pervis folds his arms, starts stroking his chin and giving Rasheed this look, like he's one of those school counselors or something. They always give you that *you sure?* and let it sit there a minute so you know what you've been saying is good and fucked up and you can get yourself ready to hear God's own truth coming at you from the other side of the desk. "When she hears I smoked your ass twice she ain't gonna want to touch your shit for nothing. Why don't you just keep it in your pants till I get through?"

"I ain't taking your seconds," Rasheed says. He gives the big man a chest pass, hard. "We gonna play for it."

Lydell puts his arm around Rasheed. "You looking a little worked up, my man."

Rasheed shakes him off, looks at Pervis. "Check the ball in, youngster. Let's get it on."

Pervis stands there smiling, holding it.

"Look at you, getting into it with your homeboy over some pussy," Lydell says, hands in his pockets now. "If I didn't know no better, somebody could tell me you were a little soft for this girl. She make you think of your momma or something?"

"Fuck you, 'Dell," Rasheed says. "She ain't nothing but a girl."

"Then maybe I oughta get back down to school tomorrow," Lydell says. "Get me a piece of the Dominique."

Rasheed shrugs. "Don't matter. She's coming to me first."

"'Cause I ain't gonna lie to you all, I been going a little dry lately." Lydell looks around, checks who's listening. "Fact is, I been hearing from *all* my boys. Bitches got their knees locked up since school got back."

"Always talking about they on their *period*," Jenkins says from the fence, looking down and playing with the little cross on his chain. Aaron is next to him, finishing off that apple. "This keeps up, they all gonna bleed to death."

"You hear that?" Lydell says. "Brothers around here about ready to go crazy." Then he looks at me. He knows I've got my ears open. "Hey little man down there, how long it been for you?"

I can't give him the straight answer. There's this girl Keisha in the math class with me and Pervis, but I ain't done nothing about it. I've been thinking I should try to get with her—would give me something to talk about out here. But that's just me thinking. On the court, brothers want to know about the bottom line. "Long enough," I say.

"You see what I'm saying?" Lydell says to Rasheed, but everybody's listening. "Ain't right for sisters to be holding out on us like this." He waves Pervis in and stands between them, putting a hand on both of their shoulders. "Why you two dudes want to go killing each other over it? You oughta be working together. *Teammates.*" He laughs and gives them both a squeeze. "Just like a good point guard always does, Rasheed. Giving a brother an assist so he can run up his score."

The three of them walk over to the fence. Everybody pulls in tight, in a circle, even little G. Lydell has his back to me, moving his hands and talking, but then he turns around real quick. "Jake, what you waiting on?"

The way he looks at me—his eyebrows up, his lips together tight and halfway between smiling and being pissed off—makes me think about when he told me to help him get the car. He was just standing there with Aaron, leaning up against his Olds, with that look like *what's it gonna be?* I didn't really have much choice then, if I wanted to keep hanging on Archer Street. Don't have much now neither.

We follow Lydell through the fence and lean back into those soft spots from the other side, standing in front of his car. He gets a couple old parking tickets and a pencil out of his glove compartment. He licks the tip of the pencil and looks up in the air for a second like he's thinking.

"Number one," he says, writing on the back of the ticket. "Dominique." He looks up. "Who else you fellas want?"

"What you talking about 'fellas' for, Dell?" Rasheed says. "I just told you who she's coming to."

"How long you want to hold on to her?" Lydell says, tilting his head and squinting his eyes like he's trying to get a better look. "Damn, boy. You must be soft, talking like that. Like there ain't no other girl in the world. What if she don't like you?"

Rasheed laughs and shakes his head. "Don't you worry, 'cause she knows who the man is. And there's *plenty* other girls waiting in line."

Lydell smiles big and points the eraser end at Rasheed. "Now that's what I'm talking about."

He wants us to give him some names. Fine, ugly, senior, freshman, don't matter—just girls none of us have gotten some from yet. The four older dudes start ticking them off, and Lydell makes a list. Me and little G look at each other. I'm wondering if he's going to give up some girl's name—I wonder if he's seen Keisha.

I keep my ears on the fellas. The school might be too big for anybody to notice Paula and Cheryl, but when it comes to my own sisters, I don't want their names even coming out of these dudes' mouths.

"So what you writing all this down for?" Pervis says, and everybody stops talking. He's still holding the ball, palming it, and Lydell looks up at him. "Why you want to hear about all the pussy we *ain't* got?"

Lydell gets up off his Olds and puts the list in his pocket. "Gimme that ball a minute, big man," he says. "Let me tell you all boys a little story." He takes the ball in his hand, twist-pops it up in the air so it jumps up onto his finger and starts spinning. He keeps it going, slapping it with his other hand until it's so fast all the seams just blur. Lydell ain't no great player, not like Pervis or Rasheed or anybody on the varsity, but he's damn-sure got a handle. He hardly ever gets himself in games, but when he does he always plays point. Never makes a shot, but he can dribble like a motherfucker. Between his legs, around the back, right hand, left, crossover, past one dude or through three. Nobody takes it from him. He'll bring it up the court, get the defense stepping all over each other, then dish to somebody for the open jumper or the dunk. Off the court, if he ever picks up a ball, he just likes to lean up against his car and spin it. Sometimes brothers will put money on how long he can keep it going.

"Way back in the day," he says, keeping it spinning, "my daddy used to hustle tables." Lydell's got a whole book of stories about Big Dereck, and a whole mess of them have my own daddy in them too. I started hearing them after we got the car. But Dereck's pool hall days were before he and Daddy knew each other, before we had even moved out here from Chicago. I just hope he sticks to this story, *keeps* it way back in that day. Most times when he tells me some Dereck and Curtis story, by the end he's giving me that look. *We got ourselves a little family tradition—don't we now, Jake? And you and me are turning out like the spitting images. Must be in the blood.*

Lydell spins this one quick. Like taking out an old picture, but never letting anybody hold it themselves, just pointing right to the part you want folks to see. "He'd let some sucker get a couple games up on him, get himself in the hole a little bit, and then he'd really start playing. Wipe dudes out, take *all* their money. Sometimes if he was too hot, he'd start throwing again on purpose just to let the dude get back in the game. Chump would put more money down and my daddy would just run him again." Lydell pulls his hand back and lets the ball drop . If the spin isn't perfect when you do that, the ball gets away from you. But it bounces straight up off the ground, into his hand. He gives it back to Pervis. "But what the old man told me, fellas, is that he really couldn't play for shit unless he was in the hole."

"Then he wasn't no real hustler," Rasheed says.

Lydell nods. "You're right, my man. But don't you see what I'm saying? He couldn't get nothing going until his pockets were about empty. Then it was like he'd cut on a switch and he was a different player." Lydell takes the list out of his pocket and taps it with his pencil. "It's all about getting up a little motivation."

They start going back through some names. "Let's get it to twelve," Lydell says, "so we all playing the same field. And they all got to be new for everybody."

"But what's this all about?" Rasheed says, putting his hands up. "We just going around getting booty and so what? You know I *am* trying to graduate, Dell. Ain't got all the time in the motherfucking world for some game you thinking up."

"Didn't you all hear me before?" Lydell says, laughing now and shaking his head. "I'm talking about having yourself a little incentive. The clock's gonna be ticking." He taps the list again. "And we gonna see who scores himself the most points."

They start putting the list in order, finest girls at the top. Dominique, Chantal, April, Bebe, Jackie. Jenkins says some girls should be worth more than others, so Lydell says the top three count for fifty points each, next three for forty, next for thirty. Last three they decide oughta be ugly ones, just so everybody can get some easy twenties. They come up with Tami, Sharon, and this girl Gwendolyn who goes by Gwen-D. She's older too, a friend of my sisters. I've seen her at our house a couple times, and she's a sight, with those big legs and that gap running between her teeth. Hard to blame the fellas for putting her number twelve.

"Wait wait wait," Jenkins says, putting his hand over his eyes and making that thinking-face. "There's somebody else we gotta put on that list." I look down at my sneakers. I don't know if Jenkins has seen Keisha or ever heard little G talk about her. "I can see her like she's right in front of me. Damn, what's her name?"

"You think somebody's gonna read your mind, boy?" Lydell says.

"Short read, 'Dell," Rasheed says.

"Fuck all you all. Little G knows who I'm talking about." Jenkins hits him on the shoulder. "Don't you remember that girl I was showing you the other day?"

G just shrugs.

"Forget it, Jenkins," Lydell says. "We got enough names anyhow."

"Naw, man. I want a piece of *this* one." Jenkins makes that thinking-face again and looks at Rasheed. "See, I thought of her 'cause I seen her hanging with Gwen-D sometimes. Ain't you seen her, pretty little thing with the straight hair?"

I look back down at my sneakers.

"Yeah yeah. Name starts with a 'C,' don't it?" Rasheed says.

Jenkins claps his hands together, so loud it makes me jump. "Cheryl!" He smiles real big. "Put Cheryl on that list, make her count for thirty or something."

"Cheryl *Robertson*?" Lydell says, putting the pencil behind his ear and then pointing at me. "That's little man's sister. His *blood* sister." He shakes Jenkins off. "Can't put her in the game."

"Come on, man. He ain't gonna mind," Jenkins says. "Oughta be proud."

"Naw, that ain't right," Lydell says. He takes his pencil again. "But we oughta let Jake pick somebody else instead. Anybody the little man thinks he can get some points off." He looks at me. "You *do* want in the game, don't you?"

"Naw," I say. "I ain't gonna win against you fellas."

"Don't you go counting yourself out so quick, little man," Lydell says. "You get in the game and you'll maybe show us all what you got."

I know he's right. I've only dunked twice in my life, and both times it happened in big games—everything was humming and my legs just got me up. Lydell told me they call that adrenaline, and that shit don't let you think about nothing else. But when I'm out here on my own, I never get that ball over the rim. Even if I pretend like I'm back in one of those games, it doesn't work. Only the game can get me there.

"Naw," I say, looking at Lydell, knowing everybody else is looking at me. "It ain't my game."

"Well, if he ain't playing he ain't gonna hear none of us talking no shit about his sister," Jenkins says. "So put Cheryl on that list and go buy little dude here some magazines to hide under his pillow."

Lydell laughs at that. He looks at me. "What you think about that, Jake?" He puts his pencil to the paper again. "My boy Jenkins says he wants a taste of some Robertson sugar. And you just told me you ain't gotten no play in you don't know how long. This is what you call a no-brainer, little man. Just gimme a name and you're in and Cheryl's out."

Jenkins is playing with his chain again, twirling it around his finger. Lots of stories go through the fences here, and hardly anybody ever asks where they come from, so you've got to figure out for yourself what's real. Folks say Jenkins always gets out of his head when he's drinking, and one time he drove out to find this girl he'd been soft on but hadn't given him the time of day, smacked her around till her face wasn't so pretty no more. I don't know if he's gonna keep after Cheryl even if she ain't one of the twelve, but I *do* know there's no way I'm letting my own sister go down on that list so all these motherfuckers can take a shot at her like she's some bottle they put up on a fence.

"You awful quiet there, boy." Jenkins says to me.

"Let him think a second," Lydell says. "I wanna check in with my other little man over here. We ain't heard nothing from you yet, little G. You gonna step up into all this? You gimme a name right quick before Jake does, and I'll put you in."

"Keisha," I say.

"Keisha who?" Lydell says. "We all got to know."

"Just Keisha," I say. "That's it."

Pervis shrugs. "There's only one Keisha I know about. Last name's Marshall or something like that. Girl's always *always* wearing long pants, don't matter how hot it gets."

"Them long pants! I seen that bitch!" Jenkins says. He walks over to little G and slaps his hand down on his shoulder. "That's the girl you been telling me about, ain't it now?" G looks surprised. "You said you was gonna fuck her thirteen ways till Sunday."

"I ain't said that about nobody."

Jenkins steps in closer to G, and bends to catch his eyes. His chain swings back and forth in that little space between them, and he talks soft, but plenty loud enough. "I think you *know* what I'm talking about, boy."

I feel my blood start pumping like it does when I'm waiting to get in a game. I tell Lydell to put Keisha Marshall down on that motherfucking list, and I look over at Jenkins and G when I say ain't nobody touching her without my say-so, all her points gonna be mine. I hear Lydell laugh, and without even looking I can see his big ugly smile.

Looking back on it, I wish I could have seen then what I see now, how I was just starting to get off Lydell's rope when I tied myself back in, tight as ever.

* * *

Folks always say seven is such a lucky number. I'm trying to remember that when I sit down in math class across from Keisha. Pervis gives me a little nod from the back row. When he gave up Keisha's name yesterday, he knew I was maybe a little soft on her. He didn't say anything about it then, he just sat there while we all listened to Lydell come up with that name The Sevens and go on about how the five of them oughta let the two little men try to get to Keisha first. Jenkins said he'd put money on little G, but Lydell said he had a good feeling about his man Jake, number seven man in the game. Pervis didn't say anything then, and he doesn't now, just gives me that nod like he's waiting to see me make a move.

I check the clock and see it's about a minute before the period. The teacher is still playing with her papers and stirring up her coffee. Keisha is writing away. She's wearing brown pants and a white shirt open at the collar. She turns her head real quick to me.

"You got the answers to the last page?"

"Gimme your paper," I say. This is my chance now, I've got to step up to it, because G's out there in that hall somewhere looking for her.

"Just tell me," Keisha says.

I reach over and take her paper. The bell rings to start the period. I look at Keisha and hold up a finger. This should only take a minute. I take my pencil and fill in the answers real light so she can erase them and put them down in her own hand. Just some easy multiplying and adding. Just plugging in the numbers.

When I finish up, I look at her answers on the first page, just for the hell of it. One of us has it all wrong, and it ain't me. She doesn't even have the questions written out right. The teacher's putting a problem on the board, and I look at Keisha trying to figure it out. She doesn't have that wrinkled-up thinking-face like Jenkins—her mouth hangs open and her eyes look like they might not be seeing anything at all. I whisper her name real quick and hold out my paper on top of hers. "You gotta do it all over."

She gives it back to me at the end of the period, and I pass it up the row. I stand up out of my desk when the bell rings and watch her put her things together. She takes the rubber band out of her hair, and when it falls out soft and pretty on her shoulders, my stomach goes tight. She's a short little thing, and she smiles when she looks up at me. Her eyes are light brown, almost yellow, and you don't see that much in a girl with skin as dark as hers. Nice big butt too on top of those skinny legs. Not many brothers go around talking about her, saying she's fine or they want to get with her, but they ain't me.

"I didn't know you were Jake *Robertson*," she says, putting her hand on my elbow. "I mean, I must have forgot till I saw it on your paper. I guess I didn't really know who you were over there."

Everybody leaves for the next class. Pervis gives me another nod when he walks by.

"Guess you just found out," I say.

Indian summer again in California, can't see a cloud today no matter how far you look. I tell Keisha it sure would be a shame to let this one get away. We cut out early, just walk straight out of the building. Paula told me it's been a long time since they tried to keep folks from cutting—teachers always complain about the classes being too big anyhow. And I never learn a damn thing in here to save my life.

We walk to my house. I tell her nobody's home, but I don't say where they are. Don't tell her Daddy's in lock-down again, second time since we moved from Chicago. That Momma's probably cleaning houses out in Bella Vista, or that it could be her shift at the day-care today, where she's trying to get on full-time. She told us she was gonna start having to make the money around here, and me and my sisters would need to help out if we were gonna stay off the county. I'm trying to play it cool, hoping Keisha doesn't pick up on it and start asking questions I don't want to answer.

She doesn't. My hand brushes against hers when I reach down to get my key, and I get a little chill. I get it again when I put my hand on her back and let her inside before me. And when she squeezes me and we move over to the couch.

* * *

It just happened. Right afterwards, she was damn-near bouncing around, wanting to know if I liked it, if she was good, if I'd see her again. When she left, and I started putting everything in that room back in place, all this shit went flying through my head. I was gonna go right up to Lydell and tell him to mark up thirty points for me and take me out of the game because now I was gonna be with Keisha. Was gonna walk off Archer Street without looking back. Then I remember, clear as yesterday, I picked up Momma's pillow and put it back in the corner of the couch where it belonged. She'd brought it with us from Chicago. It had a pattern on the front, a picture of our old church that one of her friends had sewn in there for her. It was warm, because that's where Keisha had put her head. I brought it close to my face and caught this little fruity smell stuck in it, from Keisha's perfume or something. There I was, maybe a few minutes after my first time, hitting that pillow like an old rug to try to get the smell out, jamming it into the corner, back side out, and hoping nobody would notice.

There was a stain in the couch, too, right where you'd expect it to be. I got some paper towels and dried it up as best as I could, but it didn't help. No blood in there, so it made me think maybe it wasn't Keisha's first time. I thought that was what a dude's supposed to look for, but I wasn't sure—I heard all sorts of things on the courts. What I did know was that my sisters were the only ones who could help me out right then. Now that I'm a grown man—now that I've got Noel and William—I can finally make some sense out of what they did.

"What you doing to the couch?" Paula says, coming up those three steps with her hands on her hips. She's the shortest in the family but she's got Daddy's big bones. She's eighteen now, but she ain't grown no way but wide since we moved out here. Cheryl's right behind her, eyebrows up and her lips pressed tight, like she's maybe holding something in. "God almighty, Jake. Who told you to just go on and do whatever you want in here?"

I'm standing behind the couch, holding the blue blanket in front of me with both hands. I give it a hard snap to get some air under it and when it settles down over the couch I start tucking the edges in. "It's gonna be getting cold soon," I say. "Just wanted to warm it up a little in here."

"You drunk? I smell something in here," Paula says, sniffing loud a couple times. "It's eighty-five degrees in September, Jake, and you out here putting a blanket on the couch." She looks at Cheryl. "You smell something too?"

Cheryl waits, like she knows the answer but she's trying to figure out if she should even say it. She tilts her head and shrugs a little. "It ain't beer."

"I don't know what you all talking about," I say. "I was just hitting some homework and then I thought I'd come in here and make things a little nice."

"How'd you get home so early?" Paula says. "You cut out?"

"Just history. We never do nothing in there."

"So it ain't the first time you done this."

"No, it ain't."

"God almighty, Jake!" Paula throws her books on the floor, quick-steps to the front of the couch and stands right across from me. "We ain't hardly started the year yet and here you go." She reaches over and slaps me right on my ear. "Sometimes I wonder what you got up there."

"Don't you touch me, bitch," I say. My ear is hot. "You think you my momma?"

"That how you gonna talk to me?" She points a finger at me and looks over her shoulder at Cheryl. "You heard it yourself now, sister. Look how he acts with a woman. It's like I told you."

"What the fuck is this all about?" I say.

Cheryl looks at Paula. "We don't know nothing for sure yet."

"What more you got to know?" Paula says, turning back to me.

"But we ain't heard from him yet," Cheryl says.

"We just did! It's just like she was telling us!"

"Who?" I say, shouting it. Cheryl looks at the floor. Paula straightens up. "Who the fuck said something about me?"

"Who?" Paula presses her lips tight again and moves in smelling-close. "Who, Jake? Is that what you wanna know?" She puts her foot up, right in the middle, right where the spot is under the blanket. "You getting pretty worked up about this. Who you *think* it was?"

"Get off that," I say, and smack her ankle.

"Can't step on your little blanket, huh? Something special about it?" She looks over in the corner and sees the bulge. "You got Momma's pillow under there?"

"Just leave everything be."

She straightens up and folds her arms across her chest. "So how about it, Cheryl—think Momma's gonna like what Jake done in here? Got a blue blanket hiding her pillow and matching her brown carpet worse than a blind man would."

Cheryl looks at me. "I don't know," she says, and I can't hardly hear her. "I just don't know."

"Well *I* know it ain't right!" Paula shouts, and she grabs the blanket and pulls. All the corners come loose, and Momma's pillow falls, but I pull back before she gets the whole thing. It snaps up in the air like a bridge over the couch. Paula is strong for a girl. I let go, and she takes the whole blanket with her falling back on her ass. The spot is there now, plain as day, dark brown mark on the tan cushion.

Cheryl tries to help her up, but Paula twists free and grabs the pillow off the floor. She cocks it back and gets her aim at me, and then she just stops. She sniffs loud, in the air, then at the pillow. "So you got your points already, huh Jake?"

"Who you been talking to?" I say. My stomach goes tight.

Paula throws the pillow down again. "Who we been *talking* to, Jake?" She jumps up and looks over at Cheryl. "You hear that, sister? Wants to know who's got his number." She sweeps her hand in front of her. "Could have been about anyone by now—whole school's gonna know before the week's out. Question is, who *you* been talking to? Who *you* trying to play—"

Cheryl cuts her off. "He ain't had a chance to explain nothing yet."

"Chance *shit*, girl," Paula says. "You treating him just like Daddy. You take your brain out when Gwen-D was talking to us?"

"What's Gwen-D know?" I say. "What'd she tell you all?"

"But she said Jenkins was drunk outta his mind when he said all that," Cheryl says.

"Yeah, and liquor's the best thing around to make somebody tell the straight truth."

"What'd Jenkins say?" I hope Cheryl doesn't know what I know yet.

"Nothing you ain't heard before," Paula says.

Cheryl walks over to our big front window, takes one of the wood chairs and turns it toward me. When she and Paula bring Gwen-D back some days after school to sit out on the front step and finish a pack, they always lean back in those chairs, sometimes far enough to look straight up at the sky. But right now Cheryl sits with her back real straight, crosses her legs, and brushes her hair out of her eyes. She looks up at me, and part of her face is in shadow. "Most days I see her in the halls and we'll stop and visit for a minute, but when I saw her today she was just, 'Can't say nothing right now.' And I'm thinking, can't say nothing about *what?* Gwen-D don't ever keep quiet about nothing."

"So the three of us are just sitting there in that doorstep where you can see the field," Paula cuts in, "watching the football team beat itself up, and Gwen-D starts telling us about the Big Dick Club and how you was in it."

"I ain't running with nothing like that!" I say. "I don't even talk to Jenkins no more."

"Look, Jake," Cheryl says, "This is just what we heard, OK? Gwen-D told us she was out with her man last night just getting a burger at the Otto's stand on Temple. Right when Jimmy goes to the bathroom, some dude she knows named Jenkins pulls in with some other dude who's big as a house, she says, and they're all liquored up. The big guy goes to the counter, but Jenkins comes right over and starts talking to Gwen-D."

"There you go again, girl, covering up." Paula shoots that finger at Cheryl this time. "Tell it to him straight, the same way she told us." She looks at me and makes her eyes small. "It wasn't *talking*, it was, 'Why don't you get in my car right quick so I can get me some before I get a good look and see how ugly you are, bitch?'"

"Naw, I don't remember it like that," Cheryl says, still looking at me. She doesn't get into it with Paula when she's hot like this, because she knows Paula just rolls her. "But Jake, it must have been something outta line because I know how Gwen-D gets."

"She went upside his head, knocked that burger right out of his mouth," Paula says, smiling.

Cheryl nods along. "She said he dropped his fries too. Everything just spilled out all over the place. So it's a good thing Jimmy came back quick from the bathroom, because . . ." She looks over at Paula. "Well, I don't know this dude Jenkins from Adam, and I been around Gwen-D long enough to know how she tells a story, so—"

Paula tilts her head up at the ceiling and closes her eyes. "God almighty, sister."

"All right all *right!*" Cheryl says. She tightens her lips almost like Paula's. "Jenkins said he'd get over on her soon enough and there'd be other brothers coming right behind him." Paula nods big and slow. Cheryl looks at her own crossed-over leg, watches her foot make little circles in the air. "He wanted to smack Gwen-D for spilling everything, but the big dude held him back, and Jimmy was right there anyway. So he might have been saying all this just because he couldn't get a punch in, Jake. But he started giving names and you was one of them."

It's like getting hit in the gut. "What names?"

"I *told* you he was gonna start sounding like Daddy," Paula says. "Like he don't know nothing about nothing. You want me to name off all seven, so you know I ain't lying? First there's *you*, of course, then we got your homey Lydell Waterson, and those two chumps at the Otto's—"

Right before I cut her off, I catch a quick look down at the spot. They still haven't seen it. "I mean the *girls*," I say. "What'd Jenkins tell her?"

Cheryl's foot is still hanging in the air, making circles. I know she won't look up now, not at me. Not if she thinks I'm teaming up with Jenkins, not if he was so fucked up he spilled *everything*.

Paula steps right up to the couch again. "He told her about a couple sophomores none of us knew," she says. "But I don't even *care* if I don't know them. What you're forgetting, *little man*, is they ain't just some fucking dolls in your little *game*. Don't you got no balls? Don't you got no head of your own? What if they tell you to go get some points off one of your homey's little sisters, you gonna do that too?"

"She wasn't nobody's *sister!*" I say. I look at Cheryl.

"Who?" she asks me.

"See I told you, girl," Paula says. "But you didn't want to hear it."

"And it didn't happen with me and her the way you all heard!" My gut gets pounding now like my heart just fell down in there. "Not the way you think,

Paula. It was one or the other, that's what I had to choose, and I was thinking if I just played along for a minute I could work things my own way."

"What you talking about now?" Paula says.

"So who was it, Jake?" Cheryl says, real even and slow. The way she's sitting still like that, up on the edge of the chair with her hands folded on her knee, I know she's got it all just about figured out. I can even see her starting to squeeze the color out of her fingers. I can tell she knows, but she's still holding back, because she hasn't figured out why.

"Coulda been you," I say.

* * *

There's nothing like 'fessing up, if you know the right way to do it. Sometimes it feels damn good even if it gets you a whupping. Getting that weight off you is like dumping a load of bricks out of your shoes, belly, and head all at once—everything just flows better, like all your blood just got unclogged.

When I was running on Archer Street, I never got too worked up when I did something I knew wasn't right—most times I couldn't tell the difference. Wasn't till long past that summer of the Sevens—wasn't until I got Noel pregnant—that I started getting that *feeling*. Like I was a train and the ride was smooth as glass if I stayed on my track. But if I got off, even a little bit, things started to rattle-shake inside. I don't know where the feeling came from—if I still talked to Momma these days she'd probably say it was the Holy Spirit finally giving me some wisdom. Some people got more than others, she said one time, but God gives some to everybody when they need it.

Maybe there's something to that, but I didn't know nothing about it that summer I was fifteen. Still wasn't a man. Wasn't playin' the game I am today, but I was damn-sure playin'. When I 'fessed-up to my sisters, it was like that time Momma sprung bail for me, when I got picked up for riding drunk in Lydell's Olds. We were scoping cars in Berkeley again and got pulled over for a DWB, driving while black. When the cop found out Lydell had a record for auto *plus* all those tickets sitting in his glove compartment, we had ourselves an express ride downtown. Momma came the next morning, and soon as we got outside I got a good smack across the mouth. She told me she hoped I learned something sitting up in that jail because now our savings was gone. But that was that—she'd paid the bail, I'd done my time and taken her slap, so I got it in my head that I'd just pull another boost and give her some of that money back.

Same thing with my sisters, except I didn't even get slapped. Cheryl hugged me and said she could get the stain up so no one even knew it happened. Paula just stood there quiet. I felt real low for playin' Keisha like I did, but I got what I wanted.

But nothing like that ever kept Cheryl away. Anytime we had trouble, she would duck past that hanging sheet in our room, over to my side, and tell me what's going down. This time she says Paula sent her in here. "Got something to tell you, little brother."

"I told you I ain't gonna talk to Keisha no more," I say, but I know the plan I've got. If I could get her easy as that, I can have any girl I want. Even if she's the only one I like.

"That ain't the problem no more," Cheryl says. "It's Keisha that's coming after *you* now."

She sits closer. "You know Gwen-D is a good friend of ours. Paula thinks you put her on the list. I told her all you probably could think about was sticking up for me, but she don't want to buy that."

That's because Paula's the smart one, I think to myself. Cheryl goes on and whispers the whole story to me about what happened with Gwen-D. How Keisha's really her *cousin* and she made sure to tell her about the Sevens, even wrote down our names so Keisha could be sure to watch out for us. Because Gwen-D knows how Keisha is, don't think much of herself and always hoping some brother's just gonna sweep her away. Gwen-D knows Keisha would give it up too easy, especially if one of these ballplayers started coming on to her.

A girl like that, a sister who falls that easy, is dangerous if she picks up she's being used. That's what Cheryl says—the girl is bad, bad news. But what the fuck does Cheryl know, I think to myself. Sitting here telling me I'm a victim or something. She don't know I'm in control.

Me and Keisha go driving, and it's different this time around. In September it's hot enough to sweat just standing still in the day but at night the wind is nice and cool. We're driving with the all windows down in this car Lydell's letting me use. It's a Lazarus, those cars just sitting on the side of the freeway waiting for somebody to bring them back from the dead. Lydell and Aaron have made a lot of money driving outside the city with a can of gas and a couple screwdrivers. A lot of those cars will start right up, Lydell says. And if they don't, then you just take the radio and anything else that could score some cash. But I don't tell Keisha none of this. Tonight it's just an old green Corolla and she doesn't have to know nothing about where it came from or why she won't ever see it again when this is all over.

It's different this time because I'm nervous. The game's been going on all week, and I ain't done nothing since I got with Keisha except listen to who's putting up the most points. I'm driving this Lazarus without a license, and I'm hoping a fight or something gets going at the football game back at school tonight so all the cops stay in the city and leave me alone out here for just a little while.

"Where we going?" she asks me. The freeway's darker now, not many cars out and a long way between exits.

"Wherever," I say. I put on the radio but the antenna's broken and we're getting too far out to catch anything. So I cut it off.

She crosses her left leg over and it stretches her pants tight. Out of the corner of my eye I can make out the shape, from her ass to her knee. It's nice. Strong, not fat. She makes a slow beat on the door with her sneaker and starts humming to herself.

"What you singing?"

"Nothing. Marvin Gaye."

"I don't like it. Let the man sing it himself."

"But we ain't got no music, Jake."

"I don't like it."

She puts her foot back on the floor, and the wind starts up through her pants again and flaps them like a couple of little flags. She looks straight out the window. "Why we have to go this far?"

"I thought you wanted to." Downtown there's enough lights on the freeways to light up Vegas but once you get out of the city, out here, they just stop dead. The moon's out but it's only a little piece of it, not the whole thing, and it keeps ducking behind clouds so it's almost like it's not shining at all. About the only thing I've got are the headlights on this Corolla, and they ain't the greatest. But I see one of those blue signs coming up that says there's a view off the side of the road, so I turn off and park in the lot.

All week I've been guessing about her pants. Cheryl told me something that keeps bouncing around in my head no matter where I go. *You got to wonder about a girl like that, Jake. What kind of girl wears pants all summer if she ain't shamed of herself somehow?* I've been thinking about how it was with Keisha the other day, why it was so easy. Ain't none of the fellas moved in on her yet, and I know they wouldn't let me have her for my own so quick. They've got to know something— must be seeing something I don't.

"Watch me," Keisha says. She gets out, moves through the grass up to the hill where you catch the view.

"Watch me walk," she says. She takes some steps across the hill, long ones, then she turns around. The wind is all up and through her now, puffing up her shirt, flapping her pants. She's close, but all I can really make out is her shape, like somebody took a black ink-pen to a black piece of paper and just followed it around her nose, her hair, her arms and legs.

"Are you looking, Jake?" She keeps walking, the other way now. She doesn't turn her head to me.

"I don't see nothing." Just that shape, smooth as can be, just walking. That shape that moved under me on the couch. I point at her, behind her. "What's up there?"

"Come look for yourself," she says.

I walk up through the grass. The wind is cold and it whips those weeds on my legs but it feels good. Keisha stops walking. I'm close now and I can see everything I need to. It's all dark out there, no view at all. "Guess it's better in the day," I say. We're side-by-side, almost touching now. Just a little space for the wind to get through.

"Maybe it is, maybe it isn't," she says. She looks up at me. She steps in, feet between mine. I put my hands behind her, pull her shirt out and run a finger down her backbone under her panties till it stops. "You ready?" I say.

She puts her hand on the back of my head. I can feel her nails. She pulls me to her, licks the soft part of my ear and bites down on it almost till it hurts. "No," she says. "Almost." Her breath makes my ear hot.

I pull my head back and look her straight-on. She's smiling. "What you mean? You got something to tell me?"

"Not now." Her arms go tighter on my back.

"When?"

"About what?" She's so close all I can see are her eyes.

"Whatever it is."

"Jake," she says. "Why you shaking?"

"I'm cold."

She moves her arms back up, behind my neck, pulls me in again and kisses me fast. She's cold too. "Come on, Jake," she says. "Why you asking all this now?" She makes like she's starting to sit down. "Just relax."

I straighten up, and her hands fall away. "I can't," I say. "'Cause I can't see nothing."

She goes to the ground and lies back. "What you need to see now that ain't right here? You know what to do."

"What's all that walking about? 'Watch me, watch me.'" The wind is blowing harder behind me now. "Back and forth up here looking like you—"

"Like *what*? What you see?" She sits up quick.

She looks nervous. More than me and I'm the one hanging my ass out driving this car around. A minute ago she was walking around telling me to check her out like I'm supposed to take a picture or something, and now I just want to know what I'm supposed to see. When I got the car tonight, Lydell told me nobody could count their points twice off the same girl. Just so I don't forget. I told myself tonight I'd decide. If I can see what Keisha's hiding and if it doesn't turn me off, then I'll make her my girl. But I want to be sure before I go taking myself out of the game.

"Go on and say it, Jake," Keisha says, leaning forward now. "What you see?"

I see a girl sitting here in front of me who gave me my first taste of sugar. I see a girl my sisters—who I ain't all that close to anyway—think is straight-up bad news. And I see a girl who's trying to show me something and hide it at the same time. "Nothing. I don't see nothing, nothing wrong with you at all."

"Don't lie," she says. "You sound just like him."

"I don't know what you talking about now, girl."

"Well let's get it over with then," she says. Another shot of wind comes in, fills up her shirt and pushes her hair off her shoulders. She grabs a fistful of those pants on her right leg and pulls till they're tight. Then she picks up a rock from beside her. One quick stroke straight down like a blade and the hole's big enough to put her hands through.

"What you doing? Those are nice pants!"

"Well you wanna see don't you?" she says. She pulls each side back from her knee and the threads pop easy. "Come here and touch me."

I sit down in front of her, right up next to her leg. She takes my hand and pulls it back to her, over her knee. Her hand's cold, shaking, but so is mine. She puts mine under the torn flap. It's light and soft, has this little blue flower print I didn't even see before. She presses my finger tips to her skin. It's bumpy, cold. I look up to catch her eyes but she won't give them to me. They follow my fingers. I touch the muscle on top, right before the bone starts, and move down. First it's soft and then the bone comes like a rock and the skin gets bunched together and raised up. I try to lift my hand to see but she just squeezes harder, and when she feels I'm not gonna fight her she moves it all the way down her knee. A long thin hill down her knee, and little grooves like tracks going across. She holds my hand, all the way down, all the way up, all the way back again.

"Didn't know I was in the zipper club, huh Jake?" She takes my hand off but keeps holding it. "Ain't it ugly?"

I shrug and shake my head. "Hardly even see it in the dark."

"Yeah but in the day . . ." she says, and turns her mouth down, looking at it like a momma does at a kid who's always acting up on the bus or someplace out in the open. "Oughta see it then."

"What's there to see?" I say. "Some doctor fixed up your knee and you got a mark. So what?"

She looks up. "It ain't like that," she says. "Not with me. Not for a girl." And then she pulls off her shoes quick as she can and stands up. "Go on over there," she says, pointing behind me. "Just a little bit. I know you gonna see this."

I take a couple steps back, then a couple more, until she puts her hand up. She walks slower than before. When she hits that little limp her face goes like a stone and she looks up and says, "Ain't never seen a girl walk so crooked, huh Jake?"

"It's nothing at all." That's the truth. Always thought that was her strut.

She doesn't buy it. "You ain't looking close enough." She goes back for her sneakers and brings one over. It's white with a red stripe and a black sole, just regular. "You got no idea what something like this costs. Huh, Jake?" She pulls out some little plastic thing from inside. It's thick and it smells like it ought to, coming out of a shoe. "And I hear about every penny of it anytime anybody goes asking him for money. Like I got an inch of gold stuck under my foot. But then he always starts off about how it don't matter what it cost because ain't nobody want nothing to do with no girl walks like a cripple." She turns away, faces out to where the view's supposed to be. Still nothing out there to see. Her chin falls on her chest. She sniffs and wipes her nose.

"He got drunk and pushed me down the stairs, Jake. Was fighting with my momma so I tried to get him off and there I went. When I was eleven. Broke it right where it's supposed to keep growing, so the doc said I'd have to get used to a short leg." She turns the plastic over in her hand a couple times. "I shouldn't be telling you this. You won't even want to take me home."

I step closer and put a finger under her chin and lift it up real soft. It's a little wet outside her eye, so I dry it. "That ain't true," I say.

"Do you think I'm pretty?" she says.

"Yeah."

"I got you fooled then," she says. "First time my daddy saw me walking with all that stitching on my leg he said that's what it was gonna take. Blind man or a fool."

"I don't wanna hear this no more," I say. "I ain't no fool."

"One of us sure is," she says, "coming up here like this." She puts the plastic in her pocket. Then she takes my hands and puts them on her hips. "Let's just do it," she says.

I smile, probably bigger than I ought to. She kisses me again and she tastes good. She puts her hands behind my neck.

"So you really think I'm pretty, Jake?" she says.

"Yeah," I say again. I do. I ain't lying.

"And you like the way I walk?"

"Uh-huh," I say. I move my hands around back and squeeze.

She pulls me in, just like before, and does the same thing on my ear. A soft little bite. And it's hot when she talks. "Tomorrow I want you to tell your big brother all about it."

"Don't talk no more right now," I say. I feel myself getting ready. "I don't got no big brother."

She moves over to the other ear. "Pervis. From our math class. Ain't he been watching you?"

The words hang there a couple seconds in my ear. It's hot from her breath, then the wind comes and everything's cold again. I pull my face away and just look at her.

"What'd he say when you told him about me the first time?" she says, trying to hold my eyes.

She looks different up close, if I really look hard. Her teeth always looked nice to me, but her lip always covered up those bottom ones. And in close like this, looking down, I can see why. A couple of them are turned all sideways, and one right near the middle is missing a chip. Looks sharp as a rock.

"He didn't say nothing 'cause I didn't tell him," I say. "Nobody else needs to know now."

"That's real sweet, Jake," she says. She tilts her head back and presses her arms down harder on my shoulders, squeezing a little tighter. "But then how you gonna get your points?"

She's cool as can be, blinking her eyes, waiting.

"What you talking about?" I say.

"How you gonna keep up with your boys if you don't tell them about me?"

She knows. Cheryl's story about Gwen-D giving Keisha the skinny on the Sevens wasn't no bullshit. She knows I'm in the game.

Nothing I can say that won't sound stupid, but I try anyway, to try to keep her from getting hot. But I ain't smart like Lydell. He always says if a girl thinks you're messing up you got to just lie, tell her what she wants to hear and don't back off your story no matter what. Sweet-talk her until she comes around. If he could hear me now, he'd laugh his ass off.

"I'm gonna tell them I'm out," I say, "'cause I found me the only girl I want right here."

I feel her hands come apart behind my neck, and I know the smack is coming. I'll take it, one time—I've got it coming. But she just puts two fingers on my mouth and says hush. "No, Jake, no," she says. "I don't wanna be no secret. I want you to let them *know*." She pulls her fingers back. "Why your lips still so cold, Jake?"

"They just are," I say. I can't think of nothing else.

She moves in so I can feel her whole body on mine. "You'll warm up soon enough," she says, and kisses me again, but I don't feel much this time. "I know there's twelve of us, Jake. So who's the number one girl?"

"It's you," I say.

She looks up and smiles. "I know that ain't true. But after you tell them they'll start knowing about me." She takes my hand off her hip and brings it up to her chest. I look at her. I wait. She undoes the buttons and her shirt opens up and she slides my hand inside. It's not like last time, on my couch, when I did everything. She doesn't feel the same. Her skin has those cold bumps all over now. "I want you to tell Pervis I'm better now, I know what I'm doing. Lydell Waterson's in charge, right? Make sure you tell him I oughta be worth more points than any of them girls."

I don't move my hand inside her shirt. She does it for me, sliding it wherever she wants and doing the same with the rest of me, putting me into place and moving me around just like she was a little girl playing in her room and I was one of her dolls.

* * *

It wasn't me that did it. When me and Noel went to the court on Archer Street that Sunday morning a couple years back and she got sick and said the game was over, I thought she was hearing what I was from those old fences. But it wasn't me, it was the baby. She was just getting what most pregnant mommas get, even worse than her first time—but I didn't know about her first time until later.

I picked up the ball and we went back to our place. We walked slow because Noel said her feet felt heavy. Mine did too. Felt like a big motherfucking pack had just got strapped to my back.

I didn't stay long because I had to get to work. And Noel just wanted to be off her feet so her stomach could settle. She lied down on the bed, and I ran cool water through some paper towels. She closed her eyes when she put them on and kept them that way when she asked me if I'd ever been a daddy before.

If she had watched me walk away she would have known that pack was feeling heavier each time I put another foot out in front of me. I wished I could call in sick that day but I knew I couldn't afford it. When I caught my bus I took a seat in front and settled in for the ride.

Of course I told her no. I hadn't been a daddy yet. I got with some other sisters in high school, and some ladies here and there around downtown after that, but I never knocked none of them up that I know about. Guess I was just lucky.

It wasn't me that did it. Keisha got with all the Sevens before too long, got pregnant and dropped out before she really started to show. That night in the dark was the last time with me—I heard about her now and again from Paula and Gwen-D, thought about her plenty, but I never saw her again. None of us Sevens ever stepped up to claim that baby, but I know it couldn't have been me.

That morning on the bus, I was caught up thinking about all that when this sister got on with her kid. That little girl was probably too young to even go to school yet, but she looked just like her momma when they both smiled big at the driver from under their hats. Their dresses had the same flowers, and they looked real pretty together, probably heading across town to go to church. I watched the lady put a dollar in the box. She smiled again at the driver while her girl jumped up in the seat by the door. The driver put his hand up. The door was still open. That brother just sucked his teeth real loud, shook his head and told her the fare was a dollar-ten. The sister said she didn't have no more, and even if she did it would be going on the worship plate when they got to service. Most drivers will let you slide on a dime like this, especially on a Sunday, *especially* a brother to a sister, but not this dude. Maybe he was one of those folks who gets a job, gets off the county, and the next day he's talking about shouldn't nobody be getting a handout for nothing in the U-S-of-A, jack. I got up and put a quarter in the box, nodded at the lady and sat down. The driver kept the door open, looked at me in his mirror and asked if I was gonna pay for the kid too. The lady just stood there looking at me, like she was counting on me now. I reached in my pocket and pulled out the other dollar I had on me. My boss at the restaurant said he didn't want me taking lunch out of the kitchen again no more, but I knew I could get away with it if I needed to, so I put it in the box. The sister and her girl sat quiet until they got off, and then I watched them slip into the crowd in front of their church, all the ladies with pretty hats and dresses with their kids all around. I watched them even after the driver closed the door and we pulled away, until the bus took a corner and they just disappeared.

CHAPTER 6
THERE DOWN DARK

Everybody's got dreams they just can't shake. Like some train you thought was long gone come rolling back again, hits you from you don't know where. You hear that whistle from someplace far off and right down close, and you know it's coming, you know it ain't lost, even if you ain't seen it in years. And you know you can't do nothing about it but let it roll on through, because it's gonna get you, gonna catch you while you're sleeping or even during the day when you thought you were already awake. It's gonna ride right through you, clack-rattling over them tracks you thought had disappeared but must have got laid in again when you weren't looking. Or maybe they've just always been there.

Long as I can remember, I've been seeing the maple. And for a few years, I think that's all I saw—just some old tree hanging there stripped-down like the wind gone robbed all its leaves, big thick dark branches and the biggest one coming straight out at me. Took a little while, but we were still in Chicago when I started getting more of the dream, and I could really feel that train rumbling in my gut. Seemed like every year I'd get something more, that train would bring in something new, and I'd go trying to put it together.

When it runs right through, comes in when I'm sleeping and plays straight out like a movie, I'm looking down the steps into the dark. I'm still a boy back in our house in Chicago, and it's end of the day getting on night. There's soup cooking in the kitchen, filling the air with that good warm smell, but I'm hungry and my bones are cold. I hear the soup bubbling soft, but then from down in the dark something scrapes over the floor, like metal maybe, and glass breaks. Going down it's like walking into an icebox, and the voices start up, a couple of men by the sound of it, but no words I can make out. Then there's a crash and I know it's all Granddad Lenny's tools done come down off the wall and I got to get down there and see. I jump down the rest of the stairs and come up against the wall, all them cement blocks Granddad Lenny put in who knows how long ago, that mortar dried up sharp between them. I knock my head and feel like shouting out but somebody beats me to it, like they done swiped my voice and made it a man's, took it over by the tools. I touch my head and come back with blood, but I shake it off and go looking for who's down there with me. Then there's light—the door opens to the outside. Through the door there's snow, the trunk of that maple, and a man dragging another one right up to it. I run past the workbench but trip over the tools, and when I look up again one dude is near bare-ass naked and getting hung up on that branch with his own shirt. The other dude fixes the knot tight, a bright white shirt, and ties that to some kind of blueblack rope. I come to the edge of the door, see its window broken out, but I can't walk through. I can't. I just look at that man hanging there, his skin same color as mine, and I can't even make out his face. All torn up, and the blood is a mess all over his chest. I just stand there and look at him and the other brother is gone, gone.

When it plays through, I just stand there looking at him, hanging but still breathing, this man that don't got no face. I make a move to start up the steps but then I hear the branch start to go, like the ice would sound in springtime when it came down off the gutter. The branch comes down on top of him, but when I turn him over he's just the same, still breathing, face all a mess of blood and snow. I work the knot out of the shirt and slip it off his neck. Then I take that rope off the branch—but it ain't no rope, it's Daddy's scarf. Full-up with sweat and blood now, but maybe it could clean his face if I tried. But soon as I bring it close the other brother is there quick as a one-car train flashing by in the night. He snatches them both and disappears before I can even get a look at his face, and he kicks up snow running off.

Some mornings I get up and it's like I'm still inside it, and I go looking. In the basement hole I go through my clothes thinking I'll come up with that scarf, or I step outside hoping one of those palm trees is a maple. When I was in the shelters, I went walking before wake-up past the bunks and through the rows of folks on the floor, looking for somebody turned over with a back like the one keeps running away, somebody with that face I still can't see. Every now and again I get my mind on heading back to Chicago, like maybe that's the only way I'm gonna get this thing gone. But what am I gonna do spending my money going back to that cold motherfucker and finding out somebody else done taken our house anyway—if it ain't been torn down already and cut into kindling. When we were still out there, I remember mornings I'd wake up and hear Momma in the kitchen, go in and see her standing in the dark, go over and look out the window at that tree and ask her was there any mens fighting out there, anybody getting killed, and she wouldn't even look at me, wouldn't turn and see what I was seeing out the window, she'd just laugh like you do when something ain't funny and say shush now you just a young boy don't go dreaming no crazy shit like that.

But when I was sixteen, there wasn't nothing she could do. When we'd been living in California and I'd been down on Archer Street enough to know, and Daddy had been in and out already, it came rolling in, ready or not. When Daddy brought the shirt home that November night, it was there for everybody to see.

* * *

When the door slams shut in our house, everybody feels it. In the day, when folks are talking and moving around, nobody pays it any mind. But when night comes around and things go still, you'd almost think a gun went off. There's times Paula or Cheryl come home and *whap*—I think I'm damn-near gonna fall outta the bed. I always tell myself that's it, I'm gonna tell her straight this time, but when morning comes, she's already in the kitchen with Momma, talking about what a damn fool she went out with last night and fixing my breakfast, and there ain't no sense taking her away from something important like that. But when I hear it tonight, whap-banging so hard it flies back open, it feels like a quake, shooting from the door through the house through me. I know it ain't one of the girls.

"I seen him!" Daddy says, and it's his drinking voice. I can see him without even looking at him, that little shade of purple in his face. His steps are big and heavy on the stairs, into the kitchen. "Train done come in and I seen him! You all gonna see him too!"

Coming out of my room I see him throw a sack on the table, and it hits down heavy. He went out a couple nights ago but I didn't think much of it till now. That ain't just some old pillow sack—he's at it again.

When he turns around to switch on the light, it's just like I've been seeing all this time—but I never thought I'd *see* it. That white shirt, torn up and shot through with blood.

The sleeves hang over his shoulders. He looks at me, and that color is in his face, and those old gray eyes burn, and I know he's done read me like a book. He lifts a sleeve up off his chest. "Got somebody for you to meet tonight, Jake."

I stand there at the kitchen door swung-out and watch him set some plates out on the table. He puts that sack right down on top of Momma's, laughs, and says she's gonna eat good tonight.

Before I even hear her coming Momma pushes me out of the doorway. "What you doing with him?" she says to Daddy. She stands in front of me, shoots her arm back and grabs my shirt tight, without even looking. I try to shake out of it, move to see Daddy again, and right then I can feel Momma knows something too. She's a strong lady for being so thin—you wouldn't want to fuck with her—but she lets go of my shirt, lets her arm go weak all over. Somehow I know just what she's looking at. Same thing I am.

Daddy smiles. "Been a long time, ain't it?"

She jumps at him, crawling over the table, reaching for it. "That don't belong to you no more!"

Daddy grabs her arm, quick-jerks her to him, punches her dead-on in the face. Just *whap* and Momma's head snaps to the side and she rolls out on the table, *whap* like stepping on glass, just *whap* and Daddy grunts and steps in like he's gonna get her again, but he backs off and I see those eyes flash quicker than that man running out of my dream. I see those eyes flash *my God what I done* when he looks at me and then it's gone, he jerks Momma's arm and says do you want more.

I quick-step to him, plant that right foot, and hit him with my best jab, straight in the chest. Quick in, quick out, just like he taught me, just like all the boys on Archer Street know. Don't know if I'm too quick or he's too drunk, but he lets go of her hand. I pick Momma up off the table and get the bag too, scoot out of the kitchen into the front room.

He laughs loud behind me, and I hear that plate kicked over the floor.

I set Momma in the blue chair by the window and throw the bag down. He got her good—her eye is red inside and all around now but soon enough it's gonna shut and go purple. She moans and she looks around at nothing and right through me. I shake her shoulders and tap her face on the good side. "Momma!"

"You oughta be thanking me," Daddy says, coming through the doorway. He's got a little gun in his hand, so small you can hardly see it, but we all know it's there like you'd know there's bad food in the house just by smelling it.

Paula and Cheryl come out of their room like they got thrown from it, still in their sleeping clothes, rushing right over to Momma. Paula pushes me away like I was nothing. "He hit her! Momma, you all right?"

They lift Momma out of the chair, say they're getting her to the hospital. She tells them she's all right, hold on now. She stands there with one under each shoulder and points sharp at Daddy. "So help me God, Curtis, I don't care what you been drinking or doing out there, you touch one of my children now I'll come back from the *grave* if I have to and kill you my *own* self."

Daddy steps closer, right to the back of that brown couch in front of us. He leans his hands down on the edge, letting the gun almost slip free, letting the nose slide out up in the air so it could smoke anybody if it went off, even him. One arm of the shirt falls when he drops into that lean, sways there in front of him. He takes it with his other hand and gives a little laugh, looks right at Momma and shakes his head. "That ain't gonna bring him back." He drops it and stands up full, and I feel myself doing the same thing, feel Paula and Cheryl come in tight on Momma. "I'm the only one can do that."

"So tonight you gonna tell it all, is that it, Big Daddy?" Momma says. She points over at me. "You gonna give Jake all that about the family roots?"

Daddy keeps his eyes straight on Momma but lifts his gun hand at me, the nose of it still looking back at himself. "I'm gonna do whatever I goddamn want tonight," he says. He wipes some sweat off his face and looks over at me, points at the bag down there in front of Cheryl. "Pick that up, Jake. Show it to your Momma."

"I don't want it," she says. "None of it, don't matter what it is. Just take it all and get on outta here."

"Go on, Jake," Daddy says. "Pick it up."

I pick it up. It ain't much, just looks like some pillow sack with something rolling around in it. I step over and give it to Momma, but she keeps looking right through me. Paula and Cheryl stand there like they ain't never gonna move neither.

"Open it up," Daddy says.

I hold the bag open, hold it tight. Momma gives me her eyes now, and it feels like they could split my head better than a shot from Daddy's gun. Cheryl gives me that look like always when she wants to be on everybody's side all at once, and over her head I can see Daddy in the window, standing behind me. Half the glass is lit up with the light from out of the kitchen, but the other part is dark as outside. Daddy's right there in the middle like some kind of shadow, one side of him cut out sharp in that bright white and the other part just fading away.

Momma looks past me. "You can't do nothing without that gun," she says.

He smiles, and I can see it big in the window. Then quick as that he throws the gun away, and I almost drop the bag when I hear it hit the kitchen floor and slide till it knocks up against the wall. I turn around and Daddy's holding up one arm of that shirt again. The blood is brown just like my eyes. "Didn't need nothing but my bare hands for this."

Momma breathes in sharp, and her face goes so tight looks like it might break. Quick as that, she grabs the sack right out of my hands and pushes past me. Quick as that, there's only that couch between them, and she swings the bag around, right up at his head, and Daddy's too slow.

When it hits him it's that same *whap* Momma got, knocking him up against the kitchen door swung-out. Gets him right in his collar, right where I hit him, and he slides on down. Paula takes off running to the kitchen, and Daddy ain't too fucked up not to know she's going for that gun. He reaches over and grabs her leg, trips her up. I hear her slap down on the floor when I jump past Momma over the couch, and right when I'm hauling back to hit him again he lets her go, whips around and backhands me with a fist dead-on in the chest.

I fall back on my ass, trying to catch a breath. Daddy whip-turns back to Paula but she's already there, standing over him, her arms out straight but shaking, holding the gun.

He makes like he's gonna stand up, but she shakes it at him. "You gonna stay right there now, Daddy."

I get up on a knee and point at her. "Don't you do nothing!"

Daddy just sits there still as a rock. Paula shakes it at him again, and he lies back real slow, till he's flat-out on the floor and his head's almost touching me.

Doesn't look like him, seeing his face upside-down like this. When he talks he looks scared, like some little kid. "This ain't about me, girl. Now you just toss that back in the kitchen and maybe you all gonna get a little lesson tonight. Hear the story you should have heard long time ago."

Now she's the one smiling. But her eyes are like Momma's. "Don't you go worrying, Jake," she says, looking down at Daddy. "When you do something to nothing, it don't add up to nothing."

I smell his breath coming up when he talks, that malt liquor you can get real cheap at the corner stores, the kind I've gotten torn up on myself nights hanging on Archer Street. I've heard stories about him and Dereck pulling boosts with a gun, but I ain't seen it like this, Daddy bringing home the goods. I put my hand down on his shoulder, on top of the shirt, keep my eyes on Paula. I make a fist with it, get a ball of it in my hand, and it feels soft like you wouldn't see a working man wear—like back in the day, this was a fine shirt. "This here's your Daddy," I say. I squeeze it tighter and feel that dark dried-up blood breaking between my fingers. "Why don't you step off and let him go get some sleep now."

Paula shakes her head, keeps the gun out. "You crazy like I don't know *what*," she says.

Cheryl is still with Momma behind the couch. "Jake don't have to get caught up in all this," she says. Paula looks back at her. Cheryl's eyes are tired, but her voice comes on strong. "Let him take Daddy on over to Lydell's. Dereck will let him stay there long as he wants."

"He's gonna stay *here* long as he wants," I say, squeezing that shirt again.

Daddy puts a hand up to Paula, who ain't moved an inch. "Just let me get on my way then, baby girl," he says. He talks low now, moves his hand like he's patting something soft. "Just let me get on outta here like your momma said."

"Yeah, you going, all right," Momma says. Her face is in the shadow sitting in the chair, but soon as she pushes off and that light hits her, soon as it catches her eye and she's coming past Cheryl and around the couch, I can see it closing up and gonna go purple. She jumps right down in between Daddy's legs, steps down hard on him right where *no* man wants to get hit. She hops back out before Daddy bunches up his legs, and right as his head's coming up off the floor she grabs the gun out of Paula's hand, clubs him right across the jaw. Daddy rolls over on his side, making all kinds of noise, and the torn-up shirt slides right off him, hangs there in my hand. Momma gets down on her knee, gets real close. "But you ain't leaving on your own feet," she says. "There ain't nothing here in this house for you no more, nothing you ain't broke past fixing."

Her eyes come up to me—like she's checking to see if I heard—and she quick-snatches the shirt out of my hand like I wasn't even holding it. She stands up, and her face goes cold, almost smooth in all that shadow. She puts her hand over that eye. Paula pulls the bag up off the floor, holds it in front of her and empties it out all over him, a big heavy thing looks like some kind of helmet, and all that money too, floating down like those feathers in the air that time Daddy took me under the Cliffs with the gun. Momma drops straight down, picks up two handfuls of that money and squeezes them, so tight I can hear the paper crackle. The shirt falls out of her arms, on top of the money by Daddy's feet. She looks up at me, and her mouth opens like she's gonna say something, and her eye and that side of her face is all in shadow. She looks up at Paula, over to Cheryl, back to me. She throws the money down, snaps up the shirt, and goes running outside, shuts the door loud as when this whole night got started, and the house shakes once and goes real still.

* * *

In the morning, after the police come and take Daddy but before it even gets light, I hear somebody stepping through the kitchen. Coming out of my room into the hall, the back door creaks the way it always does when it's coming shut real slow and quiet, so I slip in the kitchen and come right up to it, see if I can catch anybody out behind the house.

Can't see nothing out back till I open the door. A little light on the grass, coming up from the basement.

We don't have one like we used to in Chicago, that place Daddy kept the workbench and all Granddad Lenny's old tools up on the wall and all those scraps of wood on the floor. Can't even get to this one from inside the house—you've got to go outside like this, out back, and all there is down there is one little room and one little bulb. Only time I've been in there was when I helped Daddy stack up the last of them boxes from Chicago. We filled up that space pretty good, left a little room for the door to swing open. When I went to cut off the light, he smacked my hand away. He locked the door, put the key in his pocket, said that light was gonna stay on 'cause you gotta have something lets folks know to stay away.

Momma is in there, down on the floor. On her knees, her back to me, just wearing her sleeping clothes. I know she's got to be cold, but she ain't shaking and jitterbugging like somebody trying to stay warm. Got her face down in her hands, still as a rock.

Then real quick her head snaps up, her hands shoot out, and she's got the shirt right there. She snaps it open, hard like she wants to make that old blood jump right out. She yells and whips it up with one hand and knocks the bulb clean out. No words I can make out, just some grunt from up inside her that she hits right when the glass breaks and the room goes dark and all those pieces go hiding behind boxes where they ain't never gonna get found.

Hard to see anything down in there, but I ain't moving, ain't going in. I see Momma's bare feet, that underneath part we always joke about looks like God couldn't get to the store for more paint and had to leave something white. I hear a scrape and burn, see a match coming to life in Momma's hand. The flame throws a little light on her, and then the shirt catches, and I see her face full-on. Shadows start kicking around on the floor. Only takes a minute of watching till I can't watch no more, till the shirt's all caught up and Momma is gonna get it too.

"Get outta there!" I say, jumping down to the door. "Let go that mother-fucker!"

Momma just turns her head. Keeps that arm out straight, that shirt burning right up to her hand.

I run at her. I grab her arm and my hand damn-near gets burnt shaking that shirt from her and pulling her up on her feet. "Momma," I say. "What you doing?"

She doesn't even look at me. Her eyes are down on the floor in all those flames and the light goes crazy jumping across her face.

I swing her around, get in front of that flame. Her eyes go dark. "Momma, look at me!"

She does, and it comes quick. Hot right across my face, like her hand was stuck in that fire all night long. Stings like a motherfucker, and I let her go. She pushes past me like I was nothing, and goes over to the shirt, nothing but a little flame now, like that match all over again. She stomps down on it, doesn't even cry out like anybody else would burning their foot, and the smoke comes up quick and damn-near fills the room. She runs out, past me and through the door, leaves me there coughing all by myself.

* * *

I couldn't shake it, even after all that. Seeing it real like that, finally putting some of it together, I thought I'd sleep easy. But the dream came in like a train loose down a hill that night, right down into my belly and rumbling all around till I didn't think I'd ever want to eat no more. And it changed on me—maybe because now I'd seen the shirt, held it in my own hand. Now when that arm comes in, reaches in and takes the shirt off the body in the snow, I grab it. It shakes me off quick, slips out, but not before I get a look at who it is running away. It's Daddy. When the shirt goes over his shoulder it flaps out in the breeze like always, and it's torn and all shot-through with blood. And the scarf is trailing out behind. Daddy disappears right quick, but the color of the blood is up in that tree now—it's got leaves now—and now I know it's that maple we had out back our house in Chicago. Those leaves always went blood-red in early November, and ever since that night the tree is full of them in the dream, full-up with leaves that ash and fall like black snow when Daddy runs, like the ashes that morning in the basement room where Momma left me coughing, falling down out of my hand soft and quiet just like they were nothing.

Anytime anything happens around here there's always stories, and didn't take but till the next day for me to hear all about Daddy down on the courts. Lydell leaned back into that fence and let his shit fly—said what kind of pussy motherfucker brings a gun in on his own family and don't even know how to use it, said Daddy's the one got Dereck locked-up 'cause he don't know how to run a score right. All them stories buzzed around Archer Street like a mess of bees knocked fresh out of their hive, but I knew better. I went down and saw him in the county bullpen that same week, up on the fifth floor wearing his blues. When I saw him, he told me why he busted up that shop where Momma always got her hair done, told me it was about time somebody showed her she wasn't gonna look like no woman outta no magazine, and about time she stopped spending his money trying. He didn't say nothing about the gun, but it didn't matter. I was there with him under the Cliffs that night when I was eleven—I knew he wasn't no natural shot like me, but you don't need to be if you get in close. And he did—I held that shirt in my own hand, and I wasn't some stupid kid no more who don't know how blood gets there.

Daddy killed a man. I didn't know who, still don't. He wouldn't say it at the window because them guards always listen in, and he didn't say it that night because it ain't something you tell your boy when there's women around. But I knew he did, still do.

Must have been almost a year went by before Daddy came back around to Valley Street again, his last go-through. I was sixteen, and it's seven years back now, but it's here just the same. That night is there down in me just like the dream. Can't shake it, don't matter where I run. Shelters, SROs, Misery Accordion—wherever I've been since then, if a handle rattle-squeaks like a motherfucker, I'm right back in it. If a door bangs home dead in the night, I'm up out of my bed, running past the sheet past my sisters, and he's right there waiting.

His eyes don't meet mine no more, like the last time—I'm taller now. They're red, like he ain't slept good since God knows when. He gets smelling-close, and it's like he's been drinking and shoveling shit all in the same day. Black jacket open, black shirt out of his pants, shoes torn up and talking, the rubber coming off the leather good and wide. Some kind of black beret hat on his head, tilted instead of straight, but not even the way you'd do it to look good. His hands are low—one hand in a fist, the other holding the long end of a hammer, a big motherfucker he must have used breaking in here. He puts his fist up in front of my face but I don't back off. He opens it, and some balled-up bills drop to the floor.

"Go on, boy, take it," he says.

Momma's door opens quick, Paula and Cheryl's too, like maybe we've all been waiting for this.

"You son of a bitch," she says. The hallway is dark but her voice is clear as day. "What's it gonna be now?"

"Stay on back there, Momma," I say, putting my hand up.

Daddy laughs short and lifts the hammer up, points it back to the front room. "You come on out here and you gonna see yourself. I done got you plenty of what you want."

Momma steps right up to my hand till it comes flat on her shoulder. She feels cold. I turn to look at her. Her voice goes low, real still. "You ain't got nothing," she says, squeezing my hand but looking right past me. "*I'm* in this house with my children now, and that shirt's good and gone."

I hear Daddy's jacket rustle, and before I can even look back at him that free hand is up tight on my throat and my head snaps back on the wall. "This boy's *mine!*"

I grab his arm but it's like trying to break out of cement fixing to dry. I can't breathe, can't think, I just swing my other arm up and it catches him in the side of the head, and that gets it loose. He falls back a couple steps, keeps his feet, then brings that hammer up in front of him.

Paula and Cheryl come up behind me, but I just put that hand up again, tell them stand off now you all 'cause this here is between Daddy and me.

I step at him and he steps back. We do it again, and again until we're in that front room, right up along the couch, the light in the hallway throwing our shadows up on the window, the money Daddy dumped out swish-crackling when we step on it. He picks up the phone, pulls it out of the wall, throws it up in the air and swings through it with the hammer like he used to hit me fly balls back in Chicago, and the pieces go every which way and there ain't no sound at all when that ring dies out.

He smiles at me big, and his teeth shine in the dark. He kicks his foot over the floor, and some of them bills come up and dance around and I hear him *come on boy you my boy let's get on outta here and I'll show you how to take it I'll show you a way up outta here.* He steps in and I stay put and he steps in and steps in.

He puts his hand on my shoulder right where Momma did and he's stinking and he gets my eyes and I hear him *move on over now and I'll take you boy move on over and I'll give your momma a good whupping and you gonna see how it's done and we'll be up on outta here. Move on over 'cause she knows I ain't no pretty boy no rich man but I got this hammer and I know how to use it.*

I grab that arm and it's still a rock and he's still stinking as a motherfucker and strong enough to kill a man, but I throw it off and step in to him put my hands right up on his chest and push off with all I got. He's quick, he holds on falling back, one arm one hand, teeth shining in the dark and eyes that ain't never seen sleep, brings that hammer up falling back and there ain't nothing I can do. He's got me. I'm his.

It comes down on bone, the collar of my shirt, and I let go and the room is purple and I fall.

I'm that body now, under the maple full-up with blood, face down in the snow.

The shirt's around my neck, it's warm and I'm cold, Momma's there and Daddy's set to run.

I roll over and the tree goes to ash, just disappears to black, to nothing just like that, and I kick out and hit bone.

Daddy falls, the floor shakes. Momma yells, the girls yell.

I've got one good arm still and I push myself up and snatch at that hammer down by his feet. When he rolls over and reaches for it I bring it down flat on his hand and I know he's done punching with that one now.

I tell him to get up if he don't want the other one broke.

He gets up, and I get up with him. I toss the hammer back behind me, and before he can even open that mouth again I punch it shut. My hand comes back with blood. Daddy wipes his lip, looks at his hand, then the other one, then up at me like he don't know me no more.

He says this is it, last chance, looking over at the window, at them shadows on the glass. *Get on outta here with me and I'll make you a man.*

I run at him, swing at his head. He's quick but not that quick, and I land one right square on his chest, right over his heart. He stumbles back, trips on his feet, spins to the window and comes up against the glass. It cracks, sends lines every-whichway and looks like some spider gone took a hit of crack, but it holds him.

I stand in front of him, and my shadow is still there in the cracks with his.

You shoulda killed me when you could have, I say, and push him through.

* * *

Momma went real quiet after that. I don't mean the rest of that night, or the next day—just right on out from there she cut me off, like *I* was the one who fucked her up, like she couldn't see I had marks on my neck same color as her eye, like that hammer didn't come down on me too.

I don't think I even paid my shoulder any mind till they took him away. Out on the ground, I didn't see him moving, and I just stood there till finally I had to get down and get my hands bloody and see if that motherfucker could still breathe. I picked his head up and just let myself feel it, that skin opened up in back and that blood flowing on my hands, let him feel me holding him even if I still didn't know if I should kill him. Would have been so easy, and who would have cared after all this?

He went upstate for breaking the no-contact, and they threw all the rest at him too, hitting Momma and all them boosts. I got my arm in a sling and didn't even get a charge, but seems like can't nobody do nothing to a man like Daddy that the police give a fuck about. That sling got me in all the stories on Archer Street after that, but I didn't stick around long to hear them. Couldn't play no ball, and I wasn't gonna be one of those brothers that get old at twenty and just go there for the blunts and beers and stories and leaning back into that fence.

But back home I might as well have been some dude off the street. Momma took care of me some, made sure I was eating something, but didn't never ask how was that bone of mine or was I playing ball again or did I ever want to go visit Daddy upstate—not because I did. She took us all up the next year, though, for his fortieth, even though Paula said she didn't want to go, even though Momma sang the blues all the way up and back about we ain't got no money for no bus fare like this even if it only was once a year. She opened a bottle on the way home, sipped it all the way till we were back in our kitchen and something just set her off laughing crying at the same time saying what a way for a man to spend his birthday all locked-up and how we gonna make the rent now we just gave it all to Greyhound. Must have been that liquor in her, but what did I know then? I was just standing in that doorway, and all I saw was her looking at me, and that eye hadn't been touched in months but just then it was big and purple and shut-tight like the morning after, all I heard was her laughing getting Paula and Cheryl going too saying now you gonna have to play the thief to pay the rent Jake—or we gonna kick you outta here. I looked at her, sitting laughing at that table, that eye all healed but I swear it was busted-up again, heard her laughing crying what's a man good for anyhow, felt that crying screaming again right in that same doorway where I'd pulled her away from him before he could kill her. I was almost seventeen, and I thought I'd saved her, but standing in that doorway I knew she wasn't never getting healed. The door was still wide open and Momma wanted me out, so I just got up the next morning and ran.

CHAPTER 7
FORTY WEEKS

The day after we went to see the doc, Noel snuck a little calendar home from work, the kind you can fit in your back pocket. One for her, one for me too, but I told her I didn't have no appointments to keep track of like she did. She laughed at that and said I'd better start filling it up with interviews for a better job if I was gonna raise a kid proper. I laughed back, told her watch who you telling what to do.

The way I saw it, we had some time to make it work. Forty weeks, the doc said, and he helped us figure out the date. March 20, first day of spring.

That Sunday we came back from Archer Street to our basement hole on the Misery Accordion, Noel asked me if I'd ever been a daddy. She said she wanted to have it but not by herself. She was scared because you never knew when a brother was gonna take off, no matter how close you got to him. But she knows I'm not like those motherfuckers at the labor hall, smoking their checks and running from the state when it comes knocking. She knows because I've told her.

But there's other stuff I didn't talk about back then, things I needed to keep to myself. Anywhere I went those days, I'd see them—babies and little kids, running squirming shouting, getting off buses on Third Avenue and shooting over to the ice cream man or the window of the toy store and saying this is what they want. Daddies too, some with a woman, some without. Carrying their kid on their shoulders, holding their hand. And every time, I'd ask myself, what the hell kind of life is my kid gonna have? I didn't know if I'd be any good at those daddy things or if I'd get too tired to carry him around when he started to get heavy.

We were hiding from each other. She didn't know me, didn't know about my time in the shelters and SROs, about Lydell or Daddy. There was plenty I was set to find out about her too, but it would be a long time coming. We were going to need the forty weeks. When Noel gave me the calendar she said I ought to write down little things from each day, keep a record like she was. But when I asked her if I could see what she wrote she smacked my hand away and said there wasn't nothing in there for me. Maybe that's what really set me off, not just being told what to do but knowing that she had secrets just like me. And maybe that's why I'd try to steal a look at that book every chance I'd get.

* * *

"Goddammit, Jake!"

I freeze with my hand in the air, and for a second it feels like one of those times I got cuffed. But when I peek back over my shoulder the bathroom door's still closed, no way for Noel to see out.

"Goddammit!"

It's still real early, even for Noel, and the only light in this place good enough to read by right now is with her, behind that door. So it's no use sliding her calendar book out from under her pillow.

She keeps it there when she's sleeping and puts it in her bag first thing in the morning so she can have it at work, if something happens that she wants to get down. I know because she's told me, and because I've been watching.

I get up to see what she wants. Or maybe just to see *something*. I got my first look at her book this weekend. Noel was in the bathroom with the door closed, getting sick again. It said *mine—don't look* on the front. But she'd just puked on me, so I figured I'd paid my dues. I wiped my hands clean on the sheets, opened it, and flipped through quick. The pages were full-up with all this tight writing in pencil and blue and black and red ink, lists of what she was eating and when she got sick. Except for one thing—at the top of four or five pages in a row, she's got this little *almost there, almost there.* I've been guessing at what it could be—but I ain't seen nothing yet.

I push the door open. Noel's sitting on the floor in her T-shirt, and the toilet seat is up. "Look at this," she says.

The smell's always the first thing to hit you—catches me like somebody going upside my head. Works better than any damn alarm clock I've ever had.

"The soup?" I say. Noel fixed some chicken soup last night before we went to bed. But when she was done cooking she gave me everything, all the meat and vegetables, and just left herself some of the water. Said this lady at work told her it would help her get settled.

"Don't ever get no recipes from nobody skinny," Noel says, and leans back on the wall. "My momma told me that a time or two. Don't know why I forgot it till now."

"'Cause then we wouldn't be eating *your* cooking," I say, thinking it might get her to smile. Or reach in the shower and throw the soap at me. But she just keeps her eyes down. It's too early to be up, too late to be out, even around here, and I can hear the streetlights buzzing outside. Noel takes the bottom of her shirt and wipes her tongue hard enough to almost pull it out, then tries to spit in the bowl but can't put out anything I can see, just air that moves the water around a little then leaves it still.

She leans back on the wall again. She moves one knee up and in close to her body, puts her elbow up on top of that, and leans into her hand. "I'm calling in sick," she says.

She did that yesterday, and once last week. "Lemme get you something," I say, and go to the fridge, open up a Coke.

She shakes her head. "Don't tell me you forgot already."

"Forgot what?" I say. "Look baby, it's early. I ain't used to getting no quiz right out of bed."

Noel straightens up quick. "Don't tell me about what you ain't used to. You think I'm used to this?" She wipes her mouth with the back of her hand then leans into the tub and spits. "You think I like going into that office with all those white folk watching to see if I can hold my breakfast down? Shit, they probably got a betting pool going by now. 'What's gonna come first today? She gonna fall asleep or run to the john?'"

"I thought they were all nice to you down there," I say. "What about that lady who told you about drinking the Coke? Ain't she one of your girlfriends?"

"She's just like the rest of them," Noel says, slapping her hand at the air. "Things change, Jake. She's probably the one got everyone looking at me. Those bubbles ain't done nothing but bubble me up some more vomit every time I drink that nasty shit. I ain't touching the stuff no more." She sits there a couple more seconds and takes a big breath. She puts one hand on the edge of the tub and one on the wall and pushes herself up. When she does, she gets rocks in her arms and legs—still strong, even if she says she's feeling the pounds come on. She stands up full, breathes out and looks at me. "And I ain't going in today."

The streetlights are still buzzing. Nobody's up but us. "Who you talking to?"

"You heard me. Ain't going back up in that place and answering them phones with all this vomit breath I got."

"Come here," I say. She doesn't move. I run the water in the sink. It sounds nice, so I let it go a couple seconds until it gets cold. "You can't be out any more days, baby. Let's clean you up." I put my arm around her shoulders. She folds her arms but then she steps with me back to the sink. We're in the mirror now, her white T-shirt real sharp in the light, the top of my bare black chest showing behind, my hands folded over top her stomach, my cheek scratching hers and trying to get her eyes to find mine in the glass. The water gets higher in the sink, just that quiet splashing. Noel doesn't move. She doesn't put her hands on top of mine like she does sometimes when she wants to pretend she can feel it kicking. Doc told us it's too early for that, but I go along when she does it anyway. She doesn't take one of those real big breaths like she does most times when I wrap her up nice and soft like this. Just stands there, looking away. I take her toothbrush and run it under the water.

If she'd gone in yesterday, I might not be acting so nice. If I was getting my full forty, I might not be in here just because she told me to. Might not be letting her give me this attitude if we had a little more breathing room.

But here I am, wetting down her brush, looking at her, waiting. I take my other hand off her belly and open the mirror. The toothpaste is inside, on top of Noel's comb.

"Kill it, Jake!"

Noel jumps back and knocks her head on my chin. It's a roach, a little baby one. Sitting right in the middle of that glass shelf, right on top of Noel's comb and pointing those big long ears at my razor.

I guess I don't get panicked when I'm still waking up like this, because I move slow. Most times I'll smash these motherfuckers the second I see them. Coming up out of the kitchen sink or running behind the fridge or licking out the insides of a bag of chips. In the Angelus one got in my shorts when I was sleeping, scared the shit out of me. Thought the motherfucker was gonna crawl up my asshole. But I can tell this little guy don't know what the hell he's doing—nothing to eat in here, unless he likes soap. I put the paste down and move my hand up near the shelf, just to see if I can scare him a little, maybe make him jump out into the sink so Noel can see he ain't so bad at all. But he stays in there and runs to the other side.

"It's on my *comb!*"

"He's all right," I say, moving my hand in closer from the side. He's in the corner now. "He's coming out."

"No—now!" Noel says, and she grabs my wrist and shoots my hand at the roach. The shelf breaks and the glass falls every which way. All that noise almost cuts off the feeling for a second. But then it comes—like somebody left a screwdriver in the fire and then jammed it between my last two fingers.

"What the fuck you doing, bitch?" The blood's coming now. The glass cut me a track on both sides of my hand, and it fills up quick and starts running like a motherfucker. I squeeze my other hand into it but it just runs down my thumb and drips into the sink.

Noel reaches for it but I pull it away. "Oh God, Jake. How bad is it?"

"Don't touch me," I say. I grab that little white towel she uses on her face and press it into the cut.

"I don't know what I was doing." She tries to pull my arm so she can see.

I pull back. The towel's going red. "Worrying about your goddamn hair, that's what you doing." Last week she went out and spent sixty bucks to get it straightened and she's been fussing with it ever since. "Little roach gonna eat your comb or something." I leave her in the bathroom.

"I just like my place clean," she says. "It's gotta be clean if we're gonna do this right."

I can't sit down, just keep moving, to the door and back, holding my hand tight. "Then clean it up," I say. "You the woman, ain't you?"

"Don't start that," she says, standing by the bed now. "You ain't exactly bringing all the money home."

I stop and look at her. My hands are no good now, only thing I can do is squeeze them tighter. "Ain't nothing *I* did that got my hours cut," I say. I hold my hands up. "You got so much money, why don't you gimme some to get this shit fixed?"

The blood's down my arm now, and the towel's going red. Noel walks over and tries to touch my other hand. I lift my elbow and keep her off. My hand is hot. "Come on," she says, "let's get you some ice."

She gets a plastic bag and goes to the fridge. She looks back at me. "Just sit there a second."

"Just get it," I say.

She ties off the bag. "Hold it tight. This will slow it down."

I press it in. It's colder than a motherfucker, even with the towel still on. No way I'm falling back asleep now. I look outside and see the black's getting a little blue. "Well ain't this a great goddamn morning."

"I'm sorry, Jake," Noel says, and she moves a little closer.

"Don't gimme that," I say, walking past her, to that little window.

She follows me. I'm looking out, but I can feel her behind me. "I ain't been myself lately," she says. "Feels like I'm going through the days just trying to—"

"Well who you *been* then?" I say. The ice keeps getting colder.

"Listen to me," she says. She breathes in big. "I don't know what's going on at that office. Everybody's—"

"Then you better get your ass down there and find out," I say. "They ain't gonna keep paying you to get sick." The ice almost hurts worse than that cut now. I reach up and take that piece of cardboard off the window, the same one I put there when I got this room to keep folk from looking in. I hear a car going down the street, probably headed to the freeway, but I can't see it through the glass. Only thing I can make out is a crow in the next lot, picking at a bag full-up of something somebody left for nobody at all.

"Jake!" she says. "You don't understand what's going on!"

"What you want me to understand?" I look over my shoulder. "What?" I turn back to the window. "You fuck up my hand and act like *you're* the one can't go to work. Am I supposed to wipe your nose for you while you sit up here all day 'cause your belly's aching?"

"I just said I didn't mean it."

"Well why don't you stop yapping and start dressing?" I say. "Get an early start down there today." The crow keeps picking at the bag, faster now, like he smells something good.

"Going early ain't gonna do nothing," she says. "They know, Jake."

I turn around. My hand's getting numb. "Know what?"

She bites down on her lip and looks at the floor. "I'm gonna get cut loose."

"Since when?" I say. "I thought you was doing fine down there."

"Everybody knows I got hired straight out of George's hall," she says. "And now I got this baby coming. You should see it—they're all looking at me like I'm getting set to slap on that county crown."

Something falls out of the bag outside, rings like glass, bounces a couple times and rolls away. I look out there but I can't see it, and the crow's gone. "Shit, Noel. What the hell you care what those folks think?"

"I *don't* care," she says. "I just want the job."

"Then go on in."

She looks at the floor again, and she starts putting a hand through her hair. "Not today."

"You see what I'm saying?" I go to the sink by the fridge. The ice is starting to drip. "There's no talking to you sometimes."

She follows me. "I got to think some things out. I don't know how else to say it."

I lift up the ice and the towel. There's a slot between those fingers could fit a quarter—gonna take more than some Band-Aid. I throw Noel's rag in the sink, roll up some paper towels and tie them back around my hand tight as I can, then put the ice back on. "Well go think on it at the county office," I say. "Get yourself down there if you don't want nobody looking at you. You'll be just like everybody else."

"*Fuck* you, Jake. I ain't collecting that shit."

I walk past her and pick up my pants by the bed. "Too good for it, ain't you?"

"Wouldn't need it if you was working better." She folds her arms across her chest. "You think you're such a man stepping into them pants? How about taking care of your woman?"

I pull the zipper. "Don't you go thinking I can't walk outta here," I say.

Her lips get tight and she cocks her head. "Where you gonna go?" I lace my shoes up as best I can with my hand like this. "You go now and you gonna need more than some four and a quarter job to open that door when you get back."

I stand up. "You oughta be thanking me you're getting to see any of my money at all."

She gives me a quick laugh like a little dog barking. "Who's just like everybody else *now*, Jake? Couple weeks ago it was 'Naw baby, I ain't like them motherfuckers at the hall. Gonna get you through—'"

"I know what I said. And I know who I am." I walk back over to the bathroom. The water's running over the sink. "I'm on my day off today, so I'm gonna do whatever the fuck I want." There's a little pool down on the floor, and I see the roach swimming in it. Probably just trying to get the fuck out of here, anyplace else than our damn bathroom. I stomp my foot down on him and splash the water every which way. Don't even look to see if I get him, just squeeze my hand again to feel it, and head for the front door. I look at Noel again, still with her arms folded, still with that head cocked, checking me up and down and shaking her head at all the water on my shoes. I open the door. "What you gonna do?"

* * *

When I stepped outside that morning, I didn't know where I'd end up—I was just getting *out*. Out of that goddamn basement hole. I was tired of smelling that vomit, tired of Noel acting so proud. Laurence had sniffed her, straight up, first time he met her, and he told me so too, but I didn't understand a thing until we got right down to the end of those forty weeks. *She ain't like you and me, Jake, ain't from down here.* I didn't want to believe it until it was right in my face, when Noel opened up that little book of hers and gave me the whole story about her momma, the real one. I didn't even want to believe my *own* story, and damn-sure didn't want her knowing it. That's why I never told her about what went down at the Ready Man that day she sliced my hand, after I ran into Laurence at the St. Al's.

Everybody knows St. Al's is where you go when they won't take you in noplace else. And the Birdhouse is the little clinic up inside. Passing the Angelus and heading into Parker's Alley, I can see the light in Chaka's window—maybe she can stitch me up.

I go to the door by the dumpster, and bang it good with my other hand. Just like that a rat jumps out of the dumpster, hits me smack in the chest and lands down on my foot. I kick at him, try to smash him up against the door, but all I get are some hurting toes. He shoots between my legs and gets away down the alley.

"Hey! Yo man, what you doing your kung-fu shit on that door for?"

I look over to the Wall Street end of the alley and see some big brother standing on the sidewalk, looking at me. The light ain't good, so I can't make out much. But when he starts walking, I know.

"Ain't nobody gonna hear you," he says. He takes a big step with his right foot, slides it out in front, and his shoulder kind of dips down with it. His right hand's in his pocket but his left one swings when he takes that step. It floats over, all the way to his right leg, then just floats back like some grandfather clock when he steps with his left. The left goes short, a quick step, and you can hear his shoe catch the street and see that shoulder come back up straight till he steps out with his right again and it dips and the left hand floats back over. It's Laurence. That's his strut.

I don't say anything, just stand by the door and watch him walk. Laurence gets almost close enough to spit on me, and then he stops and strokes his beard real quick, runs his fingers from his cheeks to his chin, from black to where it starts going gray. He pushes his glasses up on his nose and smiles big. "Found your way back down again, huh brother?"

I laugh. "Just trying to get me some St. Al's coffee."

"Well you ain't finding it back here," he says. "This door don't open no more." He turns around and starts that walk. "Come on with me if you want something better than that motor oil they're pouring upstairs. Man's got to have something decent to start him out in the morning." He puts a finger on his chin, right where some of that gray is, then points it at me. "What's your name again, brother?"

I tell him. "We were signing in at the Ready Man a couple months ago."

He stops and snaps his fingers. "Jake—that's right," he says. "I knew it." He makes a thinking-face and looks down a second, then back at me. "You the one was working them jobs with the *girl*. Everybody down at the hall been wondering where she took off to."

"Both of us found something full-time, so we ain't had no reason to come back."

"*Both* of you," Laurence says, nodding real slow and showing his teeth through that beard. He starts walking again, looking straight ahead. "You talking like you got yourself a little claim on that bitch. Guess you got her name too?"

"That ain't all I got," I say. "Check this shit out."

Laurence looks at my hand. "Chasing your ass out with a kitchen knife, huh? Ain't so bad, brother—least she didn't cut it off." He puts his hand on my shoulder and gives me a squeeze. "They shoulda had that in them track meets when we was back in school—hundred yards running from your woman when she gets crazy." He sticks his hand up in the air, points the finger and thumb like a gun. "Ready-set-go and all the little sisters start chasing after us with them frying pans." He laughs a little and we start walking again. "I know I woulda made out better with *my* old lady if I'd been in training," he says, looking down and shaking his head. Then he squeezes my shoulder again. "Let's go get you fixed up right."

I don't say nothing, don't tell him Noel ain't got a kitchen knife sharp enough to cut butter and that I sure as hell ain't *running* from her. I just go with him because he knows the way to Chaka now and I don't.

There's another door back down the alley, no handle or nothing. I walked right by it before—never seen anybody open it or even try. Laurence stops and goes in his pocket. "Got to open this one from the inside," he says.

He shows me his hand. Just three rocks, about as big as some pennies. "You watch," Laurence says. "Good as three little birdies."

You can tell a lot about a man watching him throw. That's one thing Daddy said that sticks with me from those Chicago days. He used to take me to the park with a glove and a ball, trying to make me a southpaw—he always said they were the best pitchers. But I never could do a damn thing with my left, so he taught me the right. We'd be there till dark sometimes, him kneeling behind me and holding my back foot in place and taking my arm all the way to the follow-through. After a while I could do it myself. You've got to be smooth, get that ball behind your head, that elbow back and roll those shoulders—don't want to look like some girl when you're throwing. Daddy would have liked Laurence, because he's a lefty, and he's got that motion down perfect. Laurence hits Chaka's window smack in the middle three times. The door creaks like a train coming in and he hops back.

Chaka sticks her head out, gives Laurence a smile. Her teeth just about sparkle off her dark skin, bright as her uniform. "Howdy," she says to him. "I got someone upstairs." Behind her, inside, it's noisy with humming, heaters or boilers or something going all-out. "I got to run—just meet me up there," she says, and swings back around. A couple of her braids fall loose from where they're wrapped up, and I see the colors she's got worked in on the ends.

I follow Laurence through the boilers until we get to some stairs. At the top there's a door and then we're in a hallway lit worse than the alley. "Where we going?" I say.

He doesn't even break stride. "Just keep following me."

We go through another door and see Chaka over on the other side of the room, bending over some white dude sitting in a chair. He's all in black. She takes a little something out of his mouth, straightens up and holds it in front of her face. Some staff here come and go quick as matches on a windy day. Dealing with all these crazy motherfuckers, you got to be a little crazy yourself to keep from burning out, but Chaka's kept on for long as I can remember.

Looks like somebody took some paint and a hammer to this room since the last time I was down. There's a couple benches now for folks to wait in, up against the walls where the old metal fold-ups used to be. And the walls have a fresh coat, so you can't see the marks from the chairs or any of the whacked shit folks would write when they were sitting in here. These benches could even be church pews, with this nice red cushion on the seat. Laurence and I sit down near the white guy, and I watch the sister with that little thing in her hand. She's over by the window now, holding it out in front of her again. Looking through that window I can see the building across the alley and that escape ladder over there with them steps missing.

Laurence slides down in the bench and puts his hands behind his head. He looks at the white dude and then at the sister. "Taking care of God's own this morning, huh Chaka?"

"Don't you know it," she says. She winks at Laurence, then she looks at the white guy like she's about to say she's sorry for something. "Ninety-eight point five," she says, holding out that stick and walking over to him. Her voice is high but it ain't soft, and I can tell she didn't come up in Oakland. Those i's give her away, just like my Auntie Thelma in Mississippi. *How you do, chi-i-i-ld?*

She stands in front of the white guy. "You'd be hotter if you'd just chased a pretty woman around the corner, Father Riley."

Laurence gets a laugh out of that but Riley's face is real still, like Chaka didn't say nothing. Young-looking too, maybe older than me, but still awful young to be wearing that collar. If you ask me, a man needs to get around the world a little before he zips up into one of those.

"I found my man Jake out doing a little early morning exercise, Chaka," Laurence says, slapping my back, maybe trying to jump-start me a smile. "Getting his miles in, shaping up to go a few rounds with his old lady once that hand of his heals up. I told him you'd give him some of that good coffee and wrap him up right."

"No one's brought me my coffee yet, miss," Riley says, shaking his head and grinning. He's got a red beard that matches his hair, and they both could use a trip to the barber's. His eyes are blue, and he blinks them a couple times and breathes in real big. "I think that instrument you used is mistaken. I'd like you to take it again."

Chaka looks right at me and pulls the air with her hand. "Come on, mister Jake," she says, and heads to that little back room with the big glass window. She walks quick, and before I even stand up she's in there and yelling back out. "You keep the holy man nice and cool, got that, Laurence? Let's hurry it up, Jake!"

I get up from the bench and I hear Laurence start in. "So mister Pope Riley, what's the Big Man been telling you lately?"

Chaka's in front of the sink, pulling things out of the cabinets. I watch her from the doorway. She takes out a long flat box, slaps it down, takes out a couple little bottles, sets them smack on the table almost hard enough to break. Those loose braids bounce on her back, and she's pretty, all in a huff like this. "Watch them bottles," I say, "or we gonna need another nurse in here."

She closes the cabinet doors real slow, one hand on each, right at the same time. She folds her arms over her chest. "You gonna tell me how to do my job too?" She picks up the box and points at me. "It's just lucky Laurence brought you up. Now sit down."

I keep quiet while she works on my hand. She cuts off the towels, wipes it clean, and looks at it with some kind of magnifying glass. I hold still. No more blood coming like before. She gets another bottle out of the box and sprays it right in. Stings like a motherfucker, but I bite my lip.

She looks at me. "How'd you get this glass in here?"

"Oh, you know," I say. It's going a little numb in there. Chaka takes some tweezers out of the box. "Just keeping the place clean, washing a few dishes. Shoulda done like my girl and worn those gloves."

"Right," she says. She moves in close with that eyeglass right by her nose and those tweezers right under it. "You came awful close to needing stitches, you know."

I close my hand. "I had it stuck under my arm the whole way down here," I say. "You don't wanna get your nose too close."

Chaka straightens up and lets out a little laugh like she's shushing me. "You better believe I smelled a lot worse in this place," she says. "At least you didn't have it up your ass. Now give it here." She takes me by the wrist. She don't have no Auntie Thelma grip, her fingers come around nice and slow and just strong enough to hold me still. They're warm, and I relax a little. But I wait. I make her put the tweezers down and un-ball my fist. I make her peel my fingers back just so I know that first touch on my wrist wasn't some accident.

She says she's gonna keep her hand there to keep mine steady. "At least you got some reason to be in here," she says. "Not like our man Riley out there, coming in every time he's fixing to sneeze, like I got his hankie waiting for him."

"That dude one of the St. Al's priests?"

"Thinks he's way beyond that." She picks up the tweezers again. "All right, just you look away now and try not to think about your hand."

I turn my head to the door. I can't see Laurence but I can hear him now out on that bench. "*Kid?*" he says. "All this time and you never told me the pope had a kid of his own?"

Chaka takes something out of my hand, and it's all I can do not to shout out till that pain passes. "One more little piece," she says, and I bite down on my lip again, waiting. "You shoulda heard that Riley first time he come down to St. Al's. We all knew he was special all right, but not the way he had in mind. Wouldn't take a mat—wanted his own bed and shower and the rest. Said a man in his position deserves a little special treatment." I feel the glass come out. "There it is," Chaka says. "That's the one."

She holds it up. I don't think I could even see it if it wasn't catching the light like it is. Don't know how something so small can feel that sharp. Chaka gets up and brings back the bottles and a roll of tape. "What sort of position this dude say he's in?" I say.

"Can't you tell? He's the pope," she says, getting a little rhythm going. "His eminence, the Rome Gnome, back again from the Vat-i-can. Just walking the streets of Oakland, spending a little time with the *people*." She shakes her head and laughs to herself while she opens the bottle up. "Tell you the truth, I feel pretty bad for the man. A fish that far out of water don't have much hope, if you ask me." She takes my hand again and her grip feels nice, good enough to take away the sting when she puts on the yellow stuff from the bottle. "That first day he was here—first half-hour, really—all he could tell us was the pope needs to be treated right, the pope needs his own place. Broken record in a jukebox with the wires all crossed up. Most times somebody like him comes in here, we call over to the sixth floor at Sinai and try to get them a time with the doc. But come the summertime they got so many folks up there they don't do assessments except on involuntaries. So we thought we'd try to get his parents to pick him up if we could. Somebody at the desk tracked them down clear out in Omaha or one of those corn towns, said this lady answered and got real quiet when they asked her if she knew her son was walking around homeless in California. Lady didn't say another word, just hung up and didn't pick up again when they kept calling back."

Chaka keeps working on my hand while she finishes the story. I hear Laurence again, but I can't make it out. She wraps me with gauze, from my wrist all the way to my fingertips. She tells me the pope dude gets under her skin sometimes but she don't mind talking to him. "Mighty tough thing when your own parents make like they never even heard of you just because you're in a fix," she says. "Mighty tough." She wraps some tape to hold the gauze. "And most folks here ain't got my patience with him. Next time he goes asking for the pope's private room they gonna put him out and let him find one his own self."

Chaka finishes and I stand up and tell her thanks. She gives me some of that gauze and tape and tells me what to do with my hand for the next couple days. Then she snaps her fingers and puts her hand on my chest. "Hold on," she says. "I forgot to get you some coffee."

Laurence was right. Before it even hits my lips I know it's *good*, a hell of a lot better than anything you can get waiting in a line downtown, even better than the kind Noel makes. Doesn't even need cream or sugar. Chaka watches me take a couple sips. "Thanks now," I say. "Real nice of you."

She folds her arms and nods back at me, then smiles a little. "You a handsome man, mister Jake. What you got troubles with your woman for?"

I take another sip. I like Chaka's braids. And that ass of hers sure would give me something more to grab than what Noel's got.

Right then something beeps in the waiting room, sharp like an alarm clock. Laurence is headed toward us, holding a pager. I didn't even know he had one, but it don't surprise me. I've seen the billboards all over the city—they're cheaper than phones now, especially for folks who ain't always in the same place from one month to the next. "Damn Jake, you got a cast on there or what?" he says. "Your old lady ain't gonna be messing with you no more." Then he looks at Chaka and holds up the pager. "Gotta use your phone," he says, and pats her on the shoulder when he walks to the back of the room. "But Riley's still out there waiting on you to take his holy temperature again."

I follow Chaka back into the waiting room. Riley is sitting in the same place on the bench, hands folded on his stomach. He's looking straight ahead, maybe out at that escape ladder or maybe at nothing at all.

"Everyone deserves to be taken care of," he says. "Especially—"

"Sing it again, padre," Chaka says, and sticks the thermometer right in his mouth. He looks up at her but she doesn't break stride, just spin-pivots right back around and comes toward me. "God's number one man on the planet deserves better than what we got at St. Al's. I keep telling you Riley—you keep up that song, you gonna be shaking a cup out on that *street*."

I hear the phone hang up. I turn around and there's Laurence, pointing at my coffee. "Finish it up," he says. "We got ourselves a big ticket."

"You leaving already?" Chaka says to him. I'm standing in the doorway between them. "You ain't even had your coffee yet."

"I'll make it up to you," Laurence says, and slides right between me and Chaka. "George told me that man Franklin on the east side just called in a job and wanted me on it."

Chaka folds her arms again, and her nose wrinkles, like she smells something. "Ain't he the one who worked you till you dropped last time?"

"Don't matter," Laurence says. He walks over to the side door where we came in and opens it. "That man *pays*, Chaka. I ain't passing it up. Neither is Jake." He gives me a quick wink then looks back at Chaka. "You gonna be at the meeting on Friday?"

Chaka cocks her head. "Ain't you the funny man today. Always telling me one day at a time and here you are talking all the way into Friday. Question is, are *you* gonna be there? Wasn't too long ago you was at those meetings regular as an Ex-Lax addict at the john."

Laurence smiles big. "Only thing that keeps me away is work," he says. "You know that. Now I told you to page me if you're in trouble. You still gonna do that, right?"

"I know the number," Chaka says. Then she looks at me. "So you pick up jobs down at the hall too, huh?"

"Not like I used to," I say, taking the last sip of my coffee. "I got a restaurant gig that keeps me floating."

"And your woman's treating you like this?" Chaka puts her hand on my arm and looks over at Laurence. Her fingers come around nice and slow just like they did when she was fixing my hand. "How many jobs does she want a man to have? I don't understand that sister at all."

"You ain't the only one," Laurence says. He looks at me. "Come on, our clock's ticking."

Chaka lets go of my arm, and I tell her thanks. No time for nothing more. I get one last look at Riley with the collar before I walk out. He's still looking out that window, and now the side of his mouth is going, even with the thermometer in, like he's trying to talk it into giving him a fever. Me and Laurence go out the way we came, through the boiler room and into the alley.

Out on the street, Laurence tells me about Chaka, says that wasn't even her name before she got here. He tells me he met her in AA at St. Al's, and I know the rule: *Talk from the meeting stays at the meeting.* I know, but I ain't gonna stop him from breaking it. I want to hear something, even if Laurence has something with her on the side. Even if he's just riffing, making shit up like those street preachers and shouting to make it sound good, I need to hear something.

We pick up the pace, hustle-step it past the Angelus on our way to the hall, and Laurence spins the story out fast, lets it zoom-clack along like the cars up above the Cliffs. Tells me about this girl Constance from some town down South who went drinking whisky like soda pop after her momma found out why she was looking a little fat in the belly. She and her boyfriend hopped a train before her momma got a chance to shoot one of them, and by the time it pulled into Oakland, Connie was going by Chaka. She went and holed up in the Luby, that shelter where women run from their men, until about six months later when the state took her baby and sent her to the desert to get clean.

"Girl got herself some church too," Laurence says. "I saw her in that St. Al's meeting, but I was on my way out, tired of hearing all them stories of motherfuckers shooting up and throwing up and waking up locked-up. If you get something out of it, good for you. And Chaka did. But it ain't for me. I've got to keep working."

We're coming up on Battery now, just a couple blocks from the hall. We cross under the freeway, and there's a whole mess of condos under here like always.

"Check this out," Laurence says, hopping off the curb, keeping that fast clip going. "My man Pope Riley just told me about this kid he sees every day in the park. You probably ain't gonna believe it but I bet it's true. He tells me he's got blond hair just like his own brother's, just sitting there with his momma on a bench, same time every day. And you know what that dude does? Brings the boy some food." Laurence stops dead right in the street, slaps me in the gut. "Pockets on a robe like his hold plenty of extras from St. Al's kitchen."

I smack his hand away. I can see those green doors from here. "Sounds like that dude ain't so fucked in the head."

"Yeah well then he started in about how the kid was his kid because all kids are God's kids. And he's God's number one man, of course, but he can't get Chaka to believe him yet." Laurence laughs a little and shakes his head. "But you got something there, Jake—you never know with him. The dude made me think about what I got to do today."

I stop, look at the light flashing off his glasses. "You going somewhere you ain't told me about? I thought we had a ticket waiting for us."

Laurence hops up on the curb. "Come on," he says. "You know what I'm talking about." I hustle to catch up to him. He holds his hands up, makes them into fists and squeezes so hard they shake. "I just got to roll up the sleeves, put in the hours. And then, first week of the month, I take a little stroll downtown, right past the county office and all those fools crying at their caseworkers. Right past it and into the post office. Take out a few bills, make out an order for the kids and send it certified." He looks at me and smiles, pushes his glasses up again. "Just like that—everybody's happy. She gets her money, and I stay out of that desert and keep clocking the hours till that year comes around."

"You starting to sound like Noel," I say, just to see how Laurence will take it. "Talking about those folks on the county like that."

He shakes me off. "Well if I do, it ain't because I'm like her. You telling me you ain't figured out where that girl's from yet?"

Ain't no time for that one now. One of the dudes standing in front of the hall starts yelling Laurence's name and waving us in. "*Vamos!* George calling for you!" Laurence takes off running, and I'm right behind.

He slaps hands with the Mexican who was yelling to him. I hardly recognize any of these dudes standing out here today, except for that one in the black jacket. But George told me they got so many folks going in and out of this place it's like a new hall every month.

The Mexican guy's standing right by those green doors now, got a pack on his shoulder and a Lakers hat on his head. I can tell he's older than me but he's damn smiley and he looks like he ain't had to shave more than twice his whole life. Laurence catches his breath a second before he can say anything. "Gus-tav-o," he says, "My main man Gus, looking out for me like always." He says something in Spanish, and Gustavo laughs and talks back. They finish their shake and Laurence grabs the door handle.

Gustavo sticks his foot right at the bottom of the door and blocks it. "George say you need for one person to help you on the job."

Laurence pats him on the shoulder. "Ain't you got yourself a ticket yet?" He points at me. "I already told this brother he's on it."

Gustavo ain't so smiley no more. He looks at me. I'm still catching my breath. He shifts his pack a little and sticks his chin out my way. "What happen your hand?"

"It ain't nothing," I say, and look at Laurence. "We gonna go to work today or what?"

"As long as you can handle it," he says. He looks at Gustavo till the dude pulls his foot away, then he opens the door.

George is right there inside, standing at the desk with Blue. He's got those little glasses on, and a tie, like always. Blue's in that real high chair he's got so he can meet you eye-to-eye even if he's sitting. George looks at us and pulls off his glasses. "Jake," he says, looking surprised. "Didn't know when we were going to see you down here again." He puts out his hand.

"I found myself something steady," I say, putting mine out too. "But I got me a day off today."

He puts his hand down on the desk. "What you got there?"

It's always loud as a motherfucker in here, especially early mornings before most of the jobs go out. But right then it feels like it gets quiet. I look at my hand. Then I look over at Blue. He's looking back. He's still got that cast on his own hand from when the brother in the black jacket tried to pull a Mike Tyson on him about getting put on restriction. I look at George and shrug my shoulders. "It's nothing to talk about."

Laurence gives a little laugh. "The brother *wishes* he got something like that," he says, and he points over at Blue's cast. "That would sure keep the bitch off him next time."

Blue laughs, and George does that thing where he turns his head and waves his hand in front of him like he's smelling something bad. "All right," he says. "I don't have time to jaw with you fellas this morning."

That's fine with me, I think. George puts those glasses back on and picks up two tickets from the desk. I just want to get *doing* something today, especially if it will get a little sweat going and take my mind off my hand and everything. He looks at Laurence. "Mr. Franklin just called in five minutes ago," he says, "wondering when the hell you're getting out there. You know how he is. Now who you want with you?"

Laurence points his thumb at me. "What you think this brother's standing here for?"

George pulls a face like he's smelling something again. He looks at Blue. "Did you hear that right?" Blue says he's not sure, and George looks at Laurence again. "We're talking about *Franklin*. I thought I told you, the man wants a gravel drive-way put down—" I hear the door open behind me, and I turn around and see Gustavo come in. George looks up at him for a second and then back at Laurence. "And a garden bed."

"Just give it to me," I say, and clap my hands together. Doesn't even hurt no more. "I'm good to go."

"Jake," George says, shaking his head just a little. "The man's got twenty yards of gravel and ten yards of soil. Needs one man on a shovel and the other running the wheelbarrow. You can't do that work one-handed."

"Let me get out there," I say, and reach for the tickets.

George snatches them up. He looks over my shoulder. "Gustavo, you ready to go?" He takes his pen out of his pocket, then he looks at Laurence. "You've worked with him before, right?"

"Oh yeah," Laurence says. "Little dude's a good worker, as long I'm helping him with the English."

I look at Laurence when he's saying that, but he's talking straight to George, like he's on a string from that brother's tie. Just for a second I feel like reaching over and knocking their heads together, but Gustavo slides right between me and Laurence. He doesn't say nothing, just puts his hand out over the desk. He's smelling-close, got about half a bottle of Aqua Velva or something on him, and if I wasn't awake before, I sure am now. George puts a ticket in his hand and the other in Laurence's. Gustavo folds it up real quick into his pocket and takes a step back. His big motherfucking pack catches me right in the chest—bangs me like he's got some bricks in there. I put both my hands on that pack and push. Gustavo goes right up against the door like a hockey player done forgot how to skate, and his pack comes off his shoulder.

Now I *know* it's quiet—ain't no feeling. Folks here always love to watch two people throw-down. Gustavo looks at his pack and then he looks at me. His eyes go small.

Laurence quick-steps right over in front of me, puts both hands on my shoulders, and talks low. "Don't start this shit now, Jake," he says. "I got a job to get to."

"*Fuck* your job," I say.

I hear somebody yell at Laurence to let 'em get it on, and then some more folk after that. It gets louder. But he doesn't budge. "You ain't getting no work fighting here," he says. "You know George will put your ass on restriction."

"Take it out of my hall, Jake!" George says. "Gustavo, you'd better—"

I knock Laurence's hands off my shoulders and turn around to the desk. "Don't tell me about *your* motherfucking hall," I say, pointing at George. "You think that tie lets you give my job to some Mexican?" I feel Laurence's hand on my arm but I shoot my elbow up quick and shake it off. I step up and slap my hand down on the desk. "I want to make some motherfucking money."

Blue jumps out of his chair and looks at George, like he's ready to whack me with that cast just as soon as George gives the word. But George just keeps looking at me and puts his hands on his hips. "One week, Jake," he says, real calm now. "Get out of here."

This time I let Laurence pull me back. Folks are still making noise but he's loud enough for me to hear him. "Tell you what," he says. "You're gonna walk right out this door with me now, go get yourself some breakfast across the street, and cool out."

George and Blue are coming around the desk toward the doors. The noise keeps up. George points at me while he's walking. "Get going."

Me and Laurence turn around toward the doors. Folks are circled up now. Gustavo is right in the middle, still looking at me. Some other Mexican dude is holding his pack. I look back at him.

"Gustavo!" George says.

"Clock's still ticking," Laurence says to me. "Let's go." He walks in front of me toward the doors.

"Gustavo! I want to talk to you," George says.

Gustavo moves out of Laurence's way, but not much. He keeps his eyes on me. I walk by, smelling-close. Laurence says something and folks start to move away from the door. I can still feel those little eyes behind me.

Then it just happens. I hear him spit, and I feel it stick right to the back of my head, and just like that, before I even look, I cock my hand over to my left side and squeeze it till it burns, whip it back across my body, turn my shoulders and hips and get everything into it, everything I've got, but it misses Gustavo and cracks George right in the jaw.

George falls back. Blue catches him. There's nothing I can do now—don't matter who I was trying to hit.

Nobody tries to stop me when I run out. I go as fast as I can up Battery, slip under the freeway and stay out of the streets, weave through the shadows in the alleys till I'm good and far gone.

* * *

That cut on my hand closed itself up pretty quick after I hit George. Chaka got all the glass out, so it just needed some time. I'd left without my key that morning so I had to waste the whole day walking around trying not to look at folks with kids, till Noel got home and I talked her into letting me back in. She didn't put up a fight—I think she felt mighty bad about cutting me, especially when I told her it cost me a ticket at the hall. And we both knew I had to get to the restaurant the next day, because there wasn't no sense in me taking a chance on losing the hours I still had left there. I remember it didn't take her but a couple of minutes to sit me down with some more ice and then head back out the door to get some fresh wrap and patches. And soon as that door closed, I started looking for her little book. Under the bed, in the pillowcases, behind the toilet, in the freezer, and all through her underwear. I wanted that calendar, wanted to see everything she was putting down. But she never left it behind, not until a couple months later.

'Fessing-up is easy with folk like Cheryl. They're soft, and they let you off so easy you know you could go back and run the whole thing over again. But Noel ain't like that, and that's why I never told her about hitting George. As soon as the cut closed up, she was on me to go back to the hall, but I kept telling her George wouldn't even let me sign in until the hand was ready to put in eight hours of man's work. But I didn't tell her what I thought he'd do if he even saw me any- where on Battery. I just kept it all to myself because I know sometimes when you open up, stories just keep coming and you end up letting something slip that you didn't want nobody to know.

"'Is he getting you a ring soon?'" Noel says, making her voice high and sounding like some bird. It's Monday morning, and she's getting ready to go in to that office. It's my day off from the restaurant, and last night I told her I'd go looking for work. But now I just feel like sleeping, and her yapping ain't helping that at all.

"That's all I heard from her last week," Noel says. I turn over, but I still hear her walk into the bathroom and start brushing her hair. "Asking me what plans I got. All this stuff that's none of her goddamned business."

Here we go. Crying about the white lady who's training her again. I know I can either lie here and pretend I don't hear or try to smooth her out a little so she doesn't go through the whole day like this. So I sit up and put my feet on the floor. "Why don't you just talk to the lady?" I say. "Makes the time go by quicker."

I hear the medicine cabinet close and she comes out, walks to the fridge. She looks good, like she usually does when she's going to work. She's wearing a pink shirt and those white pants that fit real nice—the job-service place the folks at Sal's Army told me about set her up pretty good. They called it Chrysalis, but I didn't see no records at all. She pours herself some milk. "It's only quicker if it's *real* talk. You oughta come in and hear her yourself, Jake. Always going on like she's trying to be my friend." She takes a quick swallow and puts the cup back in the fridge. "One of these days I'm gonna tell her to shut up and just teach me how to do the *work*. Just the work, lady."

I never thought I'd hear a woman complain about talking too much. But when she's in one of her little nasty spells, Noel would be the one to do it. "Why don't you just have a little fun with it?" I say. "Make up some story and keep it going."

"Make it up why? I got something to be 'shamed of?"

I shake my head. "Just tell her what she wants to hear."

"What she wants to hear." Noel looks at me a second and gives me a laugh that comes out like a cough. Then she walks past me, picks up her pocketbook, and stands by the door. "You mean that I'm just like her? Got me a nice big house like the kind I'm typing-in about every damn day with her breathing over my shoulder? She wouldn't believe it—even if it were true, Jake. She just thinks I'm token."

"Then fuck her," I say. "Why you care what she thinks?"

"'Cause it ain't just *her* thinking it," Noel says. "I see the way she's talking to the other folk there. They all think I'm a county queen."

I put my elbows up on my knees and my face in my hands. I take a big breath and let it out slow. "I don't know why I got to keep hearing this," I say, and look up at her. "There ain't no harm being on the county while you're having your kid. It ain't like they gonna want a piece of him right when he comes out."

"Yeah but they want a piece back from *me*," she says, putting her finger on her chest. "And back from you too. You ain't been around these folks like I have, Jake. I even heard this shit from my own momma." Noel opens up her pocketbook and takes out her keys. They jingle-sing in her hand. "She and her girlfriends crying about paying taxes for some sister down the street who was having a kid. Crying about having to put that sister up on the stay-out-of-school scholarship, and all the time some of them bitches know *they* was on the county themselves a few years back."

I clap my hands together and sit up straight. "That's what I'm saying, baby—easy as that. You just chime right in."

Noel gives me a frown. "The lady ain't that stupid," she says. "They got the spotlight on me. Don't make no difference anyway—they all gonna believe what they want to."

She opens the door and sticks her key in the outside lock. I tell her to hold on. "Let me come down there and give that white lady a talking-to," I say, squeezing my hand into a fist and clapping it into my other hand. "Smack a little sense into her about what she wants to believe."

I say it just to get a laugh out of her, just to get that nasty look off her face.

She puts her hands on her hips. "Ain't you got nothing better to do?" Her keys just hang there in the lock, swinging, jingle-singing. "If your hand's feeling that good why don't you get down to the hall and go to work?"

"Look, Noel," I say, unballing my hand and then squeezing it a couple times so she can see, "I done *told* you it ain't ready for—"

"You done told me, you done told me," she says, smacking the door. "I'm tired of it. I wanna hear something else, Jake."

"Sounds like you starting to take after that white lady pretty good," I say. "Now it's *you* only wants to hear what you wanna hear." Now she's got me going. Now I'm starting to let it out. "You want something else, sit your ass down and I'll give you a couple hours of something else. A little story I call, 'My daddy was a—'"

"Put your pants on!" Noel's face gets darker and her eyes open real big. "You're such a goddamn man, get outta bed and put 'em on."

I stay put. "Just get going, Noel. Don't start with this."

"I know what I'm gonna do," she says, pointing at me. "First thing when I get to the office I'm calling up George." She puts her hand on her cheek like a phone. "'Yeah, just put him on something nice and easy. You know he's got that little *hand* to watch out for—'"

I get up. I grab my pants from in front of the bed. "I'm up."

"About time," she says, and shuts the door. I hear the lock turn.

I take the 16 all the way to the freeway overpass, and get off just like usual, at Fifth and Battery, just like I'm going to the hall. The fog's real low and thick today, like it might as well be raining, and the wind makes sure that wet cold gets all the way to the bone. I look but I can't make out much happening down by the hall. Right then a van goes past me, a big white one with the back doors banging. Heads down Battery toward the hall, and the brake lights come on but it doesn't stop. There's always a few guys hanging around outside who never sign in—some crowing, some just drinking. The crows are mostly Mexicans with no ID, but I've seen some brothers and white guys doing it too, the ones who got Alcatrazzed by George. Folks call them crows because those dudes are living off the scraps. Standing out there, *hey hey HEY right here man* at every van or pickup that goes by, all of them at once and then they all run at it when it stops and start shouldering to get position so the man behind the wheel will tell them go on get in the back. I've seen them, and I've heard. That dude I know who always wears the black jacket was out there crowing for a good month when he got put on restriction for drinking in that old lady's house. He told me that was a hard month all right. Some days you got to jump at the first shit job you can, 'cause you don't know what else is coming down the street. Most times you've got to take that four-an-hour, he said, sometimes three, because if you don't the Mexicans will and you'll just be standing on the sidewalk, and soon enough you'll be back at the shelter with nothing to show for your day. Unless of course you get to drinking—then you got something. I can't see them from here, but I'm guessing it's just the drunks out there this morning. That's why the van doesn't stop. It's after eight, pretty late to be picking up work, so maybe all the crows already found something, or maybe they just gave up and figured it's gonna rain soon enough anyway.

It's been a couple months, but not long enough. I look at my hand. The scar doesn't look too bad anymore, just a line up and down between my last two fingers. Nobody would even see if they didn't know to look.

I squeeze it. Just to see how it feels. I ball it up and squeeze tight until the nail on my little finger is pressing right into the scar. I press a little harder until it stings, then harder again until it feels like the nail could break through if I'd just push it. For a second I think I could just open it up at the bottom and let all the bad blood slip out, just one little push that wouldn't hurt so much because it'd be so good to get it out. But I stop. It ain't no blister. Opening it up doesn't make no sense—I've got to give it time.

I take the calendar out of my pocket. I probably grabbed it on the way out because I could hear Noel in my head the whole time I was getting dressed, all the way till I pulled the knots tight on my shoes. When she said she was gonna call George, I knew she'd do it if I pushed her. Don't want her finding out, if I can help it.

I look down the sidewalk again. I know I could crawl through those green doors and start crying to George to let me sign in again. Could even work myself up so I come on like one of those dudes in recovery doing their Ninth Step, coming back and trying to set things straight. *O Lord, George—Jesus done showed me how I fucked up all right. Can you find your way to giving me another chance, brother?* But who knows if he'd call the cops on my ass—it ain't been all that long. Or he could just laugh me back outside again. I know I could stand out there and wait on another van to come by and give me a shot at making two-fifty an hour. I know I could wait all day for it, too, on a day like today.

So I start walking. Turn around and start walking. To the other end of downtown, looking for I don't know what, just anything else.

* * *

There's a store on Second and Olive that's got just about every little thing you can think of, and when I come up on it I get to feeling mighty hungry all of a sudden. There's a sign in the window—best dim sum. Don't know for sure, but I'm guessing it's those little things in that heat box that look like little burritos. Right next to the corn dogs, but they don't get to spin like those do.

It's just a little store, four aisles, but Laurence has been stopping in here for cigarettes and candy bars for the longest time. For beers too, before he got clean.

The door's open and I can smell that stuff in the heat box before I even walk in. A little bell goes off when I step through and I look over at the man behind the register. He's reaching up and putting packs of cigarettes in those slots that hang right over the counter. He gives me a quick little nod and a smile. "How you this morning, sir?"

"Hey I'm all right," I say. "Just looking for a little something." I'd call him by his name but I ain't sure what it is. I think it's Ho. Laurence said the dude was Korean or Chinese or something. But I ain't too sure about that either. I don't know if 'Ho' means the same thing where this guy's from as it does to me, so it won't do me no good to call him that if it ain't his name. Not if I want to lift something out of here.

I walk the aisles and check out all the stuff. Like I said, they've got a little bit of everything. Razors, pantyhose, soap, toothbrushes, and even diapers. All kinds of food too—gum and candy bars, chips, beef jerkies, and nuts, and some fruits over on a little table next to the counter. I pick up a banana and an apple but they both feel too soft, so I go back and look at the candy. The fruit's too close to the man up there anyway—I don't know if I'm smooth enough anymore to take it right out from under him. Used to be, when I was running with Lydell, but not these days.

The candy's easier, and even if it's not much it's something to get me through the morning without having to go stand in some mission line downtown. I look at Ho. From where he's standing over there he can't see my hands, so I can slip three or four bars under my jacket, no problem.

I stand still and pretend like something back in the coolers—maybe all those forty-ouncers, since that's what the man's gonna think I want anyway—is catching my eye. I just try to keep cool, but right when I'm reaching I see the little lady coming out of the back room. She steps through the black plastic hanging down in the doorway and looks right at me, like she done sniffed me from all the way back there.

Some shelves are in the way so I can't see but one side of her short little self. Her sleeve is rolled up and her arm's got some muscle on it. She's got a little gray in her hair. I take my hand back and look at her, then give her a smile like she's the damn sunshine of my life. But she doesn't bite, she just looks over at her husband and says something I can't make out, some Asian stuff that don't sound a damn bit like English—or even like Spanish. Her face tightens up while she's saying it. Her eyes shoot over to me, then back at her man.

He shakes his head, says something back, and keeps filling the slots. Doesn't even break his rhythm.

But she talks again, louder. This time Ho looks over at me, just real quick, but it's enough. He shakes his head, waves her off until she goes back through the plastic. Once she's gone he starts stocking again. I know it's time for me to try to spread a little honey.

Walking toward the counter, I'm thinking of Lydell, his no-look. He couldn't shoot, but he could pass like a motherfucker. Nobody could stop it—he'd dribble right at you and lock your eyes into his, and before you knew it the pass would go right by you to some dude cutting to the hole for the dunk. Worst thing was, he'd always smile. Eyes going one way, hands going the other—he was so smooth you almost didn't feel bad you got burned.

"Hey, you seen my man Laurence come around this morning?" I say, putting one hand on the counter.

"No," he says. He quits stocking and gives me a thinking-face. His eyes go so small I wonder if he can still see out of them at all. "Who that?"

I laugh a little. "Aw come on now," I say. "You know Laurence. Tall brother with glasses and a beard. Got this real smooth way of walking." I step away from the counter and do the strut, just to the door and back.

Ho slaps the box and starts nodding his head real fast. His eyes open up and he smiles. "Oh yes, yes," he says. "Mr. Laurence. My best customer for many year." He points over to the coolers. "I saw him just two–three day ago, I said he need start drinking again keep me in business. My boy going to college someday."

He's a funny guy. That's good for me—makes it easy. I see he's got a pen in his shirt pocket. I keep smiling, pull that little calendar out of my back pocket, and ask him if I can borrow it a second. "Just wanna get something down here before I forget. Got me an interview later for a good steady job up at the market, pays overtime and everything. If I miss that, my old lady's gonna *kill* my ass." I laugh again while he's handing me the pen, just keep looking right in his eyes while I start to take it from him, putting my fingers down on the tip. Right in that little split-second when I feel him let go I let go too, quick-turn my hand to look like I'm trying to catch it, and flick it back over the counter and on the floor. I hear it bounce away.

"I'm sorry, man," I say. "Look at me—I don't get my coffee in the morning, I can't do a damn thing right."

"No, no," Ho says, looking down around his feet. "My mistake." He looks all the way over to the little swinging door that keeps folks from getting behind the counter with him. I sneak a quick look at the fruit, but I want to wait till he bends down to pick up the pen. But when he steps over there, he's limping, and I try a little more honey.

"Say there, big man," I say. "What'd you do to yourself?"

He stops short and puts his foot up on a little shelf behind the counter, pulls up his pant leg to his knee. He's got a cast down to his toes, and it looks pretty new to me, all bright white and clean. "My wife send a ghosts for my head, but he get my foot instead," he says, knocking right where the ankle is. "But not too bad—just sprain, not broken."

He starts telling me the story. I didn't ask him to, and I don't want this to take all day. I just want him to get the pen so I can put some fruit away. Hearing about some dude's church picnic makes me hungry enough to eat anything. But then he tells me about the women, and I know it's going to be real easy if I just wait.

"Very warm day on Saturday. All the ladies wearing shorts," he says, and gives me a little wink. "Except old ones like my wife." His foot's back on the floor now, and he's leaning over the counter on his elbows, with his hands folded under his chin. He tells me they had a volleyball game going, and he stacked his team with the prettiest ladies there. "I tell my wife it was for make me play harder," he says, "but she just look at me." He squints his eyes up and tightens his whole face like she must have been doing. "Sometimes your wife see right through you."

He was having himself a good old time, he says. Watching them girls bounce around after the ball, giving them a little pinch on one cheek or another when they made a good play, or even if they didn't. Halfway through the game one of them was backing up after a ball somebody hit deep. Ho was going after it too, and neither of them saw the other one coming. The girl tripped over his foot and hit her head on a rock, busted it wide open. Nobody wanted to play after that, so he packed up the net and everything. He says he'd just pulled one of them poles up out of the ground when his old lady hit him with that look again, only this time he could *feel* the motherfucker. "Here," he says, smacking his chest. "Knock out all the air. Make me step back and *pa!*" He holds his fists together and turns them down like he's breaking a pencil, makes some noise like a kid would do, playing like a gun was going off. "My foot go right in the hole. I look at my wife and she standing there watch me fall." He rubs his chin and leans in, talks soft. He says he saw a ghost or something like that—even heard it talk to him—when he was lying there on the ground. Damn thing told him he had it coming.

Just then I hear the plastic move in the back. It's a boy, maybe a teenage kid, and he looks like the man up here, from that black hair to the apron he's wearing. "Dad," the kid says. "Mom said there's a—"

The kid looks at me and shuts up. He talks just like a normal kid, doesn't have the accent like his daddy.

The man says something to him and waves him off.

The kid holds up his hands. "But Mom said I should—"

"Go!" the man says. The kid shrugs and turns around and starts to go back through the plastic. But the man yells one more time, this time in English. "Robert! You want do something, take these cigarette back." He points to the box on the counter. "Too many extra."

Robert walks up front. He moves fast and looks down. His shoes squeak a little on the floor. He's got the new black Nikes, the ones Jordan wears now. I wonder if the kid plays ball, or if he just made his daddy buy him the shoes to impress the ladies. He steps up to the counter and the man gives him two long boxes, one on top of the other. From the back side I can see little man Robert can't be much of a regular in the back—he's wearing nice pants instead of jeans under that apron, ain't got a stain on them that I can see.

The kid pulls the boxes in against his chest and walks to the back, still making that little squeaking with his shoes. The man folds his arms and shakes his head and watches him go through the plastic. He tells me the kid's supposed to be in school today, but his wife made him bring him in to help out. He turns around and grabs one of his crutches lying up against the wall. "'How you work with one leg?' she tell me." He makes his voice high, squawks like the old lady. "'What you carry?' She say we need a *man* help out."

He puts his hands down on the counter glass between us. There's some little display down at the end, with nickels and dimes stuck in it for little kids with no daddies or something like that. Right here under his hands there's some pictures looking up through the glass—the man here with his old lady and the boy when he wasn't no bigger than his daddy's leg. Looks like they're standing outside, right in front of this store. He looks up at me, turns his hands up. "This my whole job," he says. "This everything I can do."

"Hey my man," I say. "Everybody's old lady's got it in for them now and then." I point at his leg. "At least you got yourself a little break now. Get to keep her back there doing some real work."

He leans over the counter and taps his finger on the side of his head. "Still can look," he says, talking real soft. "Many pretty lady walk by and wave at me."

He's smiling now, and I'm getting itchy. It's been a little while. I check quick with the corner of my eye to see if anybody's coming out of the back, and I say it smooth as I can. "How about that pen?"

He goes down to get it. As soon as I get my hand around the apple the music hits like a bomb. Comes out of nowhere loud as a motherfucker, makes me almost knock the damn thing off the table. For a second I think the apple's got an alarm or something, so I put it down and check around. Nobody comes out of the back, and the man's still looking on the floor. The music's coming from an old white Pontiac outside.

I keep one eye on the counter and one on the back while I pick up the apple again. It's too big not to show in my jacket pocket, so I slip it inside on the right, suck in my gut, and press my arm in to hold it there. I give the zipper a tug, but it ain't half a second before it jams. The teeth are coming open. I tug it again but it won't move, so keep my gut in and my arm pressed tight.

The store bell rings. I look over at Ho behind the counter. He's up and holding that pen, but he's looking at the door.

This young brother walks in flipping a bottle cap. It jiggles in the air when he tosses it, doesn't fall straight like a quarter. Dude's got a sharp clean white sweatshirt, some jeans big enough to hide a couple kids in the pockets, and sneakers with the laces undone. Everything right off the rack. He looks at Ho and lifts his chin a little, and he says what's up to me. He doesn't come smelling-close but I know he's had something, even if his hair's brushed neat and he keeps his stride smooth. He goes over and opens up one of the cooler doors, starts looking around.

The music is still coming from that car. I can't make out the words but it sounds like one of those jams about I'm a bad motherfucker and my dick's so big I fuck three bitches at once so don't touch my gold or I'll bust a cap in your head. I used to keep up with that scene a little, but now I can't tell the shit apart, so I don't even bother. Most all of it still has good rhythm though, so usually I won't shut it off when it comes on the radio. I listen to it now for a couple seconds, and the beat helps me relax a little. It's all right.

I look at Ho again, and he's holding the pen out. The counter comes up right about to my chest, so I press up quick against it so he can't see. I don't think he'd be looking for me to take something, but maybe that's just because I'm being stupid, because it's been a while since I ran this game. Just looking at this guy, I'm not picking up anything like I might have when I knocked down a joint with Lydell. We could sniff the bust back then—somebody breathing quicker, or doing some job didn't need doing, or somebody behind the counter all of a sudden getting their hands down out of sight. But I ain't that sharp no more. Just looking at my man Ho here I wouldn't think he'd sniffed *me* yet, but I ain't so sure. And I know I'm feeling hungry enough to take a chance this morning.

I keep my right hand in place and take the pen with my left. I look at it a couple seconds, then I just tap it against my head and look across at the man. "Know what?" I say. "I think I'll just keep it up here. My old lady says I got to get sharper with remembering stuff anyhow." I hand it back to him.

The bell goes twice now, and I look over and see two more young brothers come in. Could still be in high school if they got somebody to make them go. First one looks like he could eat the little dude behind him for breakfast. Big guy, taller than the other dude by the coolers, taller than me. He ain't fat, but I bet he weighs 250 without even stepping on the scale. Wouldn't be the kind of guy to use it, because his face is all momma's boy. He's got a Detroit cap pulled down low in front and tilted heavy to the right.

The scrawny light-skinned brother gives the big guy a push in the back. "Yo, *De*-troit, go pick yourself out some juice or something," he says. His voice is high, and damn-sure louder than you'd think from a guy that small. The little dude is wearing a T-shirt with the sleeves cut off, so I can see he's got some sharp muscles, but he's still nothing the Detroit brother couldn't kill two times in two seconds if he got worked up enough. At least that's what I'd do if he pushed me again. But when he comes over to the counter, I know he's gonna start a little something with Ho, and maybe that will give me an alley to the candy bars and I'll be out the door.

"Yo dude," he says. "What you got that's hot?" He grabs the top edge of the counter with both hands and leans back, stretching himself out.

Ho smiles big and points over to the box by the window. "Dim sum very tasty," he says. "Take one with vegetable—"

The little brother looks at the ceiling a second and then cocks his head to the side. "I ain't talking about no motherfucking egg rolls," he says. "I want some *breakfast*. Pancakes, bacon, scrambled eggs—like that."

Ho shrugs his shoulders and keeps smiling. "Sorry, don't have that," he says. He takes a step back from the counter and starts moving with that gimp leg over to the heat box. "Here, you try one—"

The dude backhands that little kid display on the counter, gives it a good crack and sends the nickels and dimes all over the glass. I feel a couple drop down on my shoes. The coins make a racket, but the brother is even louder. "Ain't you heard me? I just—"

"Smitty!" That first brother cuts him off from over by the coolers. He's standing there, next to the tall dude in the cap who's holding the door open with one hand and a pint of milk with the other. He looks at me and then he puts his head down, hiding his eyes under that red brim.

"What you acting like some little punk for?" that first brother in the white says. "Ain't nobody taught you some manners?"

Smitty's face gets tight, and he points at Ho. "But he ain't got—"

The other dude holds up his hand, and Smitty stops. "I know what he's got, and what he ain't got," he says. His voice is real smooth, quieter than Smitty's. "You're acting like you don't know what you're doing in a place like this." He looks at the brother next to him who's still looking at the ground. He takes that bottle cap and taps on the glass door the dude's holding. "What you think, Detroit? Sounds like Smitty's about playing some kind of fool up there." The Detroit brother looks up but doesn't say nothing, so the other guy keeps on, looks back up here at Smitty. "Why don't you leave the man alone for right now?"

Smitty just stands there a second. He puts his hands on his hips and kind of looks around—at Ho, at me, at the floor. There's a couple coins in front of his foot, and he kicks a nickel over to me. "Yours if you want it," he says. He walks over into one of the aisles when I bend down and start picking things up.

When I put some coins in my hand I hear the music from the car outside hit a change. That big bass booming and all that hey-ho noise lightens up, and some horns start in. Must be a sample—sounds like some of that old-time stuff Daddy used to like, one of those Miles or Bird records he'd pull out every now and again on a Saturday when he didn't feel like talking to nobody.

Ho leans over the counter and tells me to stop. "Not your fault," he says, looking at the coins and brushing at the air with his hand.

"It's all right," I say, and stand up to put some nickels on the glass.

Ho says thanks, and he picks up that display and starts fitting the coins back in the slots. "That's why my wife want move off this street," he says. "Too many customer like him."

"Wouldn't blame you if you did," I say. "It's a hard living."

He laughs a little and shakes his head. "Easy for me," he says. "I know many people, come here every day get something to eat." He leans in a little closer. "Look, I show you how easy." He pinches his cheeks and tugs up till his teeth are showing. "Make smile like this, everybody nice."

"What's your old lady think about that?" I say.

"She say everyone drunk downtown, every man look at her say 'Hey baby, you want me?'" Ho picks up another coin and shrugs his shoulders. "She still want open a lady store," he says. "Sell flower, everything smell nice. I tell her I can give flower to customer who act very asshole—smell nice then."

"Dad?"

Ho stands up straight, looks over my shoulder. Robert is standing back there with that apron still on. I see Detroit in the cap looking over at the kid too.

Robert looks real quick over at Smitty and then at Ho. "Mom wants to know what—"

Ho smacks his hand down on the glass, so hard I think he might crack it. The other coins jump up a second, and they're still making noise on that counter when Ho starts into the kid. The man's mad about something, and he sure don't want any of us black folk to know. I step away from the counter, walk over to the first aisle where all the candy is and leave the man alone.

I'm getting tired of holding this damn apple in place, but I need to keep it on my gut till I get out of here. Ho is noisy but I can still hear the music outside breaking out of that change. It starts back into the rhythm it had before, smooth and steady.

I walk down the aisle till he can't see nothing but my head, and keep working the zipper to see if it will close my jacket and hold the apple by itself. It keeps sticking, but finally I get it—it breaks through and slides right up like it's on rails, but that apple slides right out anyway, onto the floor.

I look up to see if Ho hears, but he's still talking that talk at Robert, and now he's holding up that display with the coins and pointing at it. Robert doesn't say nothing back, he just turns around and sticks his head through the plastic. Smitty is in the next aisle down. He looks over at me with one eyebrow up.

Ho's old lady comes out from the back, right past her kid. She takes a quick look around and stops and folds her arms over her chest. She breathes in loud through her nose and her whole chest goes up like she's fixing to pop. She starts up in that talk, but it's fine by me—Ho's gonna be too busy ignoring her to think to look what I'm doing over here.

I go down for the apple, dust it off a little, and press into that spot that hit the floor. The skin gives easy, the juice comes right up. Don't have no time for a bite, but I lick my finger real quick before I tuck the apple away. It's sweet, even better than I thought—but I can't think of nothing that doesn't taste good when you're hungry.

I look for something down on these shelves that's gonna stick to me, chocolate with some peanuts it in maybe. Ho and his old lady are still going at it when I take some bars off the shelf. Getting so I can't hardly hear myself think.

"Both you all shut the fuck up!"

It's Smitty. Ho and his old lady stop like somebody just pulled their plug.

I want to make it quick. The bars tuck in real nice on my waist and the zipper is up, but I know Ho's looking over this way at Smitty. He's got that cast, and I can just jump up and stroll on out if I want, but I ain't got Lydell's style—he'd go over and *show* the man the goods before he took off, smile while he was at it. This man's all right, a good dude to talk to, and I just want him to forget I was even here.

"I'm tired of hearing you all kung-fu motherfuckers talking that shit," Smitty says. "Gonna give me a headache like I don't know what."

"Smitty, Smitty," the brother with the bottle cap says, still down by the end of the coolers. "There ain't nothing you can do about that. You got what you need now?"

"Yeah, Rayful," Smitty says. He's quieter. "Just about."

"All right. Now where's that other brother who was in here?"

I look up and there's Smitty's head looking down over the aisle. He points at me and looks back. "Right here. Hiding or something."

"He nervous too?" Rayful laughs. "Just go stand back on that wall, buddy. You won't have nothing to worry about."

When I get up off the floor I see Rayful looking at me and pointing with a gun. Just with the handle—he's got the nose looking down at his feet. But it's enough.

"Go on now," he says, but when I start moving I feel one of those candy bars slip down my pant leg all the way to my shoe. I take small steps to keep it in place. Rayful looks at his buddy Detroit. "That brother thinks we gonna hurt him. Walking like he's got his ankles chained up." He knocks on the cooler door with the gun handle. "Go bring him a beer, Detroit. Tell him to relax."

Detroit walks over with a forty. I don't see his eyes until he hands it to me. They're red, like he ain't been sleeping too well. I didn't catch it before, but he's got a funny ear under that cap brim he pulled down to the side. It doesn't look like the other one—it's like something that got left out in the sun too long, all shriveled up and small. I wonder if the brother can still hear out of it.

"Go on and drink up," Rayful says. He looks over at Ho, then back at the lady and her kid. "Anybody else here nervous?" he says. Detroit walks back and stands next to him again. "Plenty of beer in here to go round. I know just looking at him my man Detroit needs one."

Smitty throws down an empty wrapper, pulls something else off the shelf and rips it open. "Give him one then," he says. "Let's get going."

"Not time for that yet," Rayful says. "Why you think the man's been driving us? Can't do no jobs like this drinking." He looks at Detroit, but the big dude just keeps his eyes on the floor. "At least not the first time."

Ho's cash register rings, and he looks at Rayful. "Not much today," he says.

His old lady shakes her head and gives him one of those looks. She starts up at him again, but as soon as she does, Smitty's on her.

"I *told* you," he says, throwing the food back down and walking to where she and Robert are standing. "Enough of that shit. Makes me crazy." He bends down so his face is right in hers and knocks on the side of his head. "You understand that, lady?"

"She understands fine," Robert says. He's looking straight ahead, at his old man maybe. The lady just keeps looking at Smitty.

Smitty straightens up. "That so?" he says to the kid. "You wanna tell me what the fuck she's been saying then?"

"She just wants—"

"'Cause if she's talking smack," Smitty says, putting a finger in Robert's face, "she better know who she's talking it at."

"Let him be," Rayful says. "He's just a kid."

Robert looks back over his shoulder at Rayful. "Just don't touch my mom."

"You mean like this?" Smitty says, and he tags the kid right upside the head. Open-hand, not hard, but enough. The kid turns around, and then Smitty does the same to the lady with his other hand. "Like this?" She takes it, moves with it, doesn't say nothing. Smitty puts his finger back up to Robert. "You making the rules now, Chinaboy? Did I say you could look over at him?"

"Enough!" Ho says. He grabs one of his crutches and bangs it on top of the register. "Take this and go."

"Now everybody's thinking they're the man," Smitty says. He looks at Rayful and puts out his hand. "Gimme that gun, Ray. I'm gonna cap all these mother-fuckers myself."

Rayful gives a laugh and shakes him off. "You know the plan—big Detroit's gotta finish the night." He flips Smitty his bottle cap. "Use this if you want."

The bass from the car is smooth and steady. Rayful leans in close to Detroit, whispers something, and squeezes him on the shoulder. This bottle's good and heavy but I don't want to set it down just yet. I hold it long-ways in my arm, pressed right on my jacket about where the apple is, and now I can feel that juice coming through my shirt.

Rayful hands Detroit the gun, and they walk up to the counter. "We gonna have a little on-the-job training this morning for big Jonathan—oop! I mean, Detroit," Rayful says. "Big man's running this now. Everybody better do what he says." He looks over at me. "I think he wants you covering the door, brother. Ain't that what you said, D?"

"If you say so," Detroit says. He ain't got much voice for a big man.

"No man, listen," Rayful says, and he lifts Detroit's hand up till the gun is point-ing at Ho. "You the one in charge. It's easy now. Just run it and let's get going."

"Look here," Smitty says. He's standing next to the lady, pointing across her at Robert, at that little shiny O in his mouth. The kid's hands are shaking at his sides, and his eyes are on Smitty. "You see this, Detroit? Any of these folks do something you don't want them to, you just shoot the cap."

Detroit keeps looking at Ho, holding the gun right on him. Ho looks Detroit straight up and stays cool, doesn't say nothing.

"You got to have somebody covering that door," Rayful says. "That brother over there will help you out. Just tell him to."

"Go do it," Detroit says. He doesn't turn around.

"You heard the man," Rayful says to me. I stay right where I am, with the bottle in my arm. He walks into the aisle. "What you got there, my man?" he says, looking down at my foot. "Making off with a little breakfast?" He steps closer, and talks low. "Why don't you just stand over there a second? I won't tell the China-man nothing."

Ho is looking straight at his kid now. I hear that music break into the riff again, and the horns start in.

"That dude deaf?" Smitty says.

"I think he just don't want no one looking at his nappy ass," Rayful says, and walks over to the door. "Look at that jacket he's wearing—dude must have lost a bet." Smitty's the only one who laughs at that. Rayful stands right inside the door and makes the bell go off. "At least the brother don't make no trouble," he says. He puts his hands on his hips. "I'll cover it myself. Let's hurry the fuck up now. Ask him for the money, nice and sweet like we went over. He don't give it up, cap his ass."

The kid spits out the cap. "No!"

Smitty goes upside Robert's head again, harder this time. The kid falls back and puts his hand to his ear. "I told you keep your mouth shut," Smitty says. "Don't hear too good, do you?"

Smitty's back is to me, and that's too bad, because I wish I could see what kind of face he pulls when that little lady goes upside his head. Ain't no love tap, nei-ther. She winds up like she's going for the fences, drills him right in the jaw. "Stop hitting my *son!*" she says, and right on the last word Smitty catches that blindside full-on and damn-near trips over himself falling into the potato chips. Detroit turns quick and points the gun at the kid. Ho puts his hands together. "Please," he says to the big dude. "Only a boy."

"You all better stop fucking around," Detroit says, louder than before. He keeps the gun up with both hands.

Rayful stays by the door. "Take it easy, man. Nobody's coming. Now you can do like Smitty said if you want. Pop the kid."

"You all trying to make me crazy," Detroit says. He takes a hand off the gun and scratches his ear.

"Go on," Rayful says. "Just do what comes natural."

This bottle still feels damn heavy. Everybody's looking at Detroit now. From where I am, it wouldn't take too much to hit him right in his fucked-up little ear with this forty. I'd just want to get to that gun first when he dropped it—it's got to be the only gun. If Rayful and Smitty were strapped they'd have pulled by now.

"Over here, brother," I say. He turns his head. "Why you messing with these folks?"

He slaps one hand on the counter and looks at Ho, then at the kid again. "Put the money out."

"That's right," Rayful says. "Keep going."

Smitty cocks back like he's set to floor the lady, but then he steps off. "Detroit, you gonna do this or what?" he says, pointing at her. "How much shit I got to take from them?"

"Gimme a bag," Detroit says.

Ho puts one on the counter, puts the money in it.

I shake the candy bar off my foot and take a good grip on the bottle. I take a couple steps closer. "These here are good people, brother. Just take what you need."

Rayful laughs like a little hiccup. "Look at you, raggedy-ass malt-liquor mother-fucker. Now you playing the Chinaman's nigger."

I keep looking at Detroit while I set the bottle down. I turn up my hands in front of me. "Guess it wouldn't mean nothing to shoot a nigger," I say. "Ain't that right?"

Detroit puts the bag back down and looks at me. He scratches that ear again and he points the gun at me sideways. "What you want?"

"Don't ask him, give it to him," Rayful says. "You done one already, Johnnie. One more ain't gonna matter."

"I wasn't talking to you," Detroit says.

Rayful shrugs his shoulders. "Nobody told you to talk anyway," he says. "Just do what you gonna do and let's go."

Detroit looks at Rayful but he keeps the gun on me. "I'm running this, right?"

"Unless you don't do it right."

"That's what I thought," Detroit says. He points over at Smitty. "Get out of the way," he says. Smitty steps into one of the aisles and leaves Robert and his momma standing by themselves. Detroit keeps the gun on them but looks at Smitty. "No, over here. Behind me."

Ho picks up the bag and shakes it. "Please," he says.

Detroit snatches it but keeps his gun up. I can see the little lady biting down on her lip and squeezing her boy's hand. The big dude points at the back, at the plastic where they came through before. "You all get back there and keep quiet. I don't want you looking."

Robert and Ho's old lady go behind the plastic. Smitty shakes his head. "Still soft, ain't you? Think it's gonna be too ugly for them when you put the old man down?"

"No nice way to do this, Johnnie," Rayful says.

Detroit points at Ho and I hear the hammer click back. I think maybe I shouldn't have put the bottle down. "He's a family man," I say.

"I know what I'm doing," he says, still looking at Ho. He shakes the bag again. "This all you got?"

Ho just nods. Detroit drops the bag on the ground. It's not tied off, and a couple bills jump out near his feet. "Then get down," he says, real steady. "Down behind there right now."

Ho slips down behind the counter, and Detroit looks at Rayful and Smitty, points back and forth at them like he's got last pick on the court and can't make up his mind. "Whichever one of you all wants this," he says, kicking the bag up against the counter wall, "get down here and get it."

Smitty steps back, but Rayful smiles big. "Stop fucking around."

Detroit points at him. "I'm serious as a heart attack. It's right here."

Smitty's face gets tight. "What you gonna do now, Johnnie-boy?" he says, and he looks quick at me and throws his chin up. "Get some four and a quarter routine like this punk? Start shaking a cup?"

"He's gonna keep trying to get into that school," Rayful says. "Learn how to be the nigger's nigger."

"You both been singing that all night," Detroit says.

"That's 'cause you need somebody to be telling you," Rayful says. "Now pick it up."

"Is that right?" Detroit says, taking a step so he's right over the bag. "Well, looks like the nigger's in charge now. You want to hear what else I got to say, you come right down here close."

"I got something for you to hear," Smitty says, "with that fucked-up little raisin ear you got." He puts his hand on the gun, pushes it out of his way and starts to go down for the bag. Detroit lets his gun hand fall to the side but he makes a quick fist with the other and tags Smitty dead in the nose, breaks it like it was nothing and knocks him flat on his ass. When Smitty looks up I see the blood coming from both sides.

Ho peeks up over the counter. Smitty gets up and sees him looking. "Fuck you," he says, sounding like a little duck or something squeezing his nose like that. "You fixing to come out and work some kung-fu with them crutches?"

"Get going," Detroit says, putting the gun back up. "I ain't running with neither of you all no more."

Rayful steps over and lets Smitty walk out first. The bell goes. "You're goddamn right you're not," he says. "You'll be lucky to be walking. Momma's gonna be feeding her Johnnie with a spoon."

Funny sometimes how a little thing makes a whole lot of noise. Most days you wouldn't hear it at all, but if you're in one of those times when everything kind of holds still, even just a little baby noise can make you snap to. That's how it was with the plastic bag that morning. I was just standing there listening to that music from the car fade off till it was nothing, so when Detroit picked the bag up off the floor and pushed it back over the counter, it was like I woke up straight out of some dream. But I knew it wasn't no dream at all. I knew it was past time for me to get going, get on outta that store. Time to get back to Noel, time to get ready for our kid like a real man.

Felt easy then, sure enough. I was leaving that shit behind, not turning into no Daddy, nohow. Ain't so easy now, though, now that I'm cut off and William is sick. Ain't so easy to know which way to go when you're walking in the dark.

* * *

When I went to Noel's office building the Friday before Christmas, I stood by the edge of the little garden they had right in the middle of the lobby and tried to dry out. Rain was coming down hard that day—that's why I didn't have no work—and by the time I made it inside I was dripping like a snowman caught out in the desert. I've never spent time in a nice building I wasn't cleaning, but I figured the best thing to do was go shake my jacket out over the dirt so I didn't make some big mess on the floor. A white guy was working on the other side, had his hands in the dirt and a little plant sitting up next to him on the edge. He laughed when he saw me with my jacket, and we got to talking some. I asked him wasn't it funny putting a plant in the ground *inside* on a day like today. I can still see that plant in his hands right before he put it in. The roots hung real low and pointed every which way, like they all had a different idea about where they were going. I've had some gigs doing landscaping, and I know sometimes, if a tree is old enough, the roots run even longer than that tree itself. I remember standing there, talking with that man, waiting for Noel and wondering about that plant, if it would make it. Roots need time to take in new soil, especially if they're old, but even if they aren't. Every now and again you get one that decides it just don't want to be someplace else.

Elevators in a place like this always have that little bell that goes when the doors are ready to open. Gives folks a chance to get ready, on both sides. When I hear this one I give my jacket one more shake and move over to the side wall, out of folks' way.

She's in the middle when she first comes out, and some lady's got her ear, a lady wearing a red sweater with a Santa on the front. They stop a second, and the lady gives Noel a little touch on her belly before she walks off. Noel smiles back and waves at her. It's nice to see her take it like that—wasn't too long ago she was ready to smack the next person who asked her when was she due and wanted to feel the little guy kicking in there for themselves. But the last few weeks it's been like when we first started out, when we could just joke around and let things flow.

I called her this morning and said let me talk with miss stretch-pants, and she laughed right out loud and said she wanted to know if it was mister job-a-month asking for her.

She looks good. She always dresses nice for work but she's something special today. Even as much as she's showing, those navy slacks still fit her nice, and her red shirt brings out that little something in her cheeks. Makes me wonder if maybe she knew I'd call her up today. I found her calendar under the pillow this morning. Could be she left it behind on purpose.

"How you doing?" I say. I look down at her belly and put my hand on it. "How's he?"

"I'm all right," she says, squeezing both my hands. "And so is *she*."

She knows I'm doing it on purpose. *How come you so sure I'm gonna give you a boy* she always says, but I know she likes me teasing her. *Somebody tell you you was a man's man?*

We go through that spinning door, Noel first, and she's got her umbrella up when I come out. I can't squeeze under, but it's all right, because she's got the nice clothes and I'm already wet anyhow. It's a long walk to where we're going—one of us might as well stay dry.

Nobody makes a sandwich like they do at Cole's. It's not all the time I can get down there, but when I saw the rain this morning I thought I might have a chance. Noel's office is having some Christmas party today, so she can take a long lunch if she wants to. Back at our place, flipping the pages in her little book, I saw she had all the 20s circled straight through to March—the day the doc said the baby was coming. Right then it all came together—she's through six months today. Last time we went to the Birdhouse the doc told me things get pretty tough on a woman down the home stretch, those last three months. Said it ain't the same for everybody, but if a man didn't know better he might think his old lady was losing it. They start dreaming about babies with three heads, or just stay in bed all day, or want to eat the damnedest stuff, like bark off a tree. When I called her, I figured I couldn't do nothing about those dreams, but I can at least take my woman to lunch and make sure she ain't eating no bark.

She made lists of just about everything she ate the first couple months. I saw when I flipped through the pages. What stayed down, what came back up, and what color it was when it did. Up through the end of August she kept writing *few more days gonna make it* and then it just dropped off. She circled my birthday in September—Labor Day this year, so we both had it off—and right under it was a list for the store: eggs, sugar, butter, all that kind of thing. She baked me a little cake. Didn't turn out so good, but she tried. It was all mostly stuff about herself, but I found one more place she put something down about me—that story I told her about Ho's store. I fixed it up right nice for the telling, and she bought it all.

Told her something I saw there woke me up about what it was gonna take to keep a family together. That was true, but I kept playin', told her a kid came in there, a little boy lost from his momma, so I bought him a candy bar and walked him all the way to St. Al's. Told her I knew somebody might think I was the one took him, giving him candy and walking with him like that, but I had to help the kid out. *Gotta take a chance sometimes to do right by your kid.* And it's true—I did learn that. I just didn't see no sense in telling her the way it really went down. Didn't want her to look at what I did in there and see part of Daddy. She didn't, and I still ain't let her, ain't told her much about him at all. After a while she hugged me and said she knew we were gonna make it, and just this morning I saw what she wrote in her book that day, just two lines. *I love Jake for telling me.* And right under that, *Does he know?*

Feels like the rain starts coming down a little harder when we turn the corner on Emmaus, but Cole's is right there. We go down the stairs, and when I open the door and smell that roast beef, I think I just about unlocked the pearly gates.

I fold my jacket under my arm, grab us a couple trays, and step up in line. They've got all the usuals today: roast beef, turkey, and ham, all right off the bone, and all the sides too—potatoes, greens, candied yams, mac and cheese. The same chef is still here, wearing his apron and that big white hat. He's Russian, I think. He told me his name once, but I couldn't say the damn thing to save my life so he said to just call him Stan.

"What you say now, Stan?" I say. Noel shakes out the umbrella and steps up next to me.

He looks up from cutting some bread, and puts the knife down. "Jake," he says, smiling, "when I saw you last time?"

"Oh, few weeks at least," I say. "Ain't been working downtown in a while."

He looks at Noel and nods real big and slow, still with that smile. He points at her belly. "Busy man, heh?"

"That's right," I say, putting my arm around her waist. "Little lady's starting to get close. I told her if she gives my boy a taste of a good sandwich, he won't give her no trouble at all coming out."

Stan gets a laugh out of that. "My wife tells me, a man, he never understand how a woman hurt for the baby."

"Ain't *that* the truth," Noel says, giving me a little elbow in the gut. She looks at Stan. "What kind of sandwiches you got that's so good?"

I move my hand in front of all the meats, each one of them sitting on its own cutting board. "Can't miss in here," I say. "Say Stan, lemme have a roast beef, French-dip."

He gives me a little nod, picks up a slicing knife and starts running it up and down the sharpener in his other hand. He looks at Noel. "For you?"

Noel looks at me. "What's that dip all about?"

Stan starts slicing the roast beef, nice and thick. It's red in the middle. The slices peel off easy and the juice runs around the sides. He picks up the bread with the tongs, one piece at a time, lifts it flat-out right over a pan of juice, sticks it in quick. That's the French-dip. Just get it in there halfway, just enough to bring out the meat but not too much to break the bread. Stan gets it perfect every time. Pretty good for a guy who ain't even French.

"It's just some juice," I say. "Makes it taste better."

"You sure?" she says. "It ain't blood from the meat?"

Just then the stereo cuts on over at the bar, a real loud scratch at first. The bar's on the other side of the room, in between the serving line and the pool room, and I look over and see Doyle messing with the dials. He's got white hair and red cheeks and he pours the drinks here. There's a couple men sitting there, and some white lady with an empty glass in her hand is leaning over the bar. Doyle takes her glass and fills it when the music kicks in. Some guitars, twanging like mother-fuckers. Country or rock and roll, the kind of thing they most always play in here. Stuff would drive me crazy if it weren't for the sandwiches.

Stan puts my plate up, and Noel tells him she wants the same as me. I grab us a couple Cokes and pay for everything down at the register. We walk past the bar and the booths and back to the pool room. It's almost closed off back there, more private, and most folks at the bar are smoking anyway. Noel don't like breathing that in these days, if she can help it.

Ain't no smoking back here, no folks to do it neither. Pool games don't usually start up till after working hours. Before me and Noel got together I used to play a little stick, but I'm glad that table's empty now—makes it easier to tell her what I want to tell her. There's a booth on each side of the doorway when you come in. The one on the right has an ashtray on the table with some butts still breathing, so we put our trays down on the left.

The music shoots up loud for a couple seconds before Doyle brings it back down again. Just like I thought, some country pick-along. At least it's something Noel won't know. Every time she hears a song she likes she chimes right in, even if she don't know half the words. And even if she can't do it pretty. One time she asked me did I think she had a little something like Aretha, and I told her ask me again in about fifty years when I'm deaf.

I bite into the sandwich and close my eyes when the juices hit. I lean back, chew it nice and slow, feel that juice run down my chin. Noel's still looking at hers. She picks up her fork and starts in on the potatoes.

The white lady from the bar walks through the doorway with a pitcher of beer in one hand and two empty glasses in the other, sits right down in the booth across from us. She's wearing a blue shirt, and that open collar lets you see some wrinkles in her neck. Her hair is brown with a little blond trying to hang on in there. She pulls it up off her back, into a ponytail, and lays it back down on her shoulder in front. Her make-up is heavy—not ugly like a pro, but I can tell she's trying too hard.

"How's that sandwich?" I say to Noel. She's still eating the sides.

"I'm getting to it," she says. She looks at my plate. "You ain't eating that mac and cheese yet, Jake? Forgot your sugar, didn't you?"

I've been doing it since I was a kid, but the first time Noel saw me put sugar on mac and cheese she thought I was trying to ruin her cooking. And every time after that she always has something to say about it. That's the way Momma always made it. It's one of the only things I still think she was right about. Cuts into that sharp cheese just right. I reach for a sugar packet but Noel snaps it up and shakes it over her plate.

"All right," I say. "Go ahead."

"What?" she says, trying not to smile.

"Come on. I'm hungry."

She opens it up and sprinkles some on. She sits back when she's done and lets the smile come now before she picks up her sandwich and takes a bite. Just a little one, but I can tell she likes it, the way her eyes get big. Feels good to see my girl eating a full plate without worrying about it. She's put on some pounds in her legs and ass, but I always tell her it's just because she's got a strong baby in there.

I take another bite. "What they got you doing in that office today?"

"The usual," Noel says, picking at her greens. "What nobody else wants to do."

From what she's been telling me lately, you'd think she was the only one in the place knows how to make copies and staple. They taught her how to use the computer when she first got there, but just for typing in files, and every time she's had a little time and tried to teach herself something new, her boss Carolyn is on her case about why don't she ask for more *work* if she's done instead of playing? Noel still thinks it's gonna be any day now when they let her go, just in time for the baby to come.

"Could even be today, Jake," she says, and looks up. "Perfect time, if you think about it. They got that big party going, music and food and everybody getting drunk probably. Be easy enough for somebody to pull me into an office and tell me to make sure I get me a big piece of cake for the road."

"Aw come on, baby," I say. "It's *Christmas*."

"So what?" she says. "That's even better. With all those folks taking vacation, by the time somebody sees I ain't been coming in for a while there'll be some story about how I must have took off somewhere because you know county queens can't hold no job anyway." She shakes her head, picks at her greens some more. "You don't know these folks, Jake."

I put the sandwich down and lean in a little closer. "What'd Carolyn say when you left just now?"

"Just now? Nothing." She puts her fork down. "Ain't minding me, huh? I told you she's walking around like she forgot how to talk."

"Right," I say. I forgot how the whole thing goes—something about Carolyn's husband passed a while back and she never gets through a Christmas without getting deep-down blue.

But I don't want to talk about all that now. Don't feel like hearing about anything from that office. I want to tell my baby I'm proud of her today, making it through six months. Want to tell her she don't have to worry—I know she loves me. But I don't want to be *saying* that kind of thing out in public. So this morning, before I came to her building, I opened her book to today's page, December 20, and put down something I thought she might like. *Your man Jake loves you baby.*

"Let me show you something," I say, and pull it out of my back pocket. The one she gave me is green, but hers is dark red.

Noel looks at me like I just pulled a gun or something. She reaches over and takes it right out of my hand. "What did you see?"

I shrug. "I looked through it."

"All the pages?"

"What you all uptight about?"

There's a bang on the other table and we both look over. The white lady is sitting there with her lips all puckered up around a cigarette, clicking her lighter. It's a big silver one, not the kind you buy in a liquor store, but it must be low on fluid. She bangs it again and shakes it and keeps clicking till it lights. She blows out a big stream of smoke and takes a sip of her beer.

I slide over to the edge of the bench. "Yo lady, can't you see me and my girl here got one in the oven? Go on and smoke at the bar."

She turns her head and looks at Noel. "This is my table," she says. Her voice sounds like she ain't just started smoking yesterday. "Has been. Every year."

"Look," I say. "I ain't asking such a big thing. Just go on in the other room."

The lady finishes off her beer, drinks down half a glass all at once. She wipes her mouth and looks at me. "What's your problem, buddy? You gonna do something you don't want me to see, or do you just like having two women listening to you at once?"

Noel reaches over and squeezes my hand. "It's all right, Jake. Don't take it out on her."

I want to ask Noel what she thinks I'm taking out, but before I can, this brother about my size walks through the doorway with a hey hey *hey* booming like it's from some speakers. He stops, looks at me and Noel and the lady. He shakes the rain off his Raiders cap real quick before he fits it back on and gives us all a little tip. "Cleo Parker," he says to me and puts out his hand. He gives a good shake, the kind you can trust right off, but I don't say nothing. He's got a good twenty years on me, easy—his voice is all bass, and the wrinkles stand out around his eyes when he smiles. But the brother looks solid, still in good shape, and his eyes are shiny as a couple of new pennies. He shakes with Noel, then looks back at me. "You all some friends of the birthday girl?"

"Sit down, Cleo," the white lady says, rubbing her eye. "You're late."

"We were just getting to know her," I say.

She looks at Cleo and points at me. "What's he know? Did *you* tell him?"

"All right, Allie, all right," Cleo says. He tries to take her hand, but she smacks him off.

"Don't touch me unless you mean it," she says. "I sure as hell ain't ending up like *that* girl. She probably ain't even sure he's the one."

"Lady," I say, "only thing I know now is you one sorry drunk bitch."

Her eyes go tight, and just like that she picks up her ashtray and tries to throw it at me. Cleo is old but he's a quick motherfucker, and he stuffs her clean. The tray hits back on the table and knocks Allie's glass off. The glass breaks, and the ashes fall slow down into the beer on the floor.

Allie stands up. So does Cleo. Me and Noel don't know what to say, we just look at them looking at each other.

Allie starts rubbing her eye, then picks up her purse and tries to walk around Cleo. He tells her it's all right he'll clean it up, but she keeps her head down and pushes through. "I got something in my eye," she says, but I hear her voice crack. When the ladies' room door closes, Cleo sits down.

He brushes the ashes off the table. His eyes are still shiny, but his voice is softer now. "You all just caught her on a bad day," he says. "I can tell just looking at you, you all are real nice folks. She didn't mean nothing by it."

Allie had herself a birthday to remember a few years back, Cleo tells us. Her husband didn't like what she fixed for supper that night so he beat her so bad she finally called the cops on his ass, and he's been locked-up since. Cleo didn't meet her until about a year later, after she ended up downtown. He was training at the night desk at his SRO, so he couldn't let her stay more than one night with no money, but he hooked her up with his friend at the county office and made sure she got everything a woman in her shoes had coming to her. Every now and again he tries to talk her into cutting herself off the check, getting back into nursing and picking up where she left off. But she won't have none of it.

"Could be why she got like that with you all," Cleo says. "Her man couldn't give her no kids, and I know for a fact Allie don't like seeing other folks with them."

The ladies' room door squeaks. Allie walks up and stops right in front of the mess on the floor. Cleo starts to stand, but she puts her hand on his shoulder, then looks at Noel.

"I got pretty much carried away there," she says. Her eyes are red around the edges. "Truth is, I'm tired of coming to this place."

"Come on, baby," Cleo says. "I'll walk you back and you can get some sleep."

"Let me finish," Allie says. She kneels down and picks up her glass. It's busted-out on one side, but the rest is still holding together. Some big pieces are laying around in the beer, and Allie picks some up and puts them inside the glass. I look over at Noel but she's watching Allie. The lady looks at one of her fingers and puts it in her mouth real quick, then she looks up at Noel with the glass in her hand. "They should make them stronger, don't you think?" she says, trying to get herself to laugh. She looks at the glass and sucks on her finger again. "One little fall and they break."

Noel tucks her bottom lip under and looks down at her food while Cleo takes the glass from Allie and helps her up nice and slow. They both step over the beer.

"You ain't even cleaning this?" I say.

Allie keeps walking, with her head down, but Cleo looks back. "I'll come back for it," he says. "Just want to get her home first."

I stand up quick and almost tell him he's a lying motherfucker. But I feel a piece of glass break under my shoe, and I ain't waiting no more, not with Noel sitting here. I take some napkins and start wiping up the floor, getting the edges first, soaking up that beer. Noel says something but I don't really hear, I just keep wiping, fresh napkins in both hands now, bringing the edges in, pushing everything to the center. She says something else, but I don't look until I feel her tapping on my shoulder with that little book and I know she wants me to listen.

"You know now, don't you?"

* * *

I didn't, but she thought I did, so she let the whole thing unwrap right there at the table. She 'fessed-up, from all the way back in her LA days till before I even met her, till the time she lost her first baby, up here in Oakland. But not the way I did with Paula and Cheryl, wasn't one of those times when you come clean just because you think it's gonna make it easier to get away with fucking up next time around. Noel kept biting down on her lip, and she only does that when she can't keep it from shaking.

Looking back on it now, it's easier to see why she was so worked up about it all. She figured I'd split quick as a rat out of a cats' alley if I knew she'd lost her first baby in her second month, because she still couldn't shake what her momma told her after the old lady kicked her out, when Noel called and said she'd lost it and she wanted to come home now. *God sure is telling you something now, girl, just like I did. You ain't fit for no man, no family, no nothing.*

Back in Cole's, I didn't really see it like I do now, it was just my girl getting some secrets off her chest. Didn't change how I felt about her. Momma told me don't never come back too, but I don't give a damn. And I didn't believe in no God's curse about her babies—I figured if God had let Noel go through all that shit already, he sure enough owed her something good this time around. When she finally had William, and I saw her holding him there in bed, I knew I was right.

She was gorgeous. She looked so sleepy lying in that bed, but she was glowing, she was *alive*. William's face looked like some old piece of fruit when I first saw it, but as soon as he was in my arms he was the best-looking kid I'd ever seen. I've never liked hospitals much, and I've never figured God owed me nothing like he did other folks, but when I think back now I guess he was giving me a little something up front, something to hold on to. When things are tough now, I try to think back to that morning. I try to remember William's little fingers and his fresh smell, and that shine in Noel's eyes when she looked up at us from the bed.

Or that walk back from Cole's. We must have been at that table an hour after Cleo and Allie left, and I was fretting she was gonna be real late, but Noel said she didn't much want to get back to that party anyhow. And we were hoping the rain would let up while we talked. But it didn't. We were halfway back to her office when the wind kicked her umbrella right out of her hands, stuck it in front of a number 16 that didn't stop. I figured Noel would chase that driver down but instead she just laughed, said sometimes the rain's gonna get you anyhow, and if you pretend it feels good maybe it will. That was a tough Christmas for us, our first one together, because everything went down at the office like Noel said it would, even that piece of cake. We both knew it was gonna happen, even before she went back through that spinning door. Maybe that's why I grabbed her, held her face with both hands and brought those wet cold lips right up to mine. Maybe that's why when I did, and I heard the rain coming down hard on the sidewalk and felt it hitting me on my head, I thought it was running down Noel's face too, and if we stayed out there long enough it would run so steady and smooth she wouldn't have to wipe her eyes.

Tonight, out here in the desert, ain't a drop of rain to be found. Stars are fading, moon is sinking low now, and the sky is warming up good and slow, not a cloud in it. Time for me to get back—back to work today, back to the Flatlands tomorrow.

I turn around, look at my steps in the sand. I know what I need to do, just ain't sure how to do it.

I walk, listen to that sand crunch and whisper-shout, and feel it under my feet. Heading back to the Peniel. I laugh at myself, thinking God let me off with my hips still in place, but what do I have to lose asking him for a blessing anyway?

Show me some kind of way, I think. Help me and Noel pull William through, but please God leave Daddy out of this.

It's bad enough that I can't shake him, don't want him chasing after the two of them. I remember what he always told me about starting your own family—you don't just get the other person, you get *all* their people, every last one. Maybe Noel's momma told her the same. I don't know, but I know what to say if she starts asking. My people ain't no trouble, they're just here and there, everyplace and noplace at all. One sister in Detroit, one in St. Louis, Momma down South somewhere, back with her family. And Daddy? Aw—he's gone, long gone.

PART III

CHAPTER 8
THEM THAT'S GOT

Crossing back over into the Flatlands, the van hits that torn-up piece on the junction that shoots you off the Golden State, and my dreaming cuts off right quick. We're going fast on the overpass, coming down to street level, and the sun ain't even up yet, but from up here I can still see the water. And for a second, while I'm still waking up, I wonder if maybe he's down there, if maybe they all are. The park slips by fast before I can catch a good look, goes the same color as the water, same deep down dark that pulls everything in. The water lets those twinkles the streetlights toss out have a good little dance on top, all the way to the shore, till those waves roll up and suck them down, quick-quiet as clouds slipping across the sky and blowing out the stars.

We pull in behind the truck out back of the warehouse, same place we started on Sunday. Last night we finished late. Should have been a short day, but Daniels and his Mrs. kept changing their minds about where they wanted everything, said they didn't care if it was Memorial Day they weren't paying a dime till we got it all in place. We drove back through the night, just like Daddy did when we came from Chicago. Bills has his car and asks me do I want a lift, but it's almost morning and the walk will do me good. I tell the fellas I'll see them in a few days, and start up Third toward Battery.

I lean into the rise on Third and get a good clip going, start clicking off the blocks, feel a little sweat rise on my back under my jacket. Feels good now to stretch the legs out, just walking, ain't got nothing to carry. I'll be home soon enough with all kinds of things to do, so might as well enjoy a piece of freedom while I've got it.

Crossing King, something catches my eye down by the water. I stop right in the middle of the street, no cars in sight and not a one making noise from the Cliffs just down the way. I look but it's nothing, nothing I can see now. Nobody down here but me.

The water comes up over the wall, smack down on the street, and something about seeing it makes me think of that dude was here few days ago with the fishing pole. It comes up and smacks down again, and the sound is like dry wood popping, bones cracking. I turn and start walking slow toward it. Still too dark down here to see much, but when it comes down again that sound is even bigger, and I half-think maybe I'm gonna see something in that water *did* get cracked, some blood or bones or glass or *something*.

But it's nothing. I walk to where the water is on the street, and it's just full-up of nothing. I even get down and put my hands in it, dip them in one of the potholes but the water just pours out clean. I smell my hands, look at them front and back, but it's just me. Same hands I had me few minutes ago when I had them in my pockets, same ones been moving furniture this whole weekend and all these months, same ones that were touching my baby telling her it's all right after they had gone and snatched that purse and gripped the wheel of that Benz.

I wipe them on my jeans and stand up. I give them a good squeeze, but they're still good and cold, and that chill starts running through me. Looking up the street, it hits me, that deep-down tired I knew would find me after this weekend. Don't care how long it's been and what Noel is wearing or ain't wearing when I walk in, I just want that bed to myself. I just want to get on home.

Coming up on Battery, getting near the same overpass I ran under running from George, I look down the street and think I see something going on, maybe the first crows lining up down on the old corner. Too dark for me to see good from here. That sleep in my head is hitting me something awful now, running through my whole body like a big bowl of St. Al's soup you drink down all at once, so I sit down, lean back on one of those bridge legs and give my own legs a little mercy. I could drop off without even closing my eyes now, but I keep looking down the street, at something moving in the dark down on that corner. A car passes over up on the freeway, and I feel it through the concrete. Then another one, then more. It's steady now, that holiday weekend long gone, the city firing up again. The shadows move like water down the block. My legs feel heavy, my feet feel heavy, my head is swimming. I want to rub my eyes to see straight but I can't even feel my hand to lift it. There's a *clack clack* from down the corner and I squint harder till I see him, that dude with the army jacket and the fishing pole. He walks across the street to the green doors of the Ready Man, knocks with that pole, waiting for somebody to open up. The shadows shake and twitch all around him and I know I'm dreaming but I know I'm *not*—I knew from up in that van they were down here. The dude with the pole steps back, lets out some line and casts it good and hard at those doors, and pulls them all out—Daddy, Laurence, George, even Noel and William, all wrapped up in that line, falling over each other and squirming on the ground like fish. I can't feel my feet to move, I can only sit here and watch them fight out of it, watch Noel roll away with our baby, looking scared as a bird in a cathouse, watch George and Laurence and Daddy jump each other and can't tell who's fighting who, can't tell whose blood is crawling up the street just one thin dark line coming right to me steady steady but it's sure Noel telling me move your ass Jake get on up and *move*. ·

A truck horn blows up above, hits me like a bat on the back of the head, and I come to. A little light starting to ease into the sky now, a few brothers standing in line down the street waiting for those doors to open, some others crowing on the corner right across. No William, no Noel, no nobody, but I've got to get to them. I need to hold them something bad. I get up and shake my legs out, and as I'm double-stepping it up the street away from the hall, that last mile toward home, I think about that month Noel tried day care, before we figured out it didn't save us a dime, those nights she'd get home and just *need* to put William to her breast, just need that baby right down to her bones. I know can't no man feel like a woman, but I sure have a feeling my boy is missing his daddy after all this time I've been away.

Been a long while since I felt so good hearing the Misery Accordion. Could even be the first time. Either way, I know it's the first time I've ever seen Jerry out on the street this time of day with his feet under him. He walks around the truck a couple times, checking all the windows, trying to get himself a look inside—or maybe he just wants some ice cream real bad. It's parked on the corner, just the way up from our building. He doesn't even see me when I slip on by, but that's plenty fine by me—ain't got time for some story. And soon as I hit that bed, I won't hear no music, no traffic, no Jerry, no nothing.

"Jake!" he says from behind me, but I just put a hand up and keep walking.

"How you feeling, Jerry," I say, hopping up the stairs two at a time. "Don't tell me about it now, just keep feeling the same till tomorrow and tell me then."

"Hold it right there," he says when I put my key in the lock. I look over, and he's coming toward me. "You need to talk to me."

"Is that right, old man?" I say. "I think I need to see Noel and my boy."

"You better be ready before you go in there, kid," he says. He's closer now, at the bottom of the steps. Those gray eyes look like a couple of new nickels under that green cap. "Don't you know what day it is, Jake?"

I pull the door open, step inside, look him right back in the eye. "Right now, Jerry, I don't know a goddamn thing. And that's how I like it."

The yellow catches my eye right as I'm pulling the door shut, turning around. The tape is in a pile on the floor, at the top of the steps that go downstairs. I pop the front door back open and look for Jerry but he's gone.

"Noel!" I say, jumping down the steps. There's more tape across our door. "Baby where you at!"

The door is open. Somebody slapped a padlock on it, and somebody else busted it off. I push through, and even in the dark I can see the cops turned this place over. "Noel!" I say, running at the crib right on the other side of our mattress, checking for my boy. My foot catches something, and I take a fall, knees to the ground but catching myself on that crib without busting my head. Something kicks at my leg, and I turn around and see somebody turning up next to our bed. I push myself up off the crib and jump on his back, pin him down on the floor, reach behind me and grab for whatever's there, a frying pan, put the handle to his head put my knee between his shoulder blades and tell him don't even think about breathing motherfucker.

He twitches his head but I grab it like a basketball and press it harder into the floor, dig that pan handle into his ear. "You stupid, motherfucker?" I say. "I'll kill your ass *right* now! Don't move no more, you hear me?"

I drive my knee in again and feel the breath kick out of him. What kind of sorry motherfucker is this, breaking into a place the police already broke into? And what am I gonna do with him now? I get that grip tighter on his head, keep pressing down. Guess these hands of mine still got some strength in them for something that ain't four-and-a-quarter work after all. Maybe they just need a chance to see what they can do.

"Thought you was gonna make this place your own, that right?" I lean forward and talk into his ear. "What you know about my woman and my boy?"

He's still now, no breathing no nothing. But I feel something. Back of this dude's head has some mean tracks running, skin all bumpy and raised-up and keeping the hair clean off. I run my finger over them. Scaly like the skin on a fish. I put the pan down and feel down to the end of the tracks, touch something warm like blood, and right here in the dark it's clear as day. Seven years and all these dreams and here he is.

Daddy's hand shoots up and grabs my arm, catches me sleeping, pulls it like a motherfucker. The pain shoots through my shoulder like a rail spike in the dead of winter, and he flips me off and hops up on his knees.

I land on my back, looking straight up at him. Can't hardly see him in the dark like this except for his shape. I grab my shoulder tight, try to squeeze the pain out. I push with my feet, try to slide away. His face is all shadow, but I can feel those eyes, looking at me just a swing away, looking at me across the glass up in Folsom showing me those scars, looking at me in our house that night I put him through the window. Those big sleepy eyes, good and awake now. Been waiting all this time to see the boy who put him away, and now he's got me, right here in my own place, broke and busted and nowhere to go.

"What you doing here, Daddy?" I say. He doesn't move. I use my good arm and sit up slow. "You want to kill me? Whup my ass? I got me a boy now, better think about that."

He gets closer, still on his knees. Still in the dark, but I see his shoulders, hear him breathing.

I straighten up on my knees. "You got me hurt here, Daddy, but I'll fight you."

He gets closer again and I go with the left. But I'm too slow, too weak with that arm—Daddy only taught me how to jab with that one, never could throw a roundhouse. He blocks it like wiping rain off a windshield. I scramble back to the doorway but he's right on me, his hands lock onto my shoulders, and his thumb digs right into that spot like a nail made of ice. I shout out, and Daddy does too. "My boy," he says, and the tears come like I've never seen from my old man.

He hugs me, squeezes hard. But he's cold, and he smells like he's been crowing like a motherfucker and sleeping inside a garbage truck. I push him away, and switch on the light. When it hits him I almost don't know him. Same hot smoke eyes, but now all that hair is gray too, and his nose is dripping blood down onto that army jacket.

"What you doing here?" I say. "You looking for money? Rock? You come hugging me crying like this, you got to be playin' me for *something*."

"Just listen to me, Jake," he says.

I stand up, look around the room. We ain't got much, but every bit of it is someplace it don't belong now. Even the bed got turned over. "You see this place, Daddy?" I say. "When you took up in here, did you notice there was nobody in it? I don't got time to listen to you, I've got to find my family."

He gets up too, runs his hand under his nose and wipes the blood on his jacket. When he stands we ain't eye-to-eye like we used to be. He takes a step at me. "I'll help you, boy. But what about me? Don't I get to find *my* family?"

"You got me right here, so take yourself a picture and get on outta here," I say. "You couldn't help me find shit right now. *You're* the one done fucked everything up and lost us."

"And what'd you do?" he says, stepping in again, right up smelling-close. "You damn-near killed me."

"You was gonna kill all of us if I didn't."

"That's what you still think? Boy, I had to teach your momma a lesson. I'm your daddy, and you didn't have nothing to do with it."

"You're my daddy!" I say, laughing and jumping back. I step out the door and yell up the stairs. "Hey you all let's get a party going down here—some dude just showed up saying he's my daddy! At least somebody around here's got one!" I step back in, step right up to him, look down right into his eyes. "I know who you are," I say. "I know goddamn straight who you are. You're Curtis Robertson. You're some sorry motherfucker I used to see around, taught me a trick or two, and done showed up here in my room today after doing seven years in the pen for being such a stand-up *daddy*. You're looking for something from somebody who ain't got nothing to give. *That's* who you are."

He shakes his head. "You're my boy, Jake," he says. "I was right there when you was coming out, right there on that bed in our old house."

"Is that right? Well I was right there too when *you* was going out," I say. "Going out getting drunk, going out sitting on the corner with no job, going out pulling a boost—"

"Come on now, Jake, look here," he says, putting his hand on my shoulder.

I knock it back. "Don't go touching me no more, unless you want to end up down on that floor again."

He steps in again, with both hands now. "Let me talk here."

"You had your chance, old man, done said *enough* now," I say, and give him the double, same way he taught me—foot to the balls, fist to the chin. Even with my left, I tag him good. He falls back on his ass, smacks his head at the bottom of William's crib. He rolls over on his side, puts a hand to his nuts and pulls those knees in, wailing like a dog got its tail run over by a truck.

"Now get on out of here," I say, but he just keeps up that groaning. "Move your ass or I'll move it for you."

"You go on and do it then," he says. His eyes are shut, his face is all twisted up and showing his teeth.

"What you know about Noel and William?" I say.

"Don't know a goddamn thing about nobody, boy."

"Lying motherfucker, what you doing here then?" I drop down and grab him by the collar. The light is bright on his face. Something drips off the bottom of his ear, and I see the blood creeping around his neck and under his chin. I look at my hand—it's there too.

I lift him up and lay him down on the bed. I grab a shirt off the floor and fold it under his head. "You all right, Daddy?" I say, but he just keeps up that groaning.

I step over to the icebox, pick up another shirt and wrap some ice in it. Turning back around I see Daddy's bleeding in his pants too.

He yells, tells me he's gonna beat the black outta me when I put him on his side and press the ice to those bleeding tracks, but I hold it tight.

"How did you get in here?" I say, and press a little harder. He jerks and then holds still. He brings his knees up tighter, and his hand is still down there.

"How am I supposed to talk when you go stomping my balls like that?"

I lean over him, gonna look him straight on and tell him better give up what he knows or he'll be singing some Shirley Temple blues all the way back to Folsom, but right then it catches my eye. Been under his jacket this whole time, just fell out on the bed now. Those torn ends, those stars shining in that old dark wool.

I bring it up to my face. Doesn't smell like Daddy's old closet or anything from back then, but it's still got that cold deep in it, that same scratch that catches your beard. I pull it to me, nice and slow, and I see it all roll up—that crazy fish, that maple and all those leaves flying around. I pull it and it slips up past Daddy's arm, around his neck to his shoulder, but his eyes pop open and he grabs it tight.

"You full of questions, ain't you, boy," he says, pulling it and tucking it under him. "Like a goddamn woman."

"Funny thing, ain't it?" I say. "You ain't seen some dude for a few years, then one day he's in your place, looking like a woman himself bleeding through his pants, and smelling even worse than her snatch. And it makes you kind of curious."

He rolls over, flat on his back. He makes a fist around the scarf and keeps his other hand over his nuts. "You calling me a woman, boy?" he says. "You don't know what it *is* to be a man. You don't know what I been through to be your daddy, getting my ass back here looking for you."

I jump off the bed. "Who the fuck told you to come back?" I stand in the doorway, point up the stairs. "You don't got to go through nothing more. Tell me what you know or get the fuck out!"

"You can't kick me out."

"Because I ain't man enough, that right?" I grab the collar of that army jacket and pull him up off the bed. I throw him up against the wall and lean in smelling-close. "Go on take your pick now, Curtis. Is this being a man?" I look back over my shoulder at the mattress, the crib, the table and chair turned-over and all of it empty. "Is taking care of your family being a man, or is this?" I say, and rock his head against the wall again. "See, I didn't have nobody to show me. You want to say I ain't no man, you ain't got nobody to blame but you."

He looks at me—and there's *something* back in those eyes. Don't know what it is. But I know he knows. Blood drips off his ear onto my hand. I let go, step back. All the pain shoots back to my shoulder, but I grind my teeth fighting it, so he can't see. "So what's it gonna be then?" I say. "You want to be out on that street again? Where they at?"

He breathes in big a couple times, snorts loud once. Sucks his teeth and steps away from the wall, fixes his jacket straight and puts the scarf back on his neck. "You know you can't put me out," he says, and walks back to the mattress, sits down and folds the ice back in the shirt all run-through with blood. He breathes in loud through his teeth and shuts his eyes down tight when he puts it to his head. "I wasn't no great daddy but I didn't raise you stupid. You know I got some kind of hand to play."

"Go on, then," I say.

"You sure now, boy?" he says. "Don't forget now—I'm your old man. I done wiped the shit off your ass and put food in your mouth. Don't you want to do a little more of that punk nigger routine on me? Make me bleed someplace I ain't already?"

"The door's that close," I say, pointing. "I picked your ass up once—"

"Aw, cut the shit, boy. If you wanted to do that, you would have done it by now." He puts the ice on the bed. "That old man upstairs told me you were down here—"

"Just get to it!" I say, and bang on the door. "You know something, say it."

"Oh, I know something, boy. You ain't got even half a notion what I know," he says, still sitting on the bed, still with that gray head I don't know but those old eyes I do. Looking at me from way back, from across all those years, all those windows, feels like from way back before I can remember. I wait, don't say a thing, because it's all I can do.

"Laurence knows," he says. "He sniffed me out pretty quick once I got back to town, told me it was just yesterday he was with a skinny-ass girl and a baby boy got a cough like a loose-trigger gun. Fact is, he was looking for *you*—got a letter from her for you."

"Motherfucker! Where's he at?"

"You want them back, that right?" he says, standing up slow now. "What about what you done? What about stealing from that lady? What about some dude named George wants a piece of you?" He steps to me and it's those eyes and my arms can't move but my hands are on his chest looking right into him ready to push him through. Something back there, and I'm on Archer Street ball in my hands watching him through the fence getting closer getting closer, and in that basement in the dark looking for the scarf and the light cuts on and those eyes, and in the room blue blue and cold the closet looking for it checking the window with the ice hanging over and the maple outside dark and moving with the wind like his arm gonna reach through gonna reach up those stairs gonna grab me choke me hug me pull me outta there, and let's play ball Jake let's learn you how to shoot now here we go just smooth and follow right through step up like a man strong and straight into the hoop good arc nice and high and drop it straight in don't miss bring it home don't miss let's hear it sing don't go hitting the tree 'cause somebody's hung up in it somebody's hung up ain't got no face no name no shirt except the one he's hanging by and don't go down in that basement ain't I told you don't go down I told you told you no Daddy you ain't told me nothing.

Now I sit down. I watch him walk over and shut the door, still holding his nuts. He tells me he can get me to Laurence, but his story is going first. Got to listen to your daddy if you want to find your boy. When we get to where Laurence is at it's all gonna come clear—he's got a plan put together to get us up outta this mess, and it ain't no punk-ass four-and-a-quarter routine. We get us a piece of George, he says, we can start living like men, get your woman and your boy and start running the family *right*.

I look down at my hands. Dirt and calluses and Daddy's blood—can't none of that help me now. But what else I got? I know he's lying, he don't know a thing, but maybe Laurence does, and maybe Daddy can bring him to me. I could beat the shit outta him till he tells me more, but he's damn-near dead already ain't got nothing to lose. What else I got but these two hands, what else do I know how to do?

We're walking outta here, he tells me, and you gonna listen. I know I oughta be *running*—out on the street, checking behind every building and down every gutter looking for something, *anything* that tells me where they are, but Daddy says I owe him, and something in me knows he's got it right. It *ain't* right, but he's right. You're all I got and you ain't even mine no more, he tells me, and I know he's right. He opens the door, and we head up the stairs, down to the water.

* * *

No matter what kind of day you got, the water down here never changes. Sun shining or hiding, rain falling or wind whipping, it's always that same color that don't even seem like one, that blueblack that just takes everything in, cleans you out like a good thief and doesn't look back.

Nobody's here. Daddy says Laurence told him he'd either meet us down at the water or up at the court on Archer Street. So now we're here and it's that goddamn waiting again.

Daddy puts a line in but I know he's playin' me. Doesn't say nothing neither, just stands there on the ledge, whistling something worse than that Misery Accordion.

"So where's Laurence at?" I say. "How long you aiming to wait on his ass?"

"He's coming," he says, tugging that pole. "Watch me catch me something now."

"Fuck that." I kick at the ground, dig out a piece without even trying. It jumps over the ledge and sounds like two hands slapping together when it hits the water. What kind of fool is he playin' me for? I try to watch it go down, but the water is too dark, waves are moving too fast. They swallow up everything but my shadow now, and Daddy's too, stretching out black on black, good and long and dancing while we're just standing still.

His pole jerks, and this time it's something. His face goes tight and he bends one knee deep and pulls it right out of his shadow. Soon as that sun comes back in my eyes my gut gets knotted-up like an old lady's hair in a hurricane—it's a bumper, the Benz bumper. Shining but bent-beat like a motherfucker, got hit something awful since I saw her last. Dripping water, and Jerry-junk hanging off her everywhere.

She must have just come off. No rust on the metal, no rot in the rubber. Good and twisted though, like an 'S' when you look at her right. Driver's side still has my mark, that place I dented her hitting the front stoop, but it's nothing against the way she's bent on the end, like she got half-ripped right off the car.

"Don't I got the luck?" Daddy says. "I keep it up out here I'm gonna catch us a bag full of money."

I look up at him, see those sleepy eyes smiling, that nappy hair like Momma's steel wool, that army jacket open and the scarf hanging down his chest. He gets down to look closer, gets smelling-close, but he can't really see it—Daddy never did know about cars. I put my hand on one end and run it toward the middle, feeling all the bruises, all the years. He does the same from his end, but it ain't the same. He can't feel it at all. He can't see how it should fit under her nose and eyes. He doesn't know she's mine. I run my hand back to that place she got tagged real good. Some sorry motherfucker got hold of her who couldn't even take care of her, couldn't keep her from going to junk. Daddy's playing the fool talking about fishing out money, but if he did I'd pick this bumper up and nail him like Reggie Jackson, put his sorry old stinking ass in that water, take the money myself and find my Benz. I'd fix her up right, get her shining purring pretty so I could drive through town and Noel would just feel me coming, just smell me like I was walking right up to her with some yellow flowers. She'd get in and sit right up front with William, leave all that money in the back, plenty to get us up out of these Flatlands, to get us someplace a man can have his family, someplace to get my boy's cough fixed and put good food in the fridge. And we'd keep driving till we found it, run that Benz with all the windows down and if some of that money flew out we wouldn't pay it no mind at all.

The bumper moves under my hand, and looking sideways I see Daddy's hand coming. I jump-turn and cock my fist back, but soon as I do I feel it in my shoulder. I stand up, kick the bumper at him, and walk away. "I *told* you don't try touching me," I say. "I'll go upside your head if I have to."

"Where you going, Jake?" he says. "I'm sorry."

"You're sorry?" I say. "Sorry for what? That what you bringing me down here to tell me? I ain't got time for sorry, motherfucker. Where's Laurence?"

"You shut your mouth now, boy," he says, standing up himself.

"You come on over here and shut it, we'll see who ends up standing." I squeeze my shoulder, know I can get a good swing in if I have to.

"I'm just trying to tell you—"

"Don't try to tell me *nothing*," I say. "I don't want to hear nothing out of you about no I'm sorry. I don't want to hear you do no two-stepping like every other motherfucker down here. You fucked up, period. Just give me what I want and get the fuck gone."

He laughs soft once, looks at the ground. He steps over the bumper and picks up the fishing pole, tosses the line in again. "I was down here last week," he says, sitting down, tucking that jacket under his ass. "Pulled up a fish like you never seen. Put it on a spit on that barrel over there, and folk come running. That's how I got this scarf back."

"Got it back?" I say. "You told me Granddad gave it to you, you wasn't letting it go out of the family for nothing."

He laughs again, keeps looking out at the water. "Boy, you ain't never done some real time like me—most you ever been in is a couple weeks, right? They *take* your shit from you. Everything—ID, clothes, right down to your shoes. They think, *shit* by the time this fool—"

"Look, what you trying to catch outta there?" I say, walking up next to him now. "'Cause I'm about tired of hearing all about what a real man—"

"That old man Jerry gave it to me," he says. "Said he found it under the freeway back long time ago, about the time I went in last. Said he found you under there back one day too."

"Jerry talks crazy. Just like you."

"Yeah well he sure got this one right." Daddy stands up, puts his pole down. "Cops had already been through your place, had your woman run off by the time I got in there, but he slipped word to Laurence, and that brother's got himself some wheels now, can get himself across town in nothing flat looking for them."

"Got some wheels?" I say. "That motherfucker ain't got a dime ain't in some bottle or some pussy."

"Shit, boy," Daddy says. "Pussy must be paying something good nowadays. Dude come down here in an old white Mercedes when we was frying that fish up."

"A *Benz?*" I say, jumping back.

"That's it," Daddy says.

"A *white* one? Old?"

"Yeah, showed me himself when he told me he had that letter. Got some new chrome on it, fixed up the seats inside. Said she's a moody cunt but when she runs she flies."

I grab the bumper, lift it up and throw it straight down on the ledge hard as I can, fuck the shoulder. Daddy jumps back. It clangs down and hangs over. I kick it good and hard, watch it hit the water and sink-slide back where Laurence put it. I step up to Daddy, nose to nose, grab that jacket good with both hands. "You get me to that car, old man. You get me to that brother right motherfucking now. I got a family waiting on me."

Daddy's eyes go sleepy, but he doesn't blink. He just looks back, doesn't move, doesn't talk. I could push him in, I could whup his ass, I could just get on home, but what good is it gonna do me? I shake him again, and again, then let go, step off.

He straightens his jacket out, pulls the scarf even on both sides, and starts walking. "Let's get to Archer Street, boy," he says, moving past me toward the wall. I quick-step catch up, we slip through the Break, and we're gone.

* * *

Getting closer, I can see the fence all around. It just stands there waiting, bored, nobody sticking their shirt through those rusty links, nobody slamming the ball off it, nobody leaning back into those soft spots. Quiet as a dead man up here.

Getting closer, I can see the buckets are sad, ain't even got no nets no more. Not even a scrap of one, like we had in Chicago. That's all we had on that rim, the one Daddy nailed to the maple once my hands got big enough to hold a ball. Even when I was playing, I can't remember a time that dream wasn't walking around in my head, that dude hanging from the big branch and the blood in the snow under him. If it was fall and those leaves were red, they'd come down in a hurry when I put up a brick, and I couldn't get my ass in the house quick enough. He tried making his own hoop for me on Valley Street, but it didn't last—I grabbed the rim once, and it all came down, nearly killed my ass. But it didn't matter, because I'd already started running here, on Archer Street.

Right up on it, I step through the fence. Same shit here—no Laurence yet, more waiting. I ask Daddy how long now but he just stays back, leans into the fence on the outside, keeps looking all over. "He's coming," he say. "You gonna see."

I'm giving Laurence five minutes and then I'm gone. Till then might as well show Daddy he's old. There's a white shirt stuck through the fence down the other end. No ball around so it's gonna have to do.

"You afraid to come in here?" I say, walking over to where he's standing, balling that shirt up tight. He doesn't look at me, just scratches his ear, then cups his hand on his neck right under those tracks.

"Come on, old man, I won't whup you too bad." I come right up on the fence, put my nose through, get a good grip, and lean. It gives, holds me, gives a little more and a little more till I'm almost on my toes, till I'd either be flying or falling down if it weren't holding me. I'm close, almost smelling-close, and my shadow walks right over his feet. "And if that shuffle-foot motherfucker comes around, I'll take you both at once."

He takes his hand off his neck, looks at it good. Then he looks up at me. "You ain't got no ball, boy."

I step to the gate and hold out the shirt. "We'll play with what we got," I say. "And I'll spot you five."

When he throws that shirt-ball back at me I look it over good and close, and see the blood. I watch him sticking his jacket into the fence and see a little shine off those tracks. He leaves the scarf on, wraps it around his neck good and thick like we were back in Chicago. Never used to see him wearing it in good light like this, just those early mornings going down the stairs headed to his shift at the rail yard. When I saw him then, I'd never catch his eyes, because he was already gone. I'd stand there at the door till I couldn't take the cold no more. Never used to get his eyes whenever he was playin' neither, old house or Valley Street, back around the maple tree or coming home from running with Dereck. He'd talk, but even if he looked at you he was already someplace else.

"You fixing to catch a cold?"

He puts his hands out. "You gimme back that ball, or whatever you call it, boy, and I'll take that smile off your face."

I shoot, and it goes through clean but comes loose when it hits the court. "You gimme that scarf," I say, "and we'll wrap this up good. Shit, that thing's stinking so bad we'll maybe get some bounce out of it."

He shoots a finger at me. "You don't know what you look like, boy, laughing at your daddy like that!"

"I know I don't look like no *boy* no more," I say, stepping up and reaching at his throat. I get the scarf but he gets my wrist. I let the ball go, try to get my other hand up but he grabs that one too. I push in toward his head but he's too strong. Those old gray eyes are burning, right dead into mine.

"What you gonna do now, Jake?" he says. His fingers are dug-in good as rail ties, and all the pain shoots back to my shoulder like it could come right off with one twist, like some no-good piece of fruit. "Gonna get your old man in the nuts again, make me bleed again? Go on now, try it if you think you're quick enough."

I try to rip my good arm free but I can't, and only the lowest motherfucker would get their own daddy in the balls twice in the same day. "What the fuck you *doing* here?" I say, but those sleepy eyes don't blink. "What you want with me? Where's my *boy?*"

His face goes tight, his breath is hot out his nose, and I think he's crazy enough to bite right down on mine. But he lets go, pushes me away.

"You and your punk niggers sure got some good shit going out here, didn't you?" he says. He picks up the white shirt, balls it tight, and walks past me to the foul line. He sets up, goes low with those knees, drills it through. He's still got that ugly jumper, elbow out and pulling the string on the follow-through, but when he's on, there's no stopping it. The shirt comes undone when it hits the court.

"You got some good stories going out here, didn't you? Talking some shit about your old man, how you put him through a window and now *you* the man on Valley. Ain't that right, boy—you know how to tell some stories?"

"Maybe I do. Now you tell one your own self. Where's Noel?"

A little sweat drips off his nose, and he snorts hard and cocks his head to the side. "Laurence knows about her, but I know about you," he says. "I know what you done. I know what a punk-ass nigger looks like. You'd kill me dead right now if I didn't have something you wanted."

"I ain't that kind of man," I say. "Ain't gonna kill nobody for nothing."

"I see those eyes, boy," he says, pulling the scarf loose and wiping his brow. "You got that look now same as when you put me outta my own house. Same as them punk-ass niggers just did to me in Chicago. Put a gun in my mouth and hauled me out to the maple."

Before I can ask him when was he in Chicago and is that hoop still up on the tree, I hear that diesel. I hear my Benz. It comes quick up the rise, and Laurence leaves it running when Daddy leans in the window.

I run right at it, slide across the hood, and pull Laurence out onto the street. His glasses come flying off.

"I'll kill your ass!" I say. He reaches for his glasses, but I step down on his hand. "You trying to take everything I got, motherfucker? You gonna give me them keys and tell me where they're at right now!"

"Easy, Jake, easy," he says with his eyes closed. "Just ease off and I'm gonna tell you all about it. Tell him to let me up now, Robertson."

"Go on and let him up, Jake," Daddy says. "The man's got something for you."

"Let him give it to me from down there, it's so good," I say, stepping down harder.

"You gonna get everything you want," Laurence says. "Just gimme them glasses and let me get on my feet, give me one minute to tell you what's going down."

I look at Daddy and he says do it so I step off and walk to the front of the car. Laurence finds the glasses, and his eyes get good and big above that beard. I look away, look back over at Daddy, who's looking at him. Laurence reaches across the roof and they shake some old-timer's way, some way they must have got going in Folsom. I never did figure how tight they might have gotten up in there. Don't matter how long or for what, when you're in the joint you're in some shit, and anybody who can get you through is somebody you need.

"Goddamn, Robertson," Laurence says, laughing without smiling, hitting Daddy with an open hand in the chest. "What you been rolling in? Thought you was gonna get yourself cleaned up."

Daddy jabs him back the same way. "You got some soap I'll let you wash my ass right now, no charge."

I slap the hood. "You all want to get each other up the ass just like old times just gimme them keys and I'll get on out of here."

Laurence laughs again, that salt and pepper beard showing teeth. "Boy's got a mouth on him, don't he," he says to Daddy. "You the one bring him up like that?"

"Blame his momma," Daddy says.

"Ain't they always the one? And always trying to stick it to *us*. But say, Robertson, ain't you told him yet?"

"I'll tell you what you gonna get stuck with is another conviction," I say. "What you doing with this car?"

Laurence looks at Daddy. "Well, ain't you?"

"Lots to tell," Daddy says. "Can't tell it all at once."

"Let's get to it," Laurence says.

"Daddy's stories can wait," I say, looking at Laurence. "I want to hear from *you*. Where they at?"

Laurence hmphs and puts his head down stepping over to me. If he had more room, he'd hit his strut, but just in these couple steps I can see it's there like his shadow at night. "You gonna hear from me all right," he says, sitting down on the hood. "But first go on and look at this." He pulls the letter out of his pocket and I quick-snatch it up.

They came looking for you Jake they said you robbed that lady. I thought you were different but maybe I just dont know you. I dont know where else to go but I cant stay in that room and I dont want you coming looking for me till you get things right. Dont come looking for me here cause I dont want no more trouble.

I just look at that paper in my hand, those ripped edges and those fold-creases and that pencil lead good and smudged but I know it's her hand. I turn it sideways and upside-down but it's still the same.

I look at Laurence. "That all you got?"

"Check that backside too," he says.

I turn it over. *Dont come back till you got something real.* I fold it up and squeeze it tight and put it in my pocket.

Laurence sits there quiet, Daddy too. Behind them I see that fence and the courts and those bare-ass buckets. "Let's hear it then," I say.

"She'll come around," Laurence says. "Don't you worry. She's downtown at the Luby now but she'll come running up outta there when this is all done."

"That so?" I say. "How you know?"

"All we got to do is get a little teamwork going." He looks back at Daddy. "Ain't that right, Robertson? We're all in this one together."

"The fuck we are," I say. "What you two care about them? This is *my* family."

Laurence looks over his shoulder, at Daddy again. "You really didn't tell this boy shit, did you?"

Daddy shrugs. "Lots to tell."

Laurence shakes his head, then cocks it at me, stops. He nods, claps those hands together, squeezes them and rubs them good like they were all soaped up. He goes to that beard with the left, strokes it hard, and those whiskers complain, then puts both his hands out like he's holding a ball. I know what's coming. Yeah I've *seen* these hands all right, seen the lines in the palms you could stand coins in and the scars on the backside he got down at the docks, and I see them smooth-soft now like the only thing they can hold anymore is a bottle. And I can smell him too—not knocking me over but it's still there, like that shadow in the dark, still sour enough to know he wasn't at no church bingo last night.

I pop up off the hood and smack them away. "Yeah I've seen those hands," I say. I look over at Daddy. "Seen yours too. Whole mess of times, and heard every story they got. But look here—you see these?" I say, holding mine out. "Now it's my turn. These are a man's hands. I know how to work. I ain't no drunk, I ain't no thief. Ain't running from shit neither—don't got to go to Fresno or Chicago to fix what I got to fix. So listen here—you all want to sit up here and tell me about let's go down to Cole's and get torn up and take some French-dip for the road whiles we pulling a boost on some Korean grocer, don't even waste my time."

Laurence slaps the hood, Daddy slaps the roof, like they had it timed, and laugh. Laurence leans back and puts a hand over his face, the other on his belly, jiggle-rolling like he was plugged into a wall.

"Well somebody sure wound this boy up," he says. "You all go up inside the Angelus this morning and didn't invite me?"

Daddy shrugs. "Better get on with it."

Laurence pushes himself up. He takes off his glasses, steam-breathes on them and wipes them clean, making nice slow circles with his shirt. "So you want a job that pays, Jake? I got one for you." He smiles and his eyebrows go up and I look at those eyes without the glasses, big heavy in the sockets and dark all under them. "What you think—you listening?"

"I'm listening," I say. "Don't know why."

"You'll see real soon here," Laurence says. He puts his glasses back on and moves back to the driver-side door. He puts his elbows up on the hood and holds his hands out palms-up like before. "But first you *gonna* hear about these hands— because it ain't like you heard before."

"Yeah I never did hear about no drinking nigger get out of the pen and slide right into a Benz," I say. "Why don't you tell me how those hands got hold of my car."

"*Your* car?" He points at me, looks at Daddy. "*His* car? He goes to his beard again. "This dude thinks he's somebody he ain't—thinks he's me. Either that or he's just some sorry thief who can't even—"

"I told you," I say. "I ain't no thief."

"That's right, you ain't," he says. "You ain't gonna take this car from me, because that's what a thief does—takes something ain't his. And that's a low motherfucker."

I laugh. "So what am I doing here listening to two low motherfuckers about?"

"I don't know," Laurence says. "Ask yourself that. But I know some stories, Jake. I know you know how to walk low too. Just because your daddy was locked-up when you ran that boost with those little niggers from this court don't mean he didn't hear about it. Word is you all took that car clean, made out nice."

I shake my head, look up at the sky. "I can't believe I'm hearing this. I ain't got time to listen to this mess."

"You ain't got time?" Laurence says. "Man, all you got is time now. Go on and read that letter again if you don't think so." He slaps down on the roof, and I look back at him. "So listen good."

Daddy is buttoning up that army jacket all the way to the neck. Laurence points across the roof at him but keeps his eyes on me. "The story's different this time, Jake. Your daddy knows it just like I do. This ain't about doing that old routine like he did, get liquored up with Dereck and go knock over Ho's store and stay out on the street till it's all spent up and ain't nothing left for your family. Ain't about breaking into no beauty parlor or hitting no woman or splitting on your kids neither. I know that routine too—you know I do, Jake. And I've seen that girl you got now, I know she don't want to get with just any brother comes walking down the street. I know she's counting on you—she *and* that boy are. If I hadn't seen them I wouldn't even be standing here telling you all this." He steps closer, shakes his head soft. "I know you can't afford to be no boy no more—you're a man. You can't do some punk nigger routine, going out and boosting shit just to get you some junk and a shot of pussy. Shit, that mess don't get you nowhere. And it ain't *right*—that's what I'm really telling you, Jake. I know in my heart all that shit I done, taking something wasn't mine just to get high, it ain't right. It ain't what a *man* does."

He pushes back from the roof, walks over close again. "So you see these hands, Jake? They haven't had nothing in them that was really mine in a long time. When I got out this time, I got me some work at the Ready Man and a room in the Houston. Wasn't but a week later that motherfucker took it from me. I was working in some lady's house and just doing my work, and that motherfucker went into a panic—got to get the nigger out of the house. I came back at the end of the day and there's my shit on the sidewalk, junkies and whores going through it said it was going a nickel a pound. I said this is my shit and some fool came up to me said man anything out on this street belongs to all of us."

Under the hood I hear something pinging. She's knocking, starts to shake a little. I spread my arms across the hood, try to hold her till she stops. She didn't do this before—Laurence can't be treating her right. "What kind of gas you putting in her?"

"Look here, Jake—you want this thing so bad I'll sell it to you when we're all through. Then you'll be happy as a pig in shit, won't you? Got some money, got some wheels, got your lady—"

"Got some *money*?" I stand up. "And who's giving me that? You?"

He nods big and slow. "It's already yours, young man. You let me finish you'll see it clear."

I look over at Daddy again, still on the other side of the car, still with his hands up on the roof. I look over at the court standing empty. What I really want now is a ball. Not some rolled-up shirt and not even some old bald one like I got for a dollar at Sal's Army. I want a real one. I want to get in this Benz, drive out to the store and buy a real one that's gonna last. A ball that bounces true up off the court, and knows how to hang soft on the rim and give you the roll. I want to buy two and keep one in the trunk to give to somebody that don't have one. I want Noel sitting next to me up front, I want to bring that ball back here and play these jokers and show them my hands when I hit eleven jumpers in a row and say *these* are some man's hands. But I know it can't come like that—can't run nowhere yet.

Laurence holds his hands up, pulls a guessing face. "So there I was, out on the street with nothing but these empty hands. Thinking what the fuck am I gonna do? You know what I'm saying here, Jake? Because I know your daddy does. I'm out there with nothing at all, so I just started walking. Didn't even know where I was going. Got a couple blocks and figured I'd get on over to the hall and give George a piece of my mind. All these years working out of there and he strips me clean like I was just some punk nigger out on his first job. So I'm walking, got my head so full of how I'm gonna kill that motherfucker I don't hear see smell nothing else, and if it hadn't been for that brother on the corner that car would have buried me right there on Battery. Dude pulled me out of the street back against the wall. My legs just gave out, and I fell down right there on the sidewalk. If I'd had anything to eat, I probably would have shit my pants. Can't even picture the dude's face now, because he didn't even stay a minute, just moved on. So I just sat there, right there on that corner where everybody crows, and for the first time I got a good look at that building."

A cloud rolls in, big enough to run shadows over us all and make me look up. Breeze must be good and stiff way up there, because it moves quick, and we get the sun back. But the light hits different off Laurence's glasses now, and no matter what way he moves his head I can't catch his eyes. A little one way, I just see my own face looking back at me. A little the other, it's just all the scratches in the lenses going white like chalk marks. Right in-between the sun hits full-on, flashes that bright light and wipes out everything.

"Let me tell you what I saw," he says, putting his foot up on the bumper and spreading his hands wide. "How many times I been in and out of those green doors and I never saw the whole thing? Just sitting there up against that wall, I saw myself going in those doors, and I could smell that floor wax like I buffed it myself, hear those chairs squeaking and that scratchy speaker like I was going up to the window to get my ticket. Going in coming out, going in coming out—only difference was coming out I had a piece of paper said I could work. And some days I didn't even have that. But *every* day, *either* way, my pockets were empty. Now I'm sitting against that wall thinking all this, getting on in the afternoon, and out comes George through those green doors. Now I know you can picture him,

Jake, can't you? He crosses the street, coming right at me. I still want to kill the motherfucker—and he knows it—but I can't get my ass up for nothing—and he knows that too. Sure that brother is ugly and maybe he's still got it in him to fuck somebody up like he could do before he put on that tie, but you got to remember the dude is *smart*. He stops right in front of me, looks me up and down and laughs. Down on your luck, brother? he says to me, drops a dollar down in my lap, and walks off. And I watch it float on down till it hits my leg, and when I see that other George looking up at me I get it. That brother knows he's getting gray, he knows he can't use those hands like he used to. And I know you can smell him just as good as me, Jake—only thing he wants to do with those hands now is give a whupping to niggers."

Laurence punches his hand. "And that's what he's doing! Pow!" he jumps back from the Benz and does a little Ali dance—shuffles his feet, bobs his head, jabs the air. "But the motherfucker is smart—he knows he can't go thirty seconds like that with me even if I'm in a wheelchair. So what's he do?" He rips off his jacket and pushes up his shirtsleeve, jams his finger to his bicep. "Makes like he's kin to Dracula and takes it outta here." He rolls up his pant leg and slaps his calf. "Next time he takes it outta here." He sets his feet wide and bends deep at the knees, circles his arms across his body like a train wheel rod. "When I'm mixing concrete, is George there bringing me some sand? No, he's taking a bite outta my back. When I'm digging that ditch, he's taking it outta my shoulders, and when I'm moving furniture he's getting me every which way. Before I know it I got nothing left, I'm just a bag of bones, ain't I? That motherfucker done beat the shit outta me, and didn't lift nothing but a telephone and a pencil. Now *that's* a smart motherfucker."

He moves back to the car, puts his hands down on the hood, and leans in slow. No light on the lenses now, just his eyes. He leans in and looks at me, looks over at Daddy, back at me. He's smelling-close, and he's sour. He talks low. "You ever read your Bible, Jake? You ever teach this boy about that, Robertson?"

"You looking at me, you can talk to *me*," I say. "I know something about it."

"So I guess you know that story about that Good Samaritan, the dude got beat up on the road and left for dead."

"Heard of it."

"Now *that* was some low motherfuckers, wasn't it?" Laurence says. "Whupped his ass and robbed him too. Took that wallet right out of that dude's pocket while he's lying there flat on his face. Killing and stealing—broke two of them commandments at once."

"But the dude pulls through," I say. "Somebody helps him."

Laurence nods big. "That's right, but hold on." He tilts his chin, looks over the top of his glasses. "Ain't you ever been down in that dirt yourself, Jake?"

"I don't know."

"Sure you have. I'm good and close, boy. I look at you right now and I can see the mud still on you. And ain't it George put you there? Ain't he the one went upside your head and picked your pocket? Every time you get some work at the hall, he's getting some of that money. Don't it belong to you, Jake?"

I shake my head. "I got another job. I don't need the hall no more."

Laurence laughs, so does Daddy. "So what you making there? They move you up to five an hour yet? You want to get treated right in a place like that, Jake, you got to be *sitting* at a desk, not lifting it."

"So what you saying?"

"What am I saying? It's real simple, Jake, real simple. I'm saying you're a young man playin' like an old one. Making like your ears and eyes done left you already. I ain't no Jesus, but I know what that story says—help your neighbor. Open your eyes, boy—I'm your neighbor. You're mine, your daddy's mine too. And George *ain't*—he's the one left us for dead." He looks over at Daddy, who's got his thinking face on, nodding big and slow. "When's the last time you checked yourself in a mirror, boy—can't you see? Can't you see what they see? You're just a replaceable nigger. That's all you are to George or that dude got you moving furniture or whoever. Might as well have a meter on your chest, because from the other side of that desk that's all they see—gonna suck the meat off them bones till you thin as toilet paper, and don't think they won't let you wipe their ass before they flush you."

I wave him off. "So what you want me to do?" I say. I'm getting ready to hear that mess about boosting George all over again. "Quit my job and work for you? Be a thief? Be *your* nigger?"

"Naw, Jake," Daddy says. "*Listen* to the man."

"Let him listen to you first," Laurence says. "Tell him how that song goes."

"*Them that's got is them that gets*," Daddy says. "I know I played that record for you a time or two."

"We're a *team*," Laurence says. "We're *men*. I told you, Jake, this ain't about being no thief, going snatching just anything. We're getting what's *ours*. What George got, he got because he took it from us—took it outta our backs and our pockets. What he got belongs to us, and we're just gonna get it back. That's what a man does. You want to be a man for that little boy of yours, this is how you gonna do it."

I look down and shake my head. That star ornament on the hood is looking right at me, so I feel it, run my finger around to those three points and back to the middle. Never done that before. Never knew it had a spring under the hood that lets you move it around, turn it backwards, lets it take a hit and bounce back in place. I stand it back up, turn it right-ways, pull my shirt tail out and give it a shine. "You know it ain't right, Laurence," I say. "You got this Benz all to yourself, and here I am a family man walking holes in my shoes."

"We're gonna work it out," he says. "This goes smooth as I'm thinking and you'll get everything you need for that boy. That's what a family man's got to do, Jake, I'm telling you. Got to take some responsibility for his future."

I look at him and those lenses are full-up with the sun again, can't see his eyes. Last time, walking those blocks down by the hall, he wasn't talking like this. Wasn't talking so clear. Maybe it's me, but maybe it's him. Funny thing about liquor, it can fuck you up and make you stupid, but with other folks it works like Momma's Joy in the sink, cuts right through all the mess. Daddy's hearing him too. That nodding is good and big now, building building making the car rock now and he slaps his hands down on the roof, makes a fist and pounds it again.

"We gonna get that house!"

He comes around to the front of the car, right up next to me, slaps hard down on my shoulder and squeezes, puts a finger in Laurence's face. "You been talking about taking this and that outta there, but fuck that," he says. "We gonna tie that nigger up and kick his ass to the curb, make that house our own. My boy needs a house and he's gonna have it."

Laurence laughs and puts his hands on his belly. I turn and look at Daddy. Army jacket open, scarf hanging uneven, hair gone gray and smelling like a dog, but those eyes are burning. My shoulder hurts like a motherfucker, but it's all right, that's a real man grabbing it. I can take it. I can take whatever he's got.

* * *

Always that rise on Alameda, always that rise. Me and Daddy are walking back to the house on Valley, and the rise slows him. Laurence went across the bridge to get one last look at George's place before dark. I told him to take Daddy with him, but he said he was setting this job himself, and better for the old man to get his legs moving so they're ready to run tonight. So now we're heading back downtown from Archer Street, and ain't no getting around Valley.

Back then, before Daddy went upstate and I left too, I used to know this street like my own hand. Halfway up, I could sit on the bumper of Mr. Petticoat's Cougar parked tight to the curb, because after his old lady got shot he kept that window shade pulled shut all day long. Up near the top, right before it flattens out onto Valley, the Gordons had a plum tree alongside their house, and if I saw that TV flashing in the window I knew I could climb high as I wanted in that tree and they wouldn't notice nothing, shake some plums out of the branches and even sit up there eating one, just looking out at our house. From there, I could see that hoop Daddy built, even when he was gone, until I went and tore it out. Walking this rise today, I know it's not there—nothing's here anymore. Daddy sits down on the curb where Petticoat's Cougar used to be, breathing hard, but I head past him, hop the Gordons' fence and get down in the grass around that stump. The grass is patchy, brown and green, and the old roots look like big bones floating in water. I move all around, feeling for some pits in the grass but there's nothing, nothing but rocks and those old roots.

I stand up, call down to him. "Come on, old man. We gonna get there or what?"

He coughs between his knees, and spits. "This some kind of race now?"

"Well *you* the one wanted to come up here and see it," I say. "I *told* you wasn't nothing to see but you didn't want to hear that."

I look back over to Valley. And I see it. The hoop is there. I hear the rocks under my feet, hear the ball bouncing, rim rattle-singing—and then it's gone.

"Should have told your friend Laurence to drive you here if you're so weak," I say.

Daddy feels the back of his head, checks his hand. He takes the jacket off and makes his way steady to me. "He ain't no friend," he says, and pulls the scarf off too. He stops in front of me, and the sweat slides down his cheek. "And I ain't weak. You got no idea what I been through."

"He ain't no friend? Then what you doing getting me in on this deal?"

"What else I got, Jake? I got nobody else in the world. What else I know?"

"So you think it's gonna go all smooth with this motherfucker? Get in there and clean the place out and do the split three ways even? If George is so smart like he's talking about, how we gonna do this clean? You think Laurence is scoping the place now? I know that motherfucker—he's on the freeway got one hand around his beer, one around some titty, and trying to reach his dick to the wheel to steer."

Daddy laughs, starts walking out ahead of me, onto Valley. "Come on now, Jake. You know good as me it's a job, don't have nothing to do with being nobody's friend."

I stand there, just watch him walk. The tracks are shining again. "They're both two-stepping, Daddy," I say. "George ain't no drunk but he can sure put on a good show, just the same as Laurence. We're in for some shit with all this, I know it."

Daddy turns around, walks back to me. He gets smelling-close, and I step back, but he puts both hands on my shoulders. "What choice we got, boy? We need some money yesterday, and Laurence knows where to get it. And we gonna get it all, put this family back together. You hear me?" He shakes me good and his eyes get big. "We're taking the whole house, and either one of them niggers tries to stop us I'll tear their throat out."

"You're bleeding," I say. It's dripping off his ear. I reach for the scarf.

He pulls it away. "Don't wipe it with that."

I shake my head. "So you think it makes you look like some bad ass? Or you want to keep me feeling sorry I whupped you this morning?"

"Boy, you didn't whup nothing. And this wouldn't *be* nothing if you hadn't gone and put it there in the first place," he says, shooting a finger at me. "And it ain't stopped since." He puts a hand to it, then wipes it on his pants and walks on again. "All I ever wanted to do my whole life was give you a good home."

I run at him. I see that blood, dark wet slow sliding down his neck when I get close. He turns and his hands are up quick as a boxer bouncing off the ropes. But I'm past him. I jump up the curb, into the dirt grass kicking it up, past one house two and getting closer, running right in front and picking up a rock, looking straight through that window like I did last week, into that room where I was when I put him through, looking down at all the glass and blood around his head, my hands full of it, holding that rock now squeezing it trying to make it bleed, past the window to the door, closer, pegging it with the rock then kicking it good till it gives and sucks me in, brings me down on my knees inside, dark cold everywhere smelling like something caught out in the rain couldn't never get dry.

His steps are quick behind me, and I'm up. "This what you talking about? This all you ever wanted? Well look how you let it get now."

Daddy stops short in front of the door. His eyes go to the window. He walks to it, looks down at the ground, drags his foot back and forth in front of him and watches the dust come up. He steps around me and up the stairs, turns left and heads to the window I brought down. Just some pieces of it there still, hanging onto the wood. I hear his foot crunch the glass on the floor, and I hustle outside, right up to it, look at Daddy's knees and all the way up to that gray hair. He bends down and brings up a piece of glass big as his face. He goes to throw it and just in that quick second when it comes in front of his face I see it—Daddy's face just disappears. Eyes, nose, mouth get wiped clean and I swear it's the face I've always seen looking up at me from the snow under the maple. When he tosses it, it lands right in front of me and goes every which way. Some pieces knock off my boots. Dust floats up. "You did this, Jake."

"I don't know you," I say, quiet, almost to myself. I go down on a knee and pick through the grass. The glass catches the sun and I put the pieces in my hand. I look up at him and squeeze until I can feel it push prick, keep going until it breaks through and I can feel the blood slide sweet slow between my fingers. "You ain't no daddy," I say. "I didn't do nothing at all. You'd gone and fucked it up good enough already." I stand up and shake the glass away and get a taste of that blood. "You never wanted no good home for nobody. You would have killed us all if I hadn't stopped you."

"Got me a good piece of steel in my toe," he says. "Bring that ugly face of yours up to this window, I'll knock your teeth out good as that glass."

"How about I come up there and we'll see if you can do it like a real man," I say, and step through the door. But not quick enough. He's at the top of the stairs already, and that kick catches me good in the chest. Daddy's steps are like thunder and all I can do is roll out onto the dirt.

"I'm gonna close that mouth up good now," he says. I keep rolling and the steps are coming faster. "You owe me, boy. I ain't gonna hear none of that outta that ugly face no more."

Blood on the shoes—that's all I can see when that step comes down. Rolling turning away, I jump up on a knee and punch without looking. Don't even know where I catch him until I see him down, knees into his chest and face right down in the dirt. Don't even see him bleeding again till one hand comes up out of his crotch and locks on to my ankle, and I see Daddy's face, just that same face I've always hated always loved, just that same face was looking up at me seven years and all those dreams ago saying what the hell did you do what the hell did I do but couldn't say a word.

But now he can. "You want my balls, Jake?" He tries to push himself up, but can't. "They're about crushed now, ain't doing nobody no good, so you might as well take them." He rolls flat on his back and pulls his knees apart, and the blood is there.

I go down on a knee, put my hand out. "Let me help you up."

He spits and catches me straight on the cheek, rolls back on his side. "Get outta here with that shit. You ain't helping nothing no more. Go ahead and rip them off, Jake. Take them down to the pawn shop, see what they're paying for some sorry old nigger nuts. Won't be much 'cause they ain't pretty—can't make no pretty face like you got."

"Fuck that," I say, taking my hand back. "You calling this pretty? Open your eyes, Daddy." I brush myself off and step in front of him. His head is down so I reach in and lift his chin, and just like that his hands lock down on my arm, and his eyes lock on mine too. "I'm ugly just the same as you."

He tugs hard, and my shoulder pops. I see colors but I can still see his eyes, burning cold and smoke-gray. "You ugly, boy, you got that right. But not like me." He pulls again, and quick as that I'm on the ground. "You *owe* me, boy," he says. "For everything, but not that face."

Just like that he's there above me. He takes the scarf in both hands, snaps it out straight, and I can see it clear as day, clear as a dream—that maple, those leaves, that water, that fish jumping clean free. I try to move but he catches me, grabs my ankle, lifts and jolt-twists so I know he could tear it off if I try moving. Then he throws it down, snaps the scarf and says it's your face on here now, Jake, and now you gonna know why.

* * *

Everybody's got dreams they just can't shake—and Daddy ain't no different. It's this house, he tells me, all busted-open like a Mississippi shotgun shack and left for dead, the house brings it back.

He went looking, but it had already found him. It was coming around before he even knew it, like a storm rolling in from far-off yonder on a sunny day. When he got back to the Flatlands, old Jerry gave it to him down at the water like it was nothing, like he was returning a tool he couldn't use. Daddy hadn't seen the scarf since he woke up with a scar across the back of his head, but the dream had been inside him since the night I put him through, and way back before.

He didn't know who he was anymore when he got out of Folsom—and he damn-sure didn't know who I was. All he could see was my face, coming around at night.

Daddy goes down on a knee right in front of me, picks up some gravel in his hand and shakes it, lets it all fall through his fingers. "I had to go back to find that face you got your face from," he says. "Had to go back to where it came from, where I came from. And not just Chicago, neither—we go back way beyond that."

Only place hotter than Chicago in the summertime is down South. Been a long time now, but nothing could make me forget that heat. Can't forget how Auntie Thelma would laugh about it neither, serve us up coffee and hot peach cobbler and say you think this is hot that sun last July woulda done burned the black off you. She never could figure how none of us could take it up North, even if you had some good layering to you like her brother Lenny.

Granddad Lenny was the one gave that scarf to Daddy, left it behind in that big blue room. I ask Daddy didn't Lenny bring it up with him from Lowell. "Was Auntie Thelma the one sewed it for him?"

"She did and she didn't," Daddy says. "She had the eyes, but she didn't have the vision. She knew the one who did, though. But not even *that* woman knew the whole story, or thought the damn thing could really be true. Nobody did, till I came to town."

He went trainin' all over the country—to LA, back to Chicago, on down to Mississippi. Came into Lowell with the rains. Jackie was there, with her man Wilbur, and when Daddy sat down dripping at their kitchen table, he knew he wouldn't hardly get that seat wet before they'd be moving him on.

"I come up to that door and see her in the kitchen, hear that bacon crackling, and I swear to God I'm a young man again. The same yellow dress, and it ain't faded a bit," Daddy says, shaking his head. "That's what I remember that day she left out of Chicago. It was raining with the sun still out, and I watched her and Wilbur go through that door and the rain stuck that dress to her legs. Left like she didn't even know me, like I wasn't the one right there with her helped her bury it by the maple and kept it all from Wilbur. Even kept it all from my own wife. And there I am in that house with no sister or brother around no more, just a wife I hardly know and a big blue room won't let me be."

Daddy used to tell me about Jackie now and again, and Malcolm too. There were other kids in the house but they were the only ones stuck around long enough to know each other. I hardly knew them either—only saw Jackie those summers we visited Auntie Thelma, and never seen Malcolm in my entire life.

A car rolls by, dark blue going black, slowing down like it might stop but it keeps rolling on. The sun bounces off the windows till it's passed and I can't see nothing inside. I stand up, and Daddy gets up too, right quick.

"You know him, don't you?" I say.

He pulls an ugly face. "I ain't been on this street in seven years, you think I know every fool comes driving down it?"

"Don't gimme that shit. You know what the fuck I'm talking about." I step up smelling-close. "The face, motherfucker! The *face!*" I say. "I want to know who I been seeing all this time! Who's been hanging in that maple? Is it Malcolm—you up and kill your own brother? Or is it *me?* You come back to bury me now?"

He shakes his head. "All that burying is done now, boy, and I didn't never kill nobody."

He steps back, looks at the house. "I don't even know where I'm going, Jake." He holds up the scarf. "Since I got out I just been following my feet, and this. I ain't making this story up, just following it. Look at us. You think this is how I wanted it? You think this is what I left out of Chicago for, so I can stand right here and smell how much you still hate me?" He shakes his head again. "This story ain't straight, Jake, but I can't tell it no other way but how it is. I could try changing it around, but that wouldn't change the truth."

He says he needs to keep moving. I want to get on back downtown, but he says he's got to get the story out before we go nowhere. He starts walking, just walking around the house, and pretty soon I'm following. Around the side where my window's boarded over, around back to that basement room with the light always on, around the other side just a wall with nothing, to the front again with the glass in the dirt and again and again, cutting a groove, lifting the dirt till it's like we're walking in smoke or a cloud and I'm just following Daddy's feet, following that story going back and around and home again.

He went looking for it, but it had already found him. Never could figure how that dream got inside him, but when it hit him, in Granddad Lenny's blue room after he'd passed, he knew it had some kind of roots. He pulled his momma's sitting chair over to the closet, started pulling things off the shelf, and there was that train—he about fell out of the chair, the whistle up in his head scared him so good. Sewn-in like it was, it couldn't have been bigger than his thumb, but it was *it.* The girl was there too, the pond and the trees. Didn't even know how much he'd been dreaming it till he saw it right in front of him.

He stops. Stands still as a post, looking at the ground. We're out back. "I can't walk no farther," he says. He drops down on his knee, takes a grass clump with each hand, and rips them up, roots and all, and slaps out a space in the dirt, wide as his arms will stretch. He spreads the scarf out in front of him, smooths it down end to end.

"I'm nothing but a kid back then," he says, looking at me, shaking his head. "What—not even thirteen when he passed? But holding this damn thing, I start thinking now I'm a man. My daddy had told me that's when I'd get it, that's when he'd pass it on. I stay in that room for hours, must be, just running my hands over it. Back then it was all still one piece, just seamless like they made it. All them colors and shapes and just the way it *feels*—I start thinking there's something *to* all this stuff's been up in my head so long."

The grass Daddy tore out sits there quiet, the roots hanging every which way, the dirt holding them dried-out and barely hanging on. He shakes his head again. "Course, the straight truth is it didn't make me a man. Didn't change hardly nothing about nothing. The dreams kept coming, and pretty soon I was on my own—Malcolm snuck out to California, and I ain't heard of him to this day. And Jackie's got her own story now."

Daddy laughs but there's nothing funny, his face is turned down. He puts his finger on the train, right there in the middle of the scarf. He squeezes it, reels it in till it's all balled under his hand, and presses it down into the dirt. Then he lets go, and the scarf rises like quick bread but falls over even quicker, and unwinds halfway like an old snakeskin left out in the sun.

"Once I get outta Folsom, and step up in that train, I know it's a long time coming. It's finally all real—*I'm* real." He smacks himself in the chest. "The old dreams, the scarf, all that shit nobody wanted to tell me, it all starts coming together. That train rattles all the way to Chicago and it's cold as a motherfucker, boy, better believe that shit. I ain't seen you since you put your hand up on the glass in Folsom, I know you're probably in California, but I got my mind on finding you—my own way." He lifts his arm and points at me. "Can't get no sleep without seeing that face, so now I'm gonna find it. Train pulls in before the sun comes up three days later, and I walk through the railyard same as I did when I worked there. Don't even have to think about it, just follow my feet through the yard and right out of it, past the streets been fixed up nice for white folk to move in, down to our corner where it's all still the same. Except now most of them houses ain't even lived in, and ours ain't no different. Just feels like ghosts all around, done taken over the whole block and maybe took all the stories with them."

Daddy looks all around him, squinting his eyes when the sun catches them, and fixes his cap down lower to block it out. "You remember that fence we had back there, ran clear around the back?" he says. It's just shadow under that brim. "You remember that maple too, don't you?"

"It's all long gone now, long gone," I say.

He laughs big and gives me his eyes. "Standing just as tall as ever, believe me 'cause I'm telling you, boy. I walk right up to that fence, give the post a good shake to make sure it's gonna hold, grab the maple limb hanging over and hop on up." He grabs my hand, brings it to his arm. "Get a feel yourself, boy, I still got working-man's arms—never lost that."

I jerk my hand away quick. "That fence ain't much," I say. "Any fool can get himself over it."

"I *built* that motherfucker!" he says, smacking the ground. "Me and my daddy put our sweat into it, and ain't nothing taken it down! We took *care* of that place, you hear? Not like that motherfucking *bank*. Take a man's home and let it go to shit."

He smacks down again, and dust comes up from the ground like some steam pot got its lid knocked off. He ducks his head and rubs his eyes, but I know that's only gonna make it worse. He goes at it a minute, keeps his head ducked and coughs hard and dry, finally comes up with his eyes wet. He looks at the house and the ground and all around again. He can't look at me now, but it's all right—I don't want to see nobody crying anyhow, because he did it all to himself.

Daddy keeps his head low, breathes in hard and coughs it out. "There I am, boy, standing back there under that maple again, leaves up over my ankles—must be ten years of them, maybe more. Just standing there looking at windows been broken, siding rotted out, gutters hanging loose. A goddamn mess, and I ain't even seen the inside yet. And I can't. I just sit there in those leaves, boy, can't move a goddamn bone to save my life. I look all around me and I think I ain't been alone like this my whole life. Ain't got nothing. *Nothing!*" Daddy's head comes up but his eyes are shut down tight. "When I was in Folsom, I thought it couldn't get no worse than that. But then I'm sitting there in those leaves thinking I'm a free man now, but what the fuck good it do me? Nobody even gonna know I'm alive till I'm dead. Looking at that house my momma and daddy bought working two jobs till they died, I can see it good as old Saul falling off his horse. All that shit I said got taken from me, *I'm* the one done lost it. I'm the chump to beat all chumps."

I want to tell Daddy he ain't right, but I don't. Because he *is* right, dead-on. I watch him get up now and brush himself off, but I stay right where I'm at.

"But I look at that house and I know one more thing too," Daddy says. "I know there's one thing got taken from me, and can't nobody tell me different."

He's still quick for an old man. He runs at the house, this one right here on Valley Street never did nobody no good, runs right to that basement door and kicks it. I try to grab him, but he won't have none of it. He shoves me straight in the chest, quick-steps back and goes at the door with his shoulder low. Hits it good, straight-on, but not hard enough. He steps off slow, squeezing his shoulder and shutting his eyes tight, backs up and has at it again, rattles the door but can't get it to fall. I look at that door and wonder what Daddy's seeing, but I figure even if I don't have one good shoulder I've got another. I step out in front of him, and just like that I run at it and drive right through, bust the hinges and about break my neck falling in.

It's cold and smells like something died in here even if I can't see nothing at all. Not one thing. This is where we kept all those Chicago boxes Daddy never wanted to open, this is where me and Paula and Cheryl hid cigarettes and beer now and again. This is where Daddy had that shirt hidden away and the light always burning.

He steps on the back end of the door, and I feel it rock. I look back and all I can see is the shape of him, his shadow standing in front of me.

"You remember how we used to have that basement?" he says. "Them tools on the wall and the workbench right under them."

"Can still see it all," I say. Even if Daddy ain't nothing but a shadow, it's all clear as day to me, clear as that dream of mine. I never forgot it, even living out here—never could. The cracked wall, the window with the molding half-broke, the tile floors and the creaks in the stairs, that was my place.

"I can too," Daddy says. "I kept it all just like your granddad had it." He moves to the wall, and his hands spread out across it. My eyes are getting used to the dark now. "You remember how we had them things up there, don't you, Jake?" he says, and his shadow bounces across place by place. "Ladder in the corner, post hole digger here, spade here, shovel and rake here, next to them—"

"T-broom, wood saw, metal saw, U-drill, and metal files on the wall, and the toolbox underneath the bench." Just saying it now, I can feel that box in my hand, that thin handle cold as a motherfucker always clanked an extra beat off the box when you let it go, that bottom corner that didn't meet right and jagged my jeans all the way through to my leg. I can feel those snap-clips and hear them bang up against the top when I'd throw them open and get that good metal smell better than Momma's best tomato soup. I can feel the hammer in my hand too, the grooves down the handle and the notches in the claw where the big nails bit in.

That shadow keeps moving. The head goes slow back and forth, and then he gets low, and lower till he's crouching right near me. I look up at him but I can't make out his eyes.

His head stops. "So go figure what I'm thinking, Jake, when I walk in there and it looks just like this place does now," he says. "Not a goddamn thing to be seen by nobody. Shit, even the smell ain't there no more."

He steps back to the doorway. He looks up at the crosspiece on the jamb, runs his hand up there, presses against it like he's checking to see it's solid. "Up in Folsom, I always thought I'd get back to this house and clean all the ghosts out. Make it my own again."

"Don't go killing yourself over it," I say. "This place ain't worth shit."

"Yeah but that Chicago house *is*," he says. "I lost two homes already, and I'm fixing to get one back before I lose no more." He turns to me again. "Shit boy, that's why I'm *telling* you this!"

"Then tell it, nigger!" I jump up and cock my fist. "Tell it! Tell it!"

"You're telling a good piece of it yourself, looking at me like that, but you don't even know it," he says, running his other hand up on the jamb and letting his eyes follow. I could drill him now, he's wide open. But what else I got?

Daddy picks his foot up and kicks out into the air. "I break that glass and I'm *in*, boy," he says. "All that shit is gone, but I think I can still smell him like I did before, all those years back." He looks at me. "But you weren't even born yet. You wouldn't know nothing about it, would you, boy?" He moves his head back and forth, moving to me, coming smelling-close. I can see him good now. I can see those eyes go small and lock on mine, like he found what he was looking for.

"So I go up the stairs, thinking maybe I'll find him. Whole thing's crazy, but *I'm* crazy. But this time if I get him there won't be no letting go—I'll look him straight in that ugly face and kill him my own self. Ain't gonna let this run around inside no more. At the top before I'm about to put my hand on the door, I hear it just like I'm talking to you right now—that same rocking in the floor upstairs, coming down through the joints. Soon as I'm through that door I can't help but start swinging. Folks are just right down on the floor, dude fucking that girl like a dog. I knock those heads together, and soon as I see that blood fly I don't even need no tool, I just beat that man with my own two hands. Girl picks up her works and goes running, and I knock that motherfucker cold and drop him out the window right on that big jiggly ass of hers. She screams, and all those junkies downstairs start coming to life. I get out into the hall, rip a piece of that broken stair railing out of the wall, and go getting my house back. Don't have to knock the teeth out of about half of them before the whole mess clears out. But I'm still crazy as a motherfucker, I snap that railing over my knee, 'cause I didn't get *him*. I looked at every one of those jokers' faces and tried to make it his but not a god-damn one was him, not even the one I killed."

Outside a car engine gets revving. The dude guns it up real big, lets off till it almost cuts out, then hits it again. He holds it, and Daddy steps outside to look but I know he can't see a thing. When it comes down now it purrs smooth and steady as a good bass in the back of the band, good and warm now, ready to go.

I step out through the doorway, till I can feel that sun on me again. "Too cold inside here," I say. "And what you doing looking for some dead man anyway? Granddad Lenny passed long time back."

That car down the street jumps into gear and roars on by. Daddy follows that sound all the way down the block like he can see it. "You don't know who he is," he says. "And I don't know if he's dead."

"You found yourself some *good* rock someplace," I say.

"Just listen, Jake," he says. "Just try to hear me." He rubs his hands and puts them up to show me. "This is all I got. Them junkie-zombies tore our house apart, so I get down to work cleaning all that shit out. Patching the walls, scrubbing the floors, putting in glass, using anything I can find and riffing the rest. Just using my own hands and working them to the bone so my mind won't run and I'll just hit that floor dead asleep come night. But it don't work, Jake—every night I get up and set out looking. Railyard, bus depot, missions and pool halls downtown, every bar I know, all the corners, and I climb up in that maple a time or two. Can't find shit till I come back and hit that floor. You're in that dream, boy, and so is he. After a while I know I got to go, can't stay in this house, even if it *is* mine." He looks out to the street again, and his mouth gets tight. "Then the junkies come back, just bust right in. And before I can get out of that room, they kick the door down. If it's just one or two you know your daddy's got a fighting chance, but they're five and they're strapped."

His hand goes to those tracks on his head. I don't want to look but I can't look nowhere else. That's my daddy's blood. What else do I got?

He sucks the blood off his fingers like he's eating ribs. "I catch a couple of them punk niggers good in the jaw 'cause I still got something in me, but what's a man supposed to do? They stomp my balls, Jake. They turn them guns around and whip me like a dog. My hands get tied, and I'm down on my knees. Bleeding bad, and got a gun nose pressing against my own. I look up at that little joker holding it and he asks me do I want to play. He takes the gun back, knocks out all the bullets but one, and slaps that chamber. It's still spinning when he presses it up in my nose again. *Punk* motherfucking nigger! Says he ain't gonna do it but once, 'cause an old man ain't worth his time, and if he don't hit it I can get on outta there. I look up in his eyes Jake and I think I see you." Daddy looks down and shakes his head. "I think it's you pushing me through but I know it ain't. Dude pulls the hammer but it just rings like a slap cross the face."

My feet are itching. I need to move. Daddy can stand here inside his shadow all he wants, but I'm gonna get some blood pumping. I get across the lot, just up and run, and there it is—I see it like it was waiting for me to find it. Out on the edge of the yard, right up against the fence the Thompsons put up the same year

Daddy got sent to Folsom, a ball is sitting quiet. Nothing good, just a tennis ball like you'd throw to your dog, fuzz all worn-down and too flat to bounce anymore. Sun sucked all the color out of the side sitting up, too—gone gray as ashes.

I throw it before he looks, hits him square in the chest. "Pick it up and run, old man." I dig my heel in the ground and drag it, cutting a line through the dirt like we used to do when the boys played football out here. "See if you can score on me."

He picks it up and throws it right at the house. "Boy, you *are* your momma's child."

I run over and pick it up. I give it a good squeeze again, then look Daddy straight up and down. Maybe he got hard in the pen, maybe he gets in a lucky punch now and then, but he's still soft. "Better get your ass set, old man. I'm coming right through you."

I run at him. Only takes me a couple steps to get my stride. Daddy pulls that pussy move trying to shuffle away, but I can dance, and I hit him dead-on. When I do, it's like one of those times when everything slows down good so you can see it—really see it. I lower my good shoulder just like a tailback would knifing through the line, hit it at an angle so nobody can get a good hold on you. I catch him high in the chest and step step and drive through and he grabs at me tries to get those arms around but I keep driving and they slip away, and when my head lifts up I see it's still him, still Daddy falling away breaking through the window, still Daddy breaking his head open hitting the ground, still Daddy got his eyes burning through me and I can't look away.

The momentum takes me. I get caught in his legs and fall. The ball rolls away slow in the dirt. I push myself up to get it, but Daddy locks onto my ankle. I kick but I can't shake him.

"This is it," he says, and jerks me to him. "Stop that shit and listen close, boy! You want to make this some motherfucking game? You want to act like some punk nigger?"

"*Fuck* you!" I push up on my hands for some leverage and swing a leg at him, hit his arm, and pull my other foot free. "That what you saying I am? I'm the one got the family now—if your sorry ass don't make me lose it. *You* the one playing to lose here, Daddy. You want to call me a punk nigger, well then *you* the one raised me." I grab a hand of dirt and throw it at him. "You don't even know who I am."

Daddy wipes his face. He looks back at me, and it's those eyes. "I sure do, Jake," he says. He moves on his hands and knees now till he's right up smelling-close. I want to split out of here but I don't know what's stopping me. "You *are* my boy. I *did* raise you. But not to be no punk. That's what I'm sitting here telling you now. I looked in that kid's eyes but there wasn't nothing there. Not a goddamn thing. If he killed me, in his head he wouldn't have been doing nothing but sweeping some shit out of the house. But that ain't what you did, boy. When you fought me that night you was fighting your *daddy*. I could see it in your eyes. You had love in those eyes, Jake. I could see it then and I can see it now. They threw me outside, and when I smelled those leaves I knew it right then."

I look past him at the house, see the ball sitting there quiet again. What kind of stupid motherfucker am I? Noel and William are still about as lost as a couple pennies in the ocean, and I ain't even in the water yet. I hear another engine, and I wonder if Laurence could be back, if he has them sitting in my car. I even think nobody ever told me Lydell went off and died, so who's saying it won't be that Olds flashing by?

Daddy sits up quick, leans forward and puts a hand down on my shoulder. "That's what I come back for," he says.

The sound runs away quick, and all that's left is me and Daddy. His throat is open, but I lock my hand down on his shoulder, and pull us tight. "Who'd you come back for?" I say. "I done told you already if you want to kill me then go on and do it. You can go on and try."

"Naw, Jake, that ain't it," he says. "I had it all turned around." He locks on hard. "All that time I was in Folsom, I was holding on to that face. All I could see was the hate, Jake. But sitting there in those leaves I could smell myself, boy." Daddy looks down, but I can hear him sniffing. His voice goes soft again. "I didn't hate nobody but myself. I knew only a boy who loved his daddy could go and do what you did."

"So you almost killed a man, that right?" I say. "You come back to finish the job? Or you thinking I'm gonna do it now?"

He shakes his head. "Naw Jake, I'm all through with that. All through for good." He looks up slow and wipes his eye. "I know that ain't who you are neither, not some kid—"

"Don't try to tell me who I am!" I push him away. "I'm trying to be a family man now and you don't know shit about that. You want to come in here and get me to say I love you because you can cry a river about what a fuck-up you was? Take that shit and get on outta here, old man. Find someplace you belong."

"You don't know the family, Jake," he says. "Not like I do."

* * *

I hear Daddy start talking, and I know I'm slipping. Can't help myself. I've been holding out good and long but I'm nothing but a man. It's like fishing—you can't just sit looking at the water if you want to go home with some supper. You've got to bait the line up, got to hang it out there and wait, long past when you want to get up and leave. And if you get lucky and something comes around, it's gonna take some work pulling it out. When he says maybe I can't remember how old Auntie Thelma could tell a story, I want to tell him story time is up, motherfucker, but I know I'm slipping, I know I can't run now, the line is tugging. Got to take a chance and pull this one up. If I don't, who knows how much longer that dream's gonna run around inside, even if I *do* find Noel and my boy. Maybe the old man is right. Maybe he *does* have something to tell me. Maybe if I really knew where I came from, I'd know my way up out of this mess. Daddy keeps talking, and soon enough I can hear that train whistle and that rattling over the rails, and smell that thick Mississippi air good enough to wipe it off my face. Soon enough it's Auntie Thelma talking, and I can see it just like he's spinning it, and I know this story is all I've got.

There was always something about Auntie Thelma, but the way Daddy told it you'd think the woman had some kind of magic. She'd sniffed him from all the way up in those hills, she told him when he finally made it to the farm. The crows filled up that maple hanging over her front porch seven nights running before she had the dream, and when she did, she knew he was coming. Two weeks later, Daddy rolled in on that train that came south along the Mississippi to a place he thought he'd seen the last of. Jackie took him in, gave him his own room, but she didn't know to keep the liquor hid. Everybody knows Egret Pond didn't sit but a few miles from Lowell—a short walk through a few long hills was how folk always told it—but Thelma don't got young legs like she used to, so she let the neighbor walk that word down himself. Wilbur was the one that opened it that Saturday Jackie was at the parlor, just him and Daddy eating the last of the bacon and grits. Auntie's looking for a strong hand to help with the planting, he told him. Daddy knew he had to get gone.

He near about sweat blood into that soil. He set out through those hills that same morning, made it there with enough light left to see the farm needed work worse than a young man on the county. Auntie Thelma hardly gave him a good how-do before she had a meal in front of him and a hoe in his hand and he'd best get that north fence fixed before sundown 'cause she was tired of calling after that horse every morning. He went right to it—didn't know where it was taking him, but what else was he gonna do? No money, no car, no gun, no house, and no juice with no-damn-body, why not haul manure out to the corn field and spread it around, why not fix the chicken coop and learn to look for the eggs, why not cut sugar cane and weed the sweet potato patch and get his hands down in the dirt up to his elbows planting seeds so come springtime at least Thelma could fix him something good to eat?

You gonna live here you better remember whose house you in. She had that finger, and she'd shoot it at him for any little thing, just like a woman can. That same first evening, he tried coming inside with the mud of those fields on him, and Thelma about bolted the door back shut. Only one way to do things in Auntie Thelma's house, and he had to learn right-quick. But soon enough he had the routine down—up at dawn, eat enough to last through the day, then walk the sleep out of you and get your hands in the ground till you sweat through one shirt and then another. If your stomach starts talking at you, break off a piece of cane and just tell it to hush now 'cause it'll get filled up good once you're scrubbed clean and the day's work is behind you.

After supper the stories started up. She spun them out slow, and they went on for days. Daddy had his own too, but once Thelma starts you've got to just sit back. Out in the fields he'd turn hers over in that soil, pull them up and chew on them with that cane to get him through the day, till he could tell them himself, till they were his own.

That first night, she shows him her hands. Sat her chair tight against his so she could look him in the eye, put her hands in his. Big and strong and aching from knowing hard work for too long, but soft at the tips, maybe a little something God gave her just so she could feel like a woman. That finger she pointed with was a story all by itself.

Gonna give it to you good and simple . . . better remember. Wasn't just the family that could see it—everybody in those parts who passed through the house said the same, even before she got her finger stuck in the door. Thelma had her Granny C-C in her something powerful. Weren't no more pure Choctaw around like the old lady, but a blind man could see Thelma had a way of looking down into something told you she was gonna be a seer just the same. When the old lady's eyes started to go, she wanted that little girl Thelma. Didn't matter that she was the blackest girl of C-C's blackest girl, didn't matter that she had to damn-near burn those naps to make them braid, Granny C-C said Thelma was the one, and they hooked those crooked fingers together and she took her home. August and Lucile thought the old lady just wanted help getting home that night, but she wouldn't let her go. Auntie Thelma told Daddy there's still nights she can hear her own daddy's voice saying you ain't gonna make no Indian out of my girl, still times in the dark she can feel those cold bony hands dig into her sides and lift her up on that porch and she can feel that voice thick as a man's hand slap August and Lucile upside the head. *This one's mine—I'm the one brought us here and I need somebody to keep us here.*

This is who we got in us, Daddy tells me. I look at my own hands, brush the dirt off, and really try to see something. No crook in my pointing finger, just that swell in my pinky from breaking it once on Archer Street. But what else I got in me? Daddy keeps spinning it out, but I hear Auntie Thelma's voice talking all the same, and I think how come I never heard this before. I know I was just a kid, but how did I end up here, playin' to save my life in these Flatlands, and I don't even know who my people are? I spit in my hands, scrub them and wipe them on my pants, and I think how come I don't even know my own story? When we went down to Egret Pond from Chicago those summers I was nothing but a kid, messing around too much to hear it. The more old Auntie goes on, the more I know there's something tugging on that line. The more I hear about my Great-Great-Granny Choctaw and those dreams she fed Thelma like milk, the more I start feeling I still got to wait this out, pull this one up and see what it is.

Daddy keeps talking but I can't believe it, even if I know it's true. Can't. Just can't. The more I pull it in, the more it runs away. I listen to it all but I know there's a lie in there somewhere. I know this house has a crack someplace down below, and soon enough it's all coming down. If I *did* have a great-great was an Indian, who am I gonna ask about it now? She's long gone, and I ain't heading back down to no Mississippi just to find out, even if I *was* running from something. Maybe she *was* the one who could see things, just like Thelma told it to Daddy. Maybe she *was* that little girl who had the dream and followed it into the woods, past the old hickory with the leaves gone yellow to the pond where the egrets picked fish out of the water all day long. Maybe it all went down like that, maybe it ain't just some noise Daddy made up to make me think I really come from something. Could be her folk did call her the seer when their men went to that pond themselves and saw they'd be eating good now, saw that little girl wasn't crazy after all. Could be, and if I believed it all like Thelma did and now Daddy too, maybe I could picture the whole thing. Maybe I'd think I was just remembering it instead of making it up. Maybe I'd see Thelma stick her finger in the door trying to follow August out into the fields, see Great-Great-Granny C-C look at that child and know this one's gonna be the one, even after twelve of her own with that slave set free and five died still inside her and not a one that lived learned how to make the old talk, and this Thelma child couldn't neither but she had two good ears and a voice loud and clear. Clear enough to tell back those stories just the way she heard them, all the dreams too, and to write them down once she had her letters learned good. If I weren't trying to sniff the lie, I'd drink down the whole thing like a cold beer in a bottle at the end of a two-shirt day. I'd see Auntie Thelma putting Great-Great to bed the night Granddad Lenny gave Jo-Jo the ring and told her he had a job waiting up the line in Chicago, even when it wasn't nothing but sweet hope. I'd see that little old lady lock her crooked finger into Thelma's and whisper-shout it so Thelma couldn't pretend *the dream is back, been back*. I'd see it myself just like she was telling it, just like she was dreaming it, and I'd know this dream was kin to the old one, the one that brought her people to Egret Pond, but it wasn't the same. Something else set this dream off, some other kind of hunger. This time, Great-Great would be old and slow, can't keep up with that little girl in front of her. This time all the kudzu and every tree in the woods would be shaking, the leaves falling yellow red rusted and black, they'd whip up when she got to the edge of that pond, when the egrets carried that little girl into the air and the fish started jumping, snapping at those leaves like they were flies full of honey, tearing them to pieces till one gets his mouth stuffed full of them and they whip him down into the dirt. He's a big fish with a man's face. A face she knows but don't know for sure, red-brown skin and Lenny's eyes and Jo-Jo's nose, but still like a picture ain't finished painting yet. His mouth is full and he's on the ground flapping and he bites down on those leaves till they bleed, turn to skin and bones. And if I were buying all this I'd buy it *all*, even say *Amen, Daddy* when I picture that fish's guts just busting open like they were shot out of a gun, and I'd see old Great-Great run at it like it was her own child, try to stuff those guts back in while they were still hot and pumping, I'd see her whip that blue scarf off her neck and wrap that fish up in it good and tight.

If this is how Daddy wants to play it, it's all right by me. All this dribbling ain't gonna help none when he goes to shoot. Any way he brings it, I'm still swatting it, gonna knock it clean into the fences and tell him to get his sorry ass *gone*.

Because I can still smell him. I can still feel the floor give when I walk in here. Don't matter how he builds it. Don't matter if he wants to take me back to that blue room in our Chicago house, I ain't going in. I'll just stand at the door and watch, let this old fool talk till he cries, let him roll this movie and give me some popcorn if he wants to—I ain't going in. But maybe I will, just to get it straight, once and for all. Just step in, tackle him down again so he can't run no more. Hold him down there in the dirt and tell him even if it's true I don't give a damn. Hold him down and look in those eyes and see it just like he's telling it. See Auntie Thelma knit that scarf just like Granny C-C tells her, just how it looked in that dream, see Daddy down in the muck of those fields day in day out weeding and planting and digging so much he can feel that soil inside him he can feel himself digging inside and pulling them rotten plants, fishing out all the roots so he can put himself right. And I'll see him wake up in the middle of that old dream, see him wake up with his head bleeding and the dream is *on* now, brother, see him walking outside and know he's still inside it, following those colored leaves through the dark, staying on the path every step like he's walked it a thousand times, all the way to the pond where the leaves whip up and the water rolls warm as can be when he strips down and steps in it, and that blood flows like sweat but it's good because it's finally letting go, he's finally there and the water gets to bubbling and he can feel it tickling him till he's so hard a cat couldn't scratch it and he's gonna come 'cause it's been so goddamn long when that fish bites him. Near bites him off and he jumps out with that fish still lockjawed on, he's bleeding like he can't believe but he pries it off, he holds that fish changing colors up out of the water green yellow red rusted like the leaves and gets it on the ground. He's bleeding but he slams it down, hits it and hits it till it spits back his blood and that face ain't no fish no more. It's a man. Daddy knows it, he can see it, and I can too.

It's that face in the maple, done stole inside Daddy's dream just like mine.

Thelma told him she knew. Knew he'd come around, knew he had to come down and get it himself. Told him ain't none of it what she expected but ain't none of it a surprise neither. Didn't know he'd be crawling back from that pond with his balls busted and that fish in his belly. Didn't figure he'd puke up blood till morning. But she was sure he'd find it somehow—or it would find him. And now that it did, it was high time to get on back. *Don't spend no more time here waiting for that bleeding to stop, these old leaves can't patch up nothing. Quit chasing after what's done and gone, get on back home and it'll stop soon enough.*

"But what I got?" Daddy looks at me—nappy gray hair and slumping shoulders and bags under his eyes you could pick a house clean with. We're just sitting here with a whole lot of nothing, no more Chicago no more Mississippi, nothing we can call our own. But I can still smell him.

"What I got to get back to?" he says. "Just my son. You're the only—"

"No," I say. "You ain't never been no kind of daddy to me. Ain't starting now."

"Boy, I'm just trying to tell you one thing—"

"What more you got to tell?" I stand up and step up. "I'm gonna kick that motherfucking mouth closed next story I hear coming from it. I don't want to hear no more *from where you done come.*" I kick the dirt at him, start walking to the street. "Trying to tell me you my daddy and you ain't even a grown man yet."

"You're right, boy, I ain't," he says, but I just keep on walking. I get near the house when that ball hits me in the back of the head.

I turn around. He's up, those eyes are burning. "Where's that line?" he says.

The ball is sitting right in it. I pick it up, kick some dirt over the line and head toward the street again.

"Maybe I ain't no good daddy, Jake, but you throw that ball on back here you gonna see what kind of man I am."

The street is quiet as can be, no cars going nowhere. I turn around. I take my jacket off, and he takes off his. I throw the ball to him and walk back to where that line was, drag my heel through it good and deep and all the way across. I step over it, keep walking till I'm halfway to him.

"I always wanted to kill you, Jake," he says. "Right from the second you were born."

"Go on and bring it."

He runs. I see those knees kicking up and arms pumping, and I know I'm supposed to dig in right here but my body just starts moving, going at him, getting dead-set and this time I'm gonna finish the job. Faster faster closer and that stiff-arm comes out but I know how to slide under because he taught me himself, I duck and turn and drive that shoulder up and in and through, right in the ribs, right in the heart, right in the jaw so he can't run no more lies. But he's got his moves, got his legs under him still, and he lays that other shoulder into mine, cracks it good so I won't forget, turns me spins me till I'm on one foot trying to stay up then stepping back and back toward the line closer now but he throws the ball down because it ain't about that no more and wraps that other arm around. Pushes me back and back and *gonna tell you something now boy* getting closer right up to the line *about a man you never knew* but I get my legs back under me and my shoulder is burning with him squeezing me *knocked your momma up before I killed him* but I don't pay it no nevermind because I'm holding my ground *and left his face in you* and stepping stepping pushing him back pushing him pushing him heavy like he's all the weight in the world now and it just comes up out of me *get the fuck back get back get* pushing him throwing him down and I'm free I watch him fall and grab at me but he can't pull me with him I'm free and he hits the ground and that dust comes up thick and I can do whatever I want now kick him slap him kill him stomp his balls he's wide open now so I lift my foot to bring it down and he's got nothing but those empty hands no ball no gun no scarf but he holds them up straight to stop whatever's coming down shoots them up empty and full of blood and it flicks me like flies lost their way in the dark hits under my eye and drips past my nose and just one drop onto my lip just one hot and sharp as a rock pulled out of the fire but quick as that it melts goes down easy and I pull my foot away.

The blood is all around his head now, pooled out in the dirt. Those eyes are still burning too much to be dead. I drop down and I pick his head up. Gentle, like he was a baby. The blood is hot on my hands and I can still taste it in my mouth and down inside.

He looks up at me. "I was gonna kill you, Jake. Soon as you come out I had a mind to break that neck before you even got a breath in you. That man Haley shamed me, boy, you got to believe me. Your momma did too but I knew by then she was already gone." He coughs, and his body jerks like a current went through it, but I hold him. "That man was a Pullman porter, and he took her heart right out of her chest, boy, made me know I never even had it. I was fixing to make you my Isaac, told myself God's telling me go on and take this child from her and teach her a lesson, don't let her see that face no more. So when the time come, I locked her in that room. Figured it happened once, it could happen again as long as she didn't get out of that room. I kept waiting all those nine months to wake up and see it happen just like with Jackie, except this time I wouldn't be helping nobody try to put nothing back in, I'd take it outside and bury it under that maple straightaway. She damn-near passed out pushing you through, couldn't have stopped me if she tried, boy. And I had you by the ankle, held you right up to her so she could get a look at your face before I threw you against the wall, but then you slipped. And I couldn't even help myself, was like the angel whipping down and stilling that knife—I caught you. Both hands—ain't never moved so quick in my life. And there you were in my hands, boy, and your eyes popped open at me, and I knew you were mine. Mine from now on, no matter who you came from."

He coughs again and his body jerks the same way. Dry as a bone now, nothing more coming up. His other hand comes up to his face, but I've held my boy enough to know that it ain't just coughing no more. But I don't need to look—a grown man don't need nobody seeing him do that, most of all another man.

This house looks small as it ever did, even from down here in the dirt. Even smaller maybe. You'd think with all that empty space in there now it would look plenty big to hold just about anybody but somehow it don't.

Another car coming—can't see it from back here but I can feel the bass getting closer. And I don't need to see, soon as I hear that engine humming. My Benz. Laurence sniffed us. Or maybe Daddy told him to come back and see if he was still here running his story. Or maybe that car just has a way of getting you where you need to go.

Laurence hits the horn, two three four times like Daddy's coughs. Or maybe it's Noel, sitting up front and can't wait two seconds for nothing, like usual. Could be my boy too, sitting up behind that wheel and making like he's driving, just like Daddy Jake.

Laurence shouts out after me and Daddy. The music goes down, and I hear the door open.

Daddy wipes his hand across his eyes and under his nose. "I know it's true, Jake," he says. "I know I didn't even do the best I could. But I've got to hear it from you, boy. You're my boy, ain't you now?"

I look up and see Laurence come around the house. I look down at Daddy and his face is a mess, gray eyes gone red, and dirt and blood besides. I reach quick out for my sleeve, loosen the button and wipe him clean, squeeze his nose, brush his mouth, press into those eye sockets and back behind the ears. "It's all right," I say, and I stand, and I pull him up with both hands, and I look at him straight and squeeze those hands till he squeezes back. "I owe you, Daddy."

CHAPTER 9
CROSS THE BRIDGE

Nobody knows where he comes from. And nobody knows where he's going, don't matter what kind of plan he's got. Only thing to do when you step out into that street is go on that hunch inside you and whichever way the wind is blowing.

Downtown, me and Daddy get out of that car, watch Laurence turn the corner and disappear. I know Daddy could ride around all day long, but I wasn't gonna take it one more minute, even if it got him to quit crying about being hungry. Can't stand being in my car if it ain't still mine.

It's getting late, and we're deep down in it. Down at the Cliffs again, under the bridge, darkest place in all the Flatlands when the day's through. Laurence drops us here and says he'll be back with all the tools in a couple hours. He wants to take us to the Ready Man but I tell him this is where I'm starting, gonna look my own way because if Noel changes her mind, if she does step out on that street, I don't want nobody finding her first. Laurence laughs at that and says just you be patient young brother, but I tell him go on and get gone.

Dont come back till you got something real. Moving, quick-stepping, I dig down in my pocket and pull out the letter. It's all I've got now—no home, no car, no job, no family I can find—and you can't even call it that. Just some words on a piece of paper. Clouds rolling in again, and this wouldn't even cover my head if they opened up on me. Just something she wrote in a hurry and tore off. I stop at Parker's Alley and read it again, but it's still the same—all my shouting about Laurence being a lying motherfucker ain't changed it one bit. I stick it back in my pocket and keep walking, move on down into the alley where it's getting dark, and just like that I see her. There she is, stepping out of that clinic, and it's just last week halfway down the alley but it's as far away as never was never gonna be no more. There he is, little William coughing and I can't keep him from it, and she takes him out of my arms and opens up her shirt. I know it's just my head playin' me, and I shake it off. How did it all get so fucked up so quick like this? *I thought you was different but maybe I just dont know you.* And I know she's right, wouldn't make no difference if she wrote it on toilet paper or the LA Times. The two of them deserve better than what I've got, oughta have themselves some nice things, live like the folk on TV do. Soon as I find them we're getting up outta these Flatlands—don't care what I've got to do no more. Ain't nobody living no kind of good life down here. Maybe up across that bridge, over there where George is, but not here.

"Got to find us some food," Daddy says. He's quick-stepping it with me now, trying to keep up and holding my shirt to his head. I gave it to him up at the house, figured I could zip my jacket up if the rain comes. It's coming, all right.

I keep on down the alley, past the door to the Birdhouse and all the folk outside. A line plenty long to make your feet hurt, but not like the snake out front, trying to get in the St. Al's. I tell him to move his ass. "You saw that line good as me. You want to wait in it, go on back there." End of the month, end of a long weekend, and all the county checks are smoked spooked drunk-up tricked-out and partied-down six feet under. Rain on top of that, and ain't a joker in town wants to be in a cardboard condo if they can help it. Folks are making like dominos all up and down the block twice back and around, probably started staking out their spots soon as the morning count was through. And at St. Al's you never know when there's gonna be a cop inside that door just waiting to check your warrants, letting you get a good sniff of that hot food before he puts you in the car and serves you up a cold plate down at the county. I've been hungry before, and Daddy has too, and we both know worst thing you can do is get your mind set on something you know you can't have.

Got to see Chaka. That's the thing right now. I come up under that window and hit it with some rocks, one two three, the way I've seen Laurence do. I was about ready to put his ass *through* a window when I looked at the Benz and didn't see nobody with him. Telling me Noel and my boy done gone lost and all he's got for me is some piece of paper—I wanted to kill that motherfucker. But the only thing I want more than that is to find them, so I just kicked out that headlight instead, let Laurence pick it up if he wanted to.

She comes to that window looking like the gloves are already off, leans up to it slow with those arms crossed and her leather zipped-up tight. Got a red umbrella tucked to her side, and it comes to the glass, pointing at me and Daddy both and then right on down the alley. She does that little chin-throw, and I can't read lips but I know this ain't no good Mississippi how-do.

"Where's she at?" I say. "Where they got them?" Laurence took Noel down here to Chaka straightaway when he found her, and Chaka took her to Luby's, that place women can go when they're running from their men folk—but nobody but those women know where it is. "I ain't hit her, I ain't done nothing!"

Chaka just points that umbrella down the alley. I spin Daddy around and hold that shirt up high. "Look at this dude—bleeding like a runaway train! Ain't time to wait in no line!"

She shakes her head and throws that umbrella down. She cuts away from the window jaw-jamming full throttle, and I know we still ain't getting no cobbler and coffee but we might just get that door open.

I put the shirt back on Daddy's tracks and walk him over to that door, flip his arm over my shoulder like he can't walk without me.

That big green door squeaks pulling open. Chaka brings it back halfway, puts her shoulder through, and shoots her umbrella right up under my chin. "You think I don't know who you are?"

I jump back, pull Daddy with me, smack that umbrella but Chaka holds it tight. "Shit, woman—put that shit down! I told you I ain't done *nothing!*" I point at Daddy's head. "Can't you see this man needs a bandage?"

"I can see it mighty fine," she says. Still got those *i-i-i*'s. She reaches out with that other hand got some gauze in it, keeps her foot in the door and pulls Daddy to her. But her eyes stay with me. "So what am I fixing him up for?" she says. "He's gonna take the TV while you jumping the car?"

I let my arm slip off his shoulder. She turns him around and tilts his head down, starts snipping that gauze. I look straight into that gray nappy mess and just for a second I think do I know who he is. Been lying all these years—Momma did too, but he should have been the one to 'fess. Don't know for sure, but maybe I don't care no more neither.

"You gonna let us in and fix him right?" I say. She puts her hands down and looks at me, braids tied-back, leather zipped-up, lips shining but I know there's some teeth behind there ready to bite. She sucks back on them then looks away, gives Daddy a little pat on the shoulder and a let's go. I catch the door and slide on through. "I don't know what all that noise is about no how." My voice bounces all around in this stairway. "I ain't *got* no car, no TV neither. Don't even got my place no more."

Chaka shoots around, and I see that face right over Daddy's shoulder. "So who you gonna blame for that? Huh? Is that the *man's* fault you went and took a lady's purse?"

"Woman, shut your ass," I say, waving at the air. "What you know about running a family when you're in the kind of mess I'm in?"

Daddy takes the last step up and opens the door. "Only thing I know is I'm fixing to get some food in me and get this head of mine patched up."

Chaka slaps his hand off the door and it suck-thwaps shut. "You don't do a thing in this building without my say-so, old-timer. Nothing but a scratch you got yourself on that big old head, won't take but a minute soon as I'm good and ready." She opens it herself, looks back at me when Daddy walks on through. "Better tell that boy of yours down there to keep his mouth shut too. He thinks he's mighty good-looking but he still don't know how to treat his lady. Might be I could tell him a thing or two would keep his ass out of jail while I'm at it."

She slides inside, and I quick-hop up those stairs, follow them down the hall but they're already out of sight. When I get to Chaka's door it's open, but I look around thinking maybe I got lost. Walls look like the roll-downs out on Third, but just black on white and every which way—no color, no style in those tags. Floor is blacked up too, the kind you can't buff out. Half those benches are gone missing, only two left and that nice red seat they had on there is torn up like somebody heard there was a fifty-dollar bill inside. Just one dude lying there asleep, and it doesn't take me but a second to know it's Pope Riley. Same black robe, same red hair and beard. Hair is long and greasy, robe is torn bad as the seat, and those feet like a couple of turtles out in the desert, hard and swollen up and some red spots and black toenails to boot.

"Don't touch it like that!" Daddy says. I follow his voice to the back room, same place Chaka fixed my hand before. Her jacket and umbrella are on the counter with a couple of open bottles. Daddy's chin is in his chest, and Chaka has one hand on his forehead and one pressing in with a pad from behind.

"Just hold still," Chaka says, and tears off a piece of tape. "Mighty close, old-timer, mighty close. Little more and you was gonna open this back up nice and big. How'd you get yourself some scars like this anyhow?"

"Go on and ask Jake. He'll tell you."

"Ain't time to be telling no David and Goliath in the hood stories now," I say. I pull the letter out of my pocket and hold it up to Chaka. "Tell me about this instead."

She rips open another gauze pad and throws the wrapper on the table. She presses it to Daddy's head. "You got something to hide? Maybe I do too then."

"What you want from me? Everything I got now is in this room!" I shake the letter at her again. "Except them!"

"I'll tell you one thing, Jake," she says. "And I'll tell it to you right now. She's scared. Can't think straight. You can thank the Lord I got her into Luby's at all—at least she had a couple days off of these streets."

I knew it. "They ain't there no more?"

"I don't *know* where they're gone to," she says. "Might still be there. All I know is it's some kind of miracle Laurence got them to me before he got to drinking that day—but Noel should have seen it in him anyhow. She's some kind of desperate, Jake." She points at my hand with that paper balled-up good and tight now. "And the half of what she's running from is you."

"Let her run then," Daddy says. "When we get hold of what we got coming to us, she'll come around right quick."

He stands up out of that chair, tries to walk but trips. His hands come out and he stumble-runs falling to me but I catch him under the arms.

Chaka laughs. She pulls the rubber gloves off, throws them on the counter with everything else. "That man needs a bed, is what he needs," she says. "That bleeding won't stop with you menfolk running all over town."

I pull him up till he's standing on his own. "Need to get me some food, that's all," he says, turning around. "What you got up in this place, pretty girl?"

She crosses her arms and cocks that chin down low. "Old-timer, what do you *think* you're looking at? I got a food bank sign hanging on me?"

If she did I'd bust on through—wouldn't think about no locks no police no nothing. I can feel it too, just like him. My belly always gets to aching first, cries at me saying it's empty, but anybody can live with that, and it goes away soon enough anyhow. But when my head starts getting light, that's when I start feeling I ain't really myself. I get to feeling like I've got some kind of cloud up in there, or maybe I'm just walking around inside it. When I get like this, anything goes—my hands, my feet, arms or legs, something's bound to start acting like it don't know how to work right no more. When I get like this, anything goes up in my head too. It's like leaning back into those fences, or standing up on the bus, or inside Ho's store or Rhonda's office—I don't know what I'm thinking or where it's coming from, I'm just following wherever it goes.

"If you don't know, then who does?" I say. I look at her and then I look at her umbrella on the table. She's a strong woman but she couldn't keep both of us back, even if she got to the table first. I step in front of Daddy. "How am I supposed to know you ain't lying?"

She laughs again. "Lying why? So I can get me a little juice with you? So I can get in on a piece of that action you're running tonight?"

"You ain't getting *shit*, girl," Daddy says, pointing at her. "This here is family business."

She shoots back, points both hands at us like a couple of guns. "*Step* back, both of you all. You can run your back-alley nigger routine up at George's place all you want, but not in here. This is *my* space, *my* rules. And don't you forget I still ain't clocked out yet—I've got a man will come looking for me soon enough if I don't."

"What's all this ruckus about?" Pope Riley is in the door behind us. Tall and skinny, and toes sticking out from under that robe.

I look back at Chaka. "That your man there?"

Daddy laughs and tugs on his scarf at both ends. "Now that's one sorry motherfucker."

"Excuse me, miss," Riley says, knocking on the door glass. "Isn't this the time when I'm permitted to *sleep*? By *myself*? What are these two doing here?"

"You gonna be sleeping with my foot up your ass, you don't get yourself gone," Daddy says. He jab-steps, jukes those shoulders, and you'd think he flashed a knife the way Riley takes off running. Feet slapping and robe blowing, the dude is out the door like a 'coon on the wrong end of a shotgun, but Daddy chases after him anyhow.

I yell at Daddy to leave him be, but it's no use. I look back at Chaka, and she's got her umbrella up and her other hand on her hip. "Get outta my way."

"You lying to me?"

"No, I ain't. But you wouldn't know a lie if it came up and bit your dick off." She waves the umbrella. "Now get outta my way."

I step to her. "Go on and take me upside the head if you want. I ain't moving till I hear something about them."

"So what you want to hear? You want to hear they're having cocktails and caviar at the Sheraton? *'Oh, and make his a Shirley Temple, he ain't but just a young-un still.'* You think just because you got me in this room you're gonna make everything turn out right?" She kicks the back of the chair and it clatter-smacks down at my feet. "I got my Jesus protecting *me*. I ain't running nowhere. I ain't scared of you. Maybe she is, but I ain't."

"That what she told you—she's running scared?"

"Any fool could see it—except you." She shakes her head, looking down now. "Good Lord knows Laurence was born with a nose for it. He can sniff a woman gone lost her way clear across town. Sure found me in my time." She looks back up, her eyes tight. "And you made it easy as could be. All he had to do was tell her you were chiefing a little run over to George's to pick the place clean, and she was right up outta that safe house and out on the street. I got the call just this morning."

I hold my hand up. "Told her *I* was chiefing it?"

"That's right," she says. "Now what—he's lying on that one too? Don't tell me you're taking orders from *his* drunk ass?"

"Ha! Woman, you crazy." I squeeze my shoulder, dig my thumb down right in the spot.

"Because you know Laurence will try nine hundred ways into a girl's pants if he has to. Came in here twice after I put her in Luby's, wanting me to take her some letters like now he's some kind of schoolboy. Course I opened them—you know I *am* a woman. Noel just sat on that bed, didn't say much of nothing but I know she read it good as I did. He's painting you like some kind of thug. Now I told her—"

"I ain't no thug! Look at me." I throw off my jacket and roll up my shirt sleeves. "What you see here? You see some tracks?" I hit one arm, then the other. "I'm Jake Robertson. You're goddamn right I'm running this boost—I'm getting what's mine and ain't nobody gonna tell me how to do it."

"So who's gonna kill George? You?"

"If I have to," I say, squeezing my shoulder again. "Gonna do what it takes." I keep digging into that spot, feeling the pain warm up and just get sweeter. My head feels clear, no more clouds. I hear a tap. A crow sets down on the windowsill, tapping that glass, looking for something, but I don't got a thing, my pockets are empty and my belly too, and I shoot my hand out and feel that pain running hot and sweet, shoot it out and if I had a rock I'd throw it, shoot it out and tell him *quit that begging shit motherfucker get gone.* He flies off, and ain't nothing else out there but that escape ladder I saw the last time when Chaka wrapped my hand, was missing some rungs before but now I don't see a one.

Chaka does a quick chin-throw and hmphs loud. "Well you better think about what it takes to find that little package of yours before you go doing that, because George might be about the only one who knows where they are." Those eyebrows go up, and she tilts her head. "Might even have them himself."

I take my hand down and give my shoulder a roll, feel it all pull and stretch and bite in there. "I'm listening," I say. "Where's he got them?"

She laughs, but her face is still a rock. "Oh is that right now, huh? Now you listening." She shakes her head, cough-laughs again good and loud. "Well you better listen good and you better know I'm only doing it because I think Noel and that little boy deserve a chance at something good, Lord knows they do. Not because I think you're the one can give it to her, especially running this back-alley nigger routine with some daddy just out of the joint."

"Just tell it," I say.

"I *am* gonna tell it," she says. "You just sit tight because I'm doing it on my say-so. That girl's got some kind of angel watching her back ain't failed her yet, ain't gonna quit now for five minutes of my time."

Chaka tucks the umbrella under her arm. She puts her other hand out, right there in front of me like she's looking for five, then cups it a little like she wants me to drop something down in it. "That girl walked in here and didn't have nothing worth nothing. Got that little boy crying on one arm and that purse empty as a well bucket in the desert on the other. Laurence came in right behind with his hand on her shoulder and I said Lord have mercy on this girl, she don't know *what* kind of mess she's in. He did his little number with me but I wasn't fooled one bit. The good Lord ain't taken my eyes from me yet and I could still see he was two-stepping just the same as he's been since I kicked him out the door. Trying to tell me God sent him some work today that don't pay in this world—ha!" She slaps her fingers down into that cup, twice and three times. "He started dropping quarters into her hand, telling her you go ahead and page me whenever you get to feeling lonely, and I knew what he had on his mind."

"That's bullshit," I say. "Noel don't take no kind of handout from nobody."

"That's what I'm standing here telling you, Jake," she says. "I've only known her these past three days, but before I ever heard her story I knew she wasn't herself. All I had to do was see that face. Girl didn't know what hit her—her man's gone and her baby's crying and she's got noplace to go. So Laurence says get in the car and she gets in. He says put your hand out and she puts it out and takes whatever he's giving."

"Damn that motherfucker!" I kick the door behind me but it smacks right off the wall and gets me back again. My hand goes straight to my shoulder, my thumb digs in quick and deep. "Soon as I see him it ain't gonna take but two seconds before I kill his lying ass! He's got her, don't he?"

She shakes her head, points a finger at me. "I'll tell you something, Jake. When I saw that girl walk through the door carrying that little boy like that, heard him coughing like I don't know what, I heard God's voice loud and clear. Said, Chaka, take care of them now like they're your own. I tried to, but maybe that's where I let Him down."

Voices coming from out the door, down the hall, mixed in and souped all together and can't make out a word. But Chaka's eyes just go to the floor, to her feet standing there holding her up. "I've been praying, but I don't know what to pray for no more," she says. "Maybe it's my fault—good Lord knows I still ain't no good mother. I told myself, I can hardly fit in this room myself, how am I supposed to take in a girl and her baby. But maybe I should have, Jake." She looks up. I almost don't know her—that face is soft all around. "Maybe then she wouldn't be running from you, looking for George."

"I got him!" Daddy backpedals through the door, dragging Pope Riley with both hands. Riley's feet are going every which way but he can't get himself up. Daddy brings him past me to Chaka and drops him. Soon as that head hits the floor Riley is howling like an alley cat. "Stop your crying, motherfucker!" Daddy says, stepping over him and back next to me. He looks up at Chaka, hits his hand to his chest. "You look at me, woman, you see a man that's still a *man*." He points at Riley. "Pope whitey here going behind your back and you don't even know it. Look." He quick-steps over to Riley and gets hold of that robe, gets a handful right on his hip and just rips it back. It tears right in two—bottom half comes off in Daddy's hand and he shakes some bread out of the pockets, four five pieces maybe, bigger than Ping-Pong balls but bouncing like they're kin to them. My hands jump out and I step to it but Daddy is already on the floor sweeping it all in. Riley flips over right quick and crawls to the corner, yelling he can't let Chaka see nothing, but if she don't see that red-hairy ass now she wouldn't see a bus was about to hit her. Daddy sees it too, and I wait for him to kick it but he's not paying that dude no nevermind. He just puts a piece in his mouth with each hand and brings the rest up to Chaka.

"You see this now?" he says, looking at me, looking at her, holding both hands in front of her, his jaw working on that bread. It snaps and cracks in his mouth and then he gets it down. "Dude is lifting food outta here. Stealing from the St. Al's! I done enough time in here to know there's some *hungry* motherfuckers sleeping in this place. You take more than your share, you gonna get it taken *back*."

"Old-timer, you ain't the sharpest knife in the drawer, are you? You want a meal, you can go get it. You all know where that line is good as I do." She points her umbrella over at Riley. "He's been feeding the birds with that bread ever since I've known him, so don't think you're some kind of Perry Mason now dragging him in here." She looks over at him curled up in the corner, that ass sticking out under that robe. She laughs. "If you believe him, he's even out there giving it to kids going hungry."

Daddy laughs back, pops another piece in his mouth. I look at his hands holding it, closed down around it. I want some. I can smell it. I can feel it breaking in my fingers, feel it in my mouth biting through. Daddy looks at me, and he knows, and he throws me one, and another.

"Well we ain't no birds, but we're long gone hungry, girl," he says. "And Jake's my kid, and he's got his own one too. So the man's done his job."

I catch the bread right out in front of me, one in each hand. Quick as that I crush them good and put them in my mouth. Feels like sand but tastes better than honey, and soon enough it softens up. Tastes so good but I can't get it down in me quick enough, almost choke myself swallowing it. Daddy puts one more in his mouth and then his hands are clean, no more. I can still smell that bread in my mouth, and I lick all around my teeth front and back and keep sucking them till it's all dry, all gone.

"I know what he's got," Chaka says, with that red umbrella looking at me now, "and what he don't got. You listen good now I'll tell you where what he don't got maybe got gone *to*. You all get your nappy asses out of my clinic over to that labor hall, you might find yourselves a clue or two."

"George!" I smack my fist into my hand. "Now I'm gonna kill Laurence two times! I bet you he put them in that Benz and drove them to George his own self."

"Laurence is smart but he ain't that smart. He can't open a door that can't be found. There ain't a man in town can find Luby's—"

"George could," I say, looking at Daddy. "Motherfucker's got himself tied in every place. I don't care if ain't no man been in Luby's in twenty years, he'd find it and walk right in the door. He swiped them outta there!"

"He didn't have to walk anyplace at all, you ask me," Chaka says, shaking me off. "If she's over there, it's because *she* found *him*. That girl told me herself only thing she had she could use any more was that ID George gave her, and wasn't he a good man who gave her some work when you all were just starting out."

I turn out, walk through the door but I spin right back in. "What kind of crackhead shit you talking now? What's she gonna run to him about?"

"Don't you pay it no nevermind, boy," Daddy says. "Makes it real easy now, don't it? We'll do it all at once."

Chaka shrugs. "What's she gonna do—go to her caseworker? The police? She'd lose that baby in a second, and you two would be blowing kisses at each other on shift change at the county kitchen."

"Let's go, boy." Daddy pulls on my jacket. "We know what we got to do now. You got any more grub in this joint, girl?"

"Get out!" I look over in the corner, and Riley's red moon is still smiling. He keeps that head tucked in at his knees and shouts at the wall. "Get out! How dare you steal from me—you scum! There's nothing here for you! Get out!"

I look at Daddy and he looks at me, and we just know. I grab Riley's feet and Daddy gets his hands. We pick him up, stretch him out, move over to the wall, to the windows. He gets flailing but me and Daddy hold on tight. Chaka's on Daddy with that umbrella but he's quick as a young man again now, he squeezes Riley's wrists in one hand, ducks that red swing, and grabs it right out of her hand. He throws the window open and puts it out, and it slaps down loud in the alley. She raises her fist at him but he puts his own up too, says back off now girl, and she does.

Daddy gets Riley's arms at the elbows and lifts the man's head through the window, then steps away so I can finish the job. Riley grabs the top half of the glass but I open his legs up, get my hips at his knees and start pushing. His ass smells like a motherfucker and he's flailing but I keep right on slow and steady so he knows. I push and push and Riley holds that glass and his face comes up looking right at me. I'm bending him in half and he can't stop me, I can keep on pushing till his legs are all out and he won't have nothing to stand on nothing to hold on to.

"You know I can kill you now." I hold his legs steady then give them a jerk. "That what you want?"

"O God, don't drop me! Let me back in!"

"God ain't gonna help you. Who the fuck are you? Some kind of loser sucking on Momma Chaka's titty in here."

He tries sliding his ass back on the sill. "Have mercy on me, please."

I push again, rock him back. "Maybe I ain't in no mood for mercy."

Riley's hands slip and he grabs at the window again but his hands are slow and just big and scared like his eyes across the glass but mine are quick and pull on those legs pull just as hard as I can and maybe too quick because his head smacks the sash coming in and maybe too hard because I pull him damn-near on top of me and maybe too scared because he couldn't hold his shit and now we're both sitting in it.

Chaka starts yelling something, but Riley doesn't make a sound, just lies there looking up at the ceiling. Daddy steps over and puts his hand down to me, and I take it. He pulls me up and says let's go, but I look down at Riley. Got blood on his forehead, shit on his legs and it's on me too. I hear Daddy or Curtis or whoever he is, calling me from the door, but I'm looking at Riley right here, whoever he is, eyes up on the ceiling maybe looking for God, but I stand where I can catch those eyes and tell him you know I coulda killed you padre whoever you are, don't you.

* * *

Out the alley, turn the corner, we're running now, going to put this family back together. This isn't how I wanted it but now it's here. Maybe he spent his whole life trying and failing, but I'm my own man now, this is my time, and I'm gonna do it right.

The Angelus—gonna get up in there first. Laurence said he'd meet us back under the Cliffs around eleven, said he'd be getting the tools together till then, getting the job set up, but if I know that motherfucker, he's up in one of these rooms right now with a girl on the bed and a bottle by the door. Maybe he's got Noel and William locked-up in there someplace too. Either way I'm gonna kill him. Don't care what Daddy says about him and Laurence being Folsom kin—he can wait on the sidewalk if he don't want no part in it. And I don't care about this boost tonight neither—me and Daddy can do it ourselves without some lying drunk motherfucker telling us how. Or I'll do it my *own* self if I have to, if Daddy gets to feeling too old.

Up on the sidewalk, but there's nobody there. Just a car going one way, a bus going the other, and folks everywhere—moving, walking, strutting, shouting laughing playin', on the walk and in the street—but nobody *here*. Nobody hanging around that door—not even the dude in the black jacket. Nobody with a key I can trade for a down on a rock and tell him Laurence is good for it. I look around, and it's just me and Daddy, whoever he is.

"What you stopping about?" he says, breathing hard enough to near knock me over. "You don't think I can keep up with you, boy?"

I look at him. Nappy gray 'fro, beat-up shoes and army jacket, and that stinking scarf hanging around his neck. Only thing smells worse than him now is me, what with the pope's shit on my pants. Standing here a minute it gets right up in my head, comes back strong as an old dream riding up on a track from way down deep. I can feel that dude's legs shaking in my arms, see those eyes popped open wide, hear him begging me. It was all in my hands—just one little push and I could have put him away. When I get hold of Laurence, I ain't gonna have no ears for mercy. George can cry all he wants too, beg me till he's ready to blow me—I ain't hearing it. But I'm gonna let him watch, tie him up where he can see me clean the whole place out, take it all back. And if I feel like it, I'll do like Daddy says—just make that place my own. But not his way. I'll pull it off clean. I'll put this family back together, first time around, won't waste no time in Folsom or noplace else I don't want to go.

I look at Daddy, breathing hard. Just standing here waiting. He knows I'm running this, I can see it in his eyes. The wind picks up, and something crackles behind me, taps me on the leg. I reach down and pull an empty potato chip bag off my ankle. I fold it up and scrape my leg, wipe off as much of that shit as I can. My jeans are still wet, and the smell is in there like cement, but there ain't time to go to Sal's Army and ain't nobody taking my credit today anyhow. I let the wind take the bag again and watch it hop on down the walk.

I look at him, and smell that shit, feel those legs in my arms, and all I can see is George. Maybe I will listen—now that I'm leaving this begging shit behind, might feel damn good hearing it from him. George is the one we want—all I need from Laurence is to get us to that house and get me to my baby.

I look up at the building. That sand brick all the way to the top, eight floors, or maybe it's nine, and all those windows. Been some years since I stayed up in there, and I never counted the rooms, but I know it's got a hundred of them if it's got a one.

There ain't time. And they ain't here. I know Chaka's right—Noel went to the Ready Man, looking for George. If Laurence is inside he can stay inside—at least I'll know where to find him when eleven comes around.

Motion and commotion here in front of the Angelus, all along First, but something tells me with all this to see there ain't nothing to see. Getting colder now, the light's starting to fade, but something tells me the quicker we get down in the dark the more we're going to see.

* * *

Running, running, down through the Cliffs, and the shadows are getting longer. Something's pulling me, and the best thing I know to do is follow it. My shoulder is aching, my belly's still empty, but I keep moving. Along the wall, under the freeway, the cars rush over from uptown, zoom-zooming clack-clacking beating steady. It gets in me, that rhythm, that rush, and I move faster.

Turn up on Wilson, in the St. Peter alley—nothing. Back to the wall, under the freeway, up two blocks to San Vicente, puddles and potholes and empty dumpsters, and nothing. Dark in the next alley, cut through to King, Daddy breathing harder and harder but just a whole lot of nothing.

The wind is picking up, a good gust of it shoots down King when we come out of the alley, kicks a plastic bottle along the curb and takes a paper bag dancing. The bag zigzags and spins right past us, hops up and down near the wall and climbs up into the Cliffs. Pigeons scatter, and me and Daddy stop right where we are to watch it come back down, but it's just gone.

The Cliffs end right here, where the freeway turns in off the water and cuts through the Flatlands, heading uptown. That zoom-clack is beating steady as ever up above, but I hear something else down here, I *feel* it, on the other side of the wall. There's a thin line of light coming through the Break, like a pole lying down on the street. I walk to it. Daddy pulls up next to me sucking wind, puts his hands down on his knees, the light running right up over his foot. He starts coughing, his back jerks. I put my hands under his shoulders, lift him up so he can get some air in that chest. He coughs again. "I told you don't try to baby me, boy. Keep moving."

I hear the water, smacking up against the wall and coming down on the street behind me. I look at the light at Daddy's feet, follow it over to the wall, to that crack I got through last week, going down into the park, following the man with the pole.

"What were you fishing for?" I say.

He cocks his head, just looks at me. He knows. "Nothing. Just my own supper—ain't got nobody to take care of but me no more."

The wind picks up. Behind me there's a crackle again, and then it's up and past me, past both of us. That bag whips by, down from out of the dark, still dancing. It hits a big loop in the air, makes it a double, then side-shuffles down to the wall, riding that light like it was sliding a stair rail.

Me and Daddy follow it through the Break, down the stairs and into the grass. I see it dancing, scooting to the edge, all full-up with nothing but I know it's something. I chase it, thinking maybe she wrote on this too, but it takes off, hops up out over the water, and slips away in the dark.

Nothing. No sign of her, my boy neither. That feeling like something pulled me down here is good as gone now. Not even Jerry around to feed me some kind of clue. Nobody but me and my old man—and he's on *my* lead now.

The water smacks the wall beneath the edge, and it sprays up, gets me good and wet. I jump back, wipe my face, throw my jacket down. Daddy comes running over, all shadows but he's wheezing like a train. I want to hit something, but there ain't nothing here to hit. I turn back to the water and swing out at it, try to punch that motherfucking wave, that bag full-up with nothing.

My shoulder lights right up. I grab it, squeeze it, but my foot slips off the edge and just like that I'm looking down at all that water. But somebody grabs my arm, throws me back down on the grass. He's standing over me, might be Daddy but he's all full of shadows and I think it could be the dude with the pipe, coming to finish the job. But then my head clears, my eyes too, and I know.

It was George. It's Daddy right now, but it was Mr. Ready Man before, had that tie tucked away and those keys in his pocket and that face behind a mask.

The water smacks in again, splashes up, but now I'm ready, I'm quick and I'm strong and I pull Daddy with me, we're across the grass, out on the street and running again. Gonna find George at the Ready Man and do what I need to do to get my baby back. Gonna look him right in the eye this time when I hit him—won't be no Gustavo there and I won't go with no backhand neither. Gonna put him down to stay, and then I'll take what's mine—all of it, because them that's got is gonna be them that gets.

And then I'll be gone—we *all* will—in the Benz, on the freeway across the bridge and wherever we want to go. When we're set to leave Daddy can come if he wants but I won't wait long, because I ain't no nothing no more, I ain't gonna get stuck in that family run, ain't gonna lose my shot at being free.

* * *

Running, running, up to Vine and those same bridge legs I hid out in before, through them and straight to Battery because now I'm the chief. George can hide if he wants, but it won't last long. Crossing Lincoln and one block to go, and I'm close—I can *smell* her now, and William too.

Lights hit us from behind then sweep on by, and an engine guns. Doesn't sound like my Benz, but I turn and look. A van turns left off Lincoln onto Third, swings wide and whips past us, hopping the curb a second before it rights itself. The brakes light up soon as it crosses Battery, and me and Daddy keep running. The doors open, and I'm right behind it. They climb out—dude in the black jacket, brother with the Dodgers cap, crows, rats—six or seven folks, enough to hold down the old corner.

I grab the door, pull myself inside. Nobody, nothing—no Noel, no William, no Laurence or George. Just some joker up front with straight blond hair and a big nose, playing that country-honk music and staring me down.

"Where they at?" I step up in his face, but he sees it coming, puts his hand to my forehead. "Fuck you, jerk-off!" he says, and guns it good, and I hit the curb hard on that shoulder. The van door comes shut when it turns the corner, and then those lights are gone.

The laughing starts before I can even look up, and when I do the dude in the black jacket is at the window of the Korean breakfast joint, holding his gut. I squeeze my shoulder, and I'm up and on him, pushing him flat up against the glass. He tries his whoa nigger but my hands get his throat and squeeze it out, and I hear Daddy yelling and somebody knocks into me but I just keep squeezing till Daddy pulls me off. Quick as that two brothers are on him, pulling his arms back and putting a knee in his gut. But the dude in the black jacket calls them off.

He steps over to Daddy. Some of the brothers tell him to go on and whup my ass, but he shakes them off. "I think I know this motherfucker." He lifts Daddy's chin up. "What you doing round here in the dark like this, old-timer? Can't get you no mop jobs no more?"

I'd jump in there and start swinging, but there's too many of them. These dudes all just worked, but everybody knows rats get hungry at night, and a little money in your pocket is just like some salt on your tongue.

"Where they at?" I say. "Where's George?"

The dude in the black jacket lets Daddy's chin fall back and turns to me. "George is long gone, bro."

"You seen my girl?"

"Girl with them titties? Damn right I seen her!" He does that running shuffle in place, jumps up, and lands with both hands out front. "But every time I want to get me a squeeze that little baby's already sucking on them. And George says he's next, but I'm fixing to fight him for it if I got to!"

"You seen her with him?" I say.

The brother in the Dodgers cap pushes Daddy at me. "Shit, motherfucker— we *all* done seen that bitch."

They all crack up again, and the dude in the black jacket claps his hands, shakes his head. "She came round here looking for some work, and George done gave it to her. You better get with what's going on here, bro."

Daddy straightens up, and I look him in the eye. He's tired—just looking at him I can feel it in my own bones too. His face is sweating, he's got snot out his nose, and I know he'd just about eat a brick right now if I pulled one out of the wall. I take one end of the scarf and hold it up to him. "Wipe your face now."

"Leave me be, boy. Let's go find them."

"That's your boy, old-timer?" The dude in the black jacket laughs then looks over at me. "So this your daddy, bro? Or you just his bitch for tonight?"

I step up to all of them, and the laughing cuts off quick. "Fuck you, mother-fucker," I say. "When this is all through I'll come back around and let you suck me, after I knock your teeth out. Now tell me where Laurence is at."

He cocks his chin. "I ain't telling you shit, *boy*. All this I already done told you, and look at this smack you talking. Looks like your daddy ain't learned you nothing about being grateful." He leans in close, his voice goes low. "Come on, bro, just tell me—he your daddy?"

I look past him, look past those other brothers standing and laughing behind him. No lights, no cars coming, so I get across the street, run over to those green doors at the hall. I pull the handles but they're locked tight. I look up in the windows but it's just empty chairs in the dark. I kick through what's there on the ground—newspapers, bottles, butts—in front of the doors and out along the building, looking sniffing searching. *Ain't nothing, ain't nothing to find,* I hear the dude shouting. But what's he know? What's he know about what I'm looking for—he don't even know who I am. I know there's something to find here, George can't wipe the whole place clean. I hear glass breaking down the block, quick-step get running follow it around the corner, down Battery into the alley behind the hall. In the alley, I hear it again and I can smell my boy. I keep on in the dark, come out the other side and up the block to those green doors again—but nothing, not a goddamn thing. Just Daddy at the doors, dude in the black jacket at the curb.

"Let's go, Jake," Daddy says. "What she gonna come around here for anyhow? Let's go wait it out at St. Al's, get us some food and see if we can't get one of them cots for a couple–three hours."

"You heard that woman good as I did!" I kick a bottle against the doors, and it shatters. "What else Noel got going? Only place she figures she got ID for and won't get arrested for having it is here. She figures George treated us both good before, he's gonna do the same now."

"Come on, boy. Let's get outta here."

"Goddamn right we're getting outta here!" I step out of the doorway and look that building up and down, from the green doors to the corner and back, all these bricks and windows in between. "Who the hell is anybody down here except who George says we are?"

I start walking, past Daddy, going back to the Angelus, but I ain't stepping inside St. Al's and taking nothing I can't pay for myself—gonna wait it out but I'm doing it like a man. The dude in the black jacket cocks his head when I come up on him, digs down in his pocket and pulls out some bills.

"Here you go now, bro—I just got paid." He puts a ten in my hand before I even know it. "Go on and get your old man a hot plate and some decent threads."

I ball that money up, keep on moving, but it's heavy as a rock. I smooth it back out, and I know it's some other prez now but it's sure a lot like them three Georges I had looking at me before. I rip it up and throw it to the curb. The fellas break out laughing from across the street, and the dude calls me a motherfucker but I know he's staying put. I keep walking, good smooth and cool now because I know right where I'm going. Leaving this begging shit behind now, and at the corner Daddy is right there with me.

* * *

Rain starts in walking back, but it doesn't come heavy, and by the time we get to the Angelus it's still worth it to try staying dry. But the St. Al's stoop is full-up already, the doorway to the Birdhouse too, so we turn down Wall to the Cliffs and let the dice roll. Never know what's gonna fall on you under here, but most all the birds are sleeping by now, and if one of them gets a funky dream and drops down on me it won't be the first time I got shit on today. This is the only roof we've got right now, and better to take a chance under here than sit out in that street and get wet for sure.

Daddy sits up against a bridge leg, but I can't keep still. I walk up and back, up and back, looking down at the ground, up at him, out to the street. We ain't seen nobody with a watch, but I know it's got to be getting near eleven soon. We're gonna play it cool when Laurence comes around, don't even ask about Noel and just go get the job done, but if I saw a clock around I'd spin those hands forward and get him here *now*.

"You wearing me out just looking at you, boy," he says. "Go on and sit down."

"Then quit looking at me," I say. "And quit calling me 'boy,' motherfucker."

He laughs, shakes his head. "You can't make up your mind, can you now, boy? Don't know if you want to kill me or thank me. One minute you talking about owing me and the next you don't want nothing to do with me."

I keep walking, and he stands up, looks straight at that wall, dark and full of nothing.

"Who was he?" I say. He doesn't move, so I say it again, take a couple steps closer. "All you said was he was a Pullman Porter. What else you know?"

He keeps looking at the wall. "Nothing. Just what folks told me. Didn't need to know more than that to do what I did."

"You killed a man you didn't know?"

He turns around right quick, points at me. "I told you, Jake—he shamed me! Fucked my woman—your momma! What more do I got to know?" He steps in to me, smelling-close. "Look at you, you want to kill George now. What you know about him? He's got what you want—he took something that's yours. Ain't that enough?"

I shake him off. "Naw—it ain't the same. That was a long time ago. Things is more fucked up today."

"Don't feed me that bullshit, boy. Things was fucked up back in that day too. Niggers didn't get fighting-mad just 'cause we had big afros and tight jeans. And don't try to tell me about a long time. I'd *still* kill Haley today if I could—I'd kill him right now! So don't you think I had something worth killing him about back then?"

I look up the street—still nothing. "What did Momma see in him?"

He slaps his hand at the air, steps by me. "Naw, boy—I ain't doing this!"

I follow him. "I know I owe you something but you owe me *this*! You killed him before I even knew him. What if all this shit I'm in right now never went down? You never would have told me—"

"Told you *what?*" he says, jumping back to me, putting a finger in my face. "Told you about what? Go on now, boy, I know you want to say it. Told you about your *daddy?*"

"I want to know his story."

"What you want to know that for? Some dude busts a nut in your momma and that makes him your daddy? Boy, I *raised* you!"

"I want to know where I come from."

"From your momma! And me! Same place you always come from. From Chicago. From my people down in Mississippi." He jab-points at my feet. "From right where you're standing. He gave you his face but all the rest comes from your real people. That fool never was nothing—he *ain't nothing!*"

"Now who's the one feeding bullshit?" I say. "If Joe Haley was just nothing then what's he doing stuck in my dreams all the way out here in California? And you can't get him gone neither—so what kind of nothing is that?"

He slaps down at the air again, looks away. "I knew it. I knew it. I never should have told you." He steps by me, those shoes scratching loud on the pavement. "Ain't no use asking me anyhow. I didn't know him—I told you that. He was already dead when I really found out something about him—and I've done forgot that."

I follow him. "Tell me what you forget."

He stops, looks at his feet. A car zoom-clacks overhead, getting closer, louder, then it fades away. He crosses his arms, kicks at something on the ground. "You want to know, do you now? Well I'll tell you something about old Haley. He had nice things—that's what your momma saw first. Or thought she did. Turns out he didn't have more than most folk, just a way of walking it. I wouldn't have known—I only saw him in that uniform or his bare ass. Turns out he was a family man too—but he fucked it up good for them, now didn't he? Folk told me his oldest boy found him where I left him. They had people down South someplace, and just packed it all up after that, moved on back. Might have even been Mississippi, I don't really know."

"And they never sent nobody back after you?"

"Naw," he says, slapping that air. "If they did, they never got the job done. But I think they let it go—fact is, word at the railyard got around to me. The kids and all the kin who knew were trying to shush it, but it just spread worse than kudzu come summer, turned all the folk against each other. Ripped that family up and got them kicked out of their hometown." He looks at me and smiles. "I don't really know. If that's how it went down, I'm gonna die a happy man." He puts a finger on my chest, right over my heart, points it like a gun and presses in, slow and steady. That smile goes away. "But here's what I *do* know, boy. *I* should have done it like that. I had him down on the ground, that gun in my hand. Shit, I didn't even need to shoot it—a good whack upside the head would have finished him off. Had my finger on the trigger, pulling it back. But something inside me just said leave him be, this brother's good and dead already. So I took off running. Dumbest thing I ever done, Jake. Downright dumbest. Got away from the police, but they wasn't coming anyway. Ran into a mess worse than that instead. You want to know why I still got that man inside my head, *that's* why. I didn't finish the job. I was weak. I should have stomped him out. Sometimes I think it was good because I made him die with some *pain*. But then I can't help thinking maybe he pulled out of it, maybe he still ain't dead."

Lights swing onto Wall, cut off soon as the Benz pulls into Parker's Alley behind the Angelus. Me and Daddy quick-step up the street. Laurence gets out of the car, opens the trunk.

"You all find what you're looking for?"

"You see anybody else standing here?" I say. "You know good as I do where they're at."

Laurence nods. "That's right, I do. Just drove by the Ready Man myself and got the word. I didn't make out nothing moving at his house, but that don't mean he don't have them tied down someplace you can't see." He pulls a bag out of the trunk. "So let's go get them."

I take the bag and give it to Daddy. Getting smelling-close to Laurence, I know he's been down to Cole's or Ho's or someplace that ain't just George's. His eyes are clear and he's still talking fine, but I know he's got it in him.

"What's this all about?" Daddy says. He pulls a black pair of pants out of the bag.

"Damn! I oughta make you all take the *bus* out there!" Laurence says, stepping back from me and grabbing that bag from Daddy. He throws clothes out at me, some at Daddy, all black, and throws the bag in the trunk. "You all been looking for that girl of yours down in the sewers? Hurry up and get these on and let's move on outta here. You find any potpourri in that dumpster, go on and bring that too."

Laurence slips off his shirt and puts on a black one. Me and Daddy strip down over by the dumpster. I hold my jeans up. Can't see much but I can smell that shit and I know it's deep down, won't come out. I throw them inside the dumpster, pull my shirt off and throw that in too. Daddy does the same. Soon enough I'll have nice clothes, the kind you don't hardly have to clean. The kind you don't sweat in or shit on, and if a thread starts coming loose you just throw them away because there's always plenty more.

I hold up the black shirt. Feels big, but I'll make it fit. Maybe George was wearing it when he came at me with that pipe in his hand. I bring it smelling-close, see if it's gonna tell any stories. I try to make out that rich man's cologne of his. I shake it, see if any keys come falling out. I do the same with the pants, but nothing. Just clean-clean. Might even be new. I slip them on, tuck in and zip up, and put my own boots back on. Clothes are one thing, but it takes a long time to break in a new pair of boots. Daddy throws his pants and that camouflage Army jacket in the dumpster—and we're ready. If I had a match I'd light it all up, but it doesn't matter now—once I cross that bridge I won't be back in this alley looking for nothing no more.

We get in the car. Laurence drives. I sit up front, Daddy in the back. We stay under the freeway all the way to uptown, hit the left on Olive, take the on-ramp, and we're up, moving now, over the Cliffs and out of the Flatlands and crossing the bridge.

Can't see much down below, just that water, blueblack and dancing and taking in all the light. The city is up ahead, all those hills lit up with buildings and houses and cars because over there, folks are moving, going places, over there it's late but you can still do what you want, even just stay home and get some sleep because inside that house it's cool and quiet and ain't nothing running in the walls keeping you up, nothing behind the fridge keeping you coughing, nothing out in the street shouting screaming getting sprung spooked or fixed or selling no damn ice cream. Bella Vista is up in there someplace. Can't see it from here, but I remember it right clear, and when we get close, I'll know.

Laurence starts laying out the plan. No guard at the gate, like usual, so we can drive right in, leave the Benz in the park a few streets down. We'll stay in the trees and they'll take us right up behind the house.

I remember Daniels talking about that park when we were moving him out, crying he wasn't gonna have it this good in the desert, noplace to take the kids and just get away from shit, you know brother? I played it like I needed to then, told him yeah yeah I hear you brother or something, but now the rich man is gone and the poor man is working for himself. Now I'm moving myself in, playin' it *my* way. Leaving that minimum-wage replaceable nigger routine back in the Flatlands.

Laurence says we'll need to split up when we move on the house—him and the old man will cover the ground floor, I'll get in through the basement window and come up from behind to put the squeeze on. I look back behind me at Daddy, set to shush him with my eyes if it looks like he might holler at Laurence about you ain't splitting up no daddy and his boy, but he's quiet, looks right back at me till I turn around again. He's set, he's serious, he's gonna do what it takes—I can feel it coming off him. A little of the old days coming back around. Gonna do it for the family, except this time he doesn't have no family but what I let him have. I know I owe him, but I'm paying him back my own way—this time, I'm teaching him. I look out at the water and it's still dark, still taking in all that light, and it gets me thinking of that dream last week, facing off against all of them down on the edge, getting tackled by Daddy and sinking down. But I smile, because I know it's all changed now—that's one dream that ain't coming true. Now Daddy's on my side, now I'm getting my boy back, now I'm riding up high over this water. Now I'm gonna get Noel just what she wants—just what I want too. Something real. Something we've got coming for all we've been through, something that's gonna keep us on this side of the bridge.

Getting closer, rain keeps smearing on the windshield because the wipers are sorry, and soon enough those city lights get like a roll-down everybody wants a piece of, colors jumping all over each other every which way. I roll down the window, get some rain in my eyes but I can still see, and the air is good and cool. No stars out now. Only one around is the one on the hood, the one every Benz has, and it catches some of that light from the hill. I look at it, those three points sitting up in that circle. Never thought I'd be sitting in a car like this. Noel never did neither—she probably thinks she was dreaming when she saw me with it the other day. But she'll come around quick when we get this job done. She'll see there was something about me she didn't know. I didn't even know myself. I come from three. Got Haley's face, Momma's bones, Daddy's voice. I'm all of them, but somehow I got following Daddy more than the rest. Here I am right goddamn now, doing just what he did—can't even do different if I wanted to. All my life I told myself I wasn't gonna end up like him—but won't be much longer now. It's like I'm stuck in a track, but I've got to ride it out now because it's taking me where I need to go. Just got to know when to jump off the train. Daddy ran boosts trying to put the family back together, but he never could do it right, never could put nice things in Momma's home neither. But I ain't all his son anyway—I've got Haley in me. And Momma too. She held the family together, at least till she could, and he had *style*. When I was running with Lydell, I never got caught, not like all of them three. I'm better than who I came from. I'm all of them, but soon enough I'm gonna be none of them, gonna get across the bridge jump off the train leave it all behind.

"You don't put that head of yours back in here, you gonna lose it," Laurence says. "Now shut that thing up—getting cold in here. You been following me so far? You think you can find that window?"

I shut it and wipe my face. The rain feels good. "I can find it."

Laurence paints it out for us. The house has a fence, like every one I've seen in Bella Vista, but it's only tall as a man and no wire on top, so we'll be over it right quick. When he came across this morning, he changed out the motion light and put in a dead bulb, so we can keep things dark. The yard is clear—nothing to step in or trip over—we can move right through it. George put up a bird box in the back left corner, and he must figure he can keep a thief away with bird shit, because he leaves a key in there. Or maybe he thinks all the niggers just steal from each other and won't even think about looking for nothing across this bridge. Either way he forgot what it's like being hungry, if he ever knew in the first place.

Laurence says he'll take the key and get in through the kitchen while me and Daddy go around the side. We're looking for two windows, one at the ground, one straight above it seven–eight feet up. If I can hold Daddy up long enough for him to cut a hand through and pop that latch, he'll be into that bedroom and we'll have a squeeze on—Daddy coming from the bedroom, sealing off the front door, Laurence from the kitchen, sealing off the back. They'll flush him right down the stairs. All I have to do is kick out that basement window—George won't hear it because the Cubs are playing the Dodgers, he'll have it on loud, and he's drinking himself to sleep these days anyway. Just kick it out, slide in there, and wait. If Noel and William are down there I can go ahead and kiss them quick, but don't start getting too lovey-dove till the job's done—gonna have all the time I want soon enough. Soon enough I'll see that door open, George will come right down, and I'll have my shot at him.

Coming to the end of the bridge now, we turn off and start climbing the hills. Laurence downshifts, and she wheezes from all our weight, but I know she'll get us there, she won't let us down. Rain still smearing on the windshield, but I can see that star on the hood wink at me going under the streetlights.

"So what you got for us, man?" Daddy says from the back. "We doing this with our bare hands, or we gonna get us some tools?"

"We got what we need," Laurence says, downshifting again. The Benz jumps but then she catches and keeps climbing. He arches his back, pulls a flask out of his back pocket, uncaps it between his legs and takes a slug.

Daddy laughs. "Looks like *you* got what *you* need. You gonna pass that around or what now? While you're at it, pass them guns around too."

Laurence holds the bottle out and turns it over, mouth down. It's dry. "Down to my last dollar tonight, Robertson. Couldn't even get myself a full tank of gas."

"So we ain't got no guns," I say.

"We got one," Laurence says, patting his chest under his jacket. "And we'll get us another one inside the house, if your old man can find it in that room."

"You left your mind back across that bridge?" I say. "George got a gun in the house, and we're going in after him, only got one ourselves? We don't *know* this place, don't even know he's gonna *be* there for sure. Shit, the way you planning this now, he'll be sitting up *waiting*—"

"Naw, naw, Jake. Listen now, listen up." He turns his head, and his glasses fill up with that streetlight, then let it go. Fill up, let it go, and even in that second in-between I can't make out his eyes at all. "I *know* what's going on. You want this fool bad but I do too, and I ain't fucking around with nothing." He looks back at the road, spins that wheel big and slow into a turn. "You think I just thought this shit up today? I've been watching him, Jake, a long time now. I know he's gonna be there. I know where he's gonna be sitting, I know what's gonna be on that TV and what's gonna be in that glass."

"Well, long as it ain't no cheap wine and he's got enough to go around it's all right by me," Daddy says, laughing again. He puts his hand on my shoulder and pulls up against my seat. "Don't worry none now, boy, we'll get it done. Been a long time for me but I know I still got it in me." He squeezes me good. "When I lay eyes on that man I won't need nothing but my own two hands. Shit, back then running with Dereck we was lucky if we *had* a gun, double-lucky if we could put a bullet in it."

"We ain't playing like them old days tonight, Robertson," Laurence says. "I got the car, I got the gun, and I got this job mapped out—you all just do like I tell you, you gonna get yours and plenty of it. Won't have no hungry family no more, won't be sitting in no jail cell neither."

"You want to tell me something?" I say. "Tell me this. How we getting in that house? And while you're telling me that, why don't you tell me why I ain't got the gun, if I'm the one putting him down? You starting to look like the man himself now, Laurence. You get yourself strapped and now we're supposed to be *your* niggers."

Laurence laughs good, slaps a hand down on the wheel. He looks over at me, those glasses fill up right quick and he laughs again. "You awful funny for a man so young, Jake. Awful funny." He looks back at the road. "But I thought you were smarter. Can't you see what's happening here, my man? This ain't just some holdup we're doing now. You forgot your Bible already? We been getting beat up and left on the side of that road, the whole world passing us by—and every time we go through those green doors George hits us again. And it ain't just us three." He shakes his head. "It's *everybody*, Jake. *Everybody*. All of us down here in the Flatlands, every man that goes through those doors. We're doing this for *everybody*. We're getting some *justice*." He points a thumb over his shoulder. "You ain't been a daddy too long, but just ask your old man back there, he'll tell you straight. A daddy wants to have some *stories* to tell his son. Wants some stories worth telling, ain't that right, Robertson?"

Daddy lets my shoulder go, sits back. "That's right."

"He wants a story about something that's *real*, something he's done in this life and it wouldn't be the same life if he hadn't been a man and done it." He reaches over and smacks me open-hand in the chest. "Get your head on straight, Jake. Can't you see that's what we're doing? Can't you see I'm damn-near *giving* it to you? Every good story's got something good waiting you didn't see coming, Jake. But then when it comes you see you were looking right at it the whole time, just couldn't see it. Picture this now—here I am with the gun, you hear? First man George is gonna see, right? He knows damn well he's fucked me up the ass, I got every reason to shoot him right there in his chair. But I'm gonna let him run—try to get out the door or go get his gun. Either way he's running into your old man. Don't know him from Adam but he's gonna know he ain't there to ask him can he watch the game. I'm gonna hold that gun to his head till I see the shit running down his leg, and we'll walk him right down. He ain't gonna expect you down there, Jake, but that's the beauty of it—don't you see now? It's a surprise, but it ain't no surprise at all. He thinks we're just taking him down to shoot him and do it quick, but he's going down to get it taken outta him from the man he's been taking it from most of all. Me and your old man ain't got nothing but ourselves no more. *You* the one with the family, Jake. You the one losing most of all, so you gonna be the first one gets a shot to take it back."

Laurence kills the lights, cuts the engine, and we slide right into the park. He looks past me out the window, says straight up through those trees and we'll be at George's fence. I look too, but it's just dark. Don't know if it's the rain smearing on the glass, the shadows hanging from all those trees, or just my eyes don't want to work, but I can't see a thing.

We get out. Laurence pops the trunk. He talks low. "You see it clear now, Jake? You see what I'm doing for you?" He steps in smelling-close, and he's good and sour. "So don't start no shit about I'm making you my nigger. I ain't no blind man—you got a sick baby and a girl needs some meat on her bones. I want George so bad I can taste that motherfucker's blood in my mouth, but I know what's right." He jabs his finger into my chest, and then quick as that he jabs it in his own. "I need me a good story too, just like anybody else down here, so if I've got to let you take the lead now, then that's what I'm gonna do." He points in the trunk. "Now get that box outta there."

Just shadows lying on shadows here in the park—can't make out much of nothing. Not Daddy, not inside the trunk, not Laurence either. Just the shape of things, nothing much of what's inside. Laurence smells ripe tonight, but he's driving good, he's moving good. Maybe the first little bit just clears his head and gets him running better than if he had nothing at all.

"What you standing there looking at me for?" he says. "Get that box out."

"I don't see nothing," I say. "Where's it at?"

"Put your head in there and you'll see where it's at. Then I'll tell you where it came from."

Daddy steps over. "Come on, boy, ain't you hungry?" He leans inside, and I get up next to him. I fish around—papers, bottles, something feels like a shoe, and then a corner, pokes me right in the palm of my hand. Metal, cold. I pull it out, set it on the lip of the trunk.

"So what you got in here?"

"Open it up," Laurence says.

Just a tool box, but you never know. I pop the clips and lift the lid, and think just maybe. Just maybe when I look inside it's gonna be like them movies on TV, a case full of money in the trunk. Won't have to rob nobody, kill nobody, won't have to do nothing at all.

My hand gets jabbed again—metal, cold. Couple of hammers, wrench, screwdrivers, putty knife, box of nails. I start pulling everything out, laying it all down on the bumper.

"Take whatever you want out of there, Jake," Laurence says. "It's all his anyway, it's all gonna work good. Robertson, you find yourself that glass cutter in there and you won't need nothing else. Damn-sure won't need that nasty-ass scarf."

I pick up a hammer. "It's all whose?"

Laurence laughs. I can see him smiling right through the dark. He leans in smelling-close. "George's. Who you think? This is the box he keeps at work. Didn't I tell you all we got a good story going?"

"You got in the hall tonight?" I put the hammer down. "Motherfucker, ain't you ever heard of a hardware store? Now we got two break-ins going. George is gonna have the police there watching the game with him."

Laurence reaches in the box, then he flaps something in front of my face sounds like a deck of cards getting shuffled. "You seen this too, ain't you? It's the ticket book. We're gonna write one out for George tonight, put him to work, you hear? Except then he's paying *us*."

I grab it, whip it back in the trunk. "This your game now? Your liquor's telling you so much bullshit, you ain't been thinking about the job." I throw the hammer in the box, and it knocks it over, clang-bangs down on the street like a mother-fucker.

"Who's playin' now?" Laurence says. "Why don't you just go on and ring all the neighbors' bells, tell them the niggers are here now?" He puts the tools back in the box, puts the box back in the trunk. He leaves the lid open. "Now let's get real here, fellas," he says, almost whispering but strong. "I ain't drunk, and I *know* you all know I ain't stupid. You think I'm gonna break into the hall?" He puts that finger in my chest again. "Your girl got the box out. I got a message to her, she got it out, I picked it up in my room at the Angelus."

"Good God almighty, he's talking some shit tonight! You hear what I'm hearing, Daddy?"

"Don't much matter what you hear," Laurence says, patting his chest. "Just what you believe. I'm strapped and I'm ready to go." He points at the toolbox. "You all can take this job or you can leave it right here, don't matter to me because I'll get it done myself if I have to. All I'm doing is helping you all be a couple of them that's got."

His shoes squeak hopping the curb up into the grass. Daddy reaches in the box, pulls out the glass cutter, a putty knife, and a wrench. "Don't you pay no nevermind to his bullshit, boy," he says. "I can smell him good as you. But we still got ourselves a job to do, and I ain't letting him fuck it up for you now."

I look at him standing in front of me, putting the tools in his pockets, tucking his shirt in tight all around. I can see the shadow of that scarf hanging down off his neck. I look at the toolbox sitting there open. Maybe it's George's, maybe it's not. Maybe Noel got it out to us, maybe she didn't. Wouldn't make a damn bit of sense to me, but maybe she's playin' and she's better than I knew. Noel thinks George is the only one can help her now, so I can't see her selling him out. Don't make sense, but maybe it doesn't need to right now. Laurence could be talking a bunch of shit, but maybe that one bit is right on—don't matter what you hear, just what you believe. Right now, I've gotta believe in something. I can't stand around like that dude Hamlet I heard about back in high school—he wasn't hungry, he wasn't evicted, he damn-sure didn't ride no bus. Ain't got time for no to be or not to be routine, I've got to believe in something right now and get to it. I take the hammer out of the box, close the trunk down, and we're moving, me and Daddy now, going to work.

Hop the curb, up the rise in the grass, we catch up to Laurence at the edge of the trees. The shadows hang heavy in there, and soon enough it all fades into nothing. I get behind Laurence, Daddy behind me, and we move slow, snaking tree to tree. I keep my step soft, but I still pop a branch or two, and Laurence can't keep from squeaking, and Daddy's breathing gets louder every minute. Feels like stepping out on the Archer Street courts when you ain't held a ball in your hands for who knows how long—you just fake it, run the court until that rhythm comes back, and it better come quick or you in for a whupping.

Daddy trips and falls, damn-near knocks me over trying to catch himself, but he crashes down in the leaves and they rattle-hiss good and loud. I reach to pull him up but he's moving fast, coming to a knee, and my hand just finds the back of his head and it burns, quick hot wet. I lick my fingers, and the taste of that blood puts me back under the maple, watching Haley fall, and the shirt and scarf full-up with blood, and now I know it's his and Daddy's and mine. I've been hoping I'd shake that dream, but I know I won't. I grip tight and pull him up off that knee. Laurence is out ahead, but some lights from the houses are breaking through the trees now, and I see his shadow moving quick and low, see those glasses catch the light and wink. I say let's hustle now Daddy and we quick-step it till we're out of the shadows, onto that grass, looking right at the fence.

Just like Daniels'—that six-foot skinny wood, pointy on top and laid nice and tight together, like a row of fresh-shaved soldiers ain't learned how to hold a gun yet. Daddy hunches over and webs his hands, Laurence puts his foot in there, and I hold that fence steady. Laurence hops over, then he braces it from the other side for me and Daddy. I give Daddy a lift, and when he's over I look for his hand to come through that V between two points. I take it, lock in tight, grab another point and pull myself up. If Daddy were a weaker man, his wrist would snap right off, but he's a rock tonight, and I'm up and on the other side.

Not much to the house on the back side, just a door and some windows, a little light coming through them but not much to see by. Could be Laurence got it right, and George is in the next room, passed-out in his chair with the TV watching him.

The bird box is hanging eye-level in a little tree near the house. We move steady-quick—fast but still not running, slow but not enough to keep Laurence from squeaking, but I guess that's why he gave himself the gun. George damn-well better be piss-drunk, or he's gonna be on Laurence before me and Daddy even get in the house. If he gets that gun, I'm gonna have to come up right quick and quiet from the basement, and I won't have but one shot with the hammer, so I better land it good.

Laurence pulls the key out of the box, wipes it on his pants, spits on it and wipes it again, goes down in the grass and rakes it through and wipes it one more time.

"Don't this motherfucker ever use this key?" he says. "Got more shit on it than a park bench."

"We ain't doing it like no old days, that's for damn-sure," Daddy says.

Laurence stands up, points between us. "You all get around that side now, find those windows and get yourselves in."

We start moving, but just as soon as our backs are to him Laurence grabs me, right up on the shoulder, and spins me around. I knock his hand off, and if we didn't have a job to do I'd rip his arm out and whup him with it. That pain starts pounding again and I'm ready to give it back to somebody.

"You feeling strong tonight, Jake?" He talks low. I almost can't hear him.

"Like a brand-new man."

"Can you hold him steady?"

I step in. "What the hell you talking about?"

"I'm just saying don't let go of that hammer if you can help it."

"Don't try telling me what I oughta do," I say, letting the hammer slap down in my hand. "I ain't no fool."

He nods, big and slow. His eyes are dark behind his glasses. "That's right," he says. "You ain't." His hand comes up, like he wants to set it back on my shoulder, but I step back, start moving to the house. "Let's get to work then," I say.

"Jake," he says, whisper-shouting, moving to me, but I don't stop. "Make sure you *wait* now, let your old man get all the way in before you break that window. I'm gonna watch you from the corner, and when he's inside, then I'm coming through this door."

Go on and do what you want, I say to myself, just get it done right, get me what I came for. Or some of it anyhow. Walking along the house, down the left side to where Daddy's standing at those windows, I can feel something ain't right, something's missing. Don't even have to go inside, I can just see it right here in the dark. Noel and William won't be down in that basement, won't be upstairs neither or noplace near. That ain't how I wanted it, but it's what I got. And it's all right—sometimes a man's got to take care of business before he goes home to see his family. We'll get this job done quick and good, and that's gonna take me to them, wherever they're at.

I drop the hammer in the grass and get down on my knee in front of the windows. Daddy's a big man, and I ain't had anybody but William up on my shoulders since Archer Street. And back then I didn't have these years of work in my back, damn-sure hadn't even gone near a moving truck yet.

I breathe in big and tighten up hard as I can. My shoulder would take me upside the head right now if it could. I don't even know why I'm doing this—why Laurence didn't just get us a ladder—but I know that soon as I get what's mine tonight I'm getting my ass to a *real* doc, forget the Birdhouse, and tell that dude fix me up right this time because now you looking at a man who can pay.

"Go!" I say.

Daddy puts his hand on me. "Wait now, Jake."

I let my breath out. "What you doing?" I point down at Laurence, standing at the corner of the house. "*He's* waiting on *you*. You the point now, Daddy. Let's get to it!"

"Let him keep on waiting then," he says. "Turn around and look at me now, boy."

Laurence sweeps his hand at the house *move move move*. I pivot around on my knee and look up at Daddy.

"Ain't it funny," he says. He looks at me, sets his hand on my shoulder, then looks up at the window. "Here I am letting you put me through a window again, except this time I'm going *in*." He looks back at me, and his other hand sets soft on my cheek. "And this time I'm making you work a whole lot harder."

I squeeze his hand a second, press it against my face, then push it back slow. "And you're still getting me good in the shoulder, ain't you?" I slap him in the leg. "Now get on up."

When the weight comes down it's like he has that hammer all over again, drives it right in and breaks that bone better than he ever did, and it's just colors for me now, trying to lift him up, colors right here in the dark trying to get my feet under me, Momma's purple eye and that brown couch turned over and I'm straining trying not to slip, that white shirt and that blue scarf, blue so deep you can't find your way out of, that scarf flapping when he ran around the room and falling loose when I put him through. I hear him slicing through the glass and I can't hold him much longer, the grass is slick-soft mud with all this rain and I'm sinking sinking, slicing through my shoulder filling up hot hot all the blood's running there now, slicing through and that sound cuts right through my bones slicing slicing and the glass shatters and it's straight through my heart.

"What the hell was that?" I say. I try turning my head to look but my foot slips and it's all I can do to hold him steady. The rain starts coming down harder. "You break it?"

"Putty didn't hold," he says. I hear the window click and slide up, and one foot's off and then the other. I look up and Daddy's crack is smiling right at me. I look down the way but Laurence is gone.

"You in?" I say.

Daddy comes to the window, takes the scarf off his neck, wraps the ends around his hands. "I'll see you in here, boy."

He slips into the room, into the dark.

My shoulder is numb, and I can't get the feeling back till I squeeze it. I drop down in the grass again and give that window a good look. It's a small one all right, can't be a whole lot more than a foot either way—good thing I didn't eat nothing today or maybe I wouldn't get through. I tap the glass with my finger. It's got a little something to it because it comes back low, not that tinny sound you get from glass that's thin. I grab the hammer—tomorrow I can go buy myself some new boots but I can't chance tearing my leg up just trying to get in.

Grab that hammer, flip it up in the air, and the rain spins off the head and it flips around once twice and slap-down in my hand, it's all flowing now just like hitting a baseball you toss to yourself, squeeze that handle and swing through. And I don't know what it is but that shatter-sing just fills up my head fills fills it, and I can see the head pushing through and the cracks creeping steady out every which way the glass falling one piece two falling inside shatter-singing too getting louder and I pull the hammer out and push it through again and through again getting quicker now singing louder now the pieces falling every which way too loud he's gonna hear but I can't stop just got to get in there and make things right got to make it right sweep the claw around the edges clean it out and throw that hammer inside throw my feet in push off the grass slide my legs in almost there my feet reaching for the ground reaching reaching down in the dark keep sliding in faster faster and then my feet somebody's got me clamps them together and I feel a rope go round gonna get hog-tied getting pulled in grabbing at the siding but it's wet and he's pulling strong it's Daddy I know it I feel it pulling me through been waiting all these years pulling strong can't fight it can't fight it can't—

The floor comes quick and hard, and I feel my shoulder pop out when it hits. I shout out and it bounces around and comes back laughing. Just laughing, then steps on the floor, moving scratching coming close jingle-jangle close closer *boom.*

No colors now, just dark, just that pain filling my whole body. Don't know if I'm shot or not, don't want to move to check.

Something grabs me quick, gets my shirt up around the neck, turns me face-down on the floor. Pulls my arms behind me and it feels like rope again biting into my wrists.

"What you doing in my house, nigger! You looking for somebody?"

My arm feels like it wants to come right off. "I'm sorry, Daddy! I know I ain't been a good son to you! I'm sorry!"

His knee digs into my back. "Shut the fuck up!"

"Just don't kill me now, Daddy! I wasn't nothing but a kid then. I still owe you. I still owe you!"

"Shut the fuck up or I'm gonna cut your tongue out, nigger!" His knee lifts off, and he scratch-steps across the floor, and a light cuts on. That jingle-jangle again, and he pulls me up and quick as that I see that big ring of keys catching the light like a fistful of gold and one of them jabs right into my lip. "Is this what you want? It ain't too sharp but it'll do the trick, long as you don't mind it ain't a clean cut."

The light is too bright and he's too close in, nothing but a shadow. I shut my eyes and I feel that key pushing in, trying to bite through, cold but it smells like blood.

"I ain't your daddy, fool! Don't you even know whose house you're trying to rob? Look at me now—come on!"

He grabs me by the neck again, pulls me up, and we're moving, across the floor away from the light.

"We're gonna go upstairs and turn on all the lights and you'll see good and clear who I am. Gonna show you who your daddy really is and there won't be no more mistaking."

He drags me up the stairs. I hear a door open, and light comes in the stairwell. "You boys ready up here? I got him. You ready now?"

Out onto the floor, and the room is bright, just lights and a white ceiling looking down. He drops me on my back. I hear some moaning close by, loud, somebody hurting something fierce. Close enough to touch him, if my hands weren't tied.

"Aw, Jesus Christ! You *shot* him? Here in my house?" Some movement, folks banging something, coming closer. "Look at this—it's all over the carpet! You been drinking? I *told* you leave that nigger wine back downtown."

More moaning, louder now, *oh motherfucker goddamn goddamn goddamn*—

"Just showing him I knew how to use it, that's all. Motherfucker was starting to give me trouble."

"Did I tell you to do that? *You* got the gun, how much trouble can he give you? Did you get his hands yet? Get his hands!"

More steps on the floor, hard fast coming close. And that moaning louder than ever, no words now just pain.

"Get that bag under his leg. Do it quick before I lose the whole carpet! And get them both sitting up so they can see."

Hands under my arms, lifting me, sitting me up against a wall. I don't even have to open my eyes now—I can smell Laurence.

A hand up under my chin, quick and strong. "Look at me," he says, talking soft. I look. I can see clear through his glasses now, just those big dark eyes. "You're a good kid, Jake. But I had to take the money."

"Move away now! Let me look at what we've got!"

Laurence backs away. I see that mess of blood on the floor, see Daddy's knee shot through. The ropes are still dead-solid on my hands and feet. But I need to touch it, got to get close. Soon as I see him, Daddy's moaning pulls me, that blood pulls me.

I fall over sideways, getting close but not close enough. I push myself, try to crawl on my side. "I'm sorry, Daddy! I did this to you!"

"It's all right, boy," he says. "I'll get you outta this if I can."

Hands under my arms again, and I'm back up against the wall, but it ain't Laurence this time, just that jingle-jangle and a key in my lip. "What did I tell you about talking? You forget real quick, don't you? And who you calling Daddy?" He turns my head so I'm looking at Daddy, and goes quick upside Daddy's head with the key ring on the end of that leash, lands it good and draws blood right up close to his eye. "Quit your crying, you sorry motherfucker. Just be glad I didn't pull that eye out. I've got something I want you to see." He leans in close on Daddy. "So here you are, Mr. Curtis Robertson. What you got to say for yourself now, old man? What's this about I'm getting you outta this, boy? You sound like the movies—you think this is the movies? You think you're a star?" He presses the key up in Daddy's lip now. "Let me tell you something you cocksucking train-hopping bum. This is the real world, and you're in my part of it now." Quick as that he whips those keys away, and they jingle-jangle soft hanging off his finger hanging over his knee. He looks back and forth at both of us. "You all are in George Haley's house now. And you ain't doing nothing without my say-so."

He stands up, hollers at Laurence to bring a chair. He takes it, spins it around backside to us, and slides in, legs out to the sides, arms folded on top of the chair back, gun in one hand keys in the other. He's the same George, but I know just looking at him now he ain't the same at all, or maybe I just never knew him. Daddy always said you never know a man till you see him in his own home. And there's plenty of light in here now. Same short body, same pipe arms with his sleeves rolled up, same gray hair. But no tie around his neck, no glass he can look at you through, no desk he can sit behind and listen to your *come on now brother I'm a changed man just give me one more chance.* No desk to lay that ticket down on, but all the same he's sitting on something. I know it's coming.

"You all comfortable now?" he says. "Just relax, this is gonna take us a little while." He looks at Laurence. "What you standing around for? Get yourself a chair and sit on down!" He shrugs his shoulders at us. "Hope you don't think I'm some kind of bad host—my momma *did* teach me some manners, you know. I'd let you all go on over to the couch there but you all are—" He looks at Laurence, sitting next to him now, same as George, backside forward, legs out, gun across the top of the chair. He sniffs the air, once twice and again, and louder every time. "Laurence? Do you—well, I don't know how to put it now. Just smells like—smells like *nigger* in here. Is that you?"

Laurence laughs. George slaps him on the arm. "Come on now, my man, you can tell me. You get some pussy that wasn't clean?" Laurence laughs again, looks at the floor. George keeps sniffing the air. He gets up out of his chair, bends down in front of me, good and close. "Well *here* it is," he says, snapping his fingers. "We *do* have a nigger in here! I thought—wait!" He sniffs again, steps in to Daddy. "Well, goddamn, we got *two!*" He waves his hand in front of his nose. "And this one's even worse! You smell that too, Laurence?"

Laurence laughs, looks up. "I smell it."

"New carpet, fumigating—what else now? You break anything up here in those two minutes I left you alone?" George shakes his head. "Shit, if I'd known *this* is what you were bringing me, I'd have made you *all* come in through the basement."

"I got them to you, didn't I?" Laurence says, pointing at George with his free hand.

"Did I say you could talk?" George says, pointing back with the gun, whipping it right up under Laurence's nose quicker than he can even blink, jabbing it hard. "When I told you how you were gonna do this job, did I say it involved *talking*? You're getting bad as these chumps." He pulls back the hammer, and it clicks soft. He stands close to Laurence, hangs his shadow over him, and puts out his free hand. "Now turn that gun around and give it over. Can't trust you with it, can I now?" Laurence's eyes are shut tight—I can see right through the glasses and the shadow. He moves that gun out slow. George grabs the nose, quick-flips it and catches it by the handle with his finger on the trigger, and points it at Laurence. He jabs the other one again, under Laurence's nose. "Boom!" Laurence jumps, and George laughs. "What you worried about? You wouldn't even feel it. Might even do you some good, knock all that nigger wine out of you." He kicks Laurence's leg. "Now go make me some coffee. Make yourself some too—shit, make enough for all of us, we're gonna need it. Use the good stuff, that French roast I got in there. And make it strong."

George watches him walk away and then he shrugs his shoulders at us. "You see what I'm working with? The man doesn't learn, just doesn't learn. I bet he showed up with an empty bottle, right? Or maybe one last swallow and he drank it right in front of you. Didn't even offer you all some, right? Am I right?" He shakes his head. "Same thing he did when he tried breaking in here by himself. And now look—I give him some work, set the job up for him, I even give him the *key*, for God's sake. And he still can't get it right. I don't know, I don't know—folks are right, I guess. Just hard to get good help anymore, you know?"

He shouts back at Laurence to hurry up and make his black, no sugar no nothing. He puts a gun under his arm, shakes those keys out and steps over my legs. I hear the bolt shut in the door. "You all comfortable?" he says, walking back to his chair, putting a foot up on it. "Awful quiet down there—you all ain't gonna fall asleep on me now, are you? Just when I'm getting to tell you the story I've got waiting? Aw come on now, you get some coffee in you, you'll feel better, don't you think?"

"I'll tell you what's gonna make me feel better is putting a foot up your ass," I say. "You're some kind of man, ain't you, George? Here you are got us tied up and you still got a gun in each hand. Why don't you go on and call your cops so they can haul the niggers outta here and you won't get your hands dirty? And get my girl and my little boy in here too so they can take us *all* away. Then Mr. George can tell all his nice neighbors how he did the county a favor, got a few more off the rolls."

Laurence walks in with a couple of cups, and George takes one. He tucks one of those guns behind him. "You got a mouth on you, Robertson. I ain't heard you talk like that since I watched you run out of my hall. This kid been talking like this all night, Laurence?"

"All night."

"Damn shame, damn shame," George says. He looks at Daddy. "Jake was doing all right till you came back around, wasn't he? You just had to make sure you fucked him up good. Kid's got some good blood in him, but you went and made a nigger out of him, didn't you? And he's calling you his daddy!" He takes a sip out of his cup and quick as that pulls an ugly face, spits it back. He holds the cup out and looks at it, then looks at Laurence. "What the hell you giving me here? I said strong, I didn't say put the whole can in!"

Laurence drinks his. "I didn't see no chef's hat in there."

"Didn't see no liquor in there, that's what you didn't see," George says. He breathes out loud, looks at the cup again. "Well, somebody oughta drink this, don't make sense to waste it. What about you, old man?" He steps over my legs to Daddy, and pours it right in that knee. Daddy howls like a motherfucker. His leg shakes and his whole body twists like a snake in a cage. George laughs. "What's the matter, don't you got a taste for something strong? Come on now, Curtis. We're gonna make a man out of you tonight!"

He holds the cup out to Laurence and tells him to get it right this time. He looks at me and laughs, pointing at Daddy. "So what's the problem—something wrong with your eyes, Jake? You still think somebody like this could be your Daddy? Gets a little blood on him and he's crying for an ambulance—that's being strong, Jake? That's a man, Jake? No no no—that's weak blood." He sniffs loud again. "He's sure got one thing that ain't weak. Let me tell you something about your real daddy, Jake. Joe Haley had class. Joe Haley had style. He wasn't some rich man, but he always knew how to dress himself and he always kept himself clean. And let me tell you something else, he wouldn't *ever* go fishing in some dumpster. Never. And he wouldn't ever let no son of his get down in one either."

"Don't you listen to nothing he says, boy," Daddy says, throwing his chin out at George. "Neither one of them. Only thing they know about Haley is those lies I told Laurence up in Folsom. Don't nobody here know Haley but me."

"That's all I know, huh?" George's keys flash in his hand, in the air, and quick as that they're whipping down, catching Daddy across the chest and getting him again with the backhand. "You sorry, lying motherfucker. The only reason I'm not gonna shoot your ass right now is because you got a lesson coming. You think I don't know my father's killer when he's sitting right here in front of me?"

Daddy's leg starts shaking like before, his body starts wriggling, and I look at that knee, the blood still flowing, that hole still open, I feel myself getting pulled in tipping over again and got to plug it up, and George is laughing those keys jingle-jangling, and Laurence is coming those steps rolling-rumbling, and I fall, get close but I still can't reach him, try to move but it's no use he's still all alone, he's still shouting my boy motherfucker I raised him my boy *mine* and Laurence throws me back up against the wall so I can remember how Daddy gave me that shoulder and George must know too because he gets his hands under Daddy's arms, stands him up on his feet tells him walk motherfucker walk, and Daddy howls good and loud I can feel it coming too, I can see George kick Daddy's leg, get that shot knee up in the air, I can hear him drive it home Curtis go on now just like you did before drive it home you know where he's weak where you broke him drive it home kick him and I'll set you free take this gun if you can't be a man and break him with your own hands take this gun and I'll set you free.

"Kick him!" George says, and puts the gun in Daddy's ear.

"It wasn't me!" Daddy says. He's crying now. "I lost my head but when I came to I had mercy on him!"

George goes upside Daddy's head with the gun and shoves him down, right down on me, all that weight smell blood crashing crushing smearing, knocks the wind out of me, and when Daddy rolls off those hammers click back loud as old bones breaking.

"You sorry, lying motherfucker." George's arms are out straight, the guns looking right at Daddy. "I *found* him. I found him in that lot where you left him. I watched his last breath go out of him and he didn't even know I was there. Only reason he held out that long is because you were a pussy, Robertson. You had that gun but you couldn't pull the trigger."

"I would have saved him but it was too late by the time I came to. It wasn't me, believe me now!"

"Let me tell you what I believe." George kicks Daddy's legs away from mine, and steps in right between us, squats down, and cocks his head at me. "I believe this boy Jake is pretty well caught up in the middle, don't you think?" He looks at Daddy. "I believe I know who you are better than Jake does, old man. Maybe better than you do yourself. I believe you don't know what mercy means, just like I don't. And I believe you just don't have the balls to finish the job, but I believe I do."

He sets the gun on the floor and grabs me under the chin, gets in close. "Look at me, Jake. Look good and close. I'm blood. You're kin to me. Doesn't mean I don't own you now, doesn't mean I can't still kill you. But I sure can't hold in the truth no more." He points at Daddy with the other gun but keeps his eyes locked on me. "He let your Momma get away and then he went and killed a man to get her back. That man was our father, Jake—our Daddy." He squeezes my face tighter, gets in closer. "I was there, Jake. I was seventeen. Thought I was a man, but knew I wasn't when that family fell right down on my shoulders. I knew he messed around, but I didn't know a Pullman Porter who didn't, and as far as I knew nobody else in the family would have even guessed it. So when that word got to me, you better believe I went running."

"So you some kind of hero?" I say. "Is that what you want me to think? You gonna be the good boy now and get back the man got your daddy?"

"Shut up, Jake. Don't try to act like someone you ain't." He keeps holding my chin but that other hand clocks my ear solid. "Joe Haley didn't give you no shit brain like Curtis would have, so get using it now. And he wasn't some clown either, so don't go trying to make me laugh. A hero? Is that what you think I think I am? No no no—a hero don't live with the kind of shame I've been carrying." He shifts his eyes quick at Daddy. "But who knows, maybe my number's up tonight, you think? We're gonna let him have a listen to George's story and we'll see who he believes." He clocks me again. "You listen close. That good head you got will tell you what's right."

Noise from the kitchen. George snatches up the gun and spins around. Laurence puts the cup in his hand. George tells him to go get the truck ready.

"And give me the keys to that Mercedes you found yourself, before I forget. Maybe I can help you get it fixed up."

Jingle-jangle, keys sliding off George's ring and some others sliding on, and popping up out of Laurence's hand and getting snatched again when he pulls the door shut and clicks the bolt home.

George takes a taste. "Aw goddamn!" He pulls that ugly face, shuts his eyes tight. "You get this in you, you could run through a house, Jake. Good thing I never put Laurence on any kitchen jobs, right? But hey now, didn't old Curtis say he liked it like this?" He holds the cup over Daddy's leg, pours right over that knee again. "Come on now, what you crying over? Look—you couldn't get that leg up before but now it's moving great! This coffee's got some kick—ha ha! Get it, Jake?"

I look at Daddy, but my ropes won't budge. "I'm sorry. I did it to you."

George swings that chair around again, sets it right between Daddy and me, and sets both those guns on his knees, looking at us steady. "There you go again, Jake," he says. "Being sorry again. It's real nice, real nice. If I were a crying man I might find some tears for you. It's real nice. But you know, that's something I've always liked about you—you own up. When you did something right, you knew it. When you fucked up, you knew that too. Took you a good little while after you got that lucky punch in, but you came around just like I thought you would. That's something we got in common, you know? We've got Crying Curtis over there trying to tell us he didn't kill our daddy, when all Chicago knows he did. Then we've got us over here—you know you dragged this sorry sack of shit along on a busted break-in, can't stop apologizing about it, and I know what I've done too. And what I'm gonna do. And I'm being a man about it, a real man."

He breathes in big, looks up at the ceiling, and when he's looking his hands just float out to his knees, float out over those guns and spin them, round and round slow and easy like he was petting a couple of cats, just smooth-swishing the metal over those pants, the noses looking here looking there till they're finally looking at us again. He puts those hammers off-duty and crosses his arms.

"You know I'm a righteous man, Jake. I can't see no wrong and have it sit right with me—least of all in myself. Even when I found Joe Haley lying there, some part of me knew he had it coming, he shouldn't have been fucking around. But what was I gonna do? Carry him home to Momma, let her see him with his dick still wet? Show her he died with that sin on his soul? I might as well have killed her too, doing that. But I couldn't go the other way either, couldn't go get the motherfucker who did this. Because I knew when I got him I wasn't gonna kill him quiet, one bullet in the head or something like you see in the movies. No no no—I was gonna tear the motherfucker apart, rip his heart out and his balls off, make him eat them and pull them out again through his asshole. And don't try telling me about cops don't care if us brothers kill each other, they were gonna *find* me for that. So there I'd be, sitting in the joint while my momma tried to figure out how to feed five kids with no man around. Only life insurance she had was me, so what was I gonna do? Couldn't go any way but right up the middle. Took my pants down right there in the snow, put my underwear on him, got him home and lied my ass off. Just ate it all. Told Momma I was too late, told her Daddy got mugged on the way home and I would have saved him like that Good Samaritan but he had the heart attack right out there in the cab, just when we were getting close, and now he's gone cold. Just ate it all, Jake, and forced it back down every time it wanted to come up."

He takes one of the guns off his knee, brings it up close and holds it, turns it slow and lets the light catch and fade again, looks at it steady like he's reading it. He breathes hot on the barrel, brings it into his chest and rubs it over his heart. He holds it out again and his eyes come to me.

"We knew we couldn't make it up in Chicago anymore after that, so we didn't even try, just went back down to Mississippi where Momma had family." His eyes swing over at Daddy and that gun does too. "Sooner or later family always finds out everything, right? But folks knew enough not to let on to Momma. Or me. They could see me working, they knew I would have been headed to college soon if it weren't for this. And they probably knew I wouldn't stick around long. Word got to me when I was out here in California, folks knew and Momma knew they did but everybody liked Momma and no one wanted to bury an old woman alive. By that time I didn't much care no more, because at least out here I could breathe. I just kept working and sending the money home and I figured just as long as I kept good and far from Chicago I'd be an old man soon enough and I could make that old story into whatever I wanted."

Some noise from the kitchen again, a door opening and shutting. George stands up quick. "You got it ready? You didn't wreck it yet?"

The keys jingle-jangle when Laurence tosses them. He leans in the doorway and blocks the light. "She sticks a little getting out of reverse."

"Sticks? Fool, that truck rides smooth as young pussy." George holds the keys up. "Now look here—look me in the eye, motherfucker. Can you get us there?"

"I told you before, I got them here, didn't I? Ain't no reason I can't cross that bridge again."

George laughs. "Well I'm glad I know how to swim, that's all I'm saying." He throws the keys back to Laurence. "Get over here, and let's get this moving."

Laurence gets down in front of Daddy, wraps the plastic bag around his shot knee and peels out some duct tape loud and long. George tells him to get it good and tight unless Laurence wants to do all the carpet work himself.

"Double-wrap it over their ropes too," he says. "But leave the mouth. I'm an American, you know, don't let anybody tell you different. I believe a man's got a right to free speech. Don't you, Jake?" I keep my head down, even when I see him step in, even when I see the nose of that gun come looking at mine and touch me under the chin. "Can't hear you, Jake. Don't you believe in that too? Free speech?" He pushes the gun in, pushes my head back, and the light is all around him but he's nothing but shadow standing in front of me. "So let me ask you something now, Jake. Who you gonna believe? You've got George your blood brother here telling you about your family, or you've got old man Curtis there pleading insane. Tell me now, who you gonna believe?"

"I raised you, boy!" Daddy says, bucking his chest out. Laurence pushes him over and gets that tape going around his hands, but Daddy's eyes stay on me. "Don't you listen to him. You're my boy! I won't let him hurt you none!"

"Hold him right there," George says. "Right there like that. Now I see something I was forgetting." He gets down on the floor and goes in Daddy's pocket, and when he pulls out that little sparkle I know he ain't using it to cut no more glass.

"Leave him be!" I try swinging my legs around but I can't do nothing but knock myself over.

George palms Daddy's head like a basketball and looks at me. "You did this to him, didn't you?" He looks over at Laurence. "That's how the story goes, right? This is what the old man got when Jake put him through the window." He presses Daddy's head to the floor, and Daddy's eyes shut down tight. "So you're telling me that's your boy over there, Curtis?" His other hand moves down slow, and I don't even have to see to know that diamond is slicing through those scars and making that blood run fresh. Daddy howls and George slaps his hand over his mouth, fishhooks him, and slices through slow and smooth again. "That ain't no kind of answer, Curtis! I asked you was this your boy over here, the one who did this to you. What do you say now? I'm asking you are you all father and son!"

"Motherfucker!" Daddy jerks his head away, and the blood sprays in my eyes and George's too. "I should have killed your whole goddamn family! I should have sniffed that pussy-ass waiter before he even met your momma and cut his dick off!"

"Aw goddamn! Get him up, Laurence! Move!" George hops over Daddy and right up to me, smelling-close, and when I see that diamond with Daddy's blood on it I think he might be fixing to cut me my own set of tracks. He takes my shirt around the collar, pulls me to him, slices it right down like pulling a zipper. He strips it off and drops me down again.

"Get outta my way now! Goddamn, Robertson, can't you bleed on yourself? Use the tape now, Laurence. Get that wrapped-up good and let's get him in the truck."

Hands under my arms, and quick as that I'm standing, bare back and arms on that cold wall, and I'm looking at the blood on George's face.

"So what's it gonna be, Jake? Who you gonna believe? I'll tell you something, you come with me I'll bring Noel and that little boy of yours right to you. Can't say she'll stay around too long, because she told me something about a better man came around. Just like happened to your own momma, right?" He looks over at Daddy, got that tape around his head and Laurence holding him up. "That's what happened to his momma, Curtis. A better man came around." He wipes his face and puts his hand flat on my chest, smears that blood right where my heart is beating hard enough to break through.

"I'll let you think on it. When we get where we're going, you can choose." He squats at Daddy's feet, tells Laurence to keep the head steady against his body, and they lift him. "Remember what I said, Jake. Joe Haley didn't give you no shit for brains. You think hard now."

They move quick down the stairs. I hear their feet scratch-dragging across the basement floor, George's voice under me, doors opening. Daddy goes quiet, but I can smell him on them when they come for me, sweat and blood and even that bread we ate, smell him like he was carrying me himself, but when they throw me in the truck and I roll up against him it's so close it's not even there, can't smell nothing at all but that gun up under my nose. George gets between us, sits his ass down, and clicks those hammers back. Laurence shuts up those doors, and it's dead dark in here quick as that.

The engine kicks on. George bangs on the window and it opens. Light comes in from the cab, cuts down across his body to the floor. I feel that metal under me reach cold into my back. George tells Laurence keep it steady, middle lane, and locked on that speed limit. The gun goes back under my chin, and George tells me we're in no-man's land now, no free speech no more.

I can feel us going through the curves, down the hills, hear the engine rev high. Nothing else back in this flatbed, just us three and two guns and a little light coming through. We level out, and the light comes and goes. We get going smooth, must be crossing the bridge again, and when the light runs down George's body I try to see what I can see.

But it never catches his eyes, never catches his face at all. If I had a mirror, if we had a little light, I'd put my face right up to his and say look at those eyes brother look at that chin don't forget the nose, look how close that blood done made us. I'd tell him I never did feel like no Robertson anyhow. I'd try playin' it, even with Daddy right here—what do I got to lose? Right now, fucked-up tied-up bleeding in the back of this truck, I know Laurence had it right—we ain't nothing but replaceable niggers. Could be my blood is all I've got.

I feel us going down, taking a curve, and I don't even need to see to know we're back in the Flatlands. Maybe he's got Noel and William down there, up on the top floor of some SRO. Maybe he just wants to give us both a good whupping and leave our asses under the Cliffs someplace. Just wants to get rid of the niggers quick as he can so he can be back in the Vista getting a shower and a new carpet, let us try living with that whupping the way he did all those years. Won't matter much what he does now, because Laurence was right—George owns us.

Those doors come open, and George's hands are on my legs pulling me and under my arms sitting me up on the flap-down. Daddy howls when Laurence pulls him but George just laughs, says he can cry all he wants down here ain't a soul around who gives a damn.

I hear the water all around me like I was swimming in it, hear that wave curl up and smack the wall, hear it rain down on the street, but when I turn there's just a streetlamp throwing light down across the Break in the wall. But then the smell hits, that sweet sea salt, and I know we're going through.

"So what's it gonna be, Jake?" I can see those eyes now. Can't read them, but I'm playin'.

"I want my family back." I cock my head at Daddy. "He fucked up."

"That's a good man," George says. He stands me up, spins me around, and I feel him getting those ropes loose. My hands get hot with the blood running again. He starts working the ones on my feet, tells Laurence to get Daddy's off too.

"You're talking about overtime now," Laurence says. "The job was to here. Where's my money?"

George laughs big, throws the ropes back in the truck. "I'm talking about *George* time, motherfucker. The job is over when I say it is. If you hadn't shot the knee out of this sack of shit then maybe you'd be done. Do you think just because I put you to work now you ain't still a nigger just like them?"

He points one gun at me, one at the wall. "Get moving. We're going fishing."
He looks at Laurence. "Get that old man down there and quit talking your shit."

Laurence puts a hand out. "Give me one of them guns then. You got two—
ain't we partners?"

The light is quick and small when George moves the gun but it crack-flashes
big when the boom pops. Laurence whips his hand away, pulls it into his gut and
hops around like a rabbit on rock. "What the fuck you doing to me?"

George laughs again. "Aw quit your crying. With all that nigger wine in you it
can't hurt that much. What did you ever use that pinky for anyway? Now do like
I told you and get that crip down the stairs."

I know George has the gun straight on me, and if he shoots me now I'm going
straight to hell with what I've been doing tonight, but I ain't letting Daddy walk
on that knee nohow. I get my shoulder under his arm, my arm around his waist,
and me and Laurence lift him and take him step by step.

"What you doing?" Daddy says.

"Nothing. Only thing I can."

We hit the bottom step and set Daddy on his good leg. The water gets louder.
He grabs my arm, and his eyes go big and deep blueblack. "Don't try to save me. I
ain't nothing but an old fool."

"What we got down there? *Three* pussies now?" George's voice bounces all
around the stairwell like a ball thrown in there. "Did I say to stop?"

Laurence sets and lifts up again. "Let's go, Jake. Let's get this over with."

The wind kicks in and lifts that scarf right up off of Daddy, throws it back up
the stairs. I look back but it's gone, down in the shadows. I lean into Daddy, set
my shoulder, and talk low when I lift him. "You're an old fool but I'm a young one.
And I ain't got no ropes no more."

"Take him down to the water, Laurence," George says. "You're almost done
now."

We walk through the grass, sinking down in it, through the puddles catching
the rain and the water spraying off the wall. I step over an empty box and kick a
bottle straight at the water, and I hear the shatter get swallowed up quick when it
drops off the edge. George says stop, and we do. Daddy's good leg is on my side,
so I keep my arm around him to hold him up. George says let him stand alone.

I turn around, turn Daddy with me, hopping, splashing. George is right there,
close enough for me to pull that scarf out of his hand if he threw me the loose end.
It's hanging down like a whip, long and loose like a snake sneaking out of a tree.

He holds it out to Laurence. "Get this around Jake's neck. Knot it double so it
don't come loose."

"Motherfucker you crazy." Laurence steps right up to him, pushes the scarf
away, puts his shot hand in George's face. "What am I gonna tie with this?"

George looks over at Daddy. "If you can walk your crip self over here and finish this job, I'll give you a split of Mr. Nigger Wine's money." He goes in his pocket with his other hand, pulls out some bills, runs them right under Laurence's nose and holds them out to Daddy.

"That's mine!" Laurence tackles George. The bills fall, the scarf falls, one of the guns drops in the grass, but George keeps his feet and swings a fist into Laurence's gut. They spin around, and around again, and they both shoot an arm up with their hands locked on that other gun, whip them back down to their bodies and it goes off. George falls on his ass and hollers and Laurence looks big as a house gonna jump down on him but I just want that gun in the grass. It's right there behind Laurence's feet and I let go of Daddy and start running but quick as that the crack-flash hits. I see Laurence coming down like a bag of bricks right in front of me, right over the gun, and I look at George got his arms straight out and both hands on his gun, and he looks right back and I can't move at all.

He gets up on a knee, uses his hands to stand up full. He moves over to Laurence, dragging one leg like he was wearing a cement boot. He lets those bills fall, and the bottom one flaps open and splits off from the other two, and when they set down on Laurence's chest I can see they ain't nothing but three Georges.

"Here's your money, motherfucker. Go buy yourself some Band-Aids now."

Laurence's glasses are off, and I can see right inside his belly where George blew it open. He looks at me when those bills hit his chest, and his mouth moves but he can't say a word. His hand comes up with that pinky stub, and he puts it on my foot. I feel him squeeze tight, still something there. I still can't move, I just look back at his eyes, and I don't know if it's shadows or what but I never saw those big black bags he's carrying until the glasses came off right now.

George bends over, grabs his collar and pulls him close. But Laurence's eyes stay on me and that mouth keeps moving and that hand squeezes down tighter. George laughs and whispers loud, something about at least I taught you about an honest day's work, but those eyes don't move just keep burning into me don't know how long, and when I see that gun it's too late, the hammer quick-clicks and the crack-flash booms.

Two times. I fall back on my ass, blood hits my face. Laurence clamps down on my foot like a vise, and I look and see that old scar raised up on top of the muscles. I look at his pants and I can see the bone breaking through.

"You think you can fuck with me?" George says. "Make me shoot my own foot, I'll make you taste some pain before you die. Go on and try swimming in that water now without those knees." He looks at me. "Get on your fucking feet!"

Quick as that he has his gun at my head. I stand up slow, keep my head down, and I see the hole right through the middle of his shoe. Can't do much with that but drag it.

"Get this moaning piece of shit out of here. In the water. Move your ass now!"

I pull Laurence by the arms, look at his chest where those bills fell off, where the gun might be underneath. His mouth keeps moving, trying to say something, but he can't get it out and I don't got time to listen. I drag him and watch the ground. George can't run now, I can beat him to it. I turn Laurence and keep watching, pull him and keep watching, and there it is, right where I thought. I drop his arms and jump at it, right down and get my hands on it, but soon as I touch that cold metal I hear that click.

"That's a good man, Jake," George says. "You knew I was looking for that."

I keep my head down. He tells me to back away from it but I don't move at all. I can see that shot-through foot of his, close but maybe not too close if I'm quick enough.

"Look at my face," I say, lifting my chin, slowly now slowly, keeping my hand steady on the gun. I go up George's leg, see his gun look right down at me, keep going up past the scarf till I get his eyes. "He always said I had Haley's face. You telling me you can't see it yourself?"

He takes a step in and drags that foot. "You back away from that gun right now or I'm gonna see it looking like Mr. Laurence's belly."

I smile at him, and my thumb pushes down slow in the grass and wraps around the handle. "You can't do it, George. I'm family. You can't kill me."

"Back off, Jake!" Daddy says from the edge. "Put that shit down!"

George smiles back. "You hear that, Jake? Even that old fool is seeing straighter than you. Now do it."

I slide my finger over the trigger. "Truth hurts. He just don't want to hear it all over again. And you don't neither, but here it is, looking right at you." I come up, slowly now slowly, up on my knees and lift that gun, my finger hugging the trigger but the nose still down. "I look more like Haley than you do. I'm all you got."

"I told you, boy, don't try saving me," Daddy says. "What's done is done here, and you ain't gonna change it like that."

I keep my eyes right on George, don't even turn my head. "This is family business we're talking now, old man, so you shut that mouth good till we're finished. I ain't trying to save nobody but my own."

The gun feels good in my hand—solid, heavy, cold. Fits it just right. I ain't got no little nigger hand no more and don't need nobody to teach me how to use it. One quick cap and I'll be free, I'll get Noel and William back, and we'll be up outta this place. I hold George's eyes and I stand up, slowly now slowly, one leg then the other, I keep holding them and he doesn't blink but I don't neither, keep holding them and I feel like a man now, tighter tighter on that gun and bringing the nose up. Just keep my eyes on his, keep lifting that gun, and he won't see my other hand he won't see a thing, and even if he does I'll stay low and quick knock it out just like picking his pocket on the way to the hoop on Archer Street, and even if he gets a shot off I can take a bullet in the shoulder, I won't feel a thing because I'll be pushing him back on that bad foot and down in the grass sticking that gun up under his chin and taking back what's mine.

"So come on now, George," I say. "You ain't fooling me. If you was gonna do it I'd be dead already. Just tell me where they're at and you can go home and won't never see none of us again."

"You're wrong, Jake. You're dead wrong. I can't go home, and you can't either." George squeezes the scarf in his fist, and the loose end snake-shakes when he jabs it. "I tried my whole life to run away from Chicago, but it came and found me. And don't go telling me about family. You ain't got no family, nigger. You're all alone now."

"Houston!" Laurence's voice is soft as the rain, but it's loud enough. I look back at him, belly busted-open and glasses off and don't know if he can see me at all, but that voice comes again. "Seven—"

"No!" George jumps at me, sticks the gun past me and shoots at Laurence, keeps coming but he can't keep his feet and quick as that he's face-down in the grass and that gun is loose on the ground. I drop quick, get a knee in his back, gun to his head.

"Say your prayers and say them good, motherfucker. You gonna need them where I'm sending you." He bucks on me, tries to kick his leg up, but I press him down harder. I click the hammer and he stops. "You ready for the first one now? Where you want it?"

"Let him go!" Daddy says from the edge. "You got what you want now, boy."

"Shut the fuck up!" I say, and I smack George's head with the gun. "*What* I got, huh? Only thing I got is the motherfucker that done took everything from me! And I ain't letting that go for nobody!"

The wind picks up, the rain starts coming harder. "Then he's still got you. And you ain't never getting free. You put that blood on your hands, he's gonna own you all your life."

"Quit talking your fool shit. *You* the one wanted his house, talking all that noise about putting the family back together."

"That was a fool talking then. But it ain't now. Listen to me—"

"*Fuck* listen. All I've been doing is listening to you all fool motherfuckers telling your stories. Ain't no more listening now." I smack George's head with the gun again. "I'm the boss now, you hear? I'm gonna ask you one more time, ain't gonna be no third. How you want it? You want it like your daddy got it?"

I move my head down close and I can smell him sweating. But just like that, I catch it out of the corner of my eye, I see Daddy moving. I look up and his finger is shooting straight at me.

"You want to be like me, boy? You want to see that face all your life?" He takes a step, hollers and damn-near falls on his face but his good leg holds him, and he stands up straight again. "Leave him be now. He's finished. We beat him."

I press George's face in the grass and point the gun at Daddy. "Get your ass back!"

He does it again, half-steps, falls, and catches himself. "Put that gun down, boy."

"You quit walking or I'll shoot that other knee out too," I say. "And don't go thinking I'm carrying you outta here if I do."

He shoots that finger again. "You owe me, boy. You said so yourself."

"Well that was a fool talking then. What you ever give me that I could use? Told me about a gun, then you kept it for yourself." I pull the scarf out of George's hand and throw it in the grass. "Told me about a scarf but you went and kept that too. Told me about my daddy, but you'd already gone and killed him. So what I got to owe you? Nothing I can put my hands on." I squeeze that gun and shake it. "This is all I got, and I got it myself." I put the nose in George's ear. "This is my time now."

"*I'm* your daddy, Jake," he says. "Even if I wasn't no kind of daddy at all. You don't want to do it for me, then do it for that boy of yours. Give him a good daddy like the kind you never had."

He moves to me, half-steps, but the leg won't hold no more. George is good as dead under my knee but it just lifts, and all I know is I'm following my body over Laurence through the grass running running to the edge getting down on that concrete all slicked with Daddy's blood and the rain dripping over the edge, getting down turning him over and I know he's lost too much blood maybe he can't even see me but his hand shoots up grabs my face pulls me smelling-close and I hear glass breaking I'm falling we're both falling knocking over the kitchen table the brown couch busting through Cheryl's screams Paula's laughing Momma's purple eye going through the window both of us now right here on the ground and I get my hands under him tell him I'm getting you out Daddy but he says don't touch me don't touch me with that thing in your hand and I still feel it heavy solid cold like that body hanging from the maple like that face I never knew like that dream I just can't shake and the water is close and waiting but if I throw it I'll be dead but this is the face I always knew so I squeeze it one last time and it's gone it's gone it's gone.

I get my legs under me and start lifting Daddy, but soon as I do I hear that splash-stepping and I know it's too late, I'm a damn fool and I'm holding one too. George picks up the scarf and snaps the rain out of it, scoops up the other gun in front of Laurence and drags his foot over till he's looking right down at him. Then he does it quick, just points and shoots, and Laurence's head busts open like a watermelon.

My leg gives out and I drop to a knee. My shoulder is burning like a mother-fucker, gonna take a miracle of some kind to get Daddy out of here. But I ain't getting it. George comes slow and steady, drag-stepping and lifting the gun and breathing louder. Those eyes go tight and dark and I can't look away.

"Stand him up!"

Daddy grabs my collar. "Don't listen to him, boy."

I smack his hand away. "What choice I got?"

I get my hands under his arms and pull till he's up on that good leg. George waves the gun. "Walk him to me!"

We get close, and George pushes me straight in the chest. "Get down on your motherfucking knees." He grabs Daddy's arm and pulls him close. "I've got you now, brother."

He holds Daddy there, just looks at him, and maybe it's the dark or my head's just gone crazy but I think I see him smile. And I look at the gun, and I think it's gonna be quick, right up under the chin and blow the top off, but I wish he'd shoot me first so I don't have to see it now.

He points at me with the scarf hand. "Look at that, Curtis. Look close. That's the boy you raised?" He laughs and shakes his head. "Looks like a pussy to me. Ain't no man at all. No man a daddy could be proud of." He jerks Daddy quick, spins, and gets the gun up under the chin. "Could have saved you just now but he didn't. All he had to do was pull that trigger on me and you would've been free." He presses the gun in deep, shakes him good. "You hear what I'm saying? But don't you worry now, brother, because I'll set you free. You just finish the job now and I'll set you free."

He pulls the gun away, and Daddy's weight comes back on that knee. George steadies him when he hollers. "I've got you now, brother. I've got you." He puts the scarf in Daddy's belly. "I know why you did it. You were only doing what any man would've done, just protecting your own, that's all. Go on and finish it now."

He puts the scarf on Daddy's hand, but the hand doesn't move. Eyes don't neither. Just drilling down into me.

"Look at that face, Curtis. That's the face took your woman from you. Get a good last look now." George steps to me, snaps that scarf out with both hands and wraps it around my neck, loops it twice and holds those torn ends up. "Do it right this time and he'll be gone for good."

The scarf is cold and wet. George pulls it tight and shakes the ends at Daddy. I could run but those eyes beat down and I'm nothing but a man now can't find his way home, nothing but a little boy down here got noplace to go, looking up at my daddy knowing a whupping is coming and I can't run no more.

George pulls him to me, puts those ends in his hands. "Go on, Curtis. Set yourself free."

I look at his hands. They're smelling-close, could knock me right in the water if he wanted to. The rain hits down and makes those knuckles shine. They squeeze that scarf tighter and start shaking. I can't look at those eyes now. Ain't got no words in me and ain't no word gonna stop him anyhow.

"He's my boy."

George whips around behind him and the hammer clicks. "I can feel your heart beating right through your back, Curtis. I can give you your life back or I can take it away. Now finish the job."

Those hands get shaking good, those knuckles shining, rain dripping fast. The scarf is tight, I feel that cold cutting into my neck, and I smell Daddy's blood fresh and close.

"You're my boy, Jake."

The fingers lift up. The scarf falls on my chest. I look up, and Daddy's eyes are big and light, don't know if it's rain or sweat or what that smile is. I try to look close, but that crack-flash booms and the blood comes right out his chest and it's on me, all over me, he's falling, falling on me, I catch him, can't hold him, it's flowing, we're falling. The gun goes again and it's through to my shoulder. We fall apart, I hit the ledge and I look at George but he's dragging running gone. I feel Daddy under my leg somewhere, and I call but he can't hear. I call again but nothing. I call again and lift my head, and I see his face flat on the ledge, those eyes shut good. I can't move now, can't reach him, can't get those eyes open, but his hand is right close. My shoulder is dead but I ask God just give me an inch now, and I move it, I feel him, I squeeze him, I ain't letting go.

CHAPTER 10
FOOL DON'T KNOW

Don't know how I got here. Where I am ain't where I was, I can see that, but it's the in-between I can't get straight.

I know I'm in the Houston, seventh floor. I know that's Noel putting clothes in a bag, I know that's my boy William sitting next to her at the end of this bed, coughing just like he was when we came out of the Birdhouse, back before I took Rhonda's purse and started this whole mess. I know they walked me in here and I lied straight down, and the way the light is now I must have slept right through to the next day. The plastic sheet on the window keeps the sun out about as good as praying for rain.

That's what I was doing when Jerry found me at the water—sleeping. Looked dead when he first saw me, but when he got close he knew I still had something left. He got me on my feet, to the street, in an ambulance. Saved my ass, and the rest of me too. But lying here, with my arm in a sling, and my whole body feeling like forty bags of cement left out in the rain, I ain't sure I want to thank him.

Noel rubs William's chest and makes him sip his bottle. I remember some things. I woke up with him biting down on my nose, couple days ago in the hospital. I opened my eyes and saw Noel pulling him off, laughing good, and looked at that spit hanging all the way back to his lip like a spider web line. "Night-night," he said—or that's what Noel told me he was trying to say. "Daddy night-night." She didn't want to wake me up, but she was holding him close so he could touch me, and he just jumped. He's getting like that, getting a mind of his own, she said. I had to laugh too—laughed so good I clear forgot why I was even in that bed, till I went to wipe that spit off my nose with the wrong hand and the pain shot back full-on.

The doc told me about the bullet the day before. Didn't break the bone clean because it only caught the top of it, but it would have been better if it did. He found some chips in there, and most of the bullet, but the rest I'm just gonna have to live with. Told me it went through somebody first, heart and maybe a rib too, and he went looking for that but it's the same thing, you never know if you get it all. He started telling me it wouldn't do me no harm to have it in me, but that's when I told him get your lying ass outta my face. Didn't nobody else get shot and that's a motherfucking fact.

Jerry came back on my last day in that ward—I think it was yesterday. Noel was with him, she brought William too, told me all the nurse-folk said time was up for the fool with no Medicaid and no manners. But Jerry walked in first, and I asked him straight-up about my hand. Lying in that bed, I kept wondering if it all really happened like I had it playing in my head—if maybe it was just a dream. I'm still wondering. I know I got this shoulder, and that ain't changing no time soon, but what about this hand? I look at it, I hear what it's telling me, but I don't believe it. Did it really throw that gun in the water, same one that went upside George's head? Did it really feel that old scarf again, same one was around Daddy's neck when I pushed him through, same one was around my own neck with Daddy holding the ends? Same one Daddy tore open and tied to the shirt when he hung Haley up in the maple? I remember some things, but I don't know what to believe. Ain't this the same hand was squeezing Daddy's?

He found us right where we fell, except Daddy was half over the ledge, hanging in the water. George must have come back and tried to push him in—that's how Jerry sees it. Probably wanted to put Laurence in too, cover the whole thing up, but he took off running again when my hand wouldn't give, got back across the bridge quick as he could and got that foot fixed up. But Jerry could have been drinking—what else was he doing down there? He told me he was stone-cold sober, told me he just couldn't sleep that night, said he had a feeling something was out there. But why should I believe him? I looked him in the eye and he looked me right back, and I knew he believed it himself. But that don't mean a thing. A man like him can think up any damn thing and make it real if he wants to. He can take something he dreamed or remembered or just thought it ought to be—any story he wants—and tell himself *it was it was it was* till it *is*. I can too. Any fool can.

But I still feel it. Still feel his hand in my hand. I squeeze and it's not there, but then I open up and there it is, squeezing me back. And I know I didn't get that from some dream. I don't know about all the rest—Jerry pushing Daddy in the rest of the way and Laurence too so the crows wouldn't get at them, me looking up at him half-dead and saying the Houston, and that picture I got running around my head of Daddy lying there cold like the man under the maple. Jerry always talks crazy, and I do too now and again. But maybe I'll believe what he told me about damn-near needing a crowbar to pry my fingers back. I don't want to, but maybe this hand is telling me I ain't got no choice.

I squeeze again and try to lift it close, to give it a good listen, but my shoulder ain't playin' today and I suck back on my teeth. Noel looks up.

"You awake?"

"I'm getting there."

She puts the clothes down and looks at William, gives him that smile like only my girl knows how. "You want to show him? Let's go."

William puts his arms out to her, but those eyes look back at me when she picks him up. Big and dark enough to see yourself in when you hold him close. He doesn't smile, doesn't talk, just looks right at me till Noel sets him on the floor at the end of the bed. She lets him stand on his own, and she backs up to the wall, right here next to me. She says go but my boy's already off, he jumps the gun and starts coming. Arms pumping, feet slapping the floor, that pamper swishing, and *now* he's laughing, now he's making some noise. He wobbles a little halfway, grabs my bed and gets straight again, pushes off and boom boom boom, just like that he brings it home, right to Noel. I try to reach him with my good arm but Noel scoops him up. She puts a wet one right on his cheek and sets him in my lap.

"See what a good boy he is?"

"Sure enough is," I say. I spread my hand out on his back to steady him, lean him back and watch him smile. I bounce him a little with my leg and get him laughing again. "This his first time right now?"

Noel shakes her head. "Almost. Few days ago."

I stop bouncing and look at her. "Where were you all at? With George?"

"No, Jake. Right here in this room."

"But was he here? Don't run from me, girl."

"Was just me and your son. And we sure wasn't gonna be back in that basement no more, after you went purse-snatching."

"What you talking about? I did that for you!"

She cocks her head, puts her hands on her hips. "For me? So that yellow tape was party ribbon? You lost your check *and* our place, Jake. That was for *me*?"

"Naw, naw," I say. "That shit was stupid, I know that. I'm talking about *this*." I look quick at my shoulder.

"I'm talking about that too," she says. "How you figure you did that for me?"

"I did it for *all* of us, goddammit! I'm trying to get us up *outta* this shit! *You* the one always talking about you want nice things—"

"Aaaah!" William lets one fly. Quick as that, his face goes dark and wrinkled like an old plum, and the tears come right behind. Noel reaches for him, but I pull him to me. "Let Daddy hold him now," I say.

He snake-squirms and bangs his head on my chest and leaves me a good little wad of snot, but I start bouncing him nice and soft, start humming something, just riffing it, and it takes a minute but he slows down, cools off. He puts his head flat on my good shoulder, keeps moaning, but his mouth is closed now, and it gets quieter, quieter, till it's nothing but a hum, almost like mine. When he breathes in big I can hear it, that little wheeze and catch. I know he's got that damn thing inside him, even when he's quiet. That's why I did this.

I keep bouncing him, keep that humming going, and try to check his eyes to see if he'll go to sleep. "You think I want him to live like this?" I say, looking at Noel. "Little man can't even breathe right. Nobody can down here."

She keeps looking at William. "I know it, I know it."

William's head slides up, his eyes pop wide open. "Daddy ow-ee?" He looks at my shoulder, and puts his hand out to touch the sling. "Ow-ee?"

I shift him, get his butt in the crook of my good arm, take his hand in mine and lay it down soft right on my shoulder. His fingers spread out and he pats me, nice and soft. All those bandages are thick, but somehow I can feel his hand right through, that little pat pat pat, right where the bone got broke, right where I've got Daddy inside.

"That's it," I say. "That's a good boy now."

He laughs, he looks at me, he pats me again. I lift my good arm some more and bring him right up to me, smelling-close, and I kiss his ear. He smells good, brand-new, just like the day we brought him home. "I love you, boy," I say, soft as I can.

A bus roars outside, revs good and then it fades, quick as it came. The window is open at the bottom, not much but enough to let it all in and that breeze too. The plastic sheet flaps out, and I feel that cold air right on my face. The scarf is hanging on the back of the chair right under, and my boots are on the seat.

"What you got that window open for?" I look at Noel. She's crying. Quiet, just one tear falling down her cheek. She wipes it back and sniffs, shakes her head. "He was hot."

"Well he ain't no more," I say. "I ain't neither. What you crying about anyway, girl? Go close it."

She takes a couple steps away but then she stops, looks at me. "I wanted you to see it, Jake, I really did," she says. "I thought he wouldn't make it till you were out but he was just quicker than I thought." She points down and another tear comes. "It was right here, right here on this floor. He was even saying 'Daddy' when he did it."

I lean William back, let him slide down till he's on his feet, between my legs. "Let's make like it's the first time, huh boy?" I tell Noel to stand him up at the end of the bed. "Let's start over then, right now. *This* gonna be the first time."

Noel's mouth goes tight. She smiles small but not with her eyes, and she picks him up. "He don't know—"

"That's right," I say. "He don't know. We gonna make it right, and then he *will* know. *This* is the story his daddy's gonna be telling him. Now put him over there and let him walk."

"This bed's too soft, Jake. He'll fall."

"Don't start with that. My little man can do it. Let's go now."

She moves to the end of the bed but she stops again. "Why you got to—"

"Why I got to what? I ain't seen my boy in I don't know how long. Now let him walk to me!"

Noel puts the bag on the floor, and I pull the sheet off. I spread my legs out so William can drive the lane. He starts shaky when she sets him down, takes a second to get his feet under him, but then he gives me that smile.

"That's my boy," I say, reaching out my hand. "Now come on."

He steps, holds it, steps again, holds it, throws his arm up and laughs.

I shake my hand, stretch it out a little more. "That's it. Keep coming."

He steps again, and now I pull my hand back. Just a little. He can almost reach it, but I make him keep coming. He comes, and then he just hits it, starts running like he did on the floor. But the bed shakes him, he can't hold it. I grab his hand but his head's already knocking my knee, and he cries good and loud.

I try to lift him, but soon as I do Noel gets in with those two good arms and scoops him up. "Let me look at that head," she says, stepping away from me. He keeps crying, and she bounces him, rocks him, says *now now now*. She kisses him on the head, then looks up at me. "You see now, Jake? What I tell you?"

"My little man's a fighter," I say. "He ain't hurt. Sounds hungry to me."

"Hungry, my ass, boy. I just fed him before you woke up."

"Feed him again then!"

"That how you think it's gonna be now? You just gonna lie in that bed and tell us what to do?"

"Well I'm a little tied down at the moment," I say, pointing at my shoulder. "I took a bullet for you all."

"That ain't all you took." William's still crying, and Noel walks him to the end of the bed. She bends down, and I hear that zipper run and close that bag, and she says *now now now*. "What you do with that car you stole?"

"Oh fuck that!" I smack my hand down on the bed. "You know I didn't steal shit. That thing was just sitting there for me."

A bus horn blows in from outside, the brakes squeak, and then it revs and it's gone again. William coughs, harder this time, two three and then he's on a roll.

"I told you that boy is cold," I say. "Now get that window shut."

"And I told you don't go giving orders from that bed," she says. "I ain't shutting nothing." She rubs my boy's back, nice smooth circles, and he quiets down. He lays his head on her chest.

She throws her chin at the window. "You want it shut, do it yourself. It ain't got nothing to with being cold. He needs some good medicine, and he's got to get outta here, simple as that."

I nod big. "That's what I'm saying too, baby. You think I don't know that?"

"Well you ain't been doing much about it."

"You don't know a goddamn thing about what I been doing." I grab my shoulder. "You want me to take this off for you? Go on, stick your finger in here! I still got it in me!"

"I don't know what I know no more, Jake." She bends down, comes back up with her purse. She puts it on the bed, takes her wallet out. "This ain't how I wanted this to go." She takes a paper out of the wallet, unfolds it. "George sent me this the other day."

"So he *was* here," I say. "Why you been lying to me?"

"I said he *sent* it," she says. " It was down at the front desk. Manager told me somebody dropped it off." She laughs, quick-looks around. "You think he'd come here? To this mess?"

"A man will go about anyplace to get some."

She turns sideways, tucks William out of sight and gives me her shoulder. "Fuck you, Jake," she says, soft but loud enough. "You left. We were out on the street. I didn't know if you were in the desert or in jail. Who was I supposed to ask—your caseworker? And then I get up in that Luby house, I see that girl using, you think I'm gonna stay there? You think I'm gonna keep my *son* there? George gave me some work before, and I thought he'd help me again. And he did. He got us through what we needed, and that was that."

"I didn't leave shit!" I say. "I was working. I didn't steal but three dollars off that bitch."

"Yeah, while you was working we was starving, if it hadn't been for George." William pops his head up. Noel puts the paper on the bed and rubs his head till it's back on her chest. She looks at me again and bites on her lip. "Look, this ain't how I wanted this to go. We're supposed to be talking about our boy."

"Fine by me," I say. "That's what I've been trying to talk about. Soon as I get healed up, I'm getting us outta here."

"How you gonna do that? You think the good jobs are just sitting out there like that car, waiting for you to pick one up? Besides," she says, pointing at the paper. "You got two warrants on you."

"What you talking about?"

She points at it again. "George put out the second one. Read it right there. He says you came in shooting, tried to rob him, killed Laurence and your own daddy so you could keep it all yourself. Says he shot you back before you could kill him too."

"I should have *killed* that motherfucker!" I say, punching the air. "You believe that shit?"

William bucks in her arms and starts into his crying again.

"You gonna listen to me now?" I say. "Feed that boy!"

"With *what?*" She walks fast to the window, head down, saying *now now now.* The breeze comes again, and the plastic flaps, and the paper goes to the floor. She walks back to the bed, bouncing him, but he ain't having it—just cries louder.

"Here," I say, putting out my arm. "Let me hold him. You go get something."

Noel turns, walks back to the window. "No."

"I'll go then. I'll go across to Jimmy's and get us some milk. Crackers too."

"That ain't gonna do it."

"It won't take but a minute. I know that manager's got a dollar he can give me. If he don't, somebody out there will." I sit up, and my head goes light. I swing my legs over the side of the bed, and they still feel like all that cement still trying to dry out.

"No," she says. "Just stay where you're at."

She bends down and picks up the paper, puts it back on the bed. It shakes in her hand. She bounces William, keeps looking at the paper. "I didn't want it to be like this," she says. William keeps crying, but that bus going by honks good and loud, and she looks up quick at the window. Then she looks at me.

"I don't know what to believe," she says. Her face goes tight. "My daddy said family always takes you back." She shakes her head. "I still believe in you, Jake, but not like this."

I put my hand out to her. "What you want me to do, baby? Give me a little time now—I'm gonna get healed up and we gonna make it."

She pulls away, shakes her head again. "I don't want you to do nothing. Just take this." She puts some bills out of her wallet, puts them on the paper. "George gave me a couple hundred dollars. I got ninety-seven left, and I don't need it. My momma's paying for the Greyhound."

"You going home?" I try to get my legs under me, but my head goes light again. "I thought she kicked you out!"

"They're doing it for him," she says. "So am I."

A bus honks again. She puts her bag on her shoulder. "I got a cab waiting, Jake. Take that money and take that address on the paper."

"You can't take my boy from me!"

"Phone number is there too. You can call us. But give yourself some time. Get yourself back together."

"Don't give me no fucking money! What am I gonna do with that?" I reach over and grab it, grab that paper too, ball it and throw it at her, but she's moving, she's gone. I see William's eyes crying over her shoulder but he's too far to grab him, can't even see myself in them before they're out the door. I push myself off the bed, get out into the hall, hear those footsteps moving, that crying ringing, but it's too dark to see. I move to that exit door, feel that blood coming back in my legs, hear that crying on the stairs, those shoes slapping, and I start running, jumping down in the dark, running hearing that door shut hard and then I'm through it and out in all that light but that cab ain't nothing but a blur, nothing but a noise and it's gone quick as that. And I can't run, can't get it, because I'm nothing but a man.

* * *

I ran anyhow. All the way down the block, and the next one and the next one too. Ran till my breath gave out and my arm near came out of the sling. Didn't see nothing, just the same old shit—folks walking and talking, smoking and doping and playin'. One bus running up the street, another one running back down. But no cab. Nobody that's mine.

I looked down at my feet and saw the blood. My boots were still sitting back in that chair by the window. I sat down on the curb and picked the glass out from between my toes. Put my finger in the cut but it wouldn't stop. When I got back to this room I washed it out in the sink and stuck a sock on it. I picked the money up off the floor, the paper too, and put them in my boots. I took the scarf off the chair, I shut the window, and shut my eyes.

It's night now. Don't know what time but it's got to be one of those in-between hours. You don't know if you're closer to the sun going down or coming back up again.

I don't know what I'm doing here. I'm tired but I can't sleep no more. I didn't dream at all, but even if I did all I'd have to do now is empty out those boots to know what's real. And I've got the scarf right here too, right around my neck, Daddy's blood and sweat deep down in it.

My legs are heavy again when I get them under me, but I can still move. The blood in the sock is still wet, and I can feel the floor right through, but I ain't got another. I go to the chair, shake my boots out and put them on, put that money in my pocket and that paper too. I lift the plastic flap, open the window good and high, and I walk out the door.

Outside it's cold. I wrap the scarf tight up around my neck. I start walking, and the blood gets moving, makes my legs a little lighter and my head a little clearer. I can't go fast but I get a good rhythm going, and after a couple blocks I loosen it up.

If I'd just pulled that trigger I wouldn't have to worry about nothing at all. Daddy would be right here, wearing this thing instead of me. If I'd just pulled it we wouldn't even be here at all, walking this street with noplace to go. We'd be in that Benz, Noel and William in the back, crossing the bridge. No—we'd be a week gone now, maybe even two, heading anyplace we wanted, starting all over.

But I was a fool, a goddamn fool. I listened to him. I owed him, but this ain't how I was gonna pay.

I turn the corner and see the Angelus. I keep walking, turn the corner again and head down to the Cliffs. Where else I got to go?

He told me to do it for my boy. *Give him a good daddy like the kind you never had.* What's my boy got now? So what if I killed a man to put food on the table— I'd still have William now if I did. Even if I got locked-up, at least he could come see me, come put his hand up on the glass same time every year till it got near as big as mine. And by that time I'd be free again. Now what do I got? When am I ever gonna see him?

Rain starts falling, and I duck in Parker's Alley, looking for that dumpster. Maybe Daddy's jacket could keep me dry a little while, even if it smells bad enough to burn it. I climb up the side, but I know it's empty even before I look in—I can just feel it. I tell the dumpster it's a motherfucker, but that bounces right back at me, and I step down and keep heading for the Cliffs.

I walk slow, just one foot at a time, and every now and again a car zoom-clacks up above. Rain drips off the sides, and when I get to the wall some drops come right down on my head, roll in my eyes. I take the scarf and wipe them away, then I put it in my sling hand and squeeze. Just to feel it, see what my shoulder can take. It gets hot quick, starts pounding. Maybe the doc was right—this bone ain't healing no time soon, and the rest I'm gonna have to live with. I let go, and I know he ain't around but I can feel Daddy's hand squeezing mine back, just like up in the room.

I walk through the Break, down the steps and through the grass, out into the open where I can feel that wind. The sky is good and dark up above, but out on the horizon I see a little blueblack, a little light creeping up. The waves are good and smooth, whoosh-sweeping up and slapping the edge.

I walk all the way out and try to find the spot. A wave smacks in and gets me good, and that rain keeps falling light on my head.

No blood on the grass, none on the edge neither. I get down on my knees, but it doesn't get me nothing but wet. I can hear Daddy laughing at me, saying *what you trying to find?*

I pull the scarf off, spread it out on the edge. I look at that old maple, those leaves flying around, and that fish with no face, and I hear him laughing again. *Now you know it's mine?*

"I don't know a goddamn thing!" I say, slapping the ground. But nobody listens. Another wave smacks in. Maybe Daddy hears me.

I dig in my pocket, set the money and the paper on the scarf. This is all I've got now. I unball the paper so I can see those lies George put down, and something falls loose, a little bent-up strip of nothing. Maybe a bus transfer, maybe a receipt out of Ho's register. I pick it up, and there's that address. I turn it over, and there's my boy.

They went to a booth, one of those you sit in and feed quarters while it flashes away. Ain't like a rich folks' camera, nobody waiting there till you're ready and sitting pretty. Ain't but one good picture out of all of them—but that's how it goes, you get your chance and that's it.

The paper isn't a warrant at all. Maybe the police have one but this ain't it. Just a piece of paper. George wrote out the story himself, just like Noel told it. And then he wrote some more. Told her remember what he said, she don't belong down here. Ain't she never heard of that prodigal son? Don't spend another day with that fool, get on back to your own.

I bite down on the corner and rip it back, spit the piece out and tear it again. Is that what she believes? I throw it, and the wind takes it just like it was waiting for it. I throw the money too, and just like that it's gone, the water eats it all up. She said she believed in me, so then what's she doing this for? For William? What about what I did for him?

The sun starts coming up, puts some more light in the sky across the water, but the big clouds keep a low lid on it. I look at the picture again, that one good one with them both looking back at me. I look close as I can, let it sink in good, so I can't ever forget. I wipe the rain off their faces and put it in my pocket.

The sun comes up full, and out over the water the rain lights up, almost goes gold. Won't last but a minute, till it hits those clouds, but it helps me see. I pick up the scarf, stretch it out tight again with both hands, just like he had it. He let me live. Right from the beginning, and right here, he let me live. Maybe nobody would believe it, but I can now.

But do I want to live like this? What I got now? A picture and an address. A scarf and a story.

I press my face into the scarf and close my eyes. I breathe in big, and he's more than smelling-close. He's here. *You done good, boy.*

This fool don't know. Only thing I can do is believe. All I can believe in is what nobody can take from me. All I got is our story.

I take those torn ends, tie them back together, and set the scarf down in the water. Ain't like Auntie Thelma made it no more, but it's something. It floats out, almost too dark to see, and then a wave rolls in and it's gone. I look at the sun, but it's already up behind the clouds. The sky is getting lighter though, so it must be doing something behind there.

I walk through the grass, up the steps, through the Break. The freeway is coming to life now, the street down here too. I walk through the Cliffs, try not to get hit by the pigeons, try not to step in the potholes. Still can't see like I want to, but the light's getting stronger now, and I'll make it through.

ACKNOWLEDGMENTS

No one walks alone. I thank God for the gifts, the wounds, the healing, and the strength to walk on.

This book could not have been written without the support of family, all of whom I wish to honor, and some of whom deserve special mention: Joseph V. Nichols, my great-grandfather, whose soul left this world as mine was arriving, and who gave me an example of what a writer and activist could be; Louisa Kilgour Nichols, my great-grandmother, who gripped my hand and saw that I'd be a writer; John and Ann Tully, my grandparents, whose faith and generosity have lifted me up; John Joseph McLaughlin III and Christine Tully McLaughlin, my parents, whose love has never questioned, whose support has never failed; Timothy, Maureen, Brian, and Anne, my siblings, who sustain me with laughter, devotion, and the example of their lives; Kathy Krikorian, my wife, *mariposa de sueño*, who dares to dream and hope alongside me, and whose love allows me to follow my heart without a second thought.

Many teachers of literature and writing have selflessly offered abundant gifts, and to them I owe a great debt. At Gonzaga, Dick Myers and Paul Burke planted vital seeds—the Greeks and the Bible, Shakespeare and Joyce, Dickens and Faulkner, Flannery O'Connor and Toni Morrison—and gave me *Links* to learn the rules I'd later need to break; John Hoffman showed me the center *could* actually hold, and was worth fighting for. At Virginia, Michael D. Aeschliman lit my soul on fire and saved me from pre-med; Lisa Roberts, Bernadine Connelley, Stephen Railton, and Stephen Cushman inspired me with their passion and challenged me to go deeper; Rita Mae Brown, Sydney Blair, and Christopher Tilghman encouraged me more than my work deserved; Jonathan Coleman pushed, demanded, nurtured, and celebrated as only the best teachers can. At Iowa, the late Frank Conroy laid down the law: three hours a day, process over project; Bharati Mukherjee convinced me I could fly; James Alan McPherson told me there was something in these pages, and lent generously from his storehouse of books, records, and wisdom to help it grow.

Alex Parsons, John Casteen, Antonio Jocson, and Julie Quick stuck with me during those bitter Iowa winters. They helped my work, and they got me out of the house when I really needed it.

John Zeller, Dave Averill, Dan Restrepo, Greg Martin, Justin Rosolino, Matt Fischer, and Leah Feldman have been loyal friends and great encouragers of my work for many years. Every artist needs companions such as these.

Paul Burson, Simón Bautista Betances, Richard Rohr, Steve Donaldson, John Yurich, Kathleen O'Malley, Wayne Gsell, Paul Magnano, Catuxo Badillo Veiga, William Poleyó José, and Felicia Antonia Puntiel have all provided vital mentoring and spiritual support.

I'm grateful to many people who guided and supported me as a social worker as well, particularly: George Jones, Dave McDonough, and Mike Toguchi at Chrysalis; Gregg Alex at the Matt Talbot Center; Harry Coveny at St. Vincent de Paul; Adam Vogt, Niko Colella, and Christopher Duran at New Connections.

Those who know and love Oakland will see that I've taken great liberties with many specifics—geographical and otherwise—of that vibrant city, in order to tell this story as Jake wanted it told. I ask their forgiveness.

A sincere tip of the hat to the Knoxville Writers' Guild, Jon Manchip White, and the staff of The University of Tennessee Press for giving Jake's story a chance to be heard.

This book was greatly influenced by those I encountered during my years working with the homeless and ex-offender populations in Los Angeles and Seattle. Many men and women opened their lives to me and trusted me with what was, in many cases, their only possession: their story. For the sake of privacy, they remain anonymous here, but in this book I have tried to honor and celebrate their struggles the best way I know how, by shining a light into the places where too many of us choose not to look. If nothing else, they have taught me that each of us is much more—much richer and more fully human—than the worst thing we have ever done. I have tried to reveal the truth of their reality in such a way as to evoke the same compassion and longing for understanding that I have felt in knowing these individuals personally. If I have succeeded, it is because of the hope they inspire in me; if not, the failing is mine alone.

—JJM

A portion of the author's royalties will be donated to: Chrysalis (a nonprofit helping homeless and disadvantaged in Los Angeles; changelives.org), Men as Learners and Elders (a program of Center for Action & Contemplation, in Albuquerque; malespiri tuality.org), and Matt Talbot Center (a recovery program for addicted and homeless in Seattle; matttalbotcenter.org).